ABOUT THE AUTHORS

A securities attorney by trade, DONALD J. BINGLE is best known in the gaming world as the Roleplaying Game Association's top-ranked classics player, roleplaying more than 500 characters in his tournament career. He is the author of a wide variety of gaming materials, along with movie reviews, two screenplays, and a bevy of short stories in such anthologies as *Sol's Children, Historical Hauntings,* and *The Search for Magic.* He is currently writing a science fiction novel. Contact him at *www.orphyte.com.*

Hi, this is Nog from DS9. I was asked to write a little bio on the actor I portray in the holosuites. I wrote his biography myself. And everyone thinks Jake is the only writer around here: ARON EISENBERG was born in Hollywood, California (I've always been interested in Hollywood). He was born January 6, 1969, and was adopted by his loving parents. He was also born with one kidney, which was defective and gave him his short stature (After studying my medical books at Starfleet, I found out this sometimes happens to hewmons. I wanted him to be somewhat like me!) In 1986, Aron received his kidney transplant and is still going strong. He started acting in 1987, and the very first movie he worked on was *Colors* with Sean Penn. Soon after that, while working as an extra and stand-in, he got his agent and a SAG card. As the years went by, he worked consistently in films, television and plays. He also had the pleasure of co-writing a short story with Margaret Weis called "The Traveling Players of Gilean," appearing in *The Best of Tales Volume One.* in the "business," he enjoys collectable card games, his Playstation 2 and Gamecube, and watching movies. Tons of movies! He also enjoys mountain biking, working out and martial arts—Chinese Kenpo to be exact (I've always wanted to be the first fighting ferengi, and working out in the holosuites doing Chinese Kenpo will get me there!) He lives with his two boys, Nicholas and Christopher. From what I can tell, his boys are everything to him!

RICHARD A. KNAAK is the *New York Times* best-selling author of *The Legend of Huma* and more than twenty other novels, including the popular Dragonrealm series. His works have been published in many countries, most recently in Russia and Poland, and have lately been sold in the Czech Republic, Taiwan, and Mainland China, among others. In addition to the five books and twelve-plus short stories he has written for the DRAGONLANCE® series, he is now in the midst of writing a follow-up series to the War of Souls trilogy. The first novel in the Minotaur Wars trilogy will be released in June 2003. He is also working on projects based on the worldwide best-selling computer games Diablo and Warcraft.

DOUGLAS NILES has written more than thirty novels. His DRAGONLANCE books include *Winterheim, The Golden Orb, The Messenger, Emperor of Ansalon, The Dragons, The Puppet King, Fistandantilus Reborn, Flint the King* (with Mary Kirchoff), and *The Last Thane.* He also authored the popular Watershed Trilogy for Ace books.

JEAN RABE is the author of a dozen fantasy novels and more than two dozen fantasy, science-fiction, and military short stories. Her most recent series is the DRAGONLANCE Dhamon trilogy: *Downfall, Betrayal,* and *Redemption.* When she's not writing, Jean immerses herself in war games and roleplaying games, finds places to stash her burgeoning collection of books, plays with her two dogs, visits museums, and pretends to garden. In her spare time she

edits. She is the editor of two collections for DAW Books—
Historical Hauntings and *Sol's Children*, and a horror CD
collection for Lone Wolf Publications, *Carnival*. Visit her at:
http://www.sff.net/people/jeanr/index.html

After a number of years in public service in Belfast and
resultant years in what he likes to call a "school of police
and political science" in the southern part of the right-
fully united republic, FERGUS RYAN has settled in a
large city in the eastern United States. He is the author
of *The Siege of Mount Nevermind* and is working on a
number of short stories.

PAUL B. THOMPSON is the author of a dozen novels,
including the recently concluded Barbarians DRAGONLANCE
trilogy. Though an ardent aficionado of film and theater,
he is firmly convinced his proper place is in the audience,
not on stage. Paul lives in Chapel Hill, North Carolina, with
his wife, Elizabeth.

THE PLAYERS OF GILEAN
TALES FROM THE WORLD OF KRYNN

EDITED BY

MARGARET WEIS
& TRACY HICKMAN

THE PLAYERS OF GILEAN

©2003 Wizards of the Coast, Inc.

Distributed in the United States by Holtzbrinck Publishing. Distributed in Canada by Fenn Ltd.

Distributed to the hobby, toy, and comic trade in the United States and Canada by regional distributors.

Distributed worldwide by Wizards of the Coast, Inc. and regional distributors.

Cover art by Stephen Daniele
First Printing: February 2003
Library of Congress Catalog Card Number: 2002113221

9 8 7 6 5 4 3 2 1

US ISBN: 0-7869-2920-0
UK ISBN: 0-7869-2921-9
620-17853-001-EN

U.S., CANADA,
ASIA, PACIFIC, & LATIN AMERICA
Wizards of the Coast, Inc.
P.O. Box 707
Renton, WA 98057-0707
+ 1-800-324-6496

EUROPEAN HEADQUARTERS
Wizards of the Coast, Belgium
P.B. 2031
2600 Berchem
Belgium
+ 32-70-23-32-77

Visit our web site at **www.wizards.com**

TABLE OF CONTENTS

WELCOME TO THE SHOW

Welcome, friend, to our play! Hear tales of heroics and honor, friendship and betrayal, villains and scoundrels, lovers and love lost! Revel in these incredible stories about my famous troupe of actors, revered the length and breadth of Ansalon!

I am Sebastius, the leader of the renowned band of thespians known as the Players of Gilean. We have performed for every illustrious personage in Ansalon at one time or another: Kith-Kanan himself, every single Kingpriest of Istar, Lord Gunthar Uth Wistan and Dragon Highlord Ariakas, the beautiful Laurana of Qualinesti and the sultry Blue Dragonlady Kitiara, and the infamous Raistlin Majere (whose incessant hacking spoiled my best lines).

We have performed before elves and humans, dwarves and kender, dragons and ogres, draconians and goblins, and the very gods themselves.

We are not heroes in the ordinary sense. True, we ride upon dragons and fight daring battles with cold steel (so long as the ropes hold and the prop man is sober). True,

introduction

we perform heroic acts on a daily basis (twice daily, if you count matinees), but we do this for your pleasure and edification, not to save the world.

Well, (blushes modestly) perhaps we *do* save the world in a sense. By making the world a better place in which to live. By taking you out of your world and transporting you to ours. By inspiring those who need inspiration. By helping people remember the past to forge a better future. By bringing the light of laughter to the darkness of despair.

So join us, friend, for our plays.

Thrill to "Command Performance," by Douglas Niles, wherein we prove our mettle by performing for two warring armies.

Marvel at the winsome "Papilla" by Fergus Ryan, wherein vengeance rules.

Shudder at "Enter a Ghost" by Paul B. Thompson, for who is there among us who does not enjoy being frightened out of his wits?

Weep, dear hearts, over "Perfect" by Donald J. Bingle. All the world loves a lover.

Rise in respect for "A Matter of Honor" by Richard A. Knaack, for it deals with the honor of one of our own.

View with awe "Rewrites" by Aron Eisenberg and Jean Rabe, in which—gasp—I, the great Sebastius—take to my bed and leave the play to my underlings with, as you might expect, disastrous results.

Come, friend. Here is your seat, the finest in the house. For now you are traveling with the Famous Players of Gilean.

—Sebastius
as dictated to Aron Eisenberg

COMMAND PERFORMANCE

DOUGLAS NILES

Age of Might, circa 890 PC
Thoradin—Coastal Plain

The griffon spread feathered wings, scooping the air to each side as it came to a comfortable landing before the Duke of Fredirko. The hawk-faced mount pranced and fluttered restlessly, settling its broad wings only after a stern word from the elf who rode in the steed's leather flying-saddle. In the face of that display, the duke's white stallion merely sniffed disdainfully and otherwise ignored the griffon.

"My apologies, Excellency," said the golden-haired Qualinesti elf, slipping from the griffon's saddle to bow before the great soldier and his legendary mount.

Fredirko brushed his hand in the air dismissively. "Valiant has seen many more frightening sights than one of your eagle-mounts clacking its bill. Now to business: What have you seen?"

"Yes, of course, Your Grace," the elf stammered. "The army of Axel Bloodwart continues to pursue our own forces. His scouts and cavalry you will be able to see momentarily, and the main bulk of his infantry is but two hours away from here."

"That is about what I expected," murmured the great general, speaking mostly to himself. He and his horse stood atop a gentle ridge, looking into a shallow, grassy valley that was intersected by a shallow stream. The duke's staff, elegantly dressed lords and captains, waited on mounts standing respectfully apart from Fredirko. "They are directly on our trail?"

"Indeed, Your Grace, deployed in march columns and making good time."

"The ogre king uses his usual formation—cavalry patrols on the flanks, a broad front, with his goblins interspersed among sturdier stuff?" The Duke of Fredirko frowned thoughtfully. "War machines in the center, great scads of cavalry in reserve?"

"Yes, Excellency, exactly," agreed the elf.

"What about the terrain on our flanks?"

"This streams widens into a marsh at the end of this valley. It is wet and reedy, certainly impassable. The sea, of course, lies just a few miles beyond, so there is no vulnerability there."

The duke nodded curtly. "And inland?"

"A wide stretch of hilly, broken ground extends in that direction," the elf explained, with a sweeping gesture. "The highland is entirely a maze of ravines, craggy little peaks, and swales of sucking mire. There is no trail there for an army, nor even a man or a horse."

"Yes, well, we shall be grateful for your feathers, then," declared Fredirko. The duke lifted his arms and clapped hands clad in white silk gloves.

Immediately, the nearby subcommanders spurred their mounts forward, jostling for position around the general. Each was magnificently horsed, yet the duke's stallion stood out amongst the other mounts, a prince in the midst of pack mules.

Fredirko was still interrogating the elf scout. "Now, about that little stream—how many crossings? At the flanks, and in the middle?"

"Questionable up there because of a gorge as it flows out of the highland, and downstream it deepens with a soft, muddy bed where it draws near to the marsh, Your Grace. There is a long stretch of graveled shallows in the middle of the valley, good ground to either side."

"Splendid. We know, then, where Axel Bloodwart intends to make his effort."

"I take it you plan to meet him here, then?" a young prince mounted upon a prancing palomino mare asked breathlessly. He was wearing a scarlet cloak and a broad-brimmed hat, crowned with an astonishing plume of long green feathers. Fredirko made no acknowledgement of the question, but that didn't dissuade the young lord from speaking further. "Will we finally have a battle? At last!"

The general closed his eyes and drew a long, slow breath into his nostrils. Just as slowly, he exhaled, then nodded decisively and looked behind, to the long marching column of his army.

"I think this will be the place. Yes, Prince Grayce-feather, we shall deploy on the reverse slope of yon ridge."

"On the back side of the hill? So he won't be able to see us?" The young royal seemed on the verge of a genuine pout.

The duke's lips tightened into a thin line that, if it was a smile, contained no hint of amusement. "I will show enough of my army to whet his appetite."

By now the first regiment of the army, a file of looming elephants, was trundling past with footsteps that shook the ground. Each lumbering animal was protected by great skirts of stiffened leather armor and bore a battle platform bristling with archers and pikemen. Twin tusks, extended by metal spearheads, swayed menacingly before the gray heads. The pachyderms and their riders advanced in a long column and marched resolutely through the shallow stream and up the opposite ridge.

Companies of elf archers came next, moving at a trot, spreading out to follow each section of elephants. Cavalry followed, regiments of humans on horses and several companies of fast, powerful centaurs—warriors who rode to battle on their own four hooves but bore spears, shields, and mighty bows and arrows in their humanlike hands and arms. The riders cheered, as next came twin files of knights clad in gleaming armor, astride huge horses that still managed to prance and skip like colts.

The duke and his commanders galloped past the formations, followed by the regimental standard-bearers and one grizzled legionnaire, the duke's personal bodyguard and attendant. The party splashed through the stream in shimmering curtains of spray, and the duke paused to look at a place where the current flowed around a small, flat island, a little patch of ground no larger than a typical lord's courtyard. With a squeeze of his knees, he spurred Valiant onward, the rest of the retinue hastening to stay close.

"What do you make of it, Starlack?" asked the duke a few minutes later, after the party had gained the crest of the next ridge and now looked back for the view of the pastoral stream and valley. If any of the attending officers, many of whom were themselves of lordly rank, were offended by the duke's attention to a mere centurion, they gave no sign.

The burly veteran nodded toward the dust raised by Axel's army, rising into the sky as a roiling column past the opposite ridge. "It's obvious he wants to fight us, Your Grace. There doesn't seem to be a clear advantage to his ground or ours. That field around the shallows looks good for maneuver. He's certain to check it out."

"So if I want to be done with the matter, this is the place to do it, eh?" said the duke with a crooked, almost boyish grin.

Again, Fredirko paused to concentrate on a deep breath. He looked around and gestured with his riding crop along the ridge crest to each side as he issued orders. "We'll deploy here. Take the rest of the day to mark emplacements. I don't think our ogre king is going to try anything surprising, at least not before dawn, but let's keep the pickets out and the griffons flying just in case."

With a steady tromp of booted feet, long companies of Hylar dwarves marched up the hill, then turned on the way to their position in the center, the fulcrum of the army. Fredirko watched with honest affection. His heavy infantry had been a steadfast part of every campaign, and he trusted them implicitly to follow his orders. He knew they would stand firm against crushing pressure and attack ferociously if he needed them to advance.

As the bulk of the army deployed on the far side of the ridge, the duke ordered scouts to ride forward. These green-clad men on fast mounts of brown, chestnut, and tan probed into the water, which came only to the horses' knees across the long ford. For a quarter mile of its length, the streambed proved level and solid, no obstacle at all. Around the small island in the middle of the vale the scouts were able to ride a full circuit without difficulty.

Even as they explored, the vanguard of Axel Blood-wart's army appeared on the opposite ridge crest. These were his cavalry, his so-called Skullriders, who to a man were mounted on horses of midnight black. Like a tide of ink they rode to the left and right, while a formation of armored ogres, marching on foot, plodded into view in the center of the line. Next came the war machines, several great catapults operated by dark dwarves. These artillerymen quickly unlimbered their great weapons and wheeled them onto position on either side of the ogres.

One of the ogre catapults launched a volley of small boulders, but the missiles came down well short of the farthest-ranging scout. The scout thumbed his nose glee-fully before galloping back to the river and joining his fellows in a withdrawal to the safety of Fredirko's lines.

The duke, meanwhile, was surveying the deployment of his artillery and supply train, great wagons drawn by teams of four or eight oxen. These rolled onto the rear slope of the ridge, and the siegemen began the work of assembling the ballistae. Soon the powerful pieces, each of which was like a giant crossbow on wheels, rumbled up the hill to be arrayed on each side of the well-disciplined Hylar.

Tents were raised, stews cooked, and an extra measure of rum dispensed while the duke remained on the crest of the ridge, squinting down at the clearing in the river valley. Starlack remained at his side as the minutes passed and the great general's attention remained rapt.

"You see that island there, that bit of flatness in the middle of the stream?"

"Indeed, my lord."

"Whoever commands that ground will command the ford. And of course, whoever commands the ford will win the battle," remarked the Duke of Fredirko.

"That would seem to be the case, yes."

"So to rest, Starlack. We have a busy day ahead and an early start—for I have no intention of letting Axel Bloodwart beat me to that island!"

———◆———

"Is that an island amid the shallows, there?" asked Axel Bloodwart.

"Aye, Majesty," replied the Skullrider who had ridden along both shores of the stream. "Flat and tiny it is, and you won't get yer knees wet walking to it from either bank."

The ogre king paused, squinted, and thought. The hoary monarch was reaching the later years of his life, though he still boasted a strapping figure, terrifying to behold and lethal to face in battle. A patch of soft leather covered the socket over his left eye, while a necklace of skulls—human skulls—was his favorite ornamentation. His twin tusks were inlaid with golden wire, and he wore a great breastplate of solid steel.

He commanded numerous legions of howling, spear-chucking goblins, bruising heavy battalions of ogre grenadiers, teeming ranks of dark dwarves bearing lethal crossbows, five great regiments of snorting, black-horsed cavalry, and a train of mighty siege engines capable of battering cities, castles, and enemy armies into submission.

"This place will do as well as any and better than most," he declared, huge fists planted on his hips as he looked about the ground occupied by his mighty army.

"Aye, Sire," agreed his chief lieutenant, Bloden Long-eye. "No trees to hide the cursed elves—and smooth enough ground for the Skullriders to maneuver at speed."

Nearby, one of the black cavalry horses snorted and pawed, as if sensing its role in the imminent battle.

"Good slope," Axel Bloodwart noted. The treeless ground descended gently from the rounded ridgecrest into a broad, flat valley. The tiny stream intersecting the valley would be a minor impediment to military operations, nothing more.

"We will form along the crest of the ridge," declared the ogre king, addressing the rest of his captains as they assembled for orders. "Trueblood, you and the First Goblins will have the right. Ballracker, you and the Second take the left." The two hobgoblins nodded, ears and lips flapping with bloodthirsty enthusiasm.

"I want two hundred Skullriders posted on each flank, to watch for tricks," the king continued, addressing the black-armored captain of his cavalry. "The rest of your men should mass in the middle, ready when I want to make the big punch."

"Sire," Longeye reported, turning back to the conference after a brief word with the Skullrider. "The scouts report that the stream is surprisingly deep along its upper course . . . and muddy at the far end of the valley, a marsh, really. But there—" the lieutenant commander pointed to the center of the valley, toward a flat swath of grassy ground—"the bottom is gravel for a quarter mile. Easy fording."

"And an open field for attack." The ogre king nodded grimly. "There, in the morning, is where the battle will begin."

"Let us take it now!" urged a looming veteran, a battle-scarred lunk of a brute hulking even over the huge ogre. "We hill giants are ready to attack at once!"

"No, by Gonnas!" Axel Bloodwart roared. "You are my *reserve*. You are to stay back until ordered forward!"

"Sire," moaned Greenshot, captain of the hill giants. "Our honor is at stake!"

The king snorted in contempt. He glared into the face of the brutish warrior, who was a head taller than the ogre monarch. "Your honor? Think, oaf: The whole *kingdom* is at stake! What matters your honor if you are killed, your women and babes enslaved?"

"Enslaved?" Greenshot frowned. "But . . ."

"That's enough of that. Your honor will be called onto the field tomorrow when I send you into the fight. Remember, good Greenshot, I *always* send in my reserves, for mopping up, if nothing else."

"Mopping up?" The hill giant nodded, mollified, knowing full well that the follow-up troops were the fellows who got first pick of the enemy's treasures. "Well, I guess that's important, too."

"It is, my stalwart friend. It is." The king turned his attention to the valley, which was vanishing into the growing twilight. A thousand fires marked the camp of Duke Fredirko, while an equal number of blazes sparkled along the length of Axel's deployment.

"Do you see that little island there," the ogre added, pointing with one hand while the other reached up for a friendly clap onto Greenshot's shoulder.

"Yes," said the giant, squinting.

Axel knew that even in the best light the nearsighted hulk could make out nothing beyond a hundred paces from his nose. Still, it helped the ogre to articulate his thoughts, so he continued. "That is the key piece of ground. There we will break the enemy's center and crush his reserves. There we will win the day, the campaign, and the war!"

"There?" Greenshot said tentatively.

"There," Axel agreed. "On that little island."

The evening fog was so thick that one wagon of the little caravan was barely visible from the next. The wagons plodded slowly, lurching through a shallow stream, and finally the order to halt was given.

"This little island will be perfect," Sebastius declared from the rear of his wagon, as the rest of the theatre caravan rumbled through the shallow water, the twenty wagons coming to rest in close quarters. They occupied nearly half of the dry space already, leaving barely enough room for the stage to be erected.

"For a performance?" wondered Sir Eriath as the actor sniffed disdainfully at the surroundings. "The sound of the water will drown out the subtleties of my dialogue!"

"You have a point, there," Sebastius agreed, stretching his huge form mightily then bouncing down the stairs that emerged from the beaming portrait of his own face, painted as the sun on the side of his wagon. "So it might be that we won't be able to do *The Death of Vinas Solamnus* for tomorrow's performance."

A chorus of groans greeted this unexpected announcement as the other performers emerged from their wagons and looked around at the bleary surroundings.

"It's not like we'll even have an audience," snapped Stacia Delane, who had been playing Dame Solamnus with a fervor and volume that had extended her reputation throughout Ansalon. "We must be in the absolute center of nowhere!"

"Curse this fog, too!" groused Hatch Blackbeard, the dwarf. "Everything'll be damp, and I don't see a stick of firewood on this little plot of land." He looked quizzically at Sebastius. "Why here, anyway? Even if you do find an audience, they'll have to sit on one shore or another of the stream. They won't be able to hear much."

"You know audiences," the playwright said breezily. "They'll find us here, though this is admittedly rustic. Perhaps we'll need an emphasis on physical comedy for this performance."

"But *Solamnus* was getting such fine reviews!" Eriath objected on behalf of the cast. "Why, from Palanthas to Sanction they loved me—er, us!"

"What do you mean physical comedy—a clown show?" demanded Persnick the elf.

"Wait, good players!" Sebastius held up his hands. "You know, it's been an awfully long time since we did *The First Ten Thousand Jokes of Ferret Whalewhacker.*"

"No!" The wail came from a kender in the front of the crowd of troupers. He pulled on his topknot with one hand while the other flailed around in the air, frantically waving off the suggested topic. "That play gives kender a bad name!" he insisted, "and the last time they threw more than just ripe tomatoes. Remember that spring melon? It nearly broke my arm!"

Sebastius chuckled in genial sympathy. "Ah, that was a performance to remember. Of course, the dark dwarves were a tough audience . . . almost impossible to entertain. I remember there were predictions that not one of them would crack a smile, but you, Strawfellow Slipknot, *you* were able to make them see the humor."

"Well, that's right!" huffed the kender, though now he twirled his topknot around his fingers and remembered. "Of course, they more than smiled—at one point, I had them rolling in the aisles."

"Aye," agreed Hatch Blackbeard, the dwarf, "and later you dodged five tomatoes at once. An impressive performance."

"It was, wasn't it?" Strawfellow mused. "At least, until they started launching the melons."

"As a matter of fact," continued Sebastius, "I wrote a letter to my brother detailing your performance. It is certainly recorded in his chronicles, there for all posterity to read."

"You did? He did? It is?" Now the kender was intrigued, his objections forgotten.

"Indeed."

"Did you save a copy? Could I see it?"

"Later," replied the troupe leader. "Now it is time for you to get busy hanging the playbills."

"Where?" asked Strawfellow. "I haven't seen anyone to make up an audience."

"Or anything else, curse this fog," groused Hatch.

"Oh, people will show up," Sebastius reassured them. "Have faith. I hope to garner a large house in this great outdoors! Our island stage! Now, Hatch, I want you to go up the left hillside. Post as many bills there as you can."

"No problem," agreed the dwarf.

"And me? Do I get to go the other way?" the kender asked.

"Of course you do—you, and all your cousins. Post the bills everywhere you can, but you'd best be careful. I think you'll want to avoid getting noticed."

<hr>

"Your Grace . . . I'm terribly sorry to disturb you."

Fredirko sat up on his cot, instantly awake, eyes rapidly attuning to the flare of candlelight into his tent carried by the timid watchman.

"Don't be silly," declared the lord. "I know it must be important. Your news, man!"

"Er, it seems we've caught a prisoner, someone trying to infiltrate our picket line."

"One of Axel Bloodwart's scouts? I can't say I'm surprised. Still, don't know what he hoped to accomplish at this late hour. Tsk."

"That's just it, Excellency. It's a dwarf, a Hylar. Doesn't seem like one of the ogre's men at all."

The duke was intrigued. He didn't need to check the hourglass—his uncanny sense of time told him that it was nearing four in the morning, less than an hour until first light.

"Have the dwarf brought to my command tent. I will dress and be there shortly."

Starlack was already up and wearing his shirt of chain mail, but he smoothly knelt and helped his lord with his leggings and the knee-high boots. Fredirko donned his silken coat and the cap of black felt, capped with a griffon's feather, that completed his battle ensemble. Strapping his light rapier to his belt, the duke strode forth into the darkness, ready to make the day and the battlefield his own.

Immediately he heard hammering, the sound echoing through the night, coming up from the valley below.

"By Paladine, what's that?" he asked. "Not like our ogre friends to start construction before a battle."

"We've sent scouts to find out," reported his guard captain.

Fredirko was already moving on, striding to his command tent. He entered to find a black-bearded Hylar dwarf in animated discussion with his aides-de-camp.

"Why, 'tis the great man himself!" announced the dwarf, sweeping into a bow so deep and graceful that it was almost, but not quite, mocking. "I declare the honor and the pleasure 'tis all mine."

"I understand you were caught sneaking into my camp," declared the duke in a forthright tone.

The dwarf's eyes widened to circles, and his bearded face took on a look of wounded indignation. "Why, there's been a terrible misunderstanding!" He looked at one of the nearby guards, a man dressed in the dark robes of the night pickets. "Tell him, wouldn't you?"

"He's right, Your Grace, er, technically. That is, we caught him trying to sneak *out* of the camp."

"Going to report to your master? Details of my dispositions, my strengths?" probed the duke.

"Nothing of the sort, Your Graceful Excellence. I merely came here to do a job, and I did it, and I was going on my way when your man here apprehended me. Not that he didn't do a gentleman's job of it, no sir," the dwarf hastily amended. "A watchman for the ages, that one."

Fredirko ignored the praise, though he noted that his sentry flushed with pleasure at the dwarf's words. "What was this secretive task that you came here to accomplish? I warn you, I have little patience with liars."

"I shall strive not to take offense, Lordlyship," the dwarf reported with a huff. "Know that 'twas my sincere pleasure to post bills, Your Highnessness. I believe that I did a yeoman's job of it. After, as you may recall I have explained, I was going about me way."

"What bills? Show me," the duke encouraged, growing intrigued in spite of his initial misgivings.

"Really," the dwarf clucked, "I *did* think I had explained. I did my job *well*, and therefore I have *no* bills left, nothing to show you."

A pinch tightened his lips, as the duke allowed a momentary release of his frustration. Before he could venture another question, the door to the tent was pulled open, and Prince Graycefeather entered. His sword and belt were a tangle in his hands, but he had managed to don his scarlet cloak and lofty, feathered hat.

"I say!" he declared cheerfully, waving a parchment in the general direction of the duke. "There's to be a show! How positively splendid!"

"What?" The duke was irritated with himself as soon as the question left his mouth—he had plainly heard the prince's words and merely needed time to collect his thoughts. Before he accomplished this, another scout entered.

"Your Grace," said the man, "I have discovered the source of the hammering. It's . . . well, it's rather remarkable . . . but there's a troupe of players there, building a stage on the flat ground in the stream."

"The flat ground?" Now Fredirko was really startled. He whirled back to the dwarf. "Do you mean you intend to perform a *show*? On *my* island?"

As always, Axel Bloodwart awakened shortly before dawn. The fog of sleep was still thick in his mind, and he rubbed his eyes as he forced his old, aching body upright. He slept on a low cot in his tent, and, as he swung his bare feet to the ground he felt a twinge of sympathy for his thousands of loyal warriors. If he felt this bad after a night inside a tent, lying on a soft, portable cot, how did they feel after the same night spent under the stars, on the ground?

It hadn't been like this when he was younger, of course. There had been many nights he had gone without sleep or curled up in a nest of boulders for a few hours' rest and still fought like a bull in the morning. Some of his

greatest victories had been won when he led a party of
ogres down from the mountains, camping in the wilds
before savaging a human army, fortress, or settlement.
In this fashion, for fifty years he had maintained his
ancient realm's borders against enemy incursion.

How had he allowed things to change so much? Here
he was, hundreds of miles from any familiar landscape,
leading an army that included no more than one ogre out
of every twenty-five warriors. What use did he have for
dark dwarves and horsemen, for stubborn, petulant hill
giants and jabbering goblins? As for the Gonnas-cursed
catapults, sure, they could pound an enemy as though they
were squashing bugs, but the king himself didn't have a
clue as to how they worked. It seemed wrong, somehow,
that his army required human and dwarven technicians
with skills beyond anything an ogre could hope to grasp.

Ah, but perhaps today, perhaps here, the last battle
would be fought, the final campaign brought to conclusion. He could allow himself to hope that after fifteen
long and bloody years this great war could finally be
settled. During all those years Axel Bloodwart had never
faced a foe as diligent, as industrious and inventive, as
the Duke of Fredirko. Yet, too, never had the ogre king
commanded such an impressive array of warriors. He
might begrudge the presence of the Skullriders, but how
they could charge—a sweeping wave of black horseflesh
and keen steel that cleaned an enemy army off the field
like a breaking wave wipes a sand castle from the beach.
The dwarves too, for all their vanity and wickedness,
were as steady in a fight as any ogre and far more disciplined when it came to holding a line, or advancing and
wheeling in formation. Furthermore, he had to admit, if
only to himself, that he had come to rely upon the siege
engines, his crushing catapults that could cast a load of

stone a quarter mile or hurl barrels of oily incendiaries three and four hundred paces. Everything had changed over the years. Developments and progress made his men better at killing the enemy and the enemy better at killing them. Countless battles, innumerable miles of marching, all had led here, to this confrontation, today.

Still bleary, the king dropped his feet into his huge whaleskin boots. Clad in his woolen sleeping-tunic, he clumped to the door of his command tent and pulled aside the flap.

Already the camp was stirring. He heard horses nickering and firewood cracking as the fuel carts were unloaded and breakfast begun. An ogre sentry slept just outside the king's door, and Axel was cocking his foot for the wake-up kick when something odd caught his eye.

A paper! A thin sheet of parchment ruffled from the guard's exhalation, and the king saw that it had been attached to the ogre's helmet so that it hung down across the tusked face and fluttered with each nostril-flapping snore. In disbelief, Axel snatched the paper up and realized it had been fixed in place with a tiny piece of gum. There were words scrawled across the sheet.

The king delivered a kick, bringing his guard snorting to wakefulness, scrambling into a posture of attention.

"What is this?" Axel Bloodwart demanded, waving the parchment in the guard's pale face, as ogres, goblins, humans, and dwarves hurried to investigate the commotion.

"Sire . . . that, Your Majesty . . . er, Sire . . . ulp, I don't know!"

"You don't *know?*" The king's voice was low, a menacing purr. "I'll *tell* you what this is—it is your death sentence, fool! Someone put it on your helmet, across your *face*, and you took no note of the intrusion!"

Axel scrutinized the elaborate lettering.

"Playbill . . . stage . . ." Unfortunately, he could make out very little. "Here," he snapped, handing the sheet to a human captain. "What does this say?"

"Er, you were correct, Sire," the man replied with an irritatingly quick glance at the words. "It is in fact a playbill, announcing that a performance of 'The Players of Sebastius' will be made today, at high noon. The cast . . . in the name of this Sebastius . . . looks forward to providing us with some light diversion and buffoonery."

"What nonsense! And you allowed this to be stuck to your forehead?" Axel turned his scornful gaze on the quivering guard. "For such ineptness, you shall be drawn and quartered!"

"There seem to be more of those bills around," ventured a dwarf. "I found three of them gummed to my catapult."

"Yes, and the firewood carts, too," added a human sergeant.

"The oil wagon was virtually plastered with them," reported another man.

"Sire . . ." It was the king's lieutenant, Bloden Longeye, standing beside him, strangely hesitant to speak.

"What is it?" barked Axel Bloodwart. "Were you, too, such a sleeping lunk that they stuck one of these right on you?"

"No." Hesitantly, Bloden reached behind the king. Axel felt a slight tug, as something was pulled from the back of his sleeping tunic. He didn't need to look to see that his lieutenant had discovered another of the playbills.

"Who dared to molest the person of the king?" he growled furiously. He looked at the ogre sentry, who had sunk to his knees and begun to weep. "This fool's sentence is commuted. Instead you will go in the front line of the attack today!"

"Thank you, Sire!" groaned the warrior, falling at the king's feet. Axel kicked him away.

"Now, who is behind these bills?" demanded the monarch, stalking through the camp, trailed by Longeye and a growing retinue. Daylight was paling the sky, and when he came to the ridgecrest he was startled to see a structure occupying the flat ground below. Vaguely he made out wagons and the great square block of a platform . . . a *stage*!

"They're going to try to do their performance on my *island*?" he demanded, as his mighty jaw dropped to hang, slack and drooling, before his chest.

———◆◇◆———

"I have a feeling this will be perfect," declared Sebastius, opening the door to his sunburst-painted wagon and drawing in a deep draught of early morning air. "Smell that freedom, that freshness!"

"Smell those armies!" retorted Sir Eriath. "I swear, they both made their latrines upwind of us!"

"Small matter, that," declared the brother of Astinus with a hearty chuckle.

"What about *that*?" squawked Stacia Delane, pointing in agitation.

"Ah, our audience arrives, even if a trifle early, I daresay," fretted Sebastius. "And me without even my pancake on!"

The troupers stared, agog, as a rank of elephants lumbered into view, advancing down the eastern slope in a line. Although they plodded slowly, the beasts seemed to cover the ground with startling speed.

"Look!" cried Sir Eriath, in dismay, pointing in the opposite direction. "Cavalry! There are thousands of them!"

"Indeed, this promises to be a splendid crowd!" declared Sebastius happily. "Now, I need to get made up. Let's see, Sir Eriath. Perhaps you would do the honors of speaking to the elephants."

"Elephants?" demanded the actor. "What should I tell . . . elephants?"

"Oh, not the elephants themselves," Sebastius said dismissively. "The men *riding* the elephants."

"Well, of course, but—"

"You, Hatch . . . where's Hatch Blackbeard?"

"I don't think he has yet returned from posting play-bills," Strawfellow Slipknot announced. "I think you should have sent him with me. I would have kept an eye on him!"

"Quite," Sebastius said, looking around his troop. "Er, Stacia, it will be up to you to talk to the horses." Before the actress could utter a protest, Sebastius ran a distracted hand through his hair and turned around to disappear into his trailer.

"But—" Eriath cast a glance at the lumbering rank of pachyderms, which was drawing alarmingly close to the shallow stream. "What should we do?" he yelped, with a look at Stacia. Her face was slack, staring at the wave of black horses and scowling, bearded riders. Abruptly she turned and ran to Sebastius's wagon, pulling open the door and vanishing inside.

"You in the stage troupe," came a human's clipped, rather presumptuous voice. Sir Eriath spied a dapper man dressed in a bright cloak and seated upon a shining white stallion, advancing from among the rank of elephants. The actor was a little relieved to note Hatch

Blackbeard, apparently unharmed, clumping forward just behind this human of obviously lordly rank.

"Yes, Excellency?" the actor replied, presuming this was at least a duke if not a prince, king, or emperor.

The young lord, horse prancing anxiously, edged close to the shallow stream. "What is the meaning of this?" he shouted across the water to Eriath, who was damned if he could think of any decent answer.

Hatch Blackbeard broke the silence. "Sir Eriath! Allow me to present the Duke of Fredirko himself!" he cried, stepping forward and bowing with a flourish worthy of a standing ovation. "Come to call upon a mere knight of Palanthas!"

"Knight? Of Palanthas?" queried Fredirko. "Of what house, pray tell?"

Eriath's jaw flapped, and he tried to say something— he really did. However, no sound emerged from his mouth until he forced out a faint squeak. Fortunately or not, that sound was buried beneath a roar from the other side of the stream.

"You there? Actor!"

Sir Eriath turned to confront the largest, ugliest ogre he had ever seen—and he had seen a lot of them. This brute had a patch across one eye and two golden tusks jutting, boarlike, from his lower jaw. Behind him were numbers of horsemen, a mustachioed, swarthy lot mounted on black steeds like a sea of night flowing down the hill.

"I am speaking with the man!" declared the duke over Eriath's shoulder. "Kindly hold your tongue until I am finished."

"I'll give you a tongue—of cold steel!" bellowed the ogre in reply before turning his glowering gaze back to the actor. "Now, get these wagons out of my way, or I will have them crushed to kindling!"

Eriath spun from the ogre king back to the duke, whose horse seemed to be tapping its foot, impatient for a response. His mind spun through a thousand lines, all of them inappropriate, until a thought—a role—came to him. He straightened, seeming to grow inches in the view of the two armies. His look, cast back at the ogre again, was disdainful enough to cause that brutish monarch to shut his mouth in astonishment. Eriath turned the same look upon the duke. Fredirko pursed his lips but made no remark.

When Eriath spoke, it was not with the voice of Eriath of Palanthas but in the person of Vinas Solmanus, founder of the greatest dynasty in humankind's history. His demeanor, his tone, was enough to hold the ears of the two commanders.

"This troupe performs the epic tales of Krynn's history. Clearly, each of you is a maker of that history, but even you, kings and dukes and generals, cannot rise above that history! So I request—nay, history *demands*—that you take seats and observe. Show the respect that our world requires!"

The two army leaders remained speechless, gaping, as Eriath spun on his heel, stalking away as though he were the emperor himself. With regal strides he carried himself up the steps and through the door of the wagon. Inside, he toppled to the floor in a dead faint.

———◆◆◆———

"Of all the insolent . . . !" Axel Bloodwart was staggered beyond the capacity for cursing. He gaped in amazement as the wagon door, square in the middle of that beaming sun of a face, slammed shut.

Still groping for the words to express his colossal rage, the ogre king cast his eyes about his troops, some arrayed behind him in battle formation, others heading down the hill. Should he have the Skullriders lay waste to this troupe and collect the actors' heads on the tips of their pikes? Or should the catapults smash the caravan into kindling before his infantry marched across the bodies of the dead?

"I wanna see the show."

For a moment, Axel couldn't believe his ears, then he turned very slowly to confront Greenshot. The giant's arms were crossed on his chest, and he was scowling beneath the great cliff of his forehead.

"What did you say?"

"Wanna see-um," the hill giant repeated.

To Axel's amazement, the sentiment was echoed— albeit in dull tones—from some of the Skullriders nearby.

"Wanna see-um!" The sound was picked up and repeated, until momentarily it seemed that his whole army was murmuring the same words. They pressed closer as it built into a rumbling chant. "Wanna see-um . . . wanna see-um. . . ."

The king felt his rage slipping out of control and felt his drool and hot breath escape from his tense lips. Before he could say anything, he was distracted by a tug at the helm of his armor.

"Pssst—Sire!"

It was the fat hobgoblin, Ballracker. His eyes were squinting in the approximation of a shrewd expression.

"What?" The ogre king's fury surged at the sight of the idiot hobgoblin, but a tiny voice in the back of his mind suggested that he might need a graceful way out of this confrontation, so he leaned down, braving a waft of breath that reeked of fresh garlic and stale beer.

Ballracker lowered his voice to a conspiratorial hush, gesturing to the island, the stage, and the wagons. "What if this whole thing, this troupe, is a plot of the duke's?"

Axel liked where this was going, but he was still confused. "What does the duke have to gain by posting a troupe of players in my path?"

"You heard the men, Sire. Begging your pardon, but they want to see the show. If you blast them players to smithereens, why, they'll be disappointed. Is that the state of mind, the weight on morale, you want them carrying into the battle?"

Immediately the king saw Ballracker's logic. "Thank you for your insight, Captain—no, *General*—Ballracker." The king straightened and scowled, ignoring the suddenly puffing hobgoblin. Axel was thoughtful.

"Bring down the men and have them take seats for the show," he ordered. "Have them stay in their formations and keep their arms."

The monarch of the ogres snorted, pleased with himself. He turned to look across the stream toward where the duke was in conference with his officers and sneered.

"I wonder, my young foe: Did you have the foresight to have your players prepare an entertaining show?"

"Burn the wagons with oil-arrows—it's the only lesson for such impudence!"

"Take the lot of them and fence them in. Leave them in the stockade for a week!"

"Crush those obscene wagons into kindling and torch the actors on their own bonfire!"

"No, string up the lot of them—*that* will be a show!"

"Let my elephants march through!"

Duke Fredirko listened to the suggestions as rapidly as his subcommanders could spit them out. Each lord and captain had a more inventive means than the last for rubbing this eyesore of a troupe off the face of the Krynn. Prince Graycefeather was most ingenious, proposing they allow the ensemble to start the show then pick off each actor with a volley of arrows when he first dared to show himself on stage.

Finally they had each spoken, and the chorus of suggestions came to an end as the men waited for the duke to announce his decision. Instead, Fredirko took a long, slow breath and asked a pointed question of his grizzled centurion, who had stood silent and reflective during the long litany of violent recommendations.

"What do *you* think, Starlack?"

"Well, we could wipe them out with scarce a second thought, Your Grace, but I've been listening around . . . and it seems that some of the men would like to see the show."

"Preposterous!" sniffed Prince Graycefeather.

"Outrageous!" snapped Orik Oilsniffer, commander of the Hylar dwarves.

"If you'll look," Starlack continued, with a gesture across the stream, "it seems that Axel Bloodwart is going to let his men watch the show."

"Indeed." Fredirko, seeing the ogre activity, held up his hand, silencing any further objections. "As usual I believe my good centurion has hit the nail on the head. Indeed our noble foe is ranking his forces to see the performance."

None of the officers had in fact noticed this, but a few glances confirmed that the ogres, goblins, dark dwarves, and other scum making up Axel Bloodwart's army were arraying themselves in the field beyond the stream, sitting down and fanning outward so as to be as close as possible to the stage.

"Imagine the effect on morale, should I give the orders that so many of you are encouraging."

The duke drew a deep breath, closed his eyes, and slowly exhaled. "No," he said. "The army of our enemy will be here after the play. Let the men have some laughter and spend the heat of the day in repose. Late in the afternoon there will be time enough for violence and blood."

———◆———

"Now, we need to open with a scene that will really get their attention," Sebastius declared, nervously pacing on small floor of his wagon.

"We could do the clown scene!" Strawfellow Slipknot suggested.

The director of the troupe shook his head. "Er, no, I think we had best save the kender acts for later, with this crowd."

Stacia sighed. "I could put on the coconut shells, I suppose. This group is bound to like Yolanda the Melon Queen."

"Really?" Sebastius responded, startled. "Actually, yes, that would be splendid, if you are willing."

"I think I know how to handle these overgrown boys," the actress suggested with a throaty chuckle.

"Now, Stacy, you know what Yolanda the Melon Queen can do to military men. Surely you remember the reception in Caergoth."

"Yes. They brought the house down, almost on our ears!" Eriath agreed.

"Only because I—quite appropriately—maintained the aloofness that my profession requires," Stacia remembered. "If I do that again, we'll be fine."

"Indeed, you were quite a hit, as I recall," Hatch Blackbeard said with a chuckle.

"As was Sir Eriath, in portraying the Clownmaster," Sebastius continued. "And I do think we should do that again, though today we should reserve that for later in the show."

"No!" howled the actor, even as the kender in the troupe whooped and shouted with joy.

"Hurray for the Clownmaster!" Strawfellow Slipknot shouted gleefully. "We'll be the clowns!"

"Yes, yes of course," Sebastius said.

"I shall do it on one condition," the knight finally declared. "If we get to use real beer."

"Of course, of course. A very good idea. Now, to the wrestling match. My good Blackbeard, can you and your fellows assemble mud from downstream past these beds of gravel?"

"You want all three tubs filled?"

"Certainly."

"That'll take some time," the dwarf replied solemnly. "If you want to start at noon, maybe we should go with the streamlined version."

"Hmmm." Sebastius tapped his quillfeather against the board in his hands. "This is not an audience we would want to keeping waiting. I suppose you're right, though. We'll work without mud, today. And Hilderidge?"

"Ya?" The acknowledgment came from a great ogress who had lurked in the back of the group and thus far remained quiet. She was dressed in a great tent of gray wool and scowled, apparently in concentration, as Sebastius spoke.

"What costume today?"

"I s'pose the thong, for this group."

"Splendid!" Sebastius was beaming now. "We'll start you out with the juggling, then have you do some wrestling, too."

29

"Audience participation?" she asked lugubriously.

"Naturally!"

The ogress sighed. "How many?" she asked.

"We'll see how it goes."

Hilde nodded, but Sebastius was already moving on. In short order they lined up Hatch's juggling routine, the unicycle act, and the always stunning *Tour of Ansalon*, by the pudgy illusionist, Portentius. One after another the roles were assigned, the props listed, and the last details of costume and makeup arranged.

"Very well," Sebastius finally announced, with a businesslike tuck of the board into his flowing robe. "That's our program."

"What about the finale? What do we do for a finale?" wondered Lady Stacia. "I certainly don't want to do an encore as Yolanda the Melon Queen!"

"Tsk, no, of course not. As a matter of fact I have a finale in mind, but I think I'll keep that as my little secret for now. Everybody ready?"

With a few groans and muttered curses the troupe grudgingly replied in the affirmative.

"Very well!" declared Sebastius, clearly pleased. "Let's go out there and knock 'em dead!"

They came from their two ridgetops, great files of men, clad in armor, bearing swords—sheathed, for now—as well as unstrung bows, quivers of arrows, and great sheaves of spears. The grass was green, the sun bright in a cloudless sky, as they arrayed themselves for the show. The columns of infantry came first, lining up, taking seats on the ground with fingers close to weapons, eyes glaring distrustfully at the stage and at the army arrayed on the opposite side of the little waterway. They sat in ranks, units intact, arms at hand.

The cavalry, riders dismounted, sat higher upon the hill, while tenders held the horses nearby, at the fringes of the crowd. On each crest the great war machines, catapults and ballistae and trebuchets rose like gargantuan, skeletal constructs, framing in the shallow valley.

The two commanders were seated, each in the front of his respective army, eyes more attentive toward each other than toward the bare stage. Even when Sebastius, clad in a green silk robe that shimmered in the sunlight, emerged from his wagon, the duke and the king remained focused upon each other, eyes dark, narrowed, unblinking.

"Good warriors! Brave soldiers! Valiant elves and courageous dwarves, fierce ogres and terrible hobgoblins! I, Sebastius, extend a warm welcome to you all! We are grateful to have you in attendance today and shall do our humble best to provide for you a show that will amuse, edify, and entertain!"

The troupe leader bowed with a great flourish, sweeping through a half circle that took in the massed audiences on each side of the river. If he was expecting a welcoming round of applause, he was disappointed. There were a few jeers and catcalls, but for the most part the armies watched in ominous silence. They were a veritable blanket on the ground, these warriors who covered every patch of grassland on the two facing hills. The great arrays of horses, elephants, and war machines remained at the tops of their respective ridges, but all the ground before them was thick with men.

A hill giant stood next to King Axel Bloodwart, who glowered ominously as he sat in a great oaken chair that

DOUGLAS MILES

several of his hobgoblins brought down into the front row. Across the water and on the other side of the flat island, the Duke of Fredirko was seated in a folding camp chair, though a servant faithfully held an umbrella to keep the glare of the sun off the great man's head. Beside the duke sat a young human with a ridiculous green-feathered hat. The hatted human fidgeted and snickered nervously.

Sebastius, a veteran of thousands of productions and performances, showed neither hesitation nor reluctance. Indeed, his lips creased into a sly smile as he held up his hands and again pivoted grandly to encompass the full extent of his double audience. "But enough from me. I know you have come here to see the show, and I am not so presumptuous as to take up any more of your time than—"

"Bring on the girls!" shouted a swarthy human from the ranks of the Skullriders, who were seated in the back, having left their saddles at least for the duration of the show.

"Indeed," Sebastius said. "Let the festivities begin. Gentlemen, I give you—Yolanda, the Melon Queen!"

Hatch Blackbeard struck his deep drum with a single, resounding boom, and the curtain at the back of the wagon swept aside to reveal Lady Stacia Delane, her rouged lips curled into a fixed smile. The dwarf started a rhythmic percussion—*boom boom da-boom boom*—as she sauntered down the steps of her wagon and strolled across the stage. The men of both armies erupted into a welcome of hoots, whistles, and even—from the hobgoblins and others—a woofing chorus of imitation dog barks. On both sides of the stream, men leaped to their feet, the better to get a look at the alluring actress.

Alluring she was, even Sebastius had to admit. The twin coconut shells of her brassiere were utterly inadequate to meet the needs of modesty. They jiggled enticingly as she did a graceful pirouette in time to Blackbeard's drumming, holding the pause for a few beats longer than was strictly necessary.

Her skirt was more a collection of trailing ribbons than any actual garment. The strands gathered at her waist and fluttered around her legs in shimmering tendrils that did little to conceal her elegant calves and gracefully curving thighs. When she turned she thrust out a shapely hip, in perfect timing with an accented drumbeat. The warriors in the front row actually groaned.

Hatch kept up his drumming as Sir Eriath, in the garb of a soldier, strode onto the stage. In an effective display of arrogance he kept his nose in the air as he stalked past her. She reached out, hands clutching his arm, but he pulled roughly away.

"I have no time for you. Duty calls!" he declared haughtily. "I am off to war!"

He marched off the stage to a chorus of boos, and Sebastius smiled as he waited for the sound to build to a crescendo. Men were cursing Eriath for being a fool and a boor, and the sounds rose to a frenzy as, with perfect timing, the gentle sounds of the flute played by the elf named Persnick rose, accompanying the now soft drumbeats and carrying almost magically to thousands of listening ears.

The crowd settled now as "Yolanda" wiped away a stage tear. Her wistful gaze swept across the vast throng, and somehow she made each warrior feel as though her eyes had lingered on his alone. There was utter silence through the ranks of both armies as the flute and drum music rose and the actress began to sing.

> *He left me in the morning,*
> *Upon his horse he rode,*
> *His regiment is forming,*
> *Along Palanthas road.*

Her voice seemed as pure as any songbird's, and the trilling accompaniment of the flute formed a piercing duet with the lyrics. The men were rapt, even awestruck, as she continued through the verses. She sang a tale of war, but it was war told by a broken heart. Rumors of her beloved's travails came to her in the form of brief letters, which recounted battles with dragons and ogres, with foul undead and valiant knights.

> *But then his letters ended,*
> *No more did my love say,*
> *Upon which trail he wended,*
> *Nor where his battles waged.*

Now she paused in her singing, though the flute and drum continued through the beat and melody of another verse. Sebastius smiled privately as he saw men in the front ranks on each side of the stream actually reach forward, as if they would extend to the love-sick woman a comforting embrace.

The drum sounded a harsher boom, and the flute trilled upward into melodious and clearly delighted notes. Once more Stacia pivoted, and again that sensuous hip bumped outward, pushing aside the strands of costume. When she crossed the stage again, she undulated with a slinky sway in perfect time with the music, and the men who had moments ago reached out consolingly now shouted and cheered lustily.

And then there came another,
A soldier brave and true,
Who came to warm the bower
Within my chambers blue.

He was a warrior stalwart,
A swordsman without peer,
But in my lonely halls, hark—
He knows to use his spear!

With a flouncing of her round derriere she sashayed up the steps and disappeared into the wagon as the warriors all around erupted in whistles and hoots of appreciation. Sebastius remained behind the curtain for a few moments, allowing the frenzy to play out, knowing that his return to the stage would serve as a transition to the next act but also understanding that he needed to delay that transition until the men had vented their enthusiasm.

———◆———

"Interesting," Duke Fredirko said, a slight smile playing across his thin lips. "The men seem to appreciate her performance. I wonder how many of them fathomed the crude wit of her final line?"

"The elves, it would seem, and some of the centurions, Your Grace," Starlack said drolly, his face bland. "I don't think any of your officers did."

"Oh, this is just splendid!" exclaimed Prince Graycefeather, seated on the other side of the duke. "This is even better than a battle!"

The duke looked disdainfully at the younger man, then allowed himself a hint of a smile as he leaned toward Starlack. "Just be glad, Old Graybeard, that there are a few of us who were born to rank *and* competence."

"I give thanks daily for that fact."

The duke looked across, stonily met the eyes of the ogre king, then turned his attention to the stage. "Now, be silent. They are getting about the next act."

———◆———

"A silly waste of time," Axel Bloodwart snorted. He looked at the Skullriders and at the great swath of dark dwarves, all of whom were howling for an encore from Yolanda the Melon Queen. "I don't know how they can get so worked up over a little stick of a thing like her."

"Who can say?" agreed Bloden Longeye, wiping the foam of ale from his upper lip. "Still, there was a certain pleasing curve to her flank."

The king looked at his lieutenant in undisguised disgust. What a wasted day this would be. He snorted and leaned back in his sturdy chair, surprised to realize that he was a little curious about what would transpire next.

———◆———

"You are good warriors, loyal and true, experienced and capable. That much is apparent to me at a glance," Sebastius declared, after enduring the jeers that arose when all assembled realized that it was he and not "Yolanda" who had returned to the stage.

"No doubt your kings and captains know you to be such and pay you accordingly," he continued, with a flourishing bow first toward Axel Bloodwart, and then to the Duke of Fredirko. The two armies rumbled, chuckles and laughter rippling through the ranks.

In the meantime, Blackbeard carried a table and chair onto the stage, while Hilderidge the ogress, still dressed in her tentlike gown, rolled out a barrel, which she turned to stand upright.

"Such payrolls, of course, must travel far to reach an army in the field. In doing so, they may oft pass through the hands of a moneychanger!"

Sir Eriath stalked down the stairs from the wagon, dressed in a robe of shimmering black silk. A thin mustache and neat goatee, both of inky black, glistened as he cast a sneering glance across each section of the audience. With a sniff of disdain, he stalked to the table, pulled out the chair, seated himself, and began to count his money.

Sebastius paused, for this part needed no narration. The actor had no actual coins, nothing of any kind on the table before him. Yet his hands lovingly shaped a stack of gold, which he caressed as he carefully placed it to one side. Next he pantomimed the lifting and emptying of an imaginary sack of silver coins, which rattled and clattered on the table, some rolling away so that he had to snatch them back with quick, frantic movements. The watching men chuckled appreciatively as the pile of money grew higher and higher and the actor's efforts to keep it from toppling became more and more frantic.

"Today our moneychanger has received a delivery," Sebastius announced, crossing the stage and gesturing to the standing barrel. "A precious shipment, so the label proclaims. Yet our 'moneychanger' has no clue as to the nature of that shipment, of those important contents."

Sebastius exited, and Sir Eriath's eyes fell upon the barrel with a look of visible longing. An expectant hush cloaked the crowd as the actor took time to balance the pantomimed coins in tall stacks, then advanced toward the cask. He moved in stalking steps, like a hunter creeping toward unwary prey, and provoked a great laugh when at last he rushed up to the barrel and seized it like one grasping a slippery lover.

"What do we have?" he asked breathlessly, twirling a corner of his mustache as he scrutinized the label. "Precious . . . each is guaranteed to be one of a kind . . . quantity, unknown."

"I must see!" he declared, and with his fingers pried up a corner of the lid.

Immediately Strawfellow Slipknot emerged, squirting through the narrow opening to somersault once and bounce upward to pose with outstretched hands and cheery grin.

The moneychanger shrieked in horror and pressed down the lid, while the audience exploded into laughter.

"Thanks mister," declared the kender in a delighted squeak. "It was getting kind of stuffy in there!"

"Thief! Wretch! Scoundrel!" cried the actor.

"Who, me?" Strawfellow looked crestfallen. "I haven't stolen anything in my entire—say, is that *real* gold?"

The kender sauntered over to the table, somehow avoiding the man's frantic efforts to grapple him. He held up one of the imaginary coins, pivoting and stepping away from the table as Eriath missed him again and fell facefirst onto the stage.

"You know, this looks pretty rare. You'd be better off if you didn't leave rare things like this lying around. Why, I'm not a thief of course, but I've known some thieves, and most of them would give their left—"

"*Give that back to me!*" Eriath's scream left no room for discussion, so the kender shrugged and held out his hand.

"Sure, here. Now, where did that thing go? I could have sworn I had it right here!"

"Listen." Eriath's voice quavered. His face was pale and covered with a sheen of sweat. He hovered over the barrel, both hands resting on the lid. "Take the coin—I know you've got it somewhere. There are more of them in here. Why don't you come and have a look?"

"Sure!" Strawfellow bounced over to the barrel and helped the man lift up the lid but then skipped away as Eriath tried to snatch his topknot.

"See here," said Eriath, cajolingly. "Why don't you come and have a look."

The man held the lid, his eyes fixed upon Strawfellow. Meanwhile another kender popped out of the open barrel. He was followed by a third, and a fourth, and the troops of the two armies started to laugh harder and harder as still more of the long-haired little folk bounced and tumbled and somersaulted into view. All the while Sir Eriath's eyes remained fixed upon the sauntering Strawfellow, as the man tried to coax the kender back to the barrel.

Not until a dozen of his fellows were busily scrambling through the moneychanger's office did Strawfellow walk back up to the human. "I'll look around in there now. It will be a little easier to see."

"Yes, certainly," said Sir Eriath as the kender lifted himself into the barrel. By this time the kender were swarming around the table, toward which the knight had turned his back. Each opened a pouch or a satchel, and coins were swept inside, chased over the floor, and busily scooped until each kender was staggering around under the weight of precious metal.

Finally Sir Eriath, with a croak of cruel glee, clapped the lid down on Strawfellow Slipknot. Only then did his eyes fall upon the mob of kender in his domain. With a shriek of horror, the actor began to chase the scattering kender all across the stage. The little folk delightedly tossed their imaginary sacks of pilfered coinage in a merry game of keep-away until finally Eriath clasped both hands to his skull and was carried offstage to an accolade of laughter that rang through the valley like thunder from a spring storm.

"There is a certain appeal to their antics," admitted the duke with a wry chuckle. "To thus lampoon such an object of universal hatred."

"Bah—kender!" declared Prince Graycefeather with a shudder. "Who could wish them on anyone, even a moneychanger? Better had they all been dropped into the ocean!"

"What?" replied Fredirko, gently mocking. "You would not condemn them to the Lords of Doom?"

"Drop them into a volcano? Hmmm . . . yes, that would be even better. Don't you know, I rather like that idea! Indeed, the prospects for humor are quite plentiful."

But the duke wasn't paying attention. Instead, he had again turned toward his centurion.

"The men certainly appreciate the humor, Your Grace," Starlack noted.

"In truth. The morale effect is observable. I don't doubt that it will carry over to their bloody tasks this afternoon."

"Let's hope it doesn't have the same effect for our enemies," the centurion noted.

Axel Bloodwart snorted, working hard to keep from grinning. He glanced at Fredirko, and saw that the young lord was clearly distracted. Of course, the kender and moneychanger routine had been hilarious, but the ogre king was conscious of his place at the head of this mighty army and knew it wouldn't do to let his men see him succumb to laughter.

However, he gaped at the stage and, altogether unbidden, found himself roaring with laughter as the next act commenced.

For the stage was now occupied by a huge ogress, who was clad only in a few bits of sequined string placed provocatively across her immense bosom and around her ample hips. The ogre king had never seen such a display before and found himself utterly astounded and perfectly entertained.

"Gentlemen of two armies, I give you—Hilderidge of Bloten!" Sebastius declared, his large bulk skipping out of the way as the immense ogress swaggered around the stage. A shadow swept over the platform. Several clouds were creeping across the sky, scudding past the sun.

Hilde struck a coy pose, one leg bent slightly at the knee, both hands pressed daintily against a tree-trunk-sized thigh, while warriors shouted their appreciation. The loudest roars came from the ogres among Axel Bloodwart's troops, and the gargantuan performer flounced playfully in their direction. One rouged eyelid dropped in a showy wink, and dozens of ogres leaped to their feet, howling and stomping their approval.

"Wait!" Sebastius declared, boldly stepping in front of the still-posing ogress. "Think you that our Hilderidge is some pretty piece of fluff, all stage makeup and frills? Think this, and the opinion may well prove to be your undoing, good watchers!"

He touched the ogress's bulging bicep, allowed his hand to linger at her sinewy wrist, even toyed with one sausage-like finger. In the meantime, Blackbeard was carting props onto the stage. A moment later the dwarf and the human withdrew, leaving Hilde to stomp and prance in a circle. She flexed her muscles, went through a stretch so elaborate that an awed hush fell over the crowd, then reached into the cart to pull out her first object.

This was a hefty beam at least ten feet long and as thick around as a strong man's thigh. Hilderidge tossed it into the air, where it spun through graceful circles as it rose high above her head. Still spinning, it tumbled downward until she caught it with a smooth gesture and twirled it around as if it were a mere twig. Finally, she pirouetted, lifted the beam in both hands, then brought it down over her knee where it splintered with a loud *crack*.

Respectful applause followed, but she had already drawn from the cart three large rocks, each nearly as big as her own head. These she tossed into the air and juggled through a spinning cycle, keeping one in the air at all times while she bounced the massive boulders from one hand to the next, then upward again. Brave men gasped in fear and amazement as it seemed certain that her head would be crushed by one of these flying missiles, but she maintained the rhythm with practiced ease. When at last she finished, she let the rocks fly here and there, and each rolled off the stage to tumble onto the ground with a solid thud, scattering audience members. The noise was buried under a wave of hearty, appreciative applause.

Now she removed a barrel, the last item in the prop cart. This was a good-sized cask, and she tumbled it about the stage for a moment to demonstrate that it was indeed a solid and sturdy container. After this was clearly established she straddled the barrel and stood, holding the vessel between her muscular thighs. As the men on both sides of the stream gaped in amazement, she exerted slow, gradual pressure. Veins stood out from her forehead, and a sheen of sweat slicked her skin. Ropelike sinew bulged from her legs until, with a shout of triumph, she crushed the cask between her knees and splintered the boards into kindling.

Hilde bowed to one side then the other amidst enthusiastic applause.

"Is there among you one bold enough to come to the stage?" Sebastius asked, entering again, striding around his performer, regarding the members of the audience with a cocked eyebrow. "For you should know that Hilderidge prefers to grapple with objects of more vitality than mere props!"

"Me! I will wrestle the wench!"

The cry came from among Fredirko's Hylar, and a burly dwarf swaggered out of the band of his fellows. He was a strapping fellow, his legs bowed but sturdy as gnarled trunks, his long arms rippling with muscle as he raised them to clasp his hands over his head in a triumphant pose. "There be not an ogre, male or female, who can throw Splint Fireater!" he announced.

Cheers and whoops rose from the duke's men, while boos, hisses, and catcalls volleyed from Axel Bloodwart's army.

"Don't hurt me," Hilde said, batting her lashes and doing her best to look demure as the dwarf swaggered up the steps. He spent a moment posing and posturing for his comrades, before turning to advance on his opponent.

43

"As you look like a 'lady,' " he declared mockingly. "I will go easy on—*oof*!" The dwarf's confident expression switched to comical amazement, but he was already sailing through the air. He landed in the first rank of his fellows, who tossed him into the stream with a series of catcalls and jeers.

"I'll take a turn—let me up there!"

The next volunteer was a monstrous hobgoblin who sauntered out of the close-packed ranks of Axel Bloodwart's army. His great belly sagged over his belt, but his gangly limbs possessed the supple strength of his kind, and his wicked eyes narrowed in cunning as he regarded the great ogress. Hilde, for her part, stood with arms crossed around that massive bosom, waiting for the hobgoblin to make the first move.

Now that he was on the stage, the challenger seemed oddly reluctant to close. Perhaps he was balked by the supreme confidence of the massive ogress, who contemptuously turned her back on the hobgoblin, while she flexed and posed for the whooping humans in the duke's army. The ugly humanoid crouched, almost as if he were about to charge, then scuttled sideways and cast a confused look over his shoulder toward the rank of his fellows.

Those stalwarts only began to boo lustily, one going so far as to throw an apple core that bounced off the hobgoblin's forehead. Amid the general laughter, Hilde's booming guffaw rose like a cymbal crash, and apparently this mockery was enough to steel the wretch's spine. The hobgoblin turned, lowered his head, and charged the ogress with those long arms reaching out to clasp his foe around her muscular midriff.

He did—bouncing to a jarring stop against Hilderidge's immovable form. She made a great display of yawning while the hobgoblin locked his hands and began to squeeze with visible strain. Abruptly the ogress whirled gracefully, and her attacker's feet left the stage as, suspended from her waist by his clenched arms, he swung outward. When Hilde stopped suddenly and then reversed the direction of her twirl the challenger couldn't hold his grip and went sailing through the air to splash into the stream. The ogress bowed to the right, the left, and the right again, accepting the cheers of the admiring warriors while the vanquished hoblgoblin splashed pathetically along the shallow streambed, searching for some place where his comrades would let him out of the water and back into the ranks of the audience.

"Now me!" The next challenger was a powerful young ogre, heavier and taller than Hilde. His long black hair was contained in a thick horsetail, and tattoos depicting swords, knives, and even stranger blades were emblazoned across his broad chest, arms, and back.

"By Gonnas the Willful One, I am in love!" he roared, pushing his way toward the stage. "Have your way with me, lass. I am but putty in your hands!"

"Well, golly," Hilde declared, frowning as the newcomer splashed through the stream and, disdaining the steps, hoisted himself directly onto the stage. He knelt with a flourish and looked up at her adoringly.

"Ya won't get far on yer knees," she snapped sternly. "Get up and lemme have a look at ya."

The ogre warrior stood, raising his arms, flexing his muscles to mutters of appreciation from each side of the stream. He was in fact a magnificent specimen, and the tattoos added a barbaric and imposing element to his appearance.

"Let's see what ya got," Hilde said, stepping forward. The ogre spread his arms, ready to sweep her into an embrace, but she pivoted on one foot, pulled his weight over her jutting hip, and flipped him so that he crashed heavily onto his back. The wooden stage wobbled and creaked from the strain of his landing.

"Oh, but that's good!" groaned the ogre, rolling over and pushing himself to his hands and knees. He gazed adoringly up at the massive ogress, who lifted a shovel-sized foot, placed her heel against his forehead, and kicked him backward.

"Love hurts!" he cried, playing to his fellows now, as the ranks of ogres roared in appreciation. He rose to his feet, skipped a few steps to demonstrate that he wasn't badly injured, and then fastened his eyes upon Hilde's jutting chin. He held steady for a second or two but couldn't help dropping his gaze lower on the ogress's curvaceous form.

Faced with that distraction the warrior licked his lips and blinked, and in the space of that blink Hilderidge was upon him. She seized him about the waist, lifted, and flung him, head downward, straight into the stage. As he lay gasping upon his back she leaped into the air, like a diver aiming to make a great splash, and the prone ogre was her swimming pool. She came down across her victim's body with a timber-straining crash. She got up. He lay there, stunned, kicking feebly. She knelt to take him by the chin.

"Not a bad try, Big Fella," she said cheerfully, planting a loud, moist kiss on the warrior's leathery cheek. He sighed, jaws gaping into a tusk-baring, blissful grin.

She pushed him with a dismissive gesture, and he toppled backward to the raucous shouts and whistled cheers of the enthusiastic troops.

Hilde made deep bows in every corner of the stage, and if the stringy nothingness of her costume slipped even more revealingly she didn't seem to take note of the fact. Instead, she let the men roar their appreciation for a full minute, before making a last promenade around the stage, up the steps, and back into the wagon.

———◆———

"You know, I could use that one in my ogre brigade. I'd be tempted to make her a captain," Axel Bloodwart admitted with a rumbling chuckle.

"I'd be tempted to make her my concubine," Bloden Longeye said approvingly.

The king snorted, casting a sidelong glance at his lieutenant. Was he, Axel, the only one who had a grasp on what was really important? Sometimes he wondered if being a leader was worth the effort. He looked across, noticed that Fredirko was studying him and realized that yes, there was another who understood.

He was a little melancholy as he turned his attention back to the stage.

———◆———

Sebastius came forward again, and this time they settled to hear his introduction.

More acts moved in rapid succession, to enthusiastic response. Blackbeard juggled his hammers, working his way up to ten, then dropping them, one after the other, onto the metal cap of his helmet. Despite wearing extra padding for his skull, the dwarf as usual was wobbly and dazed as he made his way off stage.

Next came Sir Eriath in his role of the Clownmaster, and the hard-working actor bore up with surprisingly good spirits as he again occupied the stage with a dozen kender. Perhaps it was the fact that Strawfellow's flower-spray button squirted real beer, as Eriath had requested, but in any event the human and his diminutive cast mates soon had the members of both armies laughing uproariously and applauding sincerely when the kender finally carried the soaking actor off the stage.

Now it was time for Yolanda again, this time riding her unicycle while Persnick played a lively jig on his flute. Next Portentius the illusionist held the audience spellbound.

The clouds had covered most of the sky, casting the valley into shadow. Portentius began by deepening that shade, drawing a curtain of night over the field, as real as if the sun had plunged to the horizon and vanished in the matter of minutes. Magical fires came into being atop the troupe's wagons, and the stage stood illuminated in a shifting pattern of red, blue, and green light. Portentius stood in the middle of the light, and somehow the rotund, short man had taken on an image of great height, of impressive and commanding presence. He strode about the stage as if he was master of all he surveyed, and with gestures of his hands he raised a picture of a shining marble building behind him.

With regal bearing he surveyed the men of two armies, and these veterans of wars and campaigns, survivors of furious battles and high magic onslaughts, stared back in amazement at an edifice that looked amazingly real.

"It is my pleasure to extend a cordial invitation to officers and footmen alike. Come with me into this hallowed hall, and allow me to grant you a tour of the Great Library in Palanthas. I invite you to feast upon the sights that will greet your eyes, and to wonder at this place."

When Portentius turned and passed through the doors to the great structure, he did not disappear into the building. Rather, it was as though the edifice reached out to embrace the audience, and now all of the troops were inside the library with Portentius.

His voice penetrated the stillness, reaching every ear with conversational ease. "Walk with me through the vestibule of the Great Library of Astinus. Sense the presence of all history, of every life—of your *own* life— preserved."

The room was a massive vault, rising to an arched ceiling with lofty windows of stained glass softly illuminated high up on the walls. Great, shadowy alcoves led to the right and left. Each audience member felt himself a special visitor. Each could sense the long, musty halls, the hallowed rooms, and ancient volumes. Each had a sense of solitude, as if he found his own aisle in the vast stacks, free to browse, to ponder, to learn.

"But enough of this somber mood," declared Portentius suddenly. "Follow me, good guests, and we shall sample a more festive hospitality."

The next room was even larger than the library vestibule and considerably brighter. Chandeliers and lanterns blazed everywhere, like a pattern of brilliant stars just overhead. Somewhere a talented band of musicians was playing a dance with a measured beat, while men in splendid tunics and women in dazzling gowns swayed liquidly across the floor in a "*one*-two-three, *one*-two-three" cadence.

On the steps of the wagon, Persnick played his flute for all he was worth. Sebastius watched the elf as he moved deft fingers along the shaft of his instrument. Hatch Blackbeard, seated just above, thumped rhythmically on an assortment of small drums. How Portentius took these two musicians and enchanted the results of their labors into this splendid musical symphony Sebastius

49

himself didn't understand. He only enjoyed it, for it had become his favorite part of this particular show.

"Here we see the great King's Ball, an annual event during the greatest years of the Solamnic Reign," the illusionist narrated. He lingered just long enough. His watchers were entranced and amazed, for they experienced it as though they were there.

Then Portentius commanded the Solamnic Palace to fade. Moving gracefully onward, he took the armies on a tour of the Tower of Stars in Silvanesti, the fiery and volcanic interior of one of the Lords of Doom, and even the chaotic tangle of Mount Nevermind, that stronghold of the gnomish people.

Finally he escorted his many guests through the flaps of a huge tent, and Sebastius himself, watching, could almost feel the dry, desert air wafting past.

"This is the great Pleasure Dome of an early King-priest," the illusionist was explaining, in that calm and conversational voice. "Note the dancing ladies. This supposedly pious leader was famed for purchasing the prettiest young maidens he could find and imprisoning them as concubines in his lair."

Indeed, the ranks of dancers were vivacious and stunning, and if they showed too much leg with their high kicks it did not seem as though any of the military men were wont to complain.

Eventually, the illusionist's tour was over, and as the musicians allowed their plaintive notes to softly fade, Portentius gradually unveiled the cloudy afternoon sky, giving the eyes of the watchers time to readjust to the brightness. When he finally bowed and stepped off the stage, he did so to prolonged applause, an accolade that Sebastius let linger, for the audience had relished the tour as much as he himself did.

"A rather spectacular presentation, don't you think?" the duke murmured with a pleased nod.

"All tricks, I'm sure," sniffed Prince Graycefeather.

"Seriously? Do you mean he didn't transport our entire army to Palanthas, and ancient Istar?" asked Fredirko, raising his eyebrows in astonishment.

"Well, no," the younger lord began earnestly, before flushing, as he realized he was being mocked. "I wonder what they will try to do next," he concluded stiffly.

"So we come to our finale," Sebastius said, once more coming forward to take center stage. "For this, again, it is necessary that we draw upon our kind audience for volunteers."

Immediately men stood and called out their willingness to come onto the stage. A Hylar dwarf waved both arms and shouted lustily, and two cavalrymen from the Skullriders came to blows as they struggled through the crowd in an effort to reach the stage. "Pick me!" shouted the ogre who had been bested by Hilderidge. "I'm in love!" he proclaimed again, before his comrades pulled him down and genially pummeled him into silence.

Sebastius ignored all these. Instead, the manager of the troupe made a great show of carefully scrutinizing the assemblage, shading his eyes with his hands, staring up the hillsides into the farther galleries, then casting his glance across those ranked down near the front. He did this first across the Duke of Fredirko's army and turned his attention to the horde of Axel Bloodwart.

Finally he turned back to the Hylar, elves, and humans of the duke. Sebastius advanced to the edge of the stage, his attention fixed upon Fredirko himself, in his front row seat.

"Your Grace, will you please do me the honor of taking this stage?"

"Absolutely not!" Rigid, eyes wide, the man was clearly appalled at the effrontery.

Even as the duke's outraged refusal still echoed, the showman turned and crossed the stage. His outstretched hand extended clearly toward Axel Bloodwart. "Your Majesty, would you be so gracious as to also take a pose upon my playing surface?"

The ogre king glared balefully from his lone eye, but then his pointed gaze flicked away across the stage and the stream to take in the discomfiture of his rival, who sat erectly, face flushing crimson.

"It would be my pleasure," loudly declared the monarch, his voice a rumbling basso. He sneered at the duke as he rose, marching across the stream in two steps, the splashing water barely lapping over his ankles. With immense dignity he ascended the steps to stand before the suddenly dwarfed Sebastius. The ogre's eye never left Fredirko's.

Finally the duke rose stiffly and stalked up the steps on his own side of the platform. "It will not be said that the Duke of Fredirko is hesitant to face Axel Bloodwart—in anything!" he declared.

"Splendid," Sebastius chortled, rubbing his palms. "Now, come here."

He led the two commanders to the props cart, which Hatch had once again wheeled onto the stage. For a moment the three were screened from the audience then the stage manager whirled to display two long, shining swords. He whipped each through the air, as the crowd

fell silent. Each deft slash made a *swoosh*. With a great
flourish he extended the hilts of the blades toward the
two commanders.

"Your Majesty, as first to arise, do you wish first
choice of your, er, prop?"

Axel Bloodwart's tusks seemed to stiffen, as his one
good eye glared balefully at the weapons. After a moment
he shook his great head. "I will allow the duke to have
first choice."

"Splendid." Sebastius pivoted to face the human.
"Your Grace?"

Fredirko nodded acknowledgment to the ogre king
then took up one of the weapons. Axel took the other.

"I don't know what this is about," the duke muttered.
"Generals of armies have far better things to do than to
be poking at each other with swords."

"Ah, but this is theatre!" Sebastius declared heartily.
"The two of you will perform a scene that you shall
create, that is, improvise, as you progress. It is only for
me to set the scene."

"Scene? What scene?" demanded the ogre suspiciously.

"Merely imagine, my good monarch, that you are a
young buck. You are in love with a gorgeous maiden, and
she hath pledged her heart to you. But fie, her father has
secluded her and barred her from your sight. Her engagement to another, with wedding forthwith, has been most
recently announced."

The ogre king was glowering most fiercely, his hand
tightening around the hilt of the sword. "Who would
dare?" he growled.

Sebastius's attention had already turned away, and
he addressed the duke.

"You, Excellency, are a proud father, a noble of righteous station, and your daughter is a prize faithful and

true. Yet her ears have been dirtied by the solicitations of a mere soldier, and you fear her heart may have been stolen by the same."

"Indeed! No daughter of mine shall have any consort with a soldier!" the duke declared haughtily, drawing good natured chuckles from his loyal men.

With a grand sweep of his hand Sebastius turned away from the two commanders and stalked regally along the edge of the stage, a circuit that took in all of the audience. "You meet now in the city market when there are none about, and only your honor and your pride guide your hands."

Sebastius was gone, vanishing up the steps and into the wagon. The overcast sky had darkened to a steel gray, and a cool wind coursed through the valley, but none in the silent crowd took notice. Fredirko and Axel grimly regarded each other, feeling as though they *were* in a marketplace, surrounded by shuttered stalls, locked crates, and an empty stable. They held each other's gaze for a long time as, slowly, the two swords were raised.

"You!" spat the Duke of Fredirko. "Defiler of virgins! Bringer of disgrace! Be gone from my sight!"

"How dare you order me thusly?" declared the ogre in a booming voice. "Old villain! Confiner of beauty! Bechainer of freedom!"

The clang of the two swords drew a shocked gasp from the collected warriors. If these weapons were stage props, they nevertheless seemed made from strong and tempered steel. Again and again the blades met, echoes ringing through the air as the two commanders battled back and forth across the stage in a whirlwind of motion. Fredirko leaped atop the crates and slashed and parried against a frantic attack. Axel fell back, perching at the edge of the stage while he seemed to fight for his life. Each thrust was quick, each swipe powerful and dangerous.

With a sudden lunge the ogre king rushed forward, and now it was the man who defended with frantic parries, giving ground, dodging desperately. A deft sidestep lured Axel Bloodwart into a stumble forward, and the one-eyed monarch fell to his knee, leaning back against a whirling series of attacks. Grunting from the effort, he pushed himself upright, knocked the duke back with a mighty swing, and stood still, panting for breath.

"Let her choose!" cried the ogre with real passion. "He who would lock away such beauty would cast a blanket over the sun."

"Oh, bravo!" cried Sebastius, reappearing in his doorway as men on both sides of the stream applauded the ogre monarch's wit. "A king with the heart of a poet!"

"Poet?" snapped Fredirko, his tone full of fury. "You call us poets? We are generals—and I am a general who has had enough of playacting! This is a battlefield, by all the gods, and we are here to wage war!"

Steel rang with resonant force as the duke's sword swept through a vicious cut, only to meet Axel's parry.

"War it is!" roared the ogre, his own weapon coming through an overhand slash that sent the human dodging out of the way.

"I will put an end to your monstrous reign!" cried the duke, his own weapon dazzling, flashing, slashing.

Axel Bloodwart met each deft attack, strength against dexterity, power facing speed. Back and forth the two fought. For a moment the duke balanced perilously on the edge of the stage as his men fingered their weapons, but then Fredirko recovered, and it was the ogre king who fell back, and his army who tensed to spring. Sweat beaded Axel's brow even in the chilly, cloudy afternoon, while the duke drew ragged, audible breaths.

A sudden thrust, a twist, and the ogre king's sword flew from his hands, tumbling through the air, splashing into the stream. A groan rose from the ranks of his warriors who watched, spellbound and horrified, as the duke raised his blade for a killing thrust.

Fredirko's voice was a hiss that carried across the valley. "An end to tyranny!" he declared. "Let an age of freedom commence!"

That second of hesitation was enough. Something gleamed in the ogre king's hand. A knife flashed silver in the cloudy afternoon. Axel reached and plunged, and the Duke of Fredirko writhed away, doubling over as the hilt of the knife jutted from beneath his side. He gasped, trying to talk, and blood spilled from his mouth. With a convulsive gesture he toppled forward, kicked once, and lay still.

There was stunned silence.

"Foul!" cried Starlack, springing to his feet and drawing his sword. "Death to the treacherous ogre and his wicked troupe!"

"Blood!" shrieked Bloden Longeye, rising as the ogres and goblins rippled to their feet all around him. Sebastius stood like a statue as angry troops splashed into the stream, closing in on the stage from both sides. Fingers clawed at the edge of the platform, while other men raced this way and that, riders seeking their mounts, artillerists their catapults and ballistae.

Abruptly the two armies paused in confusion, every eye turning to the stage where the ogre king could be heard above the tumult, laughing loud and hard. Axel Bloodwart reached down toward the motionless form of his vanquished foe. "Look!" cried the ogre king, plucking out the knife that was clenched with the duke's armpit. He poked himself in the chest, and the blade collapsed into the hilt. "A stage knife!"

"Fake blood, as well," the duke said with a tight smile, rising to his knees and allowing the ogre to help him to his feet. "Indeed," he noted not without pride, wiping the crimson liquid from his lips, "I daresay we fooled them—though we will no longer be fooling," he added grimly, "when our armies meet in search of real blood."

Axel Bloodwart's eye narrowed, but before the ogre king could reply, before either army could attack or applaud—for the impulses warred—a crack of thunder split the air, and a bolt of lightning licked down, shattering one of the catapults. Immediately the clouds erupted, sheets of icy rain lashing the valley, hailstones drumming on armor and weapons.

Men scattered in all directions, racing for their camps, shields raised as shelter from the brutal weather. Sudden wind scoured the field, howling, piercing with icy fingers, bringing shudders to those still on stage. Sleet pummeled the ground and any man who had not achieved shelter, and bold warriors raced for tents and tarps.

The king and the duke withdrew to their sides of the stage, but before they descended the stairs their eyes met in cold appraisal.

"There will be killing here, before we march!" shouted Fredirko.

"Aye, young general," Axel agreed in a bellow. "Before we march."

The rain lashed the valley through cold evening and dark night, as the troops of both armies huddled under such meager shelter as they could hastily erect. The actors, meanwhile, dismantled their stage, packed their wagons, and before dawn were ready to depart. There was no dallying. Everyone wanted to get out of the way before the rain ceased and the two armies commenced their inevitable battle.

In the pre-dawn drizzle a figure moved through the stream and approached the great wagon with the man's sunny face painted on the side. The steps creaked under the weight of the huge person as he reached the door and knocked.

"I was expecting you," said Sebastius, pushing open the portal and inviting his visitor in.

"You were?" Axel Bloodwart asked. He hesitated then ducked his massive head and came into the wagon as the manager of the troupe moved back to make room for him.

"Yes . . . I have guessed . . . I know that you will find what you seek, with us. We have saved space for you in the third wagon with Hilderidge and Blutar, our carpenter."

The ogre king blinked his one eye, and for a moment it appeared he would change his mind. Finally he nodded. "Thank you," he finally said. "I think Bloden Longeye is more than ready for command . . . and he has more heart for it than I do these days."

Sebastius shrugged. "It is only as it should be. Welcome. You'd better get down the line to your wagon. I want us to be rolling before the catapults let fly."

Axel nodded again and turned to depart, then paused.

"Tell me," said the ogre who was formerly a king, staring earnestly into Sebastius's face, "why? Why come here, why take such risks? Your troupe was endangered, and you could have been massacred upon a whim— either mine, or my enemy's."

"We accomplished something important," Sebastius said with a sigh.

"Accomplished what? After all, there will still be battle, bloodshed, lives lost on both sides, widows and wounded made on this field."

"Yes, but for a time, for a whole day, there was laughter, diversion, and delight. We actors, we players, held death at bay . . . if only for a day."

Axel's one eye focused on the stage manager. His tusks dripped rainwater as he squinted, thinking, then nodded for a third time, not fully understanding yet. He stepped back into the rain and made his way to the wagon that would carry him away.

PAPILLA

FERGUS RYAN

*Eastern Solamnia,
circa 360 AC*

This is what they call a cautionary tale. A story told to warn children—especially young boys—against wildness or cruelty or disobedience.

Needless to say, few children—and almost no young boys—claim to believe this kind of story. They scoff it away. Dismiss it as elderly propaganda.

Yet some of them steer away from tormenting sisters and schoolmasters, from petty theft and major explosives, because of some cautionary tale they have heard and somehow credit.

———◆◆◆———

Versions of this particular tale take place in a dozen cities and towns. Villages from one coast to the other, all claiming to be the spot where the wagons stopped, where the actors set up stage, where the boys learned their lesson.

You'd almost think that the players were everywhere, performing in different places at the same time, as if they were some kind of omnipresent warning.

On a few things, though, all versions of the story agree: the names of the children, the festival, and the play itself. Almost always they say it happened before the War of the Lance.

From that point on, there are all kinds of disagreements.

Three versions of the tale are set in Solace, one in Xak Tsaroth. Since just about every story you've read or heard has something to do with Solace, I'll point you to another version. One that takes place miles away—in a little town, no more than a bend in the road, in disputed country between Coastlund and Solamnia.

Not quite Coastlund. Not nearly Solamnia.

Hollow, they called the place. You won't find it on the maps now, but it was somewhere in the foothills of the Khalkists. Hence its name, some say, in honor of the old term for a valley or a notch between mountains.

Others say that the name of the town described it in other ways. That it was called Hollow because the almost-nothing of its outsides hid the almost nothing within.

Wherever and whenever the town took shape and whatever the source of its naming, it was a place that needed a story.

Even a cautionary tale that nobody believes.

———◆◆◆———

Not that Hollow was altogether dismal. A family or two had managed to scrabble small fortune out of its few possibilities.

One of these families was that of Kaleem Bombyx, who dealt in silks.

Kaleem had been a traveler once. He had visited far-flung places and had imagined places even more far-flung. Had he lived in Istar, or Solace, or even Xak Tsaroth, they'd have called him something elegant, something distinguished, like "merchant" or "trader." In Hollow, he was a shopkeeper, almost all of his business transacted with folks who were passing through and eager to get away, who sometimes bought entirely on impulse and always at whatever outrageous prices the old shyster charged. How he acquired his goods was nobody's business and everyone's guess, but the silks were of decent quality, and the money he made was passable.

Enough so that as he settled into his early fifties, Kaleem Bombyx stumbled into a spectacular marriage.

Well, spectacular for a shopkeeper in that neck of the world.

Her name was Ilona, and she had two qualities of great note, both of which Kaleem admired greatly.

First, she was uncommonly plain. That meant, in Kaleem's reckoning, that she should be pleased to marry just about anyone, even a second-shelf merchant thirty years her senior. Furthermore, given her plainness, she would probably receive no attention from the young blades of Hollow—wild boys, chronically unemployed, blessed only with the knack of stealing chickens and wives.

Second, and more important, was Ilona's dowry. Third daughter of a Solamnic Knight who had long since given up on finding her a suitable husband, she came to Hollow with full coffers, with enough gold and jewelry to float Kaleem's business through lean times. The shopkeeper's ingenuity made much of this good financial luck: By the time his children came along, they would be set for life.

Providing, of course, that they spent that life in the dismal village of Hollow.

Meanwhile, the marriage of Kaleem and Ilona Bombyx was sound enough. Both of them loved their children fairly well, but more of that later. Each regarded the other with respectful indifference. Ilona gave up her notions and entered the life of the village, and Kaleem . . .

Perhaps he gave up something in return, though it was hard to tell. I mean, every man wants a pretty wife, doesn't he?

And well-behaved children?

After all, this is the children's story, and it is time to introduce them.

Three of them, all versions of the tale agree.

Two boys and a girl.

When the first son was born, Kaleem decided that he would name each child for a distant, exotic place. That accounted for Taladas, though the name was soon shortened to Tal. But the father gave up the notion before the second boy came along, afraid that outlandish names might set his children to wandering.

After all, he wanted them to stay in Hollow. To mind the store in his old age.

So the second son was simply Nando, like a half dozen other boys in the village.

The two sons were shaped by their naming. Tal was the wilder, the more outlandish. The one with ideas. A thin and spindly article who delighted in scenes and mischief, in finding the roundabout way to get someone else to do his dirty work.

Nando was dull and easily influenced, inventive only in petty thefts and acts of meanness. He was what the most gloomy of Solamnic philosophers had in mind when they dismissed human life as *nasty, brutish, and short.*

Then there was Livia.

There was something about the girl.

At first Kaleem was disappointed in having fathered a daughter. She wouldn't be good with numbers, he figured, and she would be less likely to lift heavy things. It's why she received a traditional Solamnic name: It was her mother's idea, because her father had lost interest in the naming and the girl herself.

But from her beginnings, it was Livia who was the eye-catcher, the charmer, the third child of all fairy tales, blessed with the beauty and innocence that neither parent had . . .

That baffled her father's plans for her future and promised (given that she was a girl from Hollow) a frustrating and unhappy life.

———◆———

Kaleem indulged his sons. He was, after all, old enough to be their grandfather, and one of the great virtues of any grandpa comes in the coddling and spoiling.

Early on, it fell to Ilona to discipline the pair. She tried her best, but when Nando was caught stealing pies or Tal devised a snare for the village barber that launched the old man into a bucket of pitch, Kaleem would overrule his wife's judgments, would set the boys scot-free after an afternoon's mayhem.

Children were children, he claimed, but what he meant was *boys were boys.* He was harder on Livia, believing that too much romping and insolence would make her an unlikely bride for the sons of tanners and rat catchers who would pay court to her in the years approaching.

Ilona would sulk, her authority muffled. She would retire to the back of the shop, where she arranged the silks in heraldic patterns and dreamed of old Solamnia, of the banquets and pageants she knew were still going on without her. Sometimes, in the early mornings when her husband and the boys were snoring in the chambers above the store front, she would drape green silks across her shoulders, brush back her long brown hair, and bathe in the quiet that she found only in the hours before the males of the house awakened.

It was then that Ilona Bombyx feared the most for her daughter.

———————◆•◆———————

It was there, on the morning of her seventh birthday, that Livia found her mother.

Ilona heard the soft padding of the girl's footsteps on the stairs. She smiled to herself—that broad-faced, cow-like smile that only her daughter found beautiful.

Behind her, Livia cleared her throat.

Ilona folded a broad swath of white silk. "Do you know what day it is, daughter?"

"My birthday, Mama!"

The voice a little breathless. The accent on the second syllable of "Mama," as they did in Thelgaard, and as Ilona had tried to teach all the children, though Livia had been the only one to pay attention.

Now Ilona turned to face the girl. "I was thinking . . . about how a new silk dress might brighten some-one's birthday."

Livia smiled. "A dress to wear to my dinner?"

"Indeed. White, I was thinking. And long."

The girl leaned against the newel post. "Not *long,* Mama. I'm not half a lady yet."

Ilona laughed softly. "Short it is, then. It will please your father. No matter what he says or does, there's something in him that wants you small a little while longer."

Livia nodded sagely, as though receiving somber wisdom. Just as suddenly, she brightened.

"Will there be other girls at the dinner, Mama?"

Ilona shook her head. "No girls. Only Yoni and Darl and their fathers."

"But Darl smells like copper, Mama. Like copper and sour fruit."

Ilona held the white silk up to the lamplight. " 'Tis the way rat catchers smell, dear. Rat catchers and their sons."

"Yoni smells worse. Like death and acid and . . . and *poop!"*

Get used to it, Livia, Ilona thought bleakly. It's the tanner's son that your father favors.

But these are not things you say to your daughter. Especially not on her birthday.

"So, short, you say? And white? You'll look charming, Livia."

"Not white either, Mama. Orange and black. Like butterfly wings."

"I believe white might be just a bit less . . . macabre, my dear. Or a pale green, to match those eyes of yours."

The child shrugged. She was accustomed to following the notions of others. Accustomed to the unconditional love of her mother, she no doubt figured that she would get to wear some orange and black monstrosity to the festival of Solinari only a few days after her birthday.

FERGUS RYAN

A rustle and thump from upstairs broke the silence of the house. Mother and daughter sighed, both able to read simple portents.

The boys were stirring.

———◆———

High in his hammock above his younger brother Nando, Tal had just concluded the first of his day's experiments in gravity and leverage.

Nando slept with a broom, its handle an imagined staff that might fend off the midnight research of his brother. By morning, when the little lout was fast asleep, Tal could pry the weapon from his hand . . .

Slip it through the hammock netting . . .

And with only a twist of the handle, send his brother tumbling to the floor.

This morning it was barely interesting. Nando hit the floor with a thump and a moan and lay there facedown, still sleeping to all intents. A handful of coins spilled out of the folds of his nightshirt. He gaped and snored. Costume jewelry glittered in his mouth—worthless stuff, but hidden in his cheeks for safekeeping.

Mouthing the bangles was common practice with Nando. Every month or so, they'd have to call in the midwife to remove a swallowed ring from his throat. Or an outcry from the backyard jakes would tell the whole family that Nando was passing a necklace again.

This morning, Tal had lost interest in Nando and in jewels. Something there was that needed his attention.

Something about the day . . .

When the thought returned to Tal—his sister's dinner, the assembled family, the presence of Yoni and Darl—it was all he could do to rein in his joy.

An occasion. An occasion highly public.

It was the kind of day when Tal did his best work.

"Nando!" he hissed at the writhing lump of blankets on the floor. "Get up, and get moving!"

Slowly, as though moving through wet sand, Nando followed his brother's orders. He moved to the great trunk at the far end of the room, withdrew two tunics— a red one for him, an orange and black one for Tal—and set them on the windowsill to air.

Meanwhile, Tal swung lazily in his hammock, his thoughts playing over the prospects.

Livia was gullible, Nando obedient. Yoni and Darl were both passing dull.

A perfect cast of characters for one of his scenarios. Everything was converging: The seventh full moon of Solinari, which marked the first day of the festival in Hollow, was only three days after his sister's birthday. Seventh moon and seventh year made the whole thing almost astrological, like the gods were telling him that a good scheme was part of the fabric of the universe. . . .

Tal could have found other reasons to justify tormenting his sister, but to be honest, he didn't need them, except as alibis to Mam and Pap.

You love Livia more than you love me.

The other children don't like me.

You dropped me on my head once.

All reasons that had worked before and were ready to work again, to forestall dire punishment when the deed was done. Instead of covering his hindparts, he would plan something that used the best parts of his players. Something simple and direct, something with great consequence.

He lay in the hammock, tilting merrily, his thoughts paring down to one uncomplicated story.

She wasn't surprised to see Tal standing in the doorway of her room.

After all, Mama had warned her.

Your brother likes to play tricks, Livia.

Don't be too quick to believe him.

Yet she was seven and adored her older brother despite his torments and schemes.

Being cautious was hard when it was Tal.

Today he was kind. He wished her "happy birthday" and agreed that she was seven and no longer six. He even gave her a pair of earrings—they were dark brown and hard and smelled a little, but he had made them all by himself.

He told her about the song and dance. She was surprised at what he told her.

Mama had never mentioned that her birthday song was too short.

Never mentioned the food dance.

"It's been a long time since Mam was seven," Tal explained. He put his fingers on Livia's clean curtains and looked out the window toward the grove at the back of the house.

It made sense, but then, her brother always made sense.

Livia squinted her eyes like folks were supposed to do when they were suspicious, but it didn't work. She wasn't suspicious. Tal looked just the same, standing there in the sunlight.

She decided that this time he was being nice.

After all, it was her birthday.

"We'll have to hurry," he said. "The food dance is not hard, but the song is long for . . . a *little* girl, and hard to remember."

Livia chewed her lip. Part of her loved to be that little girl, Mama's baby and Papa's pretty thing. But another part of her—the most of her—didn't like for Tal to call her "little."

That part longed to break free of things and be a grown-up.

"Hard for a *little* girl," she replied, "but after all, Taladas, I am no longer six."

She called him by his formal name to make a point. To show how grown up she really was.

Tal smiled at her then. "Well, Livvy," he said. "Let's begin."

———◆◆◆———

Birthday dinners were a big occasion in Hollow. Especially for the children, who marked their lives from festival to feast. Sometimes it seemed that the rest of the year was taken up either remembering the last celebration or looking forward to the next.

For Tal, all festivals meant high drama. You had the holidays that honored the gods (and there were a lot of gods, thankfully). You had rites of planting and harvest and putting away. You had family birthdays to boot, and each occasion was a chance for confusion and intrigue.

Livia's birthday promised the best of play.

Seated at the far end of the long table, Tal watched as the guests shambled in.

Yoni and Darl rushed straight for the sweets, ignoring the scolding of their parents. Unaware that what happened this evening might map out their futures, they buried themselves in the candies and dried fruit that Ilona had set carefully in bowls at the edge of the table.

At the edge, so the two little degenerates wouldn't crawl through the other food to get at the sweets.

A fine pair, his prospective brothers-in-law.

Yoni and Darl, their faces over the bowls, grunted at their parents' prompting questions and stuffed their pockets with whatever they couldn't stuff into their cheeks.

Meanwhile, old Kaleem hovered over his daughter like a stringy brood hen. His big hands clutched at her shoulders, his every word calculated to soothe and impress the sires and dams of the two pigs at the candy trough.

"Save room for the dinner at hand, Yoni!" he urged merrily. "Roast goose is a fine thing for the birthday table, but tend to the bread specially. Livia baked it herself!"

That was a lie. Everyone knew it, from most clever Tal through the haggling adults all the way down to impenetrable Nando—who by now had joined Yoni and Darl at the feeding.

Pap is lying already, Tal thought.

That meant the courtship dance had begun. For the stretch of the evening, old Kaleem would go on about his daughter's many virtues—her brains and handiness and strong back.

Her ability to bear sons, for Mishakal's fertile sake!

Oh, yes, it was dance time, and Pap would handle things like he did in his shop front, dickering over dowry and sharking at the details.

However, there was another dance in the wings, and after *it* was over, we'd see how much room Pap was left to maneuver.

The "food dance" was the part Tal had left to Nando. He didn't trust his brother's intelligence, but the dolt would do whatever Tal told him. There was no right way to learn a dance that didn't exist in the first place, so Nando couldn't really foul it up.

A few guidelines were all that Tal had given him. He trusted Nando's natural meanness to improvise.

Tal smiled at the unfolding possibilities. When all was said and done, the dinner would go down in family history, if not in the history of the town itself.

The Goosing of Livia Bombyx they would call it, and it would be worthy of its title.

It was all Tal could do to hide his growing excitement as the dinner progressed. Boiled onions and buttered carrots and baked bread began the fare, and the tanner and rat catcher, their hefty wives, and Yoni's formless lump of an older sister all took great pains to compliment the baking. Livia's future suitors, on the other hand, wrinkled their noses and stirred the vegetables on their plates, both of them looking greedily toward the door to the kitchen as the smell of roast goose floated into the room.

All through the first course, leeks and onions tumbling from his mouth as he spoke, the old silk dealer hawked the value of his daughter.

"Only eight years old!" he said, "and already frugal and pliable!"

"Seven, my dearest," Ilona corrected. "Livia is seven."

"All the more remarkable, then," Kaleem replied, glaring coldly at his wife.

Rat catcher and tanner gaped in unison, both wondering, no doubt, what *pliable* meant.

Oh, get on with it, please! Tal thought, fidgeting in his chair.

At just that moment, as though she were responding to a silent cue, Ilona rose from the table and glided into the kitchen. After a muffled rattle of crockery off-stage, she returned with the goose.

Tal smiled, curled his knobby knees beneath him, and waited for the fun to begin.

Now was the time at a Hollow girl's birthday dinner when the guest of honor was supposed to entertain. As the others waited for the main course to cool, it was customary for the birthday girl to provide a song—a simple thing, usually composed by her mother or, in some cases, a father with an imaginative bent. Needless to say, Kaleem found the whole business frivolous, so it had been left to Ilona to school little Livia in entertainments worthy of a seven-year-old. Everyone expected a short song and perhaps a dance step or two, all simple and sweet and practiced religiously for a week before the dinner.

Ilona set down the steaming goose and stood anxiously behind her husband, her red hands gripping the back of Kaleem's chair until her knuckles whitened.

Tal swallowed a laugh along with a last mouthful of onions. Poor Mam had no idea what was next on the bill.

Livia stood before the table, clutched the hem of her little white dress, and curtsied politely. Rocking slowly from foot to foot, she began the part of the performance composed by her mother.

> Welcome, welcome, all are welcome
>   North and south and west and east.
> Welcome, welcome, all are welcome
>   To my party, to my feast.

Ilona smiled proudly. Tanner and rat catcher nodded, their gazes returning to the steaming goose. Darl reached over the table toward the drumstick until the swift hand of his mother slapped him back.

Now Ilona's eyes widened, as she realized her daughter's song was not ended, not by a long shot.

> *Welcome, welcome, all are welcome*
> *To our fare of bread and goose.*
> *Welcome, welcome, all are welcome,*
> *'Scuse me while I shake this loose.*

With the second verse, Livia began to dance more wildly. First she marched like a foot soldier, then crouched like some enormous insect ready to spring. Finally, to the horror of all adults present, she waggled her bottom in the stunned face of the rat catcher's wife.

Tal wondered for a moment if Nando had gone too far. No. Not at all.

On Livia sang, the song more savage now, more particular.

> *Welcome, welcome, all are welcome*
> *Papa's fare and Papa's beer*
> *Fill your gullets, while his daughter*
> *Rides the main course out of here.*

That was it. In the last step of the Nando-invented dance, Livia leaped onto the table, twisted sinuously like a Nerakan fan-dancer through the rubble of onion and bread on the tanner's plate. Reaching the center of the table, she lifted her skirts and sat astride the goose, repeating the last verse of the song and spurring the main course like a stallion.

Kaleem's outraged eyes never left his bucking daughter. He did, however, have the presence of mind to reach out, grab Nando's hair and twist it swiftly and desperately.

Ilona gathered her daughter and fled the room.

All the rest of those present—family and guests alike—sat in silence around the table. Tal stared down at his plate, knowing the terrible, incriminating laughter that would follow if his eyes met anyone's.

It was like the aftermath of some great wind storm, when people come out to survey the damage.

"I . . . I wonder how Ilona has seasoned them onions?" the tanner's wife asked meekly in the unnatural silence. "They're the best I ever seen."

Slowly, Darl's hand stretched out toward the goose, toward the drumstick. Yoni grinned, gobbets of bread jammed in the gaps between his teeth.

"I dare ya, Darl," he challenged. "Livvy had her butt on it."

The party dissolved upon these words of wisdom.

———◆◈◆———

Kaleem maintained that there was certainly a law on the books—whether in Solamnia or neighboring Coastlund—that allowed a father to kill his sons.

"Of course there isn't, dearest," Ilona soothed.

"Would that there were," Kaleem said.

"I understand," his wife replied.

All of the children were under punishment. Tal and Nando were forbidden the festival of Solinari and confined to their room for a fortnight. Kaleem had advised them that if they strayed so far as the kitchen he would *sew them up in a silk bag and sell them to ogres.*

"I hear that they ride their main courses as well," the old man hinted darkly.

Livia was another matter. She stayed in her bedroom, wept inconsolably, and swore that at her next birthday dinner—and at all the birthday dinners that ever followed—she would never, never sing and dance.

Her parents debated her punishment. After all, it was Livia who sang the offensive song and rode the goose into village scandal. They believed her remorse was punishment enough, and yet they made her stay in her room for a crime neither of them could put words around.

Something to do with being gullible, Kaleem decided. Too much trust.

As the morning of the next day dawned, Ilona wondered if trust were something blameworthy in a girl of seven.

———————◆◆◆———————

Meanwhile, a caravan of wagons arrived in the town square of Hollow. In the early afternoon, when the townspeople dozed and gazed idly over the dusty common, their half-hearted farming done for the day and the shops closed early for the festival, an outlandish crew disembarked from the painted wagons and hammered together a wooden structure within sight of Kaleem Bombyx's shop.

The townspeople, having already heard of the monstrous behavior of the silk dealer's children, hoped against hope that the structure was a gibbet, but some among them—the most worldly, who had been all the way to Coastlund and back—soon recognized that it was a stage.

It wasn't the work that caught the townspeople's attention as much as it was the folks who did the work. Dwarves—genuine dwarves!—set the stage boards with hammers and pegs. A pair of gnomes stood by, blueprints and plumb lines in hand, jingling with tools and devices hooked to their belts and hidden in their pockets. There was even an elf—an exotic-looking fellow, draped in black robes like an evil god at a costume party, though all he seemed to do was mutter and pose.

The stage took shape quickly and efficiently under the hands of an experienced crew. Though the more sophisticated sorts in the town agreed that it wasn't a fancy theater rising in the town square, it was good enough for the festival of a minor god, good enough for Hollow.

The tanner and the rat catcher, elevated to local celebrity by the humiliation of their families at the Bombyx dinner, appointed themselves spokesmen. They walked out of the snoozing shadows, and tried to engage the players in conversation.

But they came back disappointed.

The dwarves weren't surly enough, they said. Nor were the gnomes all that frivolous or complicated. Even the elf, who was supposed to be all aloof and melancholy, was more ill-tempered than tragic.

Nobody seemed to be playing by the rules, the rat catcher said.

By evening another rumor had spread among the townspeople that the dwarves and gnomes and elves were not dwarves and gnomes and elves at all but actors in the company, each one playing the role of some exotic creature from a foreign race.

The play was beginning already, the tanner said, even before the stage was built.

It was an idea too complicated for Hollow, but it managed to catch on. Folks discussed it at the brewery, debated what it meant, and all the guessing and second-guessing sent them straight for the beer. Tired and woozy with speculations and alcohol, most of them were in bed by sunset, and their dreams that night were filled with sad elven songs, dwarven rumblings, and the endless recitals of gnomish names.

While they slept, torches blazed in the town square, and the stage rose out of a litter of boards and cloth and crepe. Awake in the midst of the sleeping town, Tal Bombyx watched from his bedroom window.

He, too, looked on with a villager's awe as an arch took shape behind the boards of the stage. Two gnomes, scrambling like spiders, draped a curtain over that arch—a curtain that shimmered in the lamplight like silk.

Or like something more than silk, Tal told himself. It was hard to tell in the distance and the darkness just what it was. He imagined dreams sewn in the hem of that curtain, that the movement of stage hands and rehearsing actors was some elaborate pattern he could follow with his eyes and thoughts, even though he could not understand it.

It was as if the stage were calling him. As if all his schemes and manipulations had been only a rehearsal for this moment in his life.

Tal's thoughts scattered and returned to Livia with a vengeance.

Mam's baby. Pap's meal ticket, offered up to the wealthy townspeople. *She* would surely have served her punishment by festival night—after all, didn't they always let her off easy?

They would let *her* venture into the town square. Let her stand among the cobblers and the vintners in front of the stage. Let her witness wonders.

Wonders he would be denied.

Well, so be it, Tal told himself. I shall make her pay dearly for it later.

At that moment, he almost resigned himself to his punishment, almost accepted it as part of the natural order of things, like rain or the change of seasons. If he had turned away from the window, climbed into his hammock, and slept the unruffled sleep of a boy who felt himself wrongly sentenced, who never did anything wrong, not really . . .

This would not have been a cautionary tale. Perhaps not even a tale at all.

But at that moment, as if on cue, the man walked into the torchlight.

———◦•◦———

He was a large man, a human. Heavy-set, inclining toward fat. His face was pale and soft, and he was smiling magnanimously.

It was more than that, of course. More than simple appearance. Because the darkness seemed to part in front of him or the torchlight seemed to follow him upstage. Tal wasn't really certain.

The boy was sure of one thing. This was the man, the one with the power. At his approach, the hammering ceased, and the clambering gnomes, up among the ropes high on the arch, paused in the tedious business of tacking and tying curtain to wood.

Tal leaned out the window for a better look. He felt giddy at once—he didn't like heights, after all. But he recovered almost as quickly, and soon he could have sworn that the man looked up at him—the briefest of glances as his eyes scanned the boundaries of the makeshift theater.

Enough to draw Tal in. To make him decide, then and there, that the next night would be *his* festival as much

as Solinari's, *his* entrance into a larger world of wonder
and intrigue.

Tal stepped back from the window, his thoughts
aflame. He heard his father snoring in the other upstairs
room, a sound that fell like cold water on his spirit.

There was no way he could ask Pap to relent. On
occasion, Kaleem would let off his older son and heir
with a warning:

You came awfully close to drowning Yoni, boy.

*Think how Darl must have felt, tied to the back of that
mule and all.*

See that it doesn't happen again.

The scandal at Livia's birthday dinner, however, had
hauled in the whole family, had embarrassed his father
and shaken his role as a public man. Furthermore, it
was too late for Tal to devise one of his elaborate plots
to trick Kaleem into letting him attend the play.

He would have to improvise, he guessed.

The hammock was just long enough that Tal could
hitch one end to the latch on his window and dangle
from the other end, ten feet or so above the ground.
Even that height unsettled him, but this was too
important, and he had learned some time ago that if
you did what you had to do in a sudden rush, you
would find yourself at the end of the ordeal before the
real fear set in.

Tal was small, and the drop to the hard earth knocked
the wind out of him for a moment. He sat on the ground
shivering, recovering his breath, then he scrambled off
into the night, headed for the lights in the village
common and toward the rising stage.

None of the players and stage hands seemed to
notice him. He passed by the downstage boards, heard
a musical voice somewhere in the shadows—an elf

rehearsing lines, he guessed—and passed silently by a trio of dwarves who were lugging a wooden castle toward the proscenium arch. His destination was a small tent, sturdy and lamplit, which he had seen the big man enter.

Breathless once more, overwhelmed by the feeling that he stood in the wings of something incredibly dramatic and important, Tal reached for the tent flap, pulled it aside, and peered in.

The man was seated at a small table, pages of parchment spread before him beneath a solitary dim lamp. The light in the tent—the light Tal had followed in his long approach over the common—seemed to come from the fellow himself. A pale light that illumined even the farthest corners of the tent. Illumined whatever it was that the man was writing.

Without looking up from the pages, the big fellow addressed the boy who stood behind him.

"By all means, come in, lad," he said. "Even the summer nights are chilly in this town."

Tal paused for a moment, gathered himself, and entered.

———◆◆◆———

It was funny, Tal thought, how the tent seemed to expand once he stepped inside. The man's smile was reassuring, and for the first time the boy saw close up the figure he had glimpsed from his bedroom window.

The big fellow was not nearly as impressive from this distance. He looked like your run-of-the-mill fat man, a dough-faced fat man at that, yet he seemed friendly enough, once you looked at him closely.

"Taladas Bombyx," the boy stammered, remembering his manners at last. "Taladas Bombyx of Hollow."

"That's a traveling name if I've ever heard one," the man said, extending his hand. "I'm Sebastius. Sebastius of . . . the country at large."

Tal clasped Sebastius's hand. His grip was soft and doughy as well.

"What brings you to see me, Taladas Bombyx of Hollow?"

A simple question. Tal was surprised that he really had no clever answer. It was as if he had been dropped into the midst of things, dropped from a great height into deep water.

Floundering before the curious stranger, the boy decided to make something up.

"Your . . . your curtains seem to be a little thread-bare. Master Sebastius. My father is the silk dealer in town, and . . . "

Here Tal paused, searching his new acquaintance for signs that the man was impressed by Kaleem's lofty station.

He found no signs.

"Anyway," he continued, his voice trailing off in a murmur, "I could . . . probably get you a good deal on some serviceable silk. Light fabric and durable. Just the thing to hold up on the road."

It might just work. A deal for curtains might soften Kaleem's heart and Tal's punishment. As long as his father didn't know who proposed the deal. . . .

The boy was suddenly proud of himself. Pretty good improvising.

Sebastius's eyebrow arched. "That would be most kind of you, sir. Curtains of blues dark and light, I'm imagining now. So that our backdrops could present both night and day. It is a splendid offer. Might I ask what you'd expect in return?"

Tal's thoughts thrashed and scrambled. If Sebastius approached his father . . . if part of the deal was the offer of front-row seats and backstage passes for the family . . .

No. He was *certain* that Kaleem would try to finagle the playmaster, and finagling would lead to questions. If the deal fell through, Pap would ask even more questions. Would end up discovering his son's whereabouts in the dead of night, how Tal had disobeyed orders and curfews.

"Oh, I could be silent about your late-night ventures," Sebastius said, answering the boy's thoughts as though he had read them on the pages behind him.

Now it was Tal's turn. He was old enough to know how *this* worked.

"In exchange for what, Master Sebastius?"

"I deal in plays, Tal, not in blackmail and betrayals. Your secret is safe with me. Still I wonder what *really* brought you here."

"A change of scenery, sir," Tal replied. He spoke before he thought, as though he had been prompted. He knew as he said the words that this was part of it, but maybe not all of it. "And . . . I love surprises."

"Well, the theater has those things aplenty, Tal Bombyx. The scenery changes from act to act. As for the surprises . . . well, what kind do you want? The ones you expect, or the ones you don't?"

It sounded like nonsense to Tal. Who ever heard of surprises you expect?

He hated paradox and mystery, unless he made them up himself.

Sebastius wasn't about to explain.

"Perhaps, then, you should sit at home until . . . the answer surprises you. I'd begin by listening a little more. Because when you listen, the surprises are . . . less unpleasant."

"Is that a dismissal, sir?" Tal asked peevishly.

"Perhaps it is, son. Perhaps it is a warning."

------◆◈◆------

Tal grumbled to himself as he returned across the village common.

It had all been a misfire. A venture into nothing.

After a brief conversation, Sebastius had turned back to that infernal scroll. Nothing Tal said would stir him from whatever he was reading.

So much for adventure. So much for grand designs.

The makeshift stage was nearly completed, and only a small crew of stagehands remained at work: a solitary gnome at the top of the arch, half-lost in an entanglement of curtain ropes, and a pair of dwarves stage right, grumbling and sweating as they hoisted the tower of the prop castle into place.

Taladas passed through them glumly, his eyes downcast and his thoughts returning reluctantly to minor ruses and to irritations.

He would have to be quiet climbing back into his bedroom. It was dangerously near dawn, and soon Ma would be up and stirring, all ears and eyes for any truant boy who had broken the family curfew.

How *dare* Sebastius brush him off? "Listen," indeed!

There was also the problem of the high window to Tal's bedroom. A simple dangle and drop was an easy escape, but climbing back up was another matter.

That Sebastius.

Tal would make sure that the old bastard purchased no good silk curtains in Hollow. He would thwart the deal somehow or see to it that the damnable fat director received damnable damaged goods. . . .

"Taladas!" someone shouted.

He looked up. Saw the wooden framework tumbling toward him. At the last moment, dove out of the way.

The prop tower never quite struck the ground. It hung at a weird tilt, tangled in ropes and pulleys, as the pair of dwarves tugged at the guy lines, growling and sweating and accusing each other as one untied his partner's legs from the painted crenels of the little castle.

The gnome high atop the proscenium arch called down to Tal.

"Are you hurt? Please tell me that you are not hurt because if you are they will hold the stage hands entirely accountable no seniority in the company you understand and it's always been the way things are done in the guild and Sebastius will be furious whether you're hurt or not but more furious naturally if you are hurt and it wasn't really my fault I promise you unless I warned you too late in which case it is my fault only in a secondary or tertiary sense and certainly not legally—"

Tal raised his hand weakly, brushed away the torrent of words. He watched the gnome gesturing from a great height like an excited bird in the eaves. He thought about cutting a deal, about getting the gnome to help him back into his bedroom in exchange for his silence.

After all, the creature was up there among cords and draw strings, and there was some kind of ingenuity involved in that, wasn't there?

Tal was envious. Rope puzzles always confused him completely.

He decided against the deal. Silence was the issue after all. The gnome might know a trick or two about climbing, but Tal doubted he could keep the little fellow quiet in a job that would demand stealth and slyness.

"No," he said at last. "No, you warned me just in time. Thank you."

The gnome was climbing down the arch and away from him now, scrambling toward the weaving tower and the two struggling dwarves. He looked like a bundle of hair and cloth amid the ropes and cables, his odd figure cinched by an oversized tool belt that jingled loudly as he hustled toward the tiring room.

Tal stood up and dusted himself off. He should have been thankful, he guessed, to escape with only a soiled jacket and skinned knees, but it felt like pure humiliation. Like an injury stacked upon Sebastius's previous insults.

As he approached the silk shop, Tal vowed revenge. If nothing else, this Sebastius would answer for his snobbery and self-importance, for his refusal to recognize Tal's gifts, not to mention the terrific importance of the Bombyx family in this backwater town.

If the old son of a bitch is such an expert in surprise, Tal thought, then I'll give him surprise, by the Red Moon! A surprise that will leave him gasping for resources.

The scheme stopped short at the open window, at the sight of the hammock—his makeshift ladder into his room—dangling a good five feet out of reach.

And that was when Nando came into the story.

After leaping vainly at the hammock, after swearing dark oaths and trying with no success to climb the clay and wattle walls of the shop front, Tal was forced to call out to his younger brother. . . .

Who came to the window at once. As though he had been waiting.

All kinds of blackmail followed, but Tal knew how the negotiations would end. Even though each brother had the goods on the other, everything came down to the simple fact that Tal was standing outside the house. He was the one who had sneaked off into the night and violated Kaleem's curfew.

And so, standing in the upper window, Nando had the upper hand. No amount of promises, briberies, and threats could finagle Tal Bombyx up the makeshift ladder.

"Here's what I want," Nando announced, raising and lowering the hammock like some sinister puppet master. "I want the bigger half of what you're getting."

"'The bigger half'?"

"You hear me. If you get a gold piece, I get two. If you get a silver ring, I get a bigger one. . . . "

"And if I get eaten by trolls, you get *boiled* and eaten?"

Nando fell silent.

"Doing the math, Nando?" Tal asked cynically.

"Er . . . no. 'Cause it all comes down to one thing. I'm up here, and I got the hammock."

"That's two things, Nando." Tal couldn't seem to resist it.

Nando backed away from the window. "D'you want me to call Ma?" he asked, his voice a little too loud for this hour and this situation.

"All right, Nando," Tal said at last. "Tie *your* hammock to *mine,* then lower the whole thing. I expect I can reach it and climb from there."

Silence from above greeted him.

"I promise," Tal conceded. "I promise that whatever I'm getting in this venture . . . that you . . . will get the bigger half."

Over the sill tumbled the hammocks, tied together clumsily by Nando's best efforts. Just looking at the knots gave Tal the shudders, but he forgot his fears when he began to climb.

Those knots. He thought of the gnome back on the proscenium arch. The little fellow who had warned him.

There was something . . .

It was suspicious. It was obvious. Yet he couldn't quite remember. . . .

Tal had one leg over the windowsill when it struck him. Struck him so firmly that he was not surprised to look over his shoulder and discover that the eastern sun had slipped above the horizon at just the moment that the memory fell in place.

How had the gnome known his name?

———————

Papilla, the playbill said. *A Comedy of Surprises.*

Livia wondered what that meant.

She was proud of her reading, but here, on the side of the cobbler's shop, was a big poster with three big words in a row.

The only one she was sure of was "Surprises."

That alone sounded like fun.

Mama and Papa had come to her door early this morning while the boys were still asleep. They told her she was sorry enough. That now she knew better.

So they had let her go to market with Mama. Who was only a few steps away, looking at the dried apples in the fruit vendor's stall.

Mama had seen some other ladies walking toward the common, and when she had said hello the other ladies had said hello as well. But they were not as friendly as usual, and it made Livia sorry again.

Because she knew why. It was because of riding that goose.

But now there was this playbill about surprises, and maybe that would make Mama happy again. Because everyone liked surprises.

"Mama!" she called, standing on tiptoe and setting her nose against the damp parchment of the playbill. Maybe if you got closer to the words you could understand them.

Mama came over. Read the playbill for her—even the little letters.

"What's a papilla, Mama?" Livia asked, taking her mother's hand.

"It's a name, dear. An old Solamnic name. I had a cousin named Papilla . . . a long time ago."

"Is the play about your cousin?"

Ilona laughed, and Livia laughed, too. Even though Mama thought what she said was silly, it was good to see Mama laugh.

"I expect not, dearest. Papilla is not an uncommon name in Solamnia. It means 'butterfly.' "

"Then the play is about a butterfly?" Livia thought of bright wings, the orange and black of the beautiful *regis* which she admired as it fluttered over flowers and weeds, as it lit on the horse dung by the stables.

"About a butterfly? Well . . . yes and no," Ilona replied, and a sly smile spread over her homely face. "But if I told you more, it would no longer be a play of surprises, now would it?"

Livia could see where this was going. It was all she could do to keep from dancing with delight—she was a little afraid of dancing so soon after her birthday dinner.

She would get to see the play! She was certain!

Mama made it even better. Leaning over her daughter, balancing her heavy market basket on her hip, Ilona whispered the words Livia had never dreamed she would hear.

"What is more, my dearest daughter . . . I think a girl of seven is grown up enough to go all by herself."

Mama looked a little sad as she said this. A little weary, as she did each morning when she heard the boys waking up.

That was part of growing up, too, Livia told herself, as they turned from the market and walked slowly back to Papa's shop.

Mothers hated for their daughters to grow.

But that was just what daughters had to do.

———◆●◆———

"What the hell is a papilla?" Nando asked, as he tugged on his muddy boots.

"Damned if I know," Tal replied.

Both of them looked around cautiously. At eleven and nine, they had only recently discovered mild oaths and were still a little afraid that their mother would catch them in the midst of swearing.

"But it's not gonna matter, Nando. On account of the play's gonna be a mess, no matter what the words mean."

Nando laughed wickedly, digging a grubby finger into his nostril.

"What we gonna do, Tal? You promised you would tell me."

Tal sat on the windowsill, looking out on the stage in the common.

"Oh, you'll see, Nando. You'll see."

"Tell me. Tell me tell me tell me or . . . I'll tell the old man about your adventure."

"All right! All right! So I *don't* know just yet! It takes time to plan these things out, Nando. But when I'm done . . . by the Book of Gilean, old Sebastius will be sorry he ever crossed me!"

Despite his threats and menacing, nothing specific occurred to Tal throughout the morning and well into the afternoon. Oh, he thought of the old tricks—of tossing a burning bag of horse dung onto the stage, of firecrackers in the torches that surrounded Sebastius's tent—but those would only be temporary measures. The show would go on in spite of them. Tal had done such things before and often, so suspicion would fall on him at once.

What was needed was a triumph. By the time the torches were lit and the people of Hollow had begun to amble toward the makeshift stage, Tal was still short an idea.

Sebastius had him daunted. He felt like the old fart was listening to his thoughts, was a plan and two guesses ahead of him, no matter where or how he turned. Now the time was short: Tal had to get out of the house or the play would be half over before he slipped through the crowd in the common.

He would have to make it up as he went along, accept whatever plan occurred to him as he stood in the wings of the stage.

Being a planner and schemer with a long view, Tal did not like that prospect at all.

Nevertheless, at sunset, when the crowd had gathered beneath the flickering torches on the common, he and Nando tied together the hammocks once again, dangled the bedding out the window, and dropped softly onto the shadowy ground next to the shop front. Still without a plan, they hastened toward the common, following the smell of torch smoke and the sounds of chatter and music.

Around the back of the stage they crept, to a fenced-in spot behind the curtains, which served as a tiring room. There the company kept stage properties and costumes, huge wooden axes and hobbyhorses leaning against crates and stepladders, threadbare garments spilling out of battered trunks.

The boys slipped behind a convenient chest, opened and spilling costume jewelry, robes, masks and dark woolen sacks. Nando pocketed a bracelet and a handful of pewter coins, then the two of them settled down and watched the actors hovering in the darkness, everyone awaiting cues in the night's festivities.

Soon the lights behind the stage were extinguished. The glow of the downstage torches reached them only dimly through the flaws and tears of the old curtain, like faint stars on a moonless night. Now they observed by hearing only, and Tal couldn't help but think of Sebastius's smug advice the night before.

I'd begin by listening a little more. Because when you listen, the surprises are . . . less unpleasant.

Well, damn Sebastius, Tal thought. Damn him and the wagon he rode in on.

Just then, the sound of the crowd subsided. Tal crept from hiding and peered through a curtain hole.

The play was under way.

Sebastius was standing upstage. He lifted his stocky arms, signaling silence.

Beyond the hulking man, Tal could see only the first two rows of spectators. The rest were lost in shadows. Nevertheless, Tal recognized the tanner and his wife, and the greengrocer leaning heavily against the stage boards . . .

And illumined by the torchlight, gaping as though she expected some kind of wonderment, was his little sister, Livia.

She looked all gaudy and foolish in her silk dress of

orange and black. Her hair was fixed in two dog-eared pigtails, and when she smiled at the approaching director you could see the gaps left by the missing baby teeth.

Livia looked ridiculous, Tal thought. She must have dressed herself.

Suddenly, as though it had come to him by divine prompting, the beginnings of a plan slipped into his thoughts.

He scuttled back into hiding as Sebastius began to speak.

The big man cleared his throat and launched into the prologue.

> "This is the story we will tell—
> applaud us if we play it well—
> of sweet Papilla and her quest
> for freedom in the ancient west,
> of a young girl, imprisoned by
> sorcery and evil eye,
> rescued in a fortunate fall.
> Enjoy this scene. Enjoy it all!"

The townspeople looked at one another nervously. They were not prepared to enjoy anything if it was in verse.

Sebastius seemed to understand. With that surprising grace that fat men often seem to have that comes from knowing how to steer around rather than through things, he seated himself on the upstage boards, his big legs dangling elegantly into the shadows. He spoke softly to the audience, even though his voice carried.

"Do not be alarmed by verse," he advised.

"For after all, it could be worse.
It could drag on throughout the play—
jostle your ears, get in the way.
Instead, it comes at crucial times.
And otherwise, to hell with rhymes."

The townspeople applauded. Yet some of them—those who were really listening—exchanged troubled glances.

Despite Sebastius's promises, the rhyming had not stopped.

Some people didn't know what to make of that. It made the play seem a little threatening.

But things *were* under way. The play was up and running, and nothing the audience could do would stop the story, even if they wanted it stopped.

In command from his station at the front of the stage, Sebastius gestured toward the wings.

Two figures emerged. One was an elf in dark robes, grayed by the smoke of incense. The other was a grizzled, haunted man in cardboard armor.

The crowd gasped—some of them at the costumes, but most of them at the simple scandal of having an elf, an actual elf, in their midst. The older races, after all, made only the rarest appearances in Hollow.

Such an exotic creature made the townspeople feel worldly and fortunate. But they also felt threatened, and nervous murmurs coursed through the crowd as the elf cleared his throat.

"I am Melchior," the elf said, in a voice dry as tea leaves. "Melchior the Dark. In a long-ago age, in a time before your remembrance, I struck a bargain with that knight over there."

The grizzled man stepped forward. "And I am Jepthah, who was in need of magic. Setting out against the ogres,

I was, and in a time when that benighted race was . . . numerous and strong."

Melchior raised his hand, and the silvery, fragrant smoke scattered through the audience. "The pact was simple," he said. "My magic would bring him victory, bring him everything his dark heart wanted. In exchange, he was to give me only 'the fare that graced his table when he returned from battle.' "

Jepthah nodded slowly. "It seemed a fair bargain to me."

"Watch out!" a boy yelled from the middle of the crowd. "It's a wizard yer dealin' with, Jebbah!"

Some in the audience laughed nervously. "It's a play!" someone hissed.

"Only a play, Darl! Now shut yer gob!"

Melchior raised his hood, his bright elven eyes glittering like pyrite in the shadows. "But of course," he announced, "a knight like Jepthah had limits to his imagination. He supposed that a fine meal would await him when he came back from the wars. That the boards of the table would sway with fruit and bread. Perhaps with sturdier fare, like a well-roasted, buttery goose . . ."

Melchior paused. You could feel the audience awaiting the end of the story.

Now the elf's voice sank to a murmur, but magically, almost unnaturally, the rest of his speech reached the deafest ears in the farthest row.

"Imagine his surprise, good people. Imagine his shock and sorrow when he entered the great hall of his castle. For there was his young daughter Papilla, crawling across the laden table, her hand extended greedily toward the drumstick of the goose in question."

"Ill-mannered little witch!" the tanner's wife scolded loudly.

Some of the townspeople laughed, having heard of

the woman's embarrassment the night before in the house of the silk dealer.

"But Papilla is just a child!" a man's voice protested from somewhere in the shadows. "The elf and the cardboard knight done said so!"

"Ill-mannered little witch or child, neither or both," Melchior said, "you can figure out what came next. I insisted on the letter of the bargain."

At that moment, the grizzled man knelt dramatically in the torchlight. The look on his face was something past mournful, as though it could not hide this deep and intimate loss.

That look seized the sympathies of the more sensitive folks in the audience. Little Livia, seated on the front row, dabbed at her eyes with the hem of her brightly colored silk dress, and from somewhere near the back of the crowd, where her father and mother stood among the tradesmen, a woman's sob arose and was immediately stifled.

"I gave my word," the armored actor proclaimed in a desolate whisper, "and a knight must stand by his word."

"Scalix could of got you off!" someone shouted from over near the apple grove on the southernmost edge of the common. "He'd have found the loophole in the bargain!"

Laughs of agreement coursed through the crowd. Scalix was, after all, the town's only lawyer and kept a great business in property disputes and domestic struggles.

But now was the time for neither Scalix nor the customary jokes that surrounded him. Slowly, melodramatically, Melchior described what happened next.

"Oh, it was a dark feast that night," he said.

Then, in response to a collective gasp from the crowd, he smiled wickedly.

"That is what we call a metaphor, people of Hollow. For I did not *really* devour the girl: that, after all, would be a tragedy. I dined most regally on bread and fruit, and the goose I left untouched. The girl was mine, mine as a gift and seal to the bargain. To my tower at the edge of Silvanost I took her, awaiting a future when Papilla would come of age, would satisfy my . . . deepest purposes."

"Whassee mean by that?" a boy's voice piped from the low branches of an apple tree, there at the edge of the common.

"By the time she comes of age, Yoni," a man's voice from the front of the crowd responded merrily, "his 'deepest purpose' may be a warm bath and warm gruel."

"Good one, Scalix!" someone called. Someone else echoed the praise, and for a moment the story of Papilla was forgotten in rising laughter.

But then the knight lay down on the stage, and bleakly closed his eyes. " 'Twas tragedy enough," he moaned. "I refused to eat and sleep. Melchior's feast was the last food to grace my table, and I dwelt alone in the sorrow of my honor, eating my promises noon and night. I did not last long."

At his words, a hush fell over the crowd. Now Sebastius stepped back into the light, soothing the audience with a wave of his large hands.

> "Remember, those who mourn and wail,
> this story is not Jepthah's tale:
> this story has a happy ending,
> not of knightly oaths unbending,
> nor of a mage's cruel power.
> For as years passed in Melchior's tower,
> Papilla simply did not grow,
> remained a little girl, as though
> something in her refused compliance
> with magic and with secret science.

So enough of sobs and tears:
the tale goes on and spans the years."

Sebastius receded into the shadows, and a handful of gnomish stagehands, dressed in black as camouflage, scurried onto the stage, dragging a brightly painted cart wherein lay a man-sized wicker dragon, rearing up menacingly, its basket-wings outstretched.

The audience babbled, sure that the wonders were about to begin.

"Whatever you do, Tal, don't let Livia figure in!" Nando begged from behind the trunk. "We allus get in trouble, and she allus wins!"

Tal had been afraid of this—that when the scheme had come to him, Nando would balk at the prospect.

Here it was, big and possible and lovely—his silly little sister in the front row, and that pompous, rhyming oaf at the front of the stage, both of them primed for embarrassment.

And Nando, predictably, was backing out.

"Get out there!" Tal hissed, seizing his younger brother by the front of his tunic, drawing him closer until their snarling faces were nose to nose. "Remember the time they found you dangling halfway down the town well?"

"Remember the grocer's gold piece?" Nando taunted.

"The tanner's donkey?"

"The seamstress's window?"

"The vintner's summer cellar?"

"Romalin's cat, rolled in honey and dropped in flour?"

"Romalin's daughter, whom you forced into the same circumstances?"

Nando fell silent. He never won these arguments because Tal remembered more and greater misdemeanors. But this time, it was a silence in which sly thoughts were swimming.

"Oh, you don't win this time, Tal!" he announced triumphantly, a little too loudly. "I got the goods on you. Remember I hauled you up through the window last night . . ."

"Those bets are off, Brother," Tal whispered. "Who's broken curfew? Who's supposed to be back at the house? If I'm caught here, you'll get what you wanted . . . The bigger half of what's coming to me."

Nando fell silent, outfoxed again.

"That's better, Nando. Remember who's the oldest. Now, go and retrieve your sister."

Tal fumbled through the chest, produced the largest of the woolen sacks.

"And take this, Nando. In case Livia resists."

Livia wondered what the strange wicker dragon had to do with the play.

She was sad for poor Jepthah because he died missing his little girl. She was so sad for Papilla, all trapped away in the elf's tower, that tears rushed into her eyes, and she dabbed them away with her orange silk sleeve.

But the big man had said it would be all right. The big man said not to cry, and after all, the story was make-believe, wasn't it? And didn't make-believe turn out happy?

She looked back over her shoulder to where Mama and Papa said they would be standing, but she could not see them through the crowd.

Now her thoughts turned back to the dragon. To a

pair of dwarves who had just stepped onto the stage dressed in ragged clothing and silly hats.

They looked so funny that Livia forgot her tears at once. Then they started talking, and even what they said was funny

Us gully dwarves, one of them said.

Us work for traveling players.

They didn't talk right, and that was funnier than anything.

For a moment, Livia was confused. Were they really gully dwarves, or were they regular dwarves just pretending? Was this part of the play, or was the play over?

She decided it could not be over because the big man had said that it would end happy, and the story was not happy yet, not really. So the dwarves were probably players pretending to be gully dwarves who were players. . . .

If you thought about it, it just got more confusing.

"Oh, I'm just going to have fun!" Livia whispered to herself. "I'm not going to think about it right now!"

She stopped looking for Mama and Papa and gave her full attention back to the stage.

Then she noticed a shadow in the wings.

It was Nando, just barely at the edge of the torchlight, standing where not many people could see him. He had one hand behind his back, and with his other hand he beckoned to her.

"Oh, you're in *big* trouble, Nando m'boy!" she whispered. That was what Papa said all the time, and Livia knew it would be worse *this* time, because Tal and Nando were supposed to be at home in their room.

For a moment she thought about telling.

But maybe Nando was sorry. Maybe he was calling her over so that she could help him stay out of big trouble.

Livia stood up quietly, took one last longing look at the

wicker dragon, and slipped toward her brother at the wings of the stage. He was welcoming her with that strange toothy smile of his that she never knew whether to believe or dread.

I'll believe you this time, she thought. Because you are in big trouble, Nando m'boy.

But as Livia approached her brother, he reached out and snatched her by her pigtail. His hand whirled out to the shadows. She felt a hot darkness smother her, she was being pulled and dragged somewhere, and for one of the few times in her short life her sweetness and trust gave way to anger.

———◆◆◆———

"Us gully dwarves," one of them said sullenly.

Instantly the audience laughed.

They knew the legends. Knew that the gully dwarves were fools and clowns, and that now the real comedy was beginning.

Three or four of the citizens of Hollow, Ilona among them, were more sophisticated than the others. They knew that these were your regular, run-of-the-mill dwarves, because no wise group of players would hire the genuine gully article, who could neither remember lines nor take direction. But that made the scene even funnier. The regular dwarves stood there like melancholy drenched cats, and part of the humor was their sheer discomfort at playing their trashy cousins.

"Us work for players," one of them said, his voice a mumble that those in the back rows strained to catch.

"Us climb up towers, put up pulleys. Make dragons jump up and curtains fall down. Today we make jump and fall for the magic elf."

PAPİLLA

His partner looked mournfully and knowingly at the audience. "This involve . . . great mechanics," he warned, gesturing toward the painted wagon. "On account of play got yer dragon in it. Not *real* dragon. Don't be scared. This dragon fly when Goggi and Bambo pull ropes."

The two waddled over to the cart and grappled with the wicker dragon. Now the device lay on the boards of the stage, staring at the audience with hollow eyes.

"Us need to hang the pulley now, Bambo," one gully dwarf said to the other. "Actors say we build big arch. Hang pulley on that."

"Only one problem, Goggi," Bambo replied after a long philosophical pause. "Us too damned lazy."

The audience tittered.

"Instead," Bambo continued, eyeing the wooden tower downstage, "us can hang pulley on window sill over there. No need to build arch, when half-good job will do."

Now Sebastius returned from the shadows. Shaking his head at the gully dwarves in mock disgust, he resumed the story.

> "And so they scale the lofty tower,
> their dwarven dispositions sour
> because they have to work at all.
> The window opens on a hall
> wherein the trapped Papilla lies,
> but other fair things catch their eyes:
> bracelets, plate, and jewelry,
> brass mirrors, and a tapestry
> all lie beyond the window sill,
> arousing greed, for good or ill. . . .

By this time, the dwarves were wrestling with a ponderous, long ladder, dancing with it awkwardly as though the two of them were romancing an ogress. It drew a chuckle from the crowd, and the chuckle became a harsh laugh when Goggi tried to ascend the ladder, slipped on the topmost rung, and fell onto the boards with a clatter.

He was slow getting up. It seemed as though the actors had not rehearsed their falls. But finally, wobbling to his feet, he spread his arms and shouted morosely, "Me have saw glories, Bambo! Magic things and jools!"

Bambo crouched in a classic pose of bad actors from Coastlund to Qualinost. "Who guard them jools?" he asked. "Warrior or dragon or spells?"

"No warrior. No dragon no spell, Bambo. Who guard them am a little girl. A little *sleeping* girl."

The dwarves rubbed their hands together in an imitation of greed and slyness.

"How us get the magic things and jools, Bambo?" Goggi asked.

"First us kill the girl?" Bambo suggested.

A chorus of "no"s floated out of the audience.

"All right then," Bambo said, gesturing toward the crowd. "they don't want us killing nobody. We just . . . climb up ladder and take them jools."

"But how we get them down, Bambo?"

"Drop them out window."

The dwarves contemplated this dilemma. Goggi scratched his head in deep thought, then reached over and scratched Bambo's head in the vain hope that if he dug deep enough he would strike a notion.

"That hurt, Goggi!" Bambo exclaimed, brushing away his comrade's hand and rubbing the injured spot. "Still, me get idea from all that scratching. What if . . . we *trick* girl into giving us magic things and jools?"

Goggi nodded excitedly. "That be easy!" he cried. "Like shooting barrels in a fish!"

Each dwarf stared at the other. They frowned, shifted from foot to foot. Sat down finally, each cupping his raggedly bearded chin in his hands.

"Tell you what, Goggi," Bambo said at last. "Since tricking girl is easy, me let you figure out plan."

"Me already got plan," Goggi replied uncertainly. "Me wonder if you can guess it."

By this time, it had occurred to even the dimmest citizens of Hollow that neither dwarf had the least notion how to proceed.

"Us do our job," Bambo said. "Us climb up tower, fix pulley to window sill. Plan will come then. Me sure."

Now the two of them looked up, craning toward the high tower window.

"Oh, lady!" Bambo called out.

Goggi placed his hand over his partner's mouth, tried to stifle the shouting, but Bambo broke away and called again.

The lady appeared. Or rather, her voice floated out of the window like a golden mist.

The voice was lovely but a little deep and also disembodied, as though it floated out of nowhere. Even the most imaginative people in the audience were troubled by its baffling, unmoored nature.

It was as if you couldn't believe what was said . . . until you saw who was saying it.

"What rough sound disturbs my sleep?" asked the woman, and some in the first row saw her hands, large for a little girl and so pale that the blue veins marbled her wrists.

> "What rough sound disturbs my sleep?
> For I have slumbered, soft and deep
> throughout five seasons, unaware
> of changes in the clouds and air,
> of summer turning into fall

> and back to winter, while these walls
> are ever changeless. Who is it calls?

"Bambo, lady. Bambo and Goggi. Us come to ask your help."

———◆———

Tal heard the laughter from the front of the stage, but he had other things on his mind.

Where was Nando?

Where, for that matter, was his sister?

It was like riding a huge, unruly horse, this making up plans as you went. How he hated to rely on anyone else! Especially that gob of a brother, who would be lucky to figure out which end of the sack to open, much less how to get Livia inside it!

Sebastius was at the front of the stage, carrying on about the two dwarves and their plan. Seems they were intent on making a deal with this Papilla.

But in a moment, Sebastius's carrying on, and all the deals he was striking, both in the play and out, would be . . .

What was Tal's father's word for it?

Null and void.

Sure enough, despite Tal's fears, here came Nando through the curtained shadows, dragging a sack behind him.

A sack that was kicking, writhing, and muttering.

Tal had never seen Livia this mad.

"Dangdang troll-faced donkey-poop of a brother!" the sack was saying.

It unsettled Tal.

Not that she was loud enough to be heard over Sebastius's booming voice, over the dwarves lugging the wicker dragon across the stage. No, it was something that Tal understood only dimly himself.

Something to do with good faith.

At that moment, the boy almost realized that the success of all his schemes and scenarios, everything involving his little sister, depended on her innocence. Depended on Livia's trust, her kindly nature, her being too young for caginess and caution.

Had Tal been able to put these feelings into words or even think them out clearly, this story might have ended far otherwise.

But Nando had arrived on cue, bearing a bagful of livid sister. And here was the prospect of embarrassing Livia and his mother and father and proving once and for all to the town and the visiting players how clever he was, how unworthy they all were of his downright cleverness.

"Give me a boost," he said to Nando. "I'm carrying the bag up the arch."

<hr/>

"The plan was simple," Sebastius said. "When it came . . .
>
> The dragon's time to rise in flame
> and entertain old Melchior,
> they needed counterbalance for
> the wicker prop. Papilla's task
> was to do simply what they asked—
> fill the bag with things of weight,
> bangles, bracelets, silver plate,
> expensive mirrors, tapestry
> and magic items, two or three
> of which they could not guess the power,
> then drop the bag straight down the tower
> drawing the wicker thing aloft.
> Its weight would make the landing soft:

No gold would dent, no glass would break,
all done for simple burglary's sake.
Upstairs, Papilla, innocent
of plot and scheme and what it meant
to throw old Melchior's riches out
would drop the bag at Bambo's shout."

As Sebastius spoke and some of the crowd nodded off at the verse, the dwarves attached a rope to the dragon and threaded it through a pulley beneath the sill of the tower window. As they did this, Melchior and a group of hooded actors crossed the stage and seated themselves. They were playing an audience who watched the dwarves' activity—an audience watched in turn by the expectant yokels of Hollow.

At the back of the crowd, old Kaleem nudged his wife.

"Where's Livvy, Ilona? I don't see her."

"I'm not sure, dearest. Watch the play."

Kaleem frowned. "It's boring. All talk and no action, except for the dwarves. I can't tell what's going on."

Ilona sighed. "It seems these gully dwarves—"

"Are they *really* gully dwarves?"

"Probably not, dearest. The eye says yes, but the nose is the true judge of their . . . gulliness, so to speak, and they smell presentable. But they're gully dwarves while on stage, you see, and they're planning to rob this Melchior . . ."

"That's the elf, right?"

"You're following the play better than you think, my love. Now the dwarves have tricked the girl . . . "

"The one we haven't seen . . . "

Ilona closed her eyes. To appreciate theater with Kaleem—even this one-act little melodrama—was a long bout of interruptions and explanations.

After all, her thoughts weren't really on the play.

"The one we haven't seen," she conceded. "It seems as though Papilla will put weight in a bag attached to the other end of the pulley rope, and as the weight draws the dragon up, the bag lands softly on the ground."

"Filled with jewels and magic things," Kaleem added. "Of course, they call them 'jools.' Gully dwarves are such fools."

"Right as always, my dear," Ilona said. She sighed again, this time mysteriously, her gray eyes focused abstractly on something beyond the stage and the back-drop. If he hadn't known better, Kaleem would have thought she was star-gazing.

"How does the play end, Ilona?"

"I'm not sure," she replied quietly. "Happily for some-one, I hope."

It seemed pretty happy for Tal at that moment.

Straddling the arch upon which the curtains were hung, puffing and sweating from having hauled aloft his bagged sister, he was marveling at how all things were coming together.

Now he would tie the bag—with Livvy inside—to one of these entangled ropes. Once that was done, he would swing the bag across the stage toward Sebastius, who was still droning on . . .

About bags and girls, of all things.

It was amazing how everything converged.

Livia kicked in the bag beside him, and Tal steadied himself on the arch. High above the activity on the stage, hidden in shadows like some naughty puppet master, he groped in the darkness for ropes and cords.

Soon, his fingers closed around a thick rope, looser than the others with which it intertwined. Tal gave it a tug, tugged again.

It was holding steady. Steady enough, that is, to anchor a swinging six-year-old girl on her flight across a torchlit stage and into further scandal.

"Hold on, Livvy," Tal whispered wickedly. "The fun's just beginning."

He tied the mouth of the bag to the loosened rope. Thought about it and doubled the knot.

Now he dropped the loose end of the rope to his brother, who stood in the darkness below.

"Ow! Watch where you drop things, Tal!"

"Quiet, Nando!" Tal whispered. "Now, just grab hold of the thing."

"Why?"

"Has to be something holding the other end. You're as good a dead weight as anything, Nando."

"Dead weight for what?"

"Oh, you'll see, brother. It's a wonderful trick, I promise."

The rope, descending into shadows, strained and tautened. Nando had grabbed it. He was following orders again.

For a moment, only briefly, it passed through Tal's obsessed imaginings that Livvy might be seriously injured in her starring role as a pendulum of vengeance. For a longer moment Tal paused and pondered, as he stood in the wings of a whole new way of thinking.

Sebastius started up again. Something about Papilla and weight. The previous night's insult rushed back into Tal's memory, blocking out everything but a desire for revenge.

Get ready, Sebastius, he thought darkly.

Get ready, you old bastard, for a change in the script.

———◆◆◆———

The townspeople were restless.

It wasn't the worst story, but it seemed as if the actors were talking rather than acting.

Sebastius was explaining again. Another long, rhymed speech about the scheme of the gully dwarves.

It seemed that the dragon was supposed to rise at the climax of the play—not the play they were watching, but the play that Melchior was about to see. Of course, what would haul the dragon to the top of the tower would be the weight of whatever Papilla had placed in that bag at the other end of the pulley rope.

Some of the audience thought the girl was foolish. Some of them thought she was just innocent. For most, however, there was no difference between innocence and foolishness, and trying to distinguish just made them tired.

"It would help," Kaleem whispered to Ilona, "if we could see the girl."

"The girl?"

"Why, Papilla, of course!" the silk trader hissed.

It was exasperating. Women and high culture didn't mix, apparently.

But part of him understood. High culture was boring him as well. Especially since he had figured out the bottom line.

"I know how this turns out," he boasted, a little too loudly in the midst of Sebastius's monologue.

"That's lovely, dearest," Ilona replied. Her plain face never turned toward him, her pale eyes fastened on the stage.

"The dwarves have duped the girl," Kaleem explained, "and as a fringe benefit, they've duped old Marmaduke—"

"Melchior, dearest." Ilona corrected. "The elf is named Melchior."

"Be that as it may," Kaleem snapped. "He gets what's due to him for tricking the knight and for keeping the girl in the castle. For cutting a deal at the expense of everyone else. Your dwarves get away, and you've got your comedy."

Ilona said nothing. Her face was unreadable as she leaned forward, listening to Sebastius.

———◆———

So the old fart was talking again.

Well, now was the time, Tal thought.

He closed his eyes and wrapped his arms around the squirming bag, ready to launch Livia into the orating old fraud, there at midstage. He imagined the sack, like a huge, writhing pendulum, descending into torchlight, catching Sebastius at the bottom of its arc, sending the fat fool hurtling into the audience with the prospect of bruises and perhaps even a broken bone or two.

He opened his eyes, took stock of the height and distance. Suddenly Sebastius seemed terribly far away, an almost impossible target to hit with a makeshift bag and rope.

Just as suddenly, Tal felt the burden of being only eleven.

It was a long shot, after all, that the sack would strike the old charlatan. More likely it would swoop through the stage lights, into the wings and back again, back and forth until it settled in full view.

Tal could feel it returning. That sense that everything was getting out of hand. That events and results had grown too large for him to figure.

He would not hear of *that*.

He would guide the weapon home.

Pulling his hood over his head, he grabbed the bag and leaped from the arch, a strong final push of his legs propelling him out into the light and over the boards of the stage, headed toward Sebastius, who had raised his hand dramatically to conclude a long-winded, clamorous speech.

Nando felt the rope turn in his hands as his brother stood atop the high arch, clutching their bagged sister, outlined in faint light.

This will be easy, he thought. All I gotta do is hold the rope.

But the world has ways of sudden temptation.

At that moment, clutching a candle and muttering something about props and prompts, a gnome waddled by, no doubt bound on some backstage duty. The creature jingled as it passed, and Nando's larcenous eye, went straight to the source of the sound. . . .

To the belt, to the dangling tools . . .

To the pouch, bulging and in full view, tied to the gnome's waist.

"Magic things and jools," Nando whispered, unconsciously quoting Goggi's line in the play.

Now one hand slipped from the rope, reached toward the pouch . . .

And something deep in the belly of the purse closed with a snap on the boy's groping fingers.

Nando cried out, removed his hand, and stared in shock at the new technology that gripped it. For nowhere in Hollow—not even in the house of Darl's father—had anyone ever seen a spring-operated rat trap.

Nando shouted again, let go of the rope, and desperately tried to pry the device off his throbbing hand.

At that very moment, his brother Tal was in mid-air over the boards of the stage.

———◆———

Sebastius kept at it, all the while Tal prepared the bag in the rafters.

> "The time came for the dragon's cue:
> upstairs, Papilla, rifling through
> the mirrors and curtains, chairs and plate,
> could not put sufficient weight
> inside the bag, and so it hung
> so it dangled, so it swung
> above the stage, till her desire
> to help the gully dwarves took fire,
> and into the half-filled sack she stepped,
> and from the windowsill she leaped."

The crowd expected nothing so sudden.

The wicker prop rose up the tower face, hoisted by unseen hands. Tied to the dragon's wings were streamers of orange and black silk, a sad simulation of the flames that were supposed to engulf the creature in the play.

Far more exciting than the dragon was the bag, hurtling out of the darkness like the counterweight of some great catapult, a small hooded figure clinging to it desperately.

One of the dwarves? they wondered.

Halfway across the stage the rope gave, and the whole apparatus—writhing sack and screaming hooded figure—fell to the boards at Sebastius's feet.

The figure lay unconscious beneath the bag. The dwarves rushed out from the wings and dragged him, hood and all, offstage.

Which left the sack. It opened, to the crowd's astonishment.

Livia emerged, dazed and decked in orange and black, like the flames on the dragon, or the bright wings of the butterfly.

For a moment, not a sound rose from the milling crowd in the village common. Livia's robes shimmered with torchlight, caught the moonlight.

Shimmered on their own.

It was as if her presence summoned the eyes, thoughts, and hearts of the town. All of them, from lawyer to merchant to rat catcher's son, were struck by the change that swept over her.

Now Livia staggered to her feet and looked out over a shadowy sea of faces. Finally she gathered the wherewithal to speak.

"I'm . . . still alive. . . . "

Sebastius, not missing a breath or a moment, picked up the verse, gathering Livia's words into the play itself.

> "'I'm still alive,' Papilla said,
> 'I'm still alive,' and rubbed her head.
> Bruised but safe on the tower ground,
> she dusted off and looked around,
> and safely clear of Melchior's sight,
> crept off to freedom in the night."

Sebastius bowed then, but the applause was only scattered. None of the folks of Hollow were quite sure whether the play was over. Many of them puzzled as well over the little girl who stood center stage.

They had thought of her so long as Livia, the silk dealer's daughter. Silly little thing. Of late, a rider of roast geese. It was hard to imagine that the play had made her someone else entirely.

Was she really Papilla? Had that been her voice, had those been her pale hands up in the tower window?

According to Sebastius, that was the story. He stepped downstage, faced the audience, and took the girl's hand. His deep, melodic voice wafted out like torch smoke over the troubled crowd.

> "Now at last our story's ended,
> Papilla free, her sadness mended,
> but some loose ends remain untied:
> the fate of others you'll decide."

If the crowd was uneasy before, they were downright unsettled now. They had come to the play not intending to think, to *decide* anything, but to be lulled by fire and magic, actors of odd appearances and races, a sword fight or two. Instead, it seemed as if almost everything had taken place off stage, except for a solitary fat man and his poetry . . .

A fat man who now was asking them to judge, by the gods!

Some of the townspeople got up and left. You could hear their muttering fade into the shadows—words like *boring* and *never again* carried back by the night air. Some of them stayed, wanting to see how things would turn out and eager somehow to be a part of it.

Now, draped in dramatic black, Melchior stepped into the light. Beside him were Bambo and Goggi, dressed in the particolored costumes that had caused such amusement only moments before.

Melchior seemed smaller somehow, as though the play's ending had stripped him of a certain magic.

But the change in the dwarves was greater still.

Even the most dim-witted of the townspeople noticed. Bambo and Goggi were, if anything, a little taller. Thinner in neck and arms, and beardless. Worse for wear, as if they had been in some kind of struggle offstage.

Bambo, it seemed, had injured his hand.

Yoni, perched on the low branches of a tree at the edge of the common, was the first to recognize them.

"Tal and Nando," he said quietly. "Them dwarves is Tal and Nando."

Whether they had been the dwarves all along or whether some bait and switch had taken place backstage, he was far too dense to determine. Instead, he started to shout their names, hoping for a wave, a shout in reply. After all, the boys were players now, stars of the stage, and Yoni *knew* them, by the Book of Gilean, he did!

But his own jealousy made him quiet, and bewilderment quieted the other townsfolk, even some who had the sense to realize that the actors had changed places.

It was not only jealousy for Yoni, though.

It was a low, malicious hope.

For hadn't the big man on the stage said something about *deciding fates?* To Yoni, such a phrase meant the prospect of punishment, pure and simple.

He sat in the tree and awaited his chance.

Now Melchior stepped downstage. He glared out over the audience with dark and fathomless eyes, and most of the people of Hollow were afraid of him—afraid that if they judged him too harshly, he would turn some kind of leftover magic upon the lot of them. Turn them into stone, or fireflies, or a bushel of apples gone bad.

Sebastius, placing a heavy hand on the elf's shoulder, addressed the crowd.

"First decide for Melchior:
Give him tender mercy, or
punish him with task or quest,
to appear before you overdressed
in silly black and orange scarves.
Have him serve the gully dwarves
or walk on water or on coals. . . .

Here he paused and awaited the crowd's response.

No matter what version of this cautionary tale you hear—
and from this point on, there are several—all versions
begin with the uncomfortable silence of the crowd.

After all, they weren't quite sure what was expected
of them.

Surely, the dullest wit among them—and Yoni,
perched in the lower branches of the distant tree, was a
prime contender for that honor—recognized that someone was supposed to judge the elf. Between too much
fear and too little imagination, most of the townspeople
were stymied.

Sebastius, ever the stage manager, prompted them
again. He repeated the speech, ending it with the same,
unrhymed line then waited, with almost godlike patience,
for someone—anyone—to speak.

Slowly it dawned upon the silent crowd that they had
become speakers in Sebastius's play. That completing
the rhyme would complete Melchior's sentence.

Sebastius cleared his throat. Even his forebearance
was wearing thin now. He repeated the last line a third
time, his melodious voice rising at the end in a sort of
irritated anticipation.

"Or walk on water, or on *coals* . . ."

An old woman in the middle of the crowd was the first to test the verbal waters.

"'Give him diarrhea and colds'?"

"No! That's no good!" Kaleem shouted, having caught at last the gist of the drama. "How about 'have his feet break out in molds'?"

The people of Hollow agreed that this was not even as good as the old woman's line. The night would have erupted in arguments among would-be judges and poets, had not Yoni, standing dangerously on the branch of the distant tree, shouted across the common.

"Let Melchior play women's roles!"

Sebastius nodded. It was bad, but it was good enough.

It seemed that Melchior took particular offense at this sentence. He glared out over the common, lifted his hands, so pale that the blue veins marbled his wrists, and muttered a spiteful phrase in Elvish at his tormentor standing in the tree.

You would have thought the elf was only an actor, but apparently, studying for his role had indeed given him some kind of residual magic.

At any rate, the tree on the far end of the common was struck by a rippling wave of air, and in some versions of the story Yoni slipped and broke his leg. . . .

Or his arm, or even his neck, depending on what account you want to believe.

Let's say his neck. There's more divine and poetic justice in a broken neck. After all, we need to move quickly to Tal and Nando.

For Sebastius had already done so. Over the screams of pain from beneath the tree, the master spoke as he gestured to the boys.

"What of Bambo and of Goggi?
Doused with water till they're soggy?
Forced the ragman's cart to follow
as he cleans the town of Hollow?
Losing hair, or teeth, or voice?"

Someone in the crowd, probably Darl, spoke out.
"Them things are bad, but something woise!"
A line that met with a long groan from the crowd.
Then silence, except for a painful, different groaning that
continued beneath the distant tree.

Then a woman's voice. Familiar to most of the town,
and most familiar to Tal and Nando.
"Let Papilla make the choice."
For the last time on this fateful evening, Livvy moved
to center stage.

Sebastius, all agree, repeated a version of the lines that
had prepared the sentence of Melchior—a list of pun-
ishments that ended, as the first had, with "walk on
water, or on coals."

All agree that the people of Hollow fell despondently
silent, having long ago exhausted all the rhymes they
knew for "coals."

But Livia, it seems, was more clever than any of them had
imagined, and more angry than any of them had dreamed.
Some say that she responded simply:
" 'Let them fall in deep dark holes.' "
Others say it was more direct and vengeful:
" 'Let them be eaten up by trolls' "
and that the sentence was carried out off-stage, as grue-
some and loud as you care to imagine.

Most say that she completed the rhyme in a manner both spiritual and dire:

" 'Let Gilean snatch up their souls.' "

Which, according to whom you believe, meant one of two things. Perhaps the boys vanished from the face of Krynn, imprisoned for eternity in some weird afterlife.

More likely, they were forever taunted from a distance. For the most common end to the story goes like this:

Released into the custody of their father, the boys found themselves locked in their upstairs room, the windows barred, and their entertainment reduced to half-hearted guesses at what they would have for supper.

Once they were released—in two months' time or so—they assumed the punishment was over and wondered why a brittle smile crossed Ilona's face each time she looked at them. Within a week, they realized the punishment had only begun.

Because news came back from Sebastius's company, when the actors played the small villages of Solamnia and Coastlund. From that day on, there was always a mysterious young actress among the players, assigned small parts at first, usually a page who held the blue train of Mishakal or the dark train of Takhisis—goddesses played by a disgruntled elf who had once trod the stage as Melchior.

Later on, it was the same young girl who played these goddesses, and the elf received at last a release from women's roles, never again having to speak in falsetto or to dangle his pale hands out the window of some flimsy wooden stage tower.

She went by many names but was adored far and wide as Papilla.

Kaleem, it is said, lived ten long and surly years and at his death passed on his business to Ilona, who had

spent those eventless years staring wistfully at the Khalkist Mountains and other distant things. She, in turn,
stayed in town only long enough to pass the inheritance
to Darl (or divide it between Darl and Yoni, in versions
of the story where the neck remains intact). She returned
to Solamnia, where she supposedly passed the rest of her
days in peace and freedom and quiet.

At least the jobs of rat catcher and tanner remained
available at her departure.

In the happiest version of this tale, Ilona was joined
years later by Livia, who was at last free of the prison of
her little home town.

Who had grown beautiful and wise from a life among
traveling players and was ready to retire, rich and still
young and famous, to a palatial Solamnic estate.

There are accounts of a fortunate marriage, and kindly,
well-behaved grandchildren.

It's been a hundred years. We cannot be certain of
the story's outcome. But everyone agrees that Ilona had
somehow known how the play would end—both *on* the
stage and in the spreading ripples of its aftermath.

Nobody knows for sure what became of Tal and Nando,
except that they amounted to nothing, more or less.

It is a cautionary tale, no matter what version you
follow. And a cautionary tale should have a moral.

*Boys, be kind to your sisters: you can never reckon what
waits in the wings.*

ENTER, A GHOST

PAUL B. THOMPSON

Nordmaar, circa 361 AC

The lead wagon in the long caravan came
to a stop. With much shouting and creaking of harness,
the wagons behind each halted in turn. All along the
line of colorfully painted conveyances, drivers and pas-
sengers craned their necks to see why the procession
had stopped.

The driver of the first wagon, a hulking minotaur, tied
off his reins and climbed down. He left behind on the
driver's box a slender woman of indeterminate age, clad
in a homespun dress and a brightly embroidered vest.

"What is it, Tog?" she asked.

The minotaur shook his broad, horned head. "Our
next stop," he rumbled. "It's always good to look a place
over before you go in."

His companion—Andura was her name—surveyed
the town spread before them. It was a faired-sized place,

with many houses of weatherworn wood and fieldstone. Many of the buildings had two stories, usually a sign of prosperity, but the town seemed to have fallen on hard times. Around the clustered houses was a defensive wall in bad repair.

Above the town to the south a lone promontory stood, surrounded by empty plain. The top had been leveled, creating a flat plateau occupied by a small but imposing fortress. Red granite walls stood straight and tall. Peering over the walls were a trio of squat towers. Their roofs had long ago rotted away—Andura could see daylight through the upper windows. Full-grown trees and scrub grew hard against the base of the castle, something no attentive commander would tolerate. Vines reached up the weathered red walls, looking from the distance like ragged green teeth encroaching on a length of raw bone.

Andura's study of the forlorn town and castle was interrupted by the arrival of several irate wagoneers. Actors all, they proclaimed their pique in no uncertain terms.

A tall, elegant man with long black hair silvering at the temples demanded, "What's the reason for this delay? Why have you stopped?"

Andura climbed down. "Tog wanted to take in the view, Thronden."

Planting fists on his hips, Thronden said, "Is that so?"

A commotion started behind them, which proved to be the contentious kender brothers, Paz and Traz Thumbcutter. They burst between Thronden and the troll tragedian Urtak, tripped on their own feet, and fell face down in the dust. Paz got up first but was dragged back down by his brother.

"I got here first! You'll not upstage me again as you did in Valkinord!" piped Traz.

"Upstage? Upstage? You were cast as Second Street Vendor. I played the First!"

The two tussled in and between the legs of the others. When they rolled under the horses harnessed to Tog's wagon, the minotaur dragged them out before the beasts trod on them. Holding up a kender in each hand, he shook them until they stopped chattering.

"Trouble?"

All eyes turned. Sebastius, master of the Traveling Players of Gilean, came around the head of Tog's two-horse team. A balding man of mature years, with a comfortable paunch and rosy face, Sebastius could have been anywhere between sixty and six hundred. The actors nearest him flinched. He often seemed to appear when no one was looking.

"No trouble, Master," Andura said. "Tog stopped to take in our next venue."

Sebastius looked over his shoulder at the shabby town. "It isn't much to look at," he said affably, "In dire need of entertainment, in fact. Just the spot for our next play."

"Just the spot for an unmarked grave," Urtak intoned.

"What is this place, Master?" asked Paz, still dangling in Tog's grasp.

"That was my question! I was going to ask that!" Traz said, indignant.

At a nod from Sebastius, the minotaur set them on their feet. Sebastius idly pulled at one pink ear. "I passed this way long ago. Now, what was it called? Oh yes, Carklin Hall."

"A gloomy town," Andura said. "I wonder what folk here do for amusement."

"Not much, by the look of it. All the more reason for us to pay a visit."

Sebastius dispersed the actors back to their wagons. Paz and Traz went, grumbling and shoving each other. When only Tog and Andura were left, the master of the troupe said, "Take us right in, Tog. Go down the main thoroughfare—let everyone in town see us."

"The first look is always free," Andura quipped. With her tugging at his massive elbow, Tog climbed back on the driver's box and took up the reins.

"*Ka-ho*," said the minotaur gruffly in his native tongue. "Giddup" was the same in any language, and the team leaned on their traces, starting the heavy wagon down the lane to Carklin Hall.

Long ago, a few wayward peaks of the Khalkist Mountains got lost on the high Nordmaar plain. Like islands in a sea of grass, these isolated pinnacles dotted the land from the Khalkist range northward to the sea. In crueler days, warrior chiefs and bandit lords were wont to seize these lonely cliffs and build strongholds atop them. By local custom, the Khalkist fortresses were called "halls," and the villages that grew up beneath them took their names from the lords who ruled them from above.

"So there must be a Lord Carklin," Andura mused.

"Once but no longer, I say," Tog grunted. "The town has gone to seed."

Andura peered up at the red granite castle. "This Carklin used to live up there, then?"

"By the look of things, no one has lived there for a long time."

"Pity."

Andura liked the nobility, even the rough, barbaric sort. They were good patrons of the stage and open-handed with money and gifts. On the other hand, town fathers, drawn from the ranks of merchants or artisans, were often stingy types, inclined to haggle over every copper they spent.

No one stopped them at the town gate—if you call two spires of fieldstone, held together by powdery white mortar, a gate. Tog guided the wagon through, dark eyes shifting from side to side, watching for curious locals. There were none.

That was strange in itself. The Traveling Players always drew a crowd wherever they went. Children trailed after the painted wagons, tradesfolk stopped to stare, even thieves brightened at the prospect of eager crowds gathering to see a play. No such interest greeted the troupe when they rolled into Carklin Hall. When they did finally encounter some locals, they were pale, strained-looking folk who went about their work with no more than a sidelong glance at the colorful caravan rolling into town.

"Is there a plague here?" Andura wondered.

The cheerless scene was brightened by the crow of a rooster. The cockerel crowed again, close behind them. Standing, Andura looked back over the wagon's shingled roof. Bounding over the top of the wagon behind them was an extraordinary looking creature. Small and compact, he had wiry brown hair, swarthy skin, and a prodigious nose. When the little man reached the front edge of the roof of the trailing wagon, he stopped, threw back his head and emitted a loud barnyard yodel, indistinguishable from a real rooster.

"Moku," Andura said, rolling her eyes. Tog just grunted.

With great agility, little Moku leaped from the wagon top to the trace pole between the horses. He scampered along the narrow bar, then launched himself onto the rear of Andura's wagon. Reaching the shingles, he crowed for a fourth time.

"Hello yourself," she replied. "Your goose call is improving."

"You only goose I see," the gulley dwarf retorted good-naturedly. "I bring message from Boss. You want hear, or make flip-flap with lips?"

He hopped down to the driver's box. Moku was no bigger than a human toddler, though he smelled a lot worse. Straining on tiptoes, he tugged Tog's ear. "Hey, Bully! Boss says, lead us to town square. Ahead straight."

The minotaur nodded.

As they penetrated deeper into the small town, the dirt street acquired a layer of cobbles. Dry brown grass poked up between the paving, and the deep ruts worn in the stones showed how many years they'd borne traffic. At last the street opened out into a modest square a hundred paces across. Taverns and shops lined all four sides.

The Traveling Players drew up their wagons in a half circle, the open end facing the west. When the last wagon was in place, the actors dismounted, stretching, yawning, and scratching their sides. It had been a long ride from their last show.

Thronden, acting as Sebastius's Master of Ceremonies, set about organizing assembly of the stage between the curving lines of wagons. The stage would be a simple platform, with a few tall poles from which to hang curtains, but it had to be sturdy enough to bear the tread of actors as weighty as Tog or Gree the centaur. Some of the burlier troupers fell to with mallets, planks, and pegs, and the platform began to take shape.

Andura opened the costume trunks stored in her wagon. Not knowing what play Sebastius would choose to perform here, she had to be ready with all the outfits she had. Lately she'd been getting a lot of what she glumly called "pork chop" roles—being the tender object of the hero's affection. She sighed. She hadn't had a lively part in months.

Opening the fourth trunk, she spotted something moving around under a pile of lace collars. They weren't real lace, just pressed paper, but they were her responsibility. Suspecting a rat, she picked up a broom and snatched the collars aside. Lying calmly on his back there was Moku. His eyes were closed. He made vague ticking sounds.

"What are you doing?" she demanded.

"Shh. Practice earwig voice."

Moku was the troupe's premiere sound maker—or as he liked to put it, he acted with his voice, while everyone else acted with their faces and bodies.

Frowning, she swept the gully dwarf aside. "Don't you have anything useful to do?"

Moku landed on his feet, somersaulted, and meowed like a cat. "I working hard!" he declared. "Bug voices hard to learn."

"How hard can they be? You are a bug!"

He had a retort nocked and ready to loose when Thronden rapped loudly on the wagon shell and said loudly, "Andura, are you there?"

"Yes, coming."

She found Thronden waiting outside with the new chap, the outcast elf Sebastius had recently taken into the troupe. The elf was a handsome, athletic sort, but sullen and rough-hewn. Sebastius had his work cut out for him if he thought he could turn him into a player. The master was seldom wrong though and had made fine performers out of less likely characters—Moku, for example.

"Who you?" said Moku, peering around Andura's legs.

The elf bowed his head slightly. "We have met, forgetful one. Camalantharas is my name, but Cam will do."

Thronden cleared his throat loudly. "The Master has assigned parts," he said gravely. Now he had their attention. Thronden held out his hand to the elf, who dipped into a large cloth bag and drew out a thick scroll. With an attempt at a ceremonial flourish, he gave this to Thronden, who passed it to Andura.

She parted the parchment and read the title: *The Iron Sack, a Comedy in Three Acts.* She'd seen this play before but never done it herself. Slipping her eyes down the cast list, she saw her part was highlighted in red ink.

"Master Tensi?" This was the lead role, an eighteen-year-old boy.

"Correct."

She'd played boy's parts before, and while her slender figure presented little problem, her mature face and voice seemed to her unsuitable to play a callow male youth.

Moku climbed her back and read over her shoulder. "Ha! Master was squinty when he choose you! Who else play?"

Andura shrugged him off. He alighted on the ancient cobblestones and cooed like a covey of pigeons.

"Gree will be Tensi's nurse, Rontz's the High Priest, Thaelix will play the Queen of Napland, and young Warkin the king," Thronden announced.

Sebastius was certainly casting against type—a 420-pound male ogre as the queen? A four-legged centaur as a nursemaid? Rontz, a goblin from Throt, had a face like a rat, so it wasn't so strange that he should play the villainous High Priest, but Warkin was a dashing young man, a bardic poet of some skill. Casting him as the King of Napland—supposedly an aged miser—was very odd, even for Sebastius.

Moku tittered. "Funny! Everybody be wrong, this play! Get big laughs!"

"There's one for you," Thronden said seriously. Cam handed him a scroll in the bag. Thronden presented it to Moku.

He spread the parchment open. Running his thumb down the page, Moku found his part.

"Scorchfinger!" he cried. "Is good, is good!" He did a jerky little dance.

"Who's Scorchfinger?" the elf asked Thronden, in what he thought was a whisper.

"Dragon! Very big, scary red dragon! Is most good part!"

So far the newcomer had held his tongue, but now his true thoughts slipped out: "How in the Abyss can anyone cast a gully dwarf as a dragon?"

Moku stopped dancing. He gazed up his long nose at the elf. "I show you, but too hungry now. Need snack," he said. "Dragon voice big strain."

"Big strain on the audience's imagination," the elf said wryly.

"Ha! I sound so real, watchers wet pants, run away." He held up a stubby thumb and forefinger, slightly apart. "Use only this much voice, is better. Scare, not scare away."

Andura said, "So thoughtful!" She appeared sincere. The elf looked at her, wondering.

Thronden left to continue his preparations. Cam folded his scarred arms and said, "I'm supposed to help. What should I do first?"

"You want help, Cam-will-do?"

He assured Moku that he did.

"Go ask cook for grub. I got to practice. Voicing dragon hungry work!"

The stage was done by mid-afternoon, and the principal actors in the forthcoming production assembled on it for a quick review of their parts. Members of the troupe not directly involved with performing *The Iron Sack* were kept busy. Crates and trunks were dragged out of the wagons, and all the costumes and props sorted and aired. The troupe's small band rehearsed lively entr'acte numbers under gray, rolling clouds all afternoon.

Sebastius had disappeared, leaving the directing to his able assistant, Thronden. Thronden told the story of the play to the cast. This was usual even for such an experienced company. All the actors knew *The Iron Sack*, and about half of them had appeared in it before, but given the special nature of the Traveling Players—tenure in the company was commonly measured in decades—it made sense for everyone to hear the story afresh.

"*The Iron Sack*, a comedy in three acts," Thronden began, rolling the R's in iron and three. Are we all here?"

"I'm not," said Rontz, the sharp-faced goblin. Moku baa'd like a sheep.

Thronden glared them into silence. "Principal cast: Master Tensi, a youth." Andura raised her hand. "Welda, his nurse since childhood." Gree the centaur, arms folded across his swarthy chest, nodded in acknowledgment.

"The King of Napland."

Warkin, short in stature but magnetic in personality, placed a gold pasteboard crown on his head and said, "His Majesty is present."

"The Queen of Napland . . ." Thronden continued down the named cast list. After the principals there were assorted bit parts—tavern loafers, bullies, street folk, soldiers, priests. Camalantharas was got his first role, non-speaking, as a palace guard.

"Tensi, an apprentice ironmonger, leaves home to find fame and fortune in the kingdom of Napland," Thronden went on. "Taking his aged nurse with him, he arrives in the royal city with little money but with a shoulder bag made of chain mail, which he keeps close to him at all times."

"What in sack?" asked Moku, getting ahead of the story.

"Iron working tools," Andura whispered. "For his trade."

"Tensi finds lodging at the Barnacle Inn, where the tavern keeper mistakes him for an infamous assassin, Black Bag Ando. To bribe the supposed assassin, he lets Tensi and his nurse lodge and eat for free. The nurse takes a dim view of this—"

" 'Only evil will come of it, Master Tensi!' " intoned Gree in his powerful baritone. This was almost the sole line the nurse had, but it was an important line, and she said it two score times in the course of the play.

"Famalun, a disgraced courtier, comes to the Barnacle Inn seeking solace in wine. As he's about to be robbed by cutthroats, Tensi happens on the scene. One thief tries to stab him, but his blade is turned by the iron sack. The nurse clubs the other robber, and the courtier is saved. The notion goes around that Tensi has subdued both miscreants with the mysterious mail sack. When the courtier regains the favor of his sovereign soon after, he summons Tensi to the palace and presents him to the king."

That was Act One. Act Two detailed Tensi's adventures in the palace. The King of Napland was an aged miser who was battling his young, scheming wife on one hand and the ambitious High Priest on the other. Thinking Tensi's sack holds treasure, he decides to

PAUL B. THOMPSON

keep the boy around by declaring him his champion. The vain, flirtatious queen tries to seduce the youth, who is so innocent he fails to even notice her efforts. Outraged, the queen reports Tensi to the high priest as a heretic. When he arrives at the Great Temple, Tensi and the nurse are seized. Tensi demands a fair trial, and the high priest, amused, says he will pardon Tensi if he does a small task for him: He must vanquish the terrible red dragon Scorchfinger, who has long decimated the southern lands of the kingdom. The high priest holds the nurse hostage to ensure Tensi's return. Gamely, the youth sallies forth to meet Scorchfinger. Death seems certain.

About the time Thronden was finishing his telling of the second act, Andura noticed two strangers skulking by the line of wagons. As no one from Carklin Hall had paid much attention to the troupe, she was surprised to see the pair. More surprising, they weren't children or busybody oldsters but young men, one dressed like a tradesman, the other in more stylish and expensive clothes.

"Only evil will come of it, Master Tensi!"

Andura missed the cue being fed to her. Moku hopped down from Gree's back and sidled over. He pursed his lips and quacked loudly.

Like a striking snake, her hand darted out and caught the gully dwarf's lips. His last quack came out as a flatulent squawk.

Turning slowly, Andura smiled serenely and said, "Why, Moku! Whatever happened to your face?"

"Meggimogu gumbum," was all he could say.

"May I please have your attention? We're almost done," Thronden said, sighing. Andura released Moku, who sat down out of her reach, rubbing his abused lips.

"Thank you. Act Three: Tensi meets Scorchfinger . . ."

Her attention drifted away again. The two men stayed there, peeking shyly around the end of the prop wagon. What were they up to? The youthful tradesman was rather handsome, in a faded, blondish sort of way. . . .

"—and so the story ends. Everyone takes a bow," Thronden was saying. Andura snapped around. What happened in Act Three? Had she been distracted that long?

"Blocking and lighting after sunset," Thronden announced, as the actors rose and began milling around. "First run-through after supper."

Luckily she knew her part and the play well enough. Andura descended the wooden steps to the cobbled square. The two men were gone. Were they only interested in a free recital of the plot?

She muttered as much under her breath.

"Nobody like to hear Throndy that much."

Moku was at her elbow, tapping the end of his long nose.

"You saw them too?"

"Smelt 'em. This nose not just for dipping in soup, you know."

She dared not think about gully dwarf eating habits too long. "I wonder where they went?" she murmured, starting toward the spot she'd last seen the men.

"Who care? Cooky is roasting a rat for me—"

"Nobody in this town so much as blinked when we arrived, then those two come snooping around. I want to know why." Andura didn't mention she found one attractive, and the other looked rich. Unaccountably, she looked skyward at the ruined castle.

"Maybe we bring Tog with us?"

"Who said 'we,' runt? Go eat your garbage before it gets cold."

Moku screwed up his wizened face and didn't make a single sound. By that she knew she'd gotten through to him.

The young men were nowhere near the wagons, but a quick look around showed them striding toward a grog shop on the east side of the square. Hitching up her skirt, Andura followed. Moku trailed a few paces behind her, essaying hunting-dog growls in the back of his throat. Andura sighed and tried to ignore the little creature.

Their quarry disappeared into the tavern. The sign over the door, much faded, showed a war club plunged into a clay cup: The Mace and Mug.

Inside, the shop was dim and crowded. Andura was surprised that the tavern had so much trade this early in the day, but the shadows were crowded with men in working clothes—cobblers in leather aprons, masons with trowels sheathed like swords, carpenters smelling of sawn wood. All eyes were on Andura as she paused in the open door. The square column of daylight she let in pierced the gloom, dividing the tavern in half.

Men coughed and shuffled their feet.

"Drop that flap!" cried the barkeep sharply. He was a fat fellow with a grizzled gray beard down to his waist.

Andura let the leather flap fall just in time to catch Moku in the face.

"Rrrak!" He squawked like a parrot. "Nice! Maybe I not come in!"

"Do us the favor," Andura said quietly. Her eyes adjusted to the poor light, and she saw the two curious townsmen seated together in a booth at the end of the bar. She went up to the bar and said, "Wine, please."

"We only serve beer," said the barkeep. Like buckeyes, his pupils seemed to fill all the white in his eyes.

"A beer, then."

He poured a leather jack full from a oaken pitcher. Andura paid him and walked deliberately over toward the two young men.

"'Ere!" exclaimed the barkeep. "This coin's a hundred years old!"

She cast a glance back at him. "Oh? It's still good, isn't it?" The proprietor blinked and put the antique silver piece on the back counter, where it glinted brightly in the gloom.

Andura hailed the two young men with false bonhomie. "Greetings, fellows! Is there room for one more?"

"Two more!" said Moku, mincing along to avoid spilling brew from his brimming jack.

"Well, one and a half."

The men smiled nervously and slid to the back of the booth. Andura sat beside the clean-shaven, well-dressed one. Moku hopped onto the bench next to the workman with the drooping blond mustache.

"Are you thinking of seeing our play?" she asked casually. Moku sucked noisily on his beer.

"Beg pardon?" said Mustache.

"Our play—in the square come tomorrow eve."

"Ah! I've heard tell of such but never seen one," Cleancheeks said. "I am Bannur of Nordling. This is my friend, Havared." The mustached man bowed his head.

"She Andura. *The* Andura," Moku said. A bead of golden beer clung to the end of his nose. He tried to lick it off, unsuccessfully. Andura shuddered and looked away.

"I Moku. We Traveling Players of Gilean." The little creature touched two fingers to his sloping brow and made a fizzing sound, like pouring beer.

"You're a gully dwarf," said Bannur.

"Aghar, you say please. I not been in gully for forty year."

Andura rolled her eyes.

The young men exchanged a look of secret significance. Andura waited for them to say something, then grew tired of their reticence. She stood up, leaving her beer untouched. "I hope you'll attend the performance," she said briskly. "Tell your friends and neighbors. Come on, Moku—" Moku pushed his empty jack away and belched.

"Wait," Bannur said, suddenly grasping her arm. She stared at his hand, but he held on. "Can we speak with you? Privately?"

"Talk is dry," said, Moku, shaking his empty cup.

Andura poured her beer into the gully dwarf's jack. "Be quick, and say what you will."

Havared and Bannur skulked outside with the actors at their heels. They ducked down the alley beside The Mace and Mug and crossed a muddy courtyard to a ramshackle frame building. From the pot and pipe on the sign, Andura recognized it as a tinsmith's shop. Bannur led them inside. Andura lingered suspiciously by the door, ready to bolt if things became ugly.

Inside, a gaunt girl child, no more than six years old, sat on the straw floor, playing with a wooden doll. When she saw Andura and Moku, she scampered away on all fours, doll clenched in her teeth. Her animal panic was so profound Andura was taken aback.

"Wait, girl—" she began.

"My daughter Sisandra," said Havared, sounding choked. "Forgive her manners. With only me to raise her, she's grown a bit wild. She has the same wasting disease that carried off her mother."

Bannur dragged up a bench for the actors. Moku sat right down, looking up with big eyes. Bannur and Havared remained standing.

"This is an old town," Bannur began, weaving his fingers together below his chin. "It was founded by my ancestor, Takin of Nordling, a vassal of the great lord Uranko, during his war with the Kingpriest of Istar eight hundred years ago—"

Moku yawned, finishing the gesture with the sound of squeaky door hinge. "You'd best leave out the history lesson," Andura suggested. "My comrade is as attentive as a bluebottle fly, and our time is short. What troubles you?"

"We are cursed!" Havared declared. "Surely you noticed the grave miasma that lies upon our town? A wasting plague hangs over us! For every two children born here, one dies before his tenth summer. Our old folks' wits fade away like summer flowers at harvest time. Crops yield so poorly we have to buy all our food from other towns."

"Too many years we've lived under this curse," Bannur added. "It exists because we are haunted—that is to say, the castle on the hill is haunted—and the specter's baleful spirit draws in all life from the town. If things go on as they are, we shall die out!"

"Why tell us?" Andura asked, puzzled.

The young nobleman said ruefully, "Strangers come here so seldom. We thought there might be a wizard among you. Your master Sebastius denied it when we asked him, however, so we left."

"You spoke to the master?"

Bannur admitted they had.

"He would not help us. Carklin Hall is doomed," Havared said with a heavy sigh.

A ponderous silence filled the shop. Fidgeting from one foot to the other, Moku made the clop-clop sounds of a horse walking on cobblestones. The townsmen looked at him indulgently.

PAUL B. THOMPSON

"If you had a wizard," Andura asked, "what would you have him do?"

In turns, the two men explained their plan, one they'd obviously worked out long ago. Some years past, Bannur's father had purchased a scroll from a passing sorcerer. It contained a spell of banishment and instructions on how to carry out the ritual. All they needed, Havared said, was someone daring enough to go to the ruined castle and try the deed.

"Do yourself," advised Moku, yawning.

"We've tried and tried," Bannur said. He frowned deeply. "We whose blood is tied to the domain of Carklin Hall cannot enter the castle and live. The wasting curse consumes us all at once, instead of bit by bit. My father tried it, and it cost him his life." He looked hollow-eyed at his friend. "Havared's brother perished too, and nine others in my lifetime. Now no one from the town dares enter the castle. Our overlord, Thane Forganon of Miernord, is a fat, dissolute old dotard who doesn't have the courage to help us. Word has gotten round the sorcerous fraternity as well, and none will come this way unless paid an exorbitant fee. We're left to beg of strangers—and your company are the first strangers to enter Carklin Hall in two years."

"We're actors, not wizards," Andura commented.

"She play one once on stage," Moku said. Andura had indeed played the Sea Witch in the famous tragedy, *The Rage of Captain Edzi*. "So-so job," he added.

She flicked a finger hard against his prominent beak. The gully dwarf hissed and retreated out of reach.

For all his rudeness, Moku raised the very point Andura was contemplating. "Why couldn't I perform the rite? I can read the scroll as well as anyone, and I have played the part of a magician before. And I'm an outsider."

Moku thumped the side of his head with the heel of one hand. "Too much ear goop," he muttered. "You want fight ghost?"

Andura considered. Did she? The townsfolk's obvious distress, poor color and thin bodies bespoke clearly of the pervasive malady afflicting them. She thought of the frightened child fleeing the room, like a startled rat. . . . These people needed help all right. Not that she intended to risk her neck for nothing. The heavy gold chain around Bannur's neck meant some wealth remained in the exhausted district.

"Why not?" she declared. "A stranger can enter the old castle with impunity?"

Both men looked uncomfortable. "We believe so," said Havared. "The wild mage who sold us the exorcism scroll went to the castle for a look around and returned alive."

"He not do spell," Moku remarked. "How come?"

"We couldn't afford his price," Bannur said. "It was all my father could do to pay for the scroll."

"I won't charge nearly so much," Andura said, smiling.

The men conferred privately. Turning back to the actors, Havared said, "Forgive us, lady, but we're not sure you can accomplish this."

"Oh? Why not?"

"Well, first of all, you're not a trained wizard," Bannur replied.

"I can read as well as any footloose necromancer!" she declared, "and I dare say I can deliver my lines better than anyone you care to name. Besides, I'm willing to try. What other choice do you have? I'm here, and I'm ready. Will you turn away from this chance?"

Bannur looked uncertain. His face reddened when Moku began clucking like a chicken. He said, "Of course, if you do this for us we'll pay what we can—"

The gully dwarf ceased his barnyard babble. "How much?"

Andura stood. "Excuse me," she said to the townsmen. Spotting a broom in the corner, she retrieved it. The others watched, perplexed, as she raised it high and aimed a swat at Moku. Screeching like an owl, he dodged the blow and ran to the shop door.

"I tell Master!" he said, putting his thumbs in his ears and flapping his fingers at her. "Troupers not work for others. You know rules!"

It was true. Sebastius's strictest rule was, his actors performed when and where he alone chose. Breaking the rule might have serious consequences.

"I wouldn't be acting," Andura said, slowly lowering the broom.

"You acting like wizard," Moku replied stubbornly.

She hated what she had to say next, but she had no choice. Andura pointed to the gully dwarf, leaning against the open door frame, whirring like a cicada.

"It's in his hands," she said to the townsmen. "If he keeps his mouth shut, I can help you."

· "I shut up if I come too," Moku declared, exploring his nose with a stubby finger.

"Aren't you afraid of the ghost?" asked Havared, wide-eyed.

"Never met ghost," he said. "Wonder, what kind noise ghost make? Good noise for actor-me to know."

"Okay, that's settled," said Andura. "Now, how much?"

Like all good actors undertaking a new part, Andura decided to research the history of Carklin Hall and the malevolent ghost holding sway over it. Bannur sent to a scrivener for a copy of the local chronicle. In it she read the tale of Thane Carklin, a minor vassal of the High Thane of Nordmaar.

During the Dragon Wars, Carklin was charged with the defense of the town against any monsters who strayed that way. All was calm until a dragon, admittedly a smallish one, arrived in Carklin territory, famished and ill-tempered. Lord Carklin led his warriors out to meet a wayward wyrm, but when the great beast attacked, he panicked and fled, leaving his men to be destroyed. Later, bursting with shame, he leaped from the battlements of his hall. A gloss in the margin of the chronicle noted, *His shade has haunted the ruins ever after*.

"Sounds like play did once in Hylo," Moku said. "Ghost come on stage with bloody head under arm—"

Andura shushed him. To the townsmen she said, "Has anyone ever seen this ghost? What does it look like?"

Havared and Bannur had both seen it at different times from a distance. From their sketchy descriptions Andura pieced together a chilling picture of the specter: squat, broad shouldered; pale, almost dead-white skin and clothing; long dark hair. The ghost-thane's forehead was smashed open, as it had been when he struck the rocky slopes below his fortress. He muttered and sighed as he roamed the grounds of castle and now and then gave vent to his death scream, a terrifying sound neither man would ever forget.

Hearing the scream brought death to any native of Carklin Hall caught inside the castle.

To Moku she said, "This does sound dangerous. You sure you want to go along?"

He waved a hand dismissively. "I not 'fraid of spooks, girl, but why you want to take risk?"

How could she explain it to him? Andura had not lost her taste for fine things—a golden chain, a bright jewel, the warm lips of a handsome man . . . nor had she lost her taste for danger and adventure. Real danger, not the stage kind.

No, Moku wouldn't understand. Instead of the truth, she said, "We can't have much of a show without an audience. If I can break the curse, think of the goodwill I'll win for the Traveling Players, and attendance will shoot up at our performance."

Andura stood up. "The play is tomorrow night, and I'm late for rehearsal. We'll have to do the job right away—tonight, in fact."

Bannur jumped to his feet. "I'll take you!"

Andura, Moku, and the two men agreed to meet at the abandoned castle when Solinari set. That would be just after midnight, an inauspicious hour, but no sooner time seemed possible.

———◆◦◆◦◆———

Rehearsal went badly. Even though she was not expected to act convincingly the first time through, Andura was so distracted by her secret mission she missed cues, violated her blocking, and was generally way off her form. Warkin, Gree, and the others took to pushing her into place and feeding her her lines and not without cutting comments.

When the run-through was done at last, Thronden threw up his hands and turned to Sebastius, who had watched the whole thing silently from the darkened edge of the square.

"What can I do, Master?" Thronden exclaimed. "Blocks of wood! Blocks of wood can act better than this!"

"Fret not," said Sebastius calmly. "We've had a long journey, and this place has had an unsettling effect on us all. By tomorrow, all will be well."

"I pray so!" Thronden faced the stage, where the cast awaited their instructions. "Get out of my sight, all of you!"

Only moments later, Andura was in her wagon, rapidly changing out of her boy's clothes into a dark dress and hooded cloak. She stuffed the flattened exorcism scroll inside her bodice and cast about for a lamp or candle. There! A copper-framed lantern, used as a prop in the seafaring play *Pirates of the Blood Sea*, was half hidden under a bundle of rags.

A rap on her door. Thinking it was Moku, she said, "Come!"

In stepped Sebastius. Andura saw the master of the Traveling Players in her tin mirror and froze, the telltale lantern in her hand.

"Good evening," he said mildly. "Going out, are you?"

"Out? No, no. I thought I would sit up a while and read through Master Tensi's lines again, then work on my blocking back on stage."

"An admirable idea." Sebastius glanced around the close confines of the wagon. "You seemed to have a lot on your mind this evening."

Andura sighed. "I shall do better in the real performance, never fear."

"I have no doubt of it." Sebastius dropped one sandaled foot on the step outside her door. "If you have any problems, you will come to me, won't you?"

"Certainly, Master."

"Good. Well, good night. Try not to stay up too late. Sleep is important to your youthful looks, you know."

She made herself laugh, and when she relaxed again, he was gone.

What was the master up to? He couldn't have been fooled by her weak lies.

Faint hearts get small parts, said the poet Warkin. Whatever her weaknesses, Andura was not faint-hearted. She tied the hood under her chin and made sure the lantern reservoir was full of oil.

Moku opened the door, then made knocking sounds while waving his fist in thin air. He was dressed head to toe in a close-fitting suit of black velvet. Only the brown oval of his face still showed.

"We go?"

Andura tied the dark cloak closed at her throat and said, "Curtain going up!"

They hurried through the empty, wind-swept streets. No dogs were abroad to bark at them. All the windows in town were dark. Weak and fearful, the villagers always bolted themselves indoors until dawn.

Solinari was dipping behind the cliff when the actors found Havared and Bannur waiting for them on the north road. Garbed in a leather coat and muffled against the chill night wind, the tinsmith carried a stout staff and a bull's eye lantern.

Havared beckoned the players forward. "Light your lantern from mine," he said when they drew near. "Do you have the wizard's scroll?"

"I do," Andura said, patting the spot.

Wind whipped at them. Havared turned his back to the breeze, shielding his lantern while he applied the burning wick to Andura's.

"I inquired of the family steward," Bannur said. "If you can best the ghost, I will give you every coin I have left, eighteen gold pieces."

Moku grunted. "Eighteen? Job more like twenty-five. Ow!" The last was in response to Andura's swift kick to his backside.

She lowered her eyes and smiled. "We can leave the exact terms to a less hurried time, can't we?"

They started for the castle. A winding path led up the steep hill. Andura soon realized why Havared needed his staff. The track was overgrown with vicious thorns and tough creepers. Once he battered these aside, a wide road appeared, paved with slabs of slate.

The path rose in a series of switchbacks, each looping twice as high as the one before it. Moku fell behind, his short legs unable to keep pace. Andura would have gladly left him, but he set up a wolfish howling that threatened to wake everyone in the province, so she doubled back and picked him up. He clasped his arms around her neck and locked his feet around her waist. Thus supported, he settled against her breast and sighed deeply.

"Don't get too comfortable," Andura chided. "I'm not carrying you once we get to the top."

"Is faster," he opined.

"I'm not your mother or your wife," she said, twisting to loosen his grip. "Take liberties and I'll boot you down the mountain!" He merely purred like a contented tomcat.

Torn clouds rolled by the sinking white moon, at times hiding Solinari so well the dark path disappeared. The way was steep, and Andura felt weighed down by her lumpish cohort. Havared and Bannur drew ahead, and soon the glow of the tinsmith's lantern was lost behind the black cedars.

A faint call, like a distant voice, reached her on the wind. Andura stopped.

"Hear that?" she whispered.

PAUL B. THOMPSON

"Wind," said Moku.

"No, someone shouting."

He let go and dropped to the ground. Standing in the center of the road, he cocked his head and held a hand to one enormous ear.

"Wind," Moku announced again. "Don't be spooky now, not to castle yet."

The path cut sharply back to the left. When Andura ducked around an ancient stone pillar marking the last bend in the road, Havared suddenly appeared before her. His eyes were wide, and his lantern dark.

"Did you hear something?" he said wildly. "I did!" He shook his head. "Thane Carklin walks tonight!"

Havared fumbled with flint and steel, trying to relight the lantern, but the wind was too strong, and his hands trembled too much. Hand on his sword hilt, Bannur paced back and forth like a captive lion.

Moku scampered into view. "Time passing!" he hissed. "Let's go!" He scooted past, vanishing into the dark gap that had once been the main gate of the castle.

"Earwig! Wait!" Andura hissed, as loudly as she dared. Havared was still trying to light his lamp. "Forget that!" she said, giving him a shove. "Come on!"

They paused at the gate, which stood open on huge, rusting hinges. Openly trembling, Bannur and Havared refused to go further.

"We can't go in," Bannur said. "It would mean our lives!"

"I understand," Andura said. She handed her light to him, while she pulled out the scroll. Wind snatched at the parchment, threatening to grab it from her fingers. Bannur closed his hands around hers, gripping the wizard's instructions.

"The ghost is powerful," he warned solemnly. "Even the night obeys his whims."

"I'll be careful," Andura answered, smiling bravely for their benefit. Underneath her cloak, however, she was shaking, and it wasn't from cold. "I have to find the earwig before he falls down a well or something."

"May the gods go with you!" said Bannur. They briefly shook hands, and the men all but ran away down the winding path.

The bailey was ankle-deep in windblown leaves. The central keep was a tall, square building with a tower at each corner. One tower had fallen, leaving the three which were visible from the town below.

"Where'd that wretched little insect go?" Andura muttered, looking around.

There was no sound in the courtyard but the wind singing over the battlement, and the dry leaves dancing to its tune. Andura essayed a soft call. "Moku? Moku, are you there?"

The leaves and wind did not answer.

She crossed the narrow bailey to the great hall. The massive doors were askew, having come off their corroded hinges. Andura held up her lantern and saw there was just enough room to squeeze between the precariously leaning panels. In the dust inside the doors was a single tiny footprint—Moku's. The gully dwarf had barged in, heedless of the danger. His only fear was of missing meals or failing to supply an adequate sound effect for Master Sebastius.

Andura steeled herself and turned edgeways to slide between the doors. Inside, she was grateful to be out of the wind. Her gratitude faded as she crossed the great room and its baleful ambience engulfed her.

The roof had come off long ago, and now the stars sailed overhead amid the black rafters. Horsehair carpets on the flagstone floor had rotted to acrid dust that rose with every muffled fall of Andura's slippered feet. The massive fireplace, blackened by decades of fire, yawned by the far wall. Now it was a haven for bats. Strewn before it were pieces of ancient furniture, square and heavy. Andura saw one chair had deep scratches in the arms, as though someone had raked his fingernails along the smooth wood. Whoever did it had a maniac's strength to gouge such deep grooves in seasoned oak.

Such anguish she sensed—such black, unadulterated despair! The room reeked of it. She was glad for once Moku had come with her into this oppressive place.

Something rustled in the gallery overlooking the great hall. Andura whirled, saying, "Moku, is that you? Don't be funny!" There was no reply.

She set the lantern on a warped and worm-eaten table, which promptly collapsed under it. Saving the light before it hit the floor, Andura stepped back, heart racing. The massive table, where enormous feasts had once been laid, had fallen to pieces. Carefully, she put the lantern on the floor. The dull orange light it cast didn't carry far.

Again something stirred in the balcony. Frightened and furious at the same time, Andura resolved to give the gully dwarf's nose a royal twisting if she found out he was behind the unsettling noises. If he was not . . . She knelt by the lantern and unrolled the scroll.

"Hear me, O Spirit!" she declaimed, reading the sepia uncials in her best back-row voice—a voice that sounded hollow, bouncing off the hard stone walls. "I, Andura, have come to charge thee! Leave this place and dwell no more among mortals. Thou art dead! Go hence from the world of the living and trouble us no more!"

The lines weren't exactly theatrical caliber, but she supposed they were chosen for their effect and not for the way they rolled off the tongue. The counterspell was repetitious, too. She was required to repeat the first injunction five times, speaking louder and more commandingly each time.

When she had said 'Thou art dead!' a fourth time, a loud crash echoed through the ruined keep. Andura flinched. Despite being shielded from the hilltop wind, the hall grew noticeably colder. Inside the glass chimney, the lantern light faltered.

"Who's there?" she called, rising to her feet. "Moku?"

An inarticulate sigh filled the hall. Andura snatched up the lantern and shone it toward the steps. A dark shape shrank from the light, towards the upstairs gallery.

"Go hence from the world of the living and trouble us no more!" she cried, thrusting the guttering lantern at the phantom.

A slow squeaking sound behind her made Andura whirl about in time to see one of the front doors break loose from its rusted hinges and fall with a boom. She leaped back as the great oaken panel, ten feet tall, half as wide and six inches thick, plunged to the floor. Unlike the decayed furniture, the door was riveted with iron and solid, and when it crashed to the ground a gust of wind poured through the yawning portal.

Andura turned away and sprang up the creaking wooden stairs. Whatever knocked down the door wasn't the wind! She halted at the top of the stairs, looking at the open doorway. Leaves from the courtyard rolled in, driven by the breeze.

Swallowing hard, she began the rite again, speaking the banishing spell, thinking, all the while, what a strange business this was, a woman of her background trying to expel a spook.

A sigh emanated from the dark end of the gallery. Andura froze. She clutched at the heavy velvet curtains hanging above the gallery rail. The decayed fabric turned to powder in her hand.

"Moku?" she whispered tersely. "I'll nail your nose to a wagon wheel if you're trying to frighten me!"

Again, no response. Andura put the lantern on the newel post at the top of the stairs and continued the incantation.

"The gods ordained that the living and the dead dwell apart," she read louder than before. "It is a sin against Those Who Reign on High to flaunt their laws and cling to the world of flesh and blood. Begone, I say, to the realm of spirits! Begone, I say, to the kingdom of the dead! Begone, I say, to the loved ones gone before you—"

Slowly she became aware of a tremor, not in her hands or body, but in the castle itself. Steady as a heartbeat she felt it through her knees and toes, pressing against the worn wooden scaffolding. As she continued to speak the spell, the shaking increased.

"Begone, in the name of all the gods! Begone, in the name of all the heroes! Begone, in the name of all the rested and lawful spirits!"

The stone walls rang as though a mighty hammer had struck them. At the other end of the gallery, a shuttered window gave way, and wind blasted down the narrow corridor. The lantern toppled over, winking out. The scroll whipped back and forth in her hand, trying to take flight. Andura threw an arm up in front of her face to ward off the ferocious blast. Something was hurtling through the air directly at her. She remembered a cautionary line from the scroll and desperately invoked it now:

"Harm me not, unsettled spirit! In the name of Paladine the Great!"

In the next moment she was struck in the face by a small, heavy object. Pitching backward under the blow, Andura lost her grip on the wizard's scroll. It fluttered away.

She pushed at the projectile, heaving it off her face. It smelled foul yet familiar.

"Ow-ow!" said the missile. The hiss of an angry tomcat followed.

"Moku, you dolt!" she cried. "It was you all along!"

"I always me," he replied. "Who else?"

She sat up, face blazing. "You've been skulking around up here, trying to frighten me!"

He backed away, waving his stubby hands. "Not this Aghar! I explore old castle, not haunt it!"

"You were up here making noises!"

"No, no! Swear on grandma's stewpot, I not!"

That was a pretty serious oath for a gully dwarf, so Andura relented. Moku claimed he'd been outside, in the south end of the bailey, looking for the ghost—

"Looking for treasure, you mean," she said.

"Hey, old castles full of old trinkets, no good to dead lords," Moku said defensively.

He'd just come to the ruins of the fourth tower when a powerful wall of wind scooped him up and hurled him through an open second story window.

"Not know anything till I hit your face." he said. Moku rubbed his side. "You got sharp chin, know that?"

"Never mind. I lost the scroll!"

"Just paper," Moku replied. "Let's hunt for dead lord's treasure. You take half, I take half?" He wiggled his fingers in the air and made a sound like the clink of tumbling coins.

"Might as well. The scroll's gone, and I don't believe there is a ghost at all, just wind and rotten timbers everywhere." She straightened her tumbled clothing.

The lantern was useless without flint or fire to relight it, but it belonged to the troupe, so Andura brought it along. They groped in the shadows and found nothing,

so she and Moku went back outside. The high walls
thrust up at the stars. The only place left to search was
the battlement itself, but Moku balked at climbing the
crumbling edifice.

"We go home? Big day tomorrow. Need my beauty
sleep," he whined.

"Shut up. You're the one who wanted to search for
treasure!"

A long set of steps led to the top of the wall. Luckily
it was made of stone and not rotted by the elements.
Holding the lightless lantern, Andura climbed, tugging
the reluctant gully dwarf.

A scrap of parchment fluttered by—the lost exorcism
scroll! It glowed pale against the red granite wall and the
menacing black tower. Andura took a deep breath and
reached for the parchment. To her surprise, Moku pulled
her back.

"Is so dark," he explained shyly. "You might trip 'n fall."

The gully dwarf was right. This high up, she didn't
want to stumble and end up a ghost herself. Andura crept
forward, sliding her feet along the stone battlement, feeling for holes or broken pavement. The wall ran straight
as an arrow to the open tower.

The scroll, wedged in a crevice, flapped in the wind
like a wounded bird. So intent on it was she, Andura
didn't notice the frantic squeeze Moku gave her hand.
Finally he gave a sharp yank on her cloak hem, punctu-
ating his gesture by whining like a whipped dog.

"What is it?" she demanded.

"Something there!"

She peered into the dark recesses of the watchtower.
Metal glinted inside.

Andura forced a laugh. "It's nothing!" she said.
"Probably an old suit of armor!"

She planted a foot on the scroll to keep it from flying off. Stooping to pick it up, she saw a rusty iron greave lying in the open doorway.

More bits of armor were dimly visible inside. She laughed again. "See? Just some old armor. It was probably set up here to scare away trespassers—"

The armor moved, assembled itself into a complete suit, and stood up.

Andura gasped and tried to run. Her feet got tangled with Moku's, and they both went down. The gully dwarf rolled to the borderless edge of the battlement and would have plunged to his death had not Andura quickly grabbed him by the collar.

He cawed like a crow and clutched fiercely at her hand. Behind her, Andura heard measured footsteps, iron on granite. The wizard's scroll was in her other hand.

"Don't let go!" Moku cried. "Too young, too talented, too handsome to die!"

True or not, she couldn't let him fall. Andura let go of the parchment. It flew off again, drifting into the courtyard depths. She grabbed the gully dwarf with both hands and hauled him to safety.

Gasping, they rolled over in time to see a ghastly apparition standing over them, dressed in the rusty armor. His black hair and beard were long and tangled. His forehead was gone, caved in and sticky with blood. His hair was clotted with blood and brains. One eye was open, the other half closed. There was no awareness in either, no life.

Andura screamed.

Sighing filled her ears. A faint, whispery voice seemed to say, "Who troubles my house? Who?"

Moku, for all his bravado, kept his face buried as deep as possible in Andura's chest.

"Begone, spirit!" Andura stammered, trying to recall the words of the lost conjuration. "You are . . . uh . . . very dead! Trouble . . . uh . . . trouble not the living with your dire presence!"

The ghost shuffled forward, its battered head lolling lifelessly on its shoulders. "I am Thane Carklin!" it cried in a stronger voice. "This is my house. Who dares order me from it?"

"You are dead!" Andura said pathetically.

The swollen, purple lips did not move, but the words sighed out. "Dead? That cannot be. I hold this place for my lord, the High Thane of Nordmaar." The ghost raised its right arm stiffly to point at Andura. Flesh had fallen from the finger joints, exposing white bone.

"Intruder! Interloper! No one may trespass in Carklin Hall!"

Up came an equally decayed left hand, reaching, reaching out for her. Andura yelped again and tried to ward off the specter with the only thing at hand—the gully dwarf. She held Moku out at arm's length.

Moku opened his tightly shut eyes. He screeched an Aghar oath and tried to run away. Arms and legs windmilling in Andura's grip, he went nowhere.

"Spook is coming—get on feet!" he urged. Andura needed no encouragement. She dropped the frightened little dwarf, and he hit the battlement running.

"Hey, wait for me!" she protested, but it was too late. The specter was nearly upon her. Something colder than ice yet hot as a branding iron touched her left ankle. Andura cried out and scrambled away.

Stumbling along, not heeding the dangers of the ancient parapet, Andura raced for the steps. She looked back just once and saw the ghost continuing its glide toward her. The greaves on its legs and sabatons on its feet were clear as glass, and the weird transparency crept up its torso as it came after her. She galloped down the steps two and three at a time, overtaking Moku before he had reached the castle gate.

The ghost of Thane Carklin materialized in front of them. "You shall not leave here alive!"

"We mean you no harm!" Andura protested, skidding to a stop. "We only wanted to bring you peace!"

"Peace?" roared the ghost, now loud as thunder. "There is no peace so long as cravens live and monsters rampage unpunished!"

Its lower half dissolving into mist, the ghost swept forward, arms upraised vengefully. Moku picked up handfuls of dead leaves and threw them at the apparition. They passed through and fluttered to the ground. When they failed as weapons, the gully dwarf threw himself on his belly and tried to cover himself with more leaves.

"Die, intruders! Thus do perish all enemies of Carklin!"

Behind the ghost, a narrow beam of golden light lanced through the open gate. Where it fell, it illuminated the angry spirit, rendering him as clear as crystal. Thane Carklin turned his shattered, lifeless head to the light.

Dawn. The sun was rising over the mountain.

Without a sound, the ghost vanished like morning dew on the grass. The awful gripping cold went with it, leaving the shivering Andura suddenly flush with relief. She almost felt like giggling.

She looked around shakily. Soft yellow sunbeams broke over the red granite wall, warming her heart and the interior of the ruined fortress.

Andura went to the quaking mound of leaves by the gate and nudged it with her toe.

"Take woman, not me!" Moku whimpered. "I too darling to die!"

"Get up, darling," she said. "He's gone."

Moku popped his head out of the leaves. "I knew that." He crowed like a prize rooster. "See? Dead man can't bear cock's crow. I chase away!"

She drew back her slippered foot and planted the pointed toe right where the gully dwarf sat. His authentic Aghar howls could be heard all the way down the mountain.

Outside the gate, Moku and Andura were arrested at spear point by soldiers of Thane Forganon, the living lord of Carklin Hall. They'd been on mounted patrol nearby and heard howling and yelling inside the old castle. They took Andura and Moku to the village guardhouse, which faced the square where the troupe was camped. Word was sent to the Traveling Players, and before long, a disheveled Thronden and sleepy Tog arrived.

"What in the Gray Voyager's name is going on?" Thronden rasped, trying to comb his long hair with his fingers. "Why have you arrested two of my actors?"

"Trespassing on thanish property and disturbing the peace are the charges," the marshal said dryly. "I may add more as I think of them."

"Andura, you? Disturbing the peace?"

"Notice you not say that to me," Moku said sullenly.

She couldn't explain without implicating Bannur and Havared, so she said nothing. Moku squirmed, trying to scratch his back. His shackles hampered him, so he slipped out his small wrists and satisfied his itch.

"Put those back on!" bellowed the marshal.

"Right-o." The gully dwarf made noises like a squeaky door swinging shut as he returned his hands to the bonds.

"This is intolerable," Thronden said to the marshal, while looking at Andura and Moku with narrowed eyes. "I need both of them for our performance tonight! Is there some fine we can pay, some promise we can give you so you'll release them? They shan't run away."

"Actors are just another breed of vagabond," said the marshal haughtily. "The miscreants must remain in custody until a magistrate arrives from Miernord."

"What? That might take days!"

The marshal stood. Burly guardsmen gathered round him. "Don't raise your voice to me!"

Tog lifted his head and stood up straighter. "The Master," he announced quietly.

When Sebastius entered the guardroom, the whole atmosphere changed. Tog melted into the background and Thronden deflated his chest. The marshal's face lost its cherry color. The master of the Traveling Players managed to dominate the room without saying a word.

He bowed slightly to Andura, saying, "Are you well, my dear?"

"Yes, thank you."

"And you, Master Moku?"

The scruffy Aghar beamed. "Fit as fiddler crab!" he replied. "Crazy night, huh boss?"

Sebastius smiled gently. "So it seems. Sir, are you the High Thane's man here?"

The marshal admitted he was.

"My people have bothered you in some way. How may I make amends?"

The question seemed to embarrass the marshal. He scratched behind one ear and said, "Two of my men were diverted from their rounds for the sake of a vagabond's prank. Perhaps it was nothing or perhaps they were vandalizing property. Am I to overlook their mischief?"

"Of course not." Sebastius slipped his right hand into his left sleeve and came out with a drawstring purse. "With this help to remedy my people's misdeeds?"

The purse clinked significantly. The marshal hefted but did not open it. Fixing Sebastius with one hard eye, he said, "How long will you be in Carklin Hall village?"

"Fortune and your good self willing, till the morning after our play."

The High Thane's man tossed the bag of coins to one of his guards. "See that you're gone before noon."

"Can make it two of clock? Moku need beauty sleep after performance—" The rest of his comment was cut off as Andura clamped her hand over this mouth.

"There'll be no trouble," she said graciously. Rising, she held out her manacles. At the marshal's nod, a guard removed them. Moku shucked his off and handed them to a fuming soldier.

"See you, marshal-man," he said. "Come to show, get big laugh."

"I don't care for theater," the marshal replied, sniffing. "Too many lies and impostures."

"Rather like life, don't you think?" Sebastius said, with half a wink. He bowed from the waist. "Good morrow to you, Sir Marshal." He shooed his people out.

Sebastius did not ask a single question on their way back to the caravan. He seldom did, yet he always seemed to know the right or wrong of a situation. This morning his silence seemed ominous.

Andura walked slowly behind Sebastius, arms folded. Her hands were scratched from running around the tumbledown castle, and she was tired beyond measure. Her left ankle ached where the ghost had touched her, and when she lifted her hem to examine it, she saw the imprint of four fingers and a thumb in her livid flesh. She didn't doubt at all that the ghost would have killed her had he gotten a firmer grip.

———◆•◆•◆———

Performance days began early. Cam and the kender brothers scrubbed the stage. Other troupe members mended costumes, polished buttons, buckles and other brightwork, and mixed makeup. A booth was set up on the opposite sign of the square. Once the sun began to set, Dashkar the dwarf's wife Telda would begin to collect admissions from the audience, and woe to any scoundrel who tried to slip past her without paying.

The actors with parts disappeared from chores early and did not appear again until an hour or so before sunset. When they did appear, they were wrapped in their personal pre-play preparations. Warkin strolled around the players' camp, clad in a loosely tied robe. He made his walk barefoot, a little ritual he did before every performance. Other actors had their own good luck superstitions. Moku came out fully costumed in his suit of black velvet, but wearing a dusty brown "good luck" cap. Gree the centaur poured two full buckets of water over his head—no more, no less. Thaelix, the ogre cast as the Queen of Napland, ate nothing but boiled potatoes before a performance. Rontz sat on the roof of his wagon and sang a Throtian battle song. The troupe's band sat on the ground in front of the stage and played several deliberately off-key songs "to get rid of all the bad notes."

Andura spent the final hours resting by the rigging wagon, watching the troupe's store of cordage being inventoried by their stage engineer, a gnome known by the uncharacteristically short name of Fitter. An odd character in a company of odd characters, Fitter claimed to have visited the red moon, Lunitari, on a flying ship invented by his fellow gnomes. Andura was polite but dubious. Not even the kender brothers believed such a whopper.

Once Fitter was satisfied all the rope was accounted for, he departed, leaving Andura alone. She catnapped, then rose to dress and don her makeup.

While Andura dozed, the anxiety level in the troupe rose drastically. Daskhar the dwarf, acting as prompter, rehearsed lines with Gree, who was only half in his nanny costume. A seamstress worked frantically at the centaur's hindquarters, trying to adjust the dress so it would cover Gree's tail. Paz and Traz had donned identical jester costumes. During the intermission, they would keep the audience laughing with juggling and tumbling tricks. As Andura crossed backstage, the kender were angrily pelting each other with the hard crabapples they should have been practicing juggling.

"Two hours to curtain! Two hours to curtain!" Thronden called striding through the melee. "If you don't have business backstage, clear out!" No one paid him the slightest heed.

Her wagon was a haven of calm. Andura's Tensi costume had been laid out for her. She dressed carefully, using long bandages to disguise her feminine figure. Combing her hair with deliberate casualness, she tied it back in a queue, apprentice-style. Sitting at her tiny makeup table, she studied her face in the tin mirror—profile and three-quarter. She still looked wan from last night. That wouldn't do. Tensi was a craftsman, a fellow of little means who traveled mostly on foot. She needed a tan face and arms. Mixing clay and ochre into small smears of greasepaint, she experimented until she found the proper shade.

A brief knock, and Moku entered. He was whistling a kender marching song and making water-drop noises at the same time, a feat Andura found both amazing and annoying.

"You can stay, but be still," she said, applying a putty adam's apple to her throat.

"Those men outside," he said, ceasing his nervous whistling.

"Bannur and Havared? What do they want?"

"Dunno."

"I can't face them," she fretted. "Not only did I fail to banish the ghost, I also lost their scroll!"

"Him very scarified," said Moku.

"Who, Bannur or Havared?"

"Naw, ghost-fella. He very scared."

She eyed him skeptically in the mirror. "What makes you say that?"

"He run away and leave his men to die, and still feared of monsters. I think that why he kill folk in his castle, so no one know how scared he is."

Andura pondered Moku's startling theory as she dotted a few reddish freckles on her cheeks, then put down her makeup pallet and stood, checking her face and figure in the mirror. Admiring her transformation, she thought, maybe dimwitted Moku was right for once. If a ghost could be frightened, maybe there was another way to get rid of him.

She turned to Moku and said, "How do I look?"

"Like bumpkin boy."

"Thanks. Shall we shout at the shadows once more?" she said, smiling.

He mimicked a tinny trumpet fanfare. "The play be done!"

Torches rimmed the square, and as soon as it was dark, a trickle of townsfolk filed in, paying their coins to Telda. There weren't many. A few tired-looking burghers drifted down front, taking the space nearest the stage. Bannur sat just beyond the footlights on a canvas camp chair, dressed in a threadbare velvet robe. Behind him were Carklin's moneyed class, the merchants and artisans. They spread sacks on the dewy cobbles and sat down, grumbling all the while about the folk in front of them, thoughtlessly blocking their view. Last to come were humbler folk: servants, navvies, and the like. They filed in at the back of the square and remained standing. Less than a hundred people showed up, looking lost in a space that could easily accommodate five times their number.

Troupe members without parts huddled together between the wagons, eyeing the meager crowd. By tradition, no one complained about the sparse, melancholy-looking audience. The stage was set, the players were girded for their roles—the Traveling Players would perform for one or one thousand just the same.

The band's drummer stood up and thumped the bass drum three times. Talk died, though not completely, so he sounded three more strokes before quiet descended on the square. The rest of the band rose and began to play a sad song known as "The Dying Knight's Lament." This further calmed the crowd. When done, the musicians swung into a livelier piece, "No Onions in the Stew." It was normally a crowd-pleaser, and Andura saw the piece brought few smiles to the townsfolk. By the time the band reached their third number, "Kick the Kender," some in the crowd were clapping listlessly in time to the brisk tune.

The last notes died, and the torches in the audience were snuffed out one by one. Thronden emerged from the curtains, elaborately dressed in scarlet and gold. With his commanding height and manly presence, he resembled a victorious general about to address his troops.

"Gentles all, I bring you greetings from our Master and all the Traveling Players of Gilean. With light hearts and ready smiles we come before you as we have so many times before, bearing in our train heroes and fools, villains and victims, the fortunate and the doomed." He paused for effect.

"Tonight bear with us as we attempt that famous story, *The Iron Sack*. Written in Ergoth two centuries ago by the playwright Ingemor Goldsteed, *The Iron Sack* has been performed for kings and emperors, high priests and holy men of every faith. Untold thousands have seen it, laughed at it, and learned its lesson. Tonight we proudly add your number to that score, no less great for lacking princes or priests, because to us, the Traveling Players, all audiences are noble, all patrons divine."

He bowed low, in his most courtly fashion. "And now, the play."

More footlights were lit, revealing the opening scene in the mythical city of Cardimore. Behind the backdrop Moku launched sounds of a city—hooves clopping on cobblestones, the creak of harness leather, footfalls of people passing near, the cry of pushcart drivers and other street merchants. His most remarkable effect resembled a crowd of people talking indistinctly in the background. The similarity was uncanny. With her eyes shut, Andura could easily believe she was on a busy city thoroughfare.

Andura and Gree entered and spoke their opening lines. Some tittering could be expected at the sight of a male centaur draped in an old dress and gray wig, but the audience was curiously attentive and calm. This was partly due to the effectiveness of Gree's acting, and partly to the very clever design of his costume. His rump and rear legs were covered in black linen, in contrast to the gray of his forelegs. In the focused light of the footlamps the centaur's hindquarters were almost invisible.

Andura swaggered out on stage and grinned, hooking her thumbs in the pockets of her vest. Before long she forgot about troubled spirits and anxious townsfolk. For the next two and a quarter hours she was Master Tensi, a cocky, good-natured young man for whom destiny was a bright and shiny toy.

Warkin played the miserly king red-faced and gasping, as though breath itself was precious. Believing the iron sack contained priceless treasure, he schemed to get it away from Tensi. His wife (played with panache by the ogre Thaelix) was a vain, fading beauty who chose to believe the sack held the secret of eternal youth. Failing to seduce the honest youth, she informed the High Priest a dangerous heretic was in their domain, bearing unholy relics in a chain mail bag. . . .

The small audience gradually began to titter, then chuckle, then roar with laughter. Gree found special favor with his constantly repeated line, "Only evil will come of it, Master Tensi!" The townsfolk took to shouting the line whenever Gree appeared on stage. Warkin earned many a hiss, but Thaelix as the queen gained particular notice as the crowd's favorite villain. Thaelix, who stood nearly seven feet tall, began to curtsy in acknowledgment every time the audience booed him.

The second act ended. The curtain fell, and local boys who had been paid a copper each moved through the square, relighting the torches. Such was the power of the play and the players, people in the audience rubbed their eyes and blinked, uncertain as to where they were or when.

Off stage, Andura gulped a cup of water while Thaelix ate fruit with both hands, devouring whole apples in one bite. Warkin sat on a bench with his eyes closed while one of the young actresses mended his florid makeup.

Thronden swept through, saying, "Very good, keep it up, keep it up. Project more, Warkin, you're sounding weak. Watch your back hooves, Gree, don't step on the extras' toes. Has anyone seen Fitter? The curtain lines look a little slack to me—"

Dashkar, who'd been out front, encouraged the cast. "I haven't seen an audience cheer up so much since Thronden took that pratfall in Palanthus."

"I've never taken a pratfall in my life!" Thronden declared huffily. The tired actors around him laughed.

Paz and Traz finished their comic juggling and scampered off stage. The band played a few tunes, then launched into its last number before Act Three, a country dance tune called "Flowers in the Window." When they finished with a flourish of pipe and drum, the audience ceased to murmur. The actors were in place, waiting for the curtain. Peeking through the curtain, Daskhar nodded his head. The audience also was waiting, expectant.

Thronden drew back the curtain himself, displaying the darkened stage set as the red dragon's lair. Upstage was a small hooded lantern, throwing a soft cone of light on the backdrop.

When Andura appeared stage left, the audience applauded and cheered. Her look of anxiety perfectly fit the moment when Tensi enters the cave of the dreaded Scorchfinger. No one but Moku knew the actress really was teetering on the brink of exhaustion.

"What a dark and fearful place!" Andura as Tensi exclaimed. "In times like this, a boy needs his faithful nurse."

"Only evil will come of it!" shouted a wag in the audience. Much laughter ensued, until an ominous shadow appeared on the canvas cave wall. A huge horned head and long snout vividly conveyed the presence of an evil dragon. Andura heard gasps. A few of the least brave onlookers bolted. Offstage, she spotted the elf Cam with his fist in his mouth to keep from laughing. From where he stood he could see the "dragon" It was Moku, making frightening shadows by modeling his little hands in the shape of the monster's head.

A serpentine hiss filled the stage, followed by a voice as deep and ancient as the ruined castle above the town. "Who speaks so loudly in my lair?" boomed the dragon.

"No one," Andura/Tensi replied timidly. "Just a moth, seeking a light in the darkness."

"Ho, ho! Come closer, morsel, and I will show you a fiery light!"

The scene unfolded from there, with much banter and by-play between the dragon and the ironmonger's apprentice. Eventually Tensi told Scorchfinger the whole, true story. When the dragon heard how all the important humans in Napland have deceived themselves over the young man's chain mail sack, he roared with delight.

The little gully dwarf, whose ordinary speech was so backward and fragmented, rolled Scorchfinger's dialogue off his tongue with such facility that it was easy to forget it was Moku. The audience was mesmerized. They were so quiet during his monologue, alone on stage, that Andura cut them a quick glance to make sure they were still out there.

Nobody noticed the figure moving onto stage from the wings. Nobody except Dashkar, watching from stage left, who thought it was Rontz and signaled the curtain.

"What's he doing?" shrilled the goblin as he raced into view, struggling with his heavy sacerdotal headdress. "I'm not in place yet!"

He wasn't. Andura looked past Rontz to the figure in white standing downstage, almost where the high priest was supposed to stand.

"Who's that?" she whispered.

Quiet consternation spread backstage. The opening curtain had revealed the temple set to the audience. The interloper stood there, unspeaking, while the actors scrambled to figure out what was happening and recover the spoiled scene.

"Who is that?" Thronden demanded. "Somebody pull the curtain and get that idiot off!"

Just then, the intruder half-turned, and the light caught his eyes. "My stars," Andura gasped.

"Who is it?" asked Thronden.

"Get the Master." She mounted the backstage steps.

"Wait, it's not your cue!"

Thronden tried to restrain her, but Andura eluded his grasp. Without looking back she walked slowly into the light. The audience cheered. Hearing footfalls, the stranger turned completely, facing the actress

"Greetings, my lord," Andura said, her voice shaking. "What brings you here?"

"Strangers have come to my domain . . . intruders."

His voice was clear if not overly loud. Andura looked past him and saw the audience was momentarily confused but faithfully following the scene as though it were part of the play.

"In life," she said with a gulp, "you were Thane Carklin." Many in the crowd gasped, looking more confused. "Why have you come here?"

The ghost looked different from last night, when she'd seen him in the castle. Gone was the matted hair, shattered skull, and dead eyes. This Carklin looked more human, clad in formless shroud, his dark hair drawn back. His eyes were sunken and colorless, but they displayed the spark of soul that had kept him earthbound.

"There were strangers in my hall last night," he said gravely. "Such insolence cannot be borne."

Behind the scenes, the actors were frantically waving to get Andura's attention. She ignored them. To her surprise, she wasn't scared. Moku was right. The ghost seemed more tragic than terrifying.

"You are dead!" she declared dramatically, thrusting a finger at the specter. "Begone to your rest, and trouble us no more!"

Like a shadow falling across the sun, the ghost's countenance darkened. "Who are you to speak to me thus?" he said, voice rising. "A whelp in workman's clothes? Tell me your name!"

The audience was absolutely quiet.

Shaking inside, Andura nonetheless bowed and said, "Master Tensi of the Iron Sack. I mean no disrespect, my lord, but hear the truth: You are long dead, and must depart the living world. Your presence brings lingering sickness and melancholy to your own people!"

The audience came back to life. Isolated cries of "Leave us!" "Get out!" and "You're dead!" punctuated the charged air. The ghost strode downstage, his translucent pall sweeping the boards. He glared at the audience, which quieted.

Andura waved for Moku. She had an idea and needed his help. If Thane Carklin would not go willingly, she meant to drive him away.

"Why do you tell me to go?" said the spirit to the audience almost pleadingly. "I am your lord!"

"Thane!" she said sharply. "Go at once, for the peace of your soul, I beg you! A monster is near and will do harm to all if he finds a warrior in his path."

He turned to her. "What monster?"

"A dragon, Scorchfinger. He comes even as we speak!"

The ghost visibly shuddered. His hideous death-wound began to reappear. He spoke, and his voice was strained. "Dragon? Do not lie to me!"

She stepped back, hand held out to Moku, secreted off stage. The gully dwarf pulled off his hood and drew a deep breath. Right on cue, Moku blasted out his best reptilian bellow. Some of the stage rigging shook loose, lines and sandbags falling to the stage. The front rows of the audience reeled away, hands over their ears. Whether out of fear or design, Moku gave them the full-throated version, louder than he ever had before, as loud as any living dragon.

Someone lit the lantern Moku used to cast shadows on the backdrop, and the image of a massive horned head appeared above the specter.

Carklin's shade drew back a step and faded almost to vanishing.

Almost unheard above the din, Andura cried, "Flee, my lord! Leave this place forever! No mortal can stand against a red dragon!"

The ghost flung out a hand to ward off the unseen monster. "No! No! I ran once! I will not flee again!"

More ropes loosened, and Andura feared the backdrop would fall, revealing the roaring gully dwarf. She strode to centerstage and held out her hand to the terrified, tormented spirit.

"Begone, my lord, begone! So long as you remain, so will Scorchfinger. He fears only you. If you leave now, he will spare all!"

Carklin was almost gone. Andura could see through him as though he were a statue made of ice.

"The beast will spare my town?" His words were but a whisper yet curiously poignant. Moku renewed his head-splitting screech.

"Your people will thank you for going," she said gently.

"I am weary." The sunken eyes closed. "My honor . . . I only wanted to protect my people."

"You have, my lord."

Moku broke his roaring to draw a breath. In that brief interval of silence the ghost's lips moved, saying something that couldn't be heard, then he vanished.

"Curtain! Bring down the curtain!" Thronden cried. Dashkar and Urtak hauled on the ropes, and the curtain closed. Bewildered, the band started to play. The audience sat stunned, darting glances around.

Andura's head swam. She sank to her knees, then a pair of powerful hands drew her to her feet again.

"Tog?"

"Don't smear your makeup," said the minotaur.

Sebastius was standing over Moku, rubbing his shoulders. The gully dwarf was purple-faced and gasping. Andura went and stood over him.

"Earwig, are you all right?"

His mouth moved, but no sound came out.

"He'll recover," Sebastius said, smiling, "but he'll speak no more tonight."

Thronden burst between them. "What shall we do? How shall we finish?" he fretted.

"Carry on," said Sebastius. He left the stage, supporting the exhausted Moku.

Andura cleared he eyes and stood up. "Right! Where's Rontz? Let's start the scene again!"

"But Moku can't make his sounds!" the goblin protested.

She cast about. The only person at hand was Thronden. Grasping his lapels, she pushed him offstage.

"You be the dragon," she said. He opened his mouth to object, and she said, "You must! Have the Traveling Players ever failed to finish a performance?"

That was just what she needed to say. Holding his chin up, Thronden took his place in Moku's cockpit and prepared to voice Scorchfinger.

The curtain opened, as the band stumbled into silence. Half the audience thought the show was over and was getting up to leave. Puzzled but curious, they streamed back.

Somehow they performed the rest of the play. Drawing on decades of experience, Thronden managed an able Scorchfinger, even with credible dragon-snoring. The play closed, as always, with Tensi married to the King of Napland's daughter. Alone with his faithful nurse, the new crown prince opens the iron sack for the first time in the play and slowly takes out the contents—ordinary metal working tools. He looks from them to the audience and bursts out laughing. From his new home in the palace cellar, Scorchfinger laughs too.

Soon everybody in the audience was laughing, then they exploded with cheers. The applause was prolonged, and the cast returned for a bow. Assembling on stage, they stood in line as the curtains were hauled back. Cheering surged even louder.

"Scorchfinger!" the crowd chanted.

Thronden came out front and held up his hands. "Good people of Carklin Hall, here is our resident dragon, Moku, alias Scorchfinger!"

The wild applause died as the gully dwarf, weaving slightly, stepped into plain view for the first time. Catcalls erupted, and someone shouted, "What kind of humbug is this?"

The Aghar stood tall, shrugging off the insults. Unable to roar, he instead held his short, thick fingers before the footlights and made dragon shadows on the backdrop. The naysayers gradually fell silent, then burst into fresh applause. Moku strutted back and forth along the footlights, basking in the acclaim.

"Tensi! Tensi! Tensi!" they now demanded.

Andura, still in costume, came out shyly, hands clasped in front of her. The crowd went wild. She bowed left and right. Her cheeks were bright with tears.

Someone shouted, "What about the ghost? Let us see the ghost!"

Andura glanced at Moku. Both looked around for Sebastius. The master of the troupe was nowhere to be seen.

"The ghost! The ghost!" the crowd called.

Andura held up her hands, "Friends, please! A word, if I may." The shouting subsided. "Good people, on behalf of the Traveling Players of Gilean, I thank you. Our comrade who portrayed the ghost of Thane Carklin has been taken ill by the strain. He now lies stricken in his wagon, but be assured I shall let him know how loudly you called for him tonight!"

She bowed deeply, legs crossed. "Good night, all!"

The crowd filed out of the square, laughing and chatting loudly.

As the torches in the square were being extinguished, Andura heard her name called. Standing by the end of the stage was the young lord Bannur. Havared was not with him.

"A word, lady, if you please," he said.

Weary to her bones, Andura trudged to him. "I have bad news," she said, sighing. "I lost your treasured scroll."

"It hardly matters now, does it?" He was smiling.

"No," she said, smiling too.

His eyes twinkled. "Will the ghost ever return?"

"That I cannot say."

Bannur said, "You've done a signal job, lady. I'm grateful, as will the whole town be once they know."

"Oh, don't tell them," she said, massaging her brow with her fingers. "Let them discover it for themselves. They'll be surprised when their lives resume a normal rhythm. One day soon the curse of Thane Carklin may be forgotten, like a bad dream that fades on waking."

"What about you? No reward? No accolades?"

She waved a hand behind her at the empty stage. "I have my accolades. As for my reward, I'm sure we can arrive at an agreeable figure."

Day came, cloudy and warm. Andura rose from bed and parted the flap at the rear of her wagon. Balmy air, scented with rain, washed over her. Though heavy with moisture, the sky seemed brighter and cleaner than it had been in many days.

The ghost had been the talk of the troupe after the show. Everybody had questions but no answers for the strange occurrence in the play. One theory going around was that somehow the whole incident had been

175

improvised by Sebastius as a means of testing their deftness on stage. Andura and Moku won much grudging praise for their neat handling of the ghostly intruder.

The troupe broke camp slowly. The actors went about their chores with great good humor, dismantling the stage, filling the water casks and provisions cart. This last task proved unexpectedly easy. A gaggle of townsfolk appeared in the square that morning, laden with goods to sell. The drab, depleted town yielded a surprising bounty, and Thronden and the others gratefully stowed away much good food for the journey ahead.

Bannur and Havared returned, looking for Andura. The tinsmith presented her with a gift suited to his skills: a new mirror, freshly tinned and polished.

"How do I deserve this?" she asked innocently. Impulsively, she kissed the handsome Havared, bringing more color to his cheeks than had been there for a long time. Bannur pressed a small cloth bag into Andura's palm, and the men departed.

She hefted the bag. It was nicely heavy.

It was good to meet a man who paid his debts.

Near noon, Moku appeared, a woolen muffler wrapped around his throat. Disdaining the heavy labor going on around him, he sat in his special undersized folding chair, hat pulled low over his eyes. At his feet was a basket brimming with fruits and vegetables. A true Aghar gourmand, he was eating the cores and seeds of the apples and throwing the flesh away.

Without saying a word, Andura saluted her colleague. Moku fingered his throat then touched two fingers to the brim of his hat.

Tog hitched the horses to the wagon. Andura climbed to the driver's box and held the reins while the minotaur made sure the harness was in place. Looking past his broad, muscular back, she watched the townsfolk as they bustled around the square, going about the business of life.

"A fine morning, don't you think?"

Sebastius was standing by the right front wheel. Andura was so content, so relaxed, she didn't even flinch at his sudden, silent appearance.

"The night's over," she replied evenly. "All the shadows have been dispelled."

A gang of children came squealing out of an alley into the square. Her attention was drawn to the girl leading the pack—Havared's daughter Sisandra. Thin as rails and poorly dressed, they ran pell-mell through the busy square, laughing as they dodged between push-carts and pedestrians.

She looked back at Sebastius, but he was no longer there. With a shrug, she peeked inside Bannur's cloth bag, slowly drawing out a thick, coiled golden chain. From the look of it, it was very old, very rare, and very expensive. She chuckled with delight as it caught the light.

"From an admirer?" asked Tog, looking up from his labors.

"From a patron of the arts, " she answered. "For a performance well done."

PERFECT

DONALD J. BINGLE

A village on the trade route
near Wyldetree
Sometime during the peace
following the War of the Lance

M̲ost tales of Krynn are set in times of conflict, war, and upheaval, but when fear and death and destruction do not weigh heavy on the mind, other things intrude themselves upon the quiet enjoyment of life—things that are not chronicled in the histories and songs of the bards but are nevertheless of concern. At least they seem that way to those involved—and perhaps to Astinus, who records all. It could be the kender are right. Even small and mundane things can be interesting and important.

Everyone in the audience was laughing and leaning forward in expectation of what was to happen next.

Crawford, the venerable actor portraying Fineous Turwillow in the ever-popular comedy, *Mistaken Identity*, tapped his fingers on a bedpost of the giant bed that dominated the set of the duke's bedroom. His face was screwed up in perplexed confusion.

"Where could that rascal have gotten to? I'm sure I heard somebody in here."

Maybar Thane, the novice actor in the role of Pinkerton Pocketpicker, the kender who foils Fineous at every twist and turn of the three-act drama, peered from beneath the four-poster, his hair and clothes blanketed in dust bunnies but his eyes bright and alert. Looking directly at the audience, he enlisted them in his next caper with a stage whisper.

"Heard me he did, but herd me he won't. I'll make my escape when he searches the wardrobe cabinet."

The audience, who had seen object after object stuffed into the ersatz wardrobe cabinet for the better part of two acts, guessed what was to come next: an open door and a deluge of objects cascading down upon the hapless Fineous. A few guffawed aloud in anticipation of the scene. Others waited expectantly, their necks craned forward to catch every detail of the broad physical comedy that was to come. Everyone was tense and alive, happy, and enthralled.

Sitting on a barrel labeled "Dried Figs" and leaning back upon a cross-strut in the wings, Zefta was languidly flipping a copy of the script on which he had noted cues and business. Not an actor or stagehand, prop handler or costume master, Zefta was a mage. His job was to conjure up the forest, castle, field, saloon, or whatever comprised the backdrop for the scenes of the play. By his magic, the sticks of wood the stagehands stuck into the floorboards were transformed into deepest, darkest forest, complete with a woodland creature or two. By his hand, the flimsy façade of a castle wall became Thelgaard Keep. By his imagination, the flickering of the oil-lamp footlights became the glint of the full moons upon the waters of Ice Mountain Bay. In this instance, a few planks and posts had been transformed into a gargantuan feather bed and a tall, tightly packed cabinet.

The magical illusions involved considerable skill, but Zefta barely even looked up as his practiced hands fluttered nimbly over arcane components and he mechanically mumbled a magical phrase, the pronunciation and cadence just so, exactly the same as he had muttered it the night before and thousands upon thousands of nights before that.

At his magical urging, the scenery did his bidding, springing to life with a vividness that contrasted with Zefta's lugubrious countenance.

Woods, night.

Woods, day.

A roadside inn.

The throne room.

A gloomy cavern.

A battlefield hillside.

A bedroom with bed, washstand, and wardrobe cabinet.

As always, he performed flawlessly—perfectly. As always, no one in the audience noticed that he even existed. As the scenes progressed, he foraged in his deep pockets for the bits of dense cracker, lint-covered cheese, and hard candy that would make up his evening meal. He usually finished eating by the middle of the third act, and retired quietly when the audience departed at the end of the play. No applause, no accolades, no bouquets of flowers, no rounds of drinks at the after-play saloon festivities. A *silence* spell eliminated the annoying clatter of post-performance celebration and stage disassembly.

He toyed for a moment with changing something, anything at all in the scene. What if, in his magical illusion, the cabinet door refused to open? How long would crotchety old Crawford play-act Fineous, tugging and pulling at the door? What if the entire cabinet came crashing down? Perhaps nothing should fall out of the opened cabinet at all, or maybe the things that fell out ought to be completely different from the various props and plot devices that had been hidden there during the course of the first two acts. Better yet, what if Fineous opened the door to find a horrible monster with three eyes, a slavering purple tongue, and long, hairy arms and fearsome claws, which attacked with a ferocious roar? How would the renowned thespian deal with that little stage mishap?

Zefta smiled for the first time that evening, but his wandering concentration had created a muted, snarling rumble behind the cabinet door as Fineous stood before it, still contemplating his options for locating his kender tormentor. Crawford/Fineous looked at the wardrobe cabinet with an expression of bewilderment, but Maybar quickly covered with a stage whispered ad lib.

"A little ventriloquism is a handy skill for a kender. Somehow, mime school just didn't work out."

The audience howled and clapped in delight.

"Kender mimes," murmured someone in the third row. "Now that's something I'd like to see more often."

His female companion tittered at his witticism, while Zefta turned his full attention back to his task. He was sure to be in for it now. The troupe's leader, Sebastius, would undoubtedly delay his bedtime by growling and lecturing at him. The door opened, the packages, props, and paraphernalia fell out as they were supposed to, and everyone in the audience had a delightful evening.

Zefta nibbled at the corners of a piece of cheese until he produced a roundish oval. Diverting an infinitesimal fraction of his concentration away from the interminable hallway door sequence on stage, he molded the cheese to match Sebastius' puffy, stern face, then crushed the glob of cheese between two crackers, and set the crackers atop his reading lamp. He watched lazily as the cheese melted in the rising heat from the oil flame until it oozed out the edges and dripped on the chimney. He popped the tasty morsel in his mouth and crunched down on the crackers, squirting the cheese over his tongue and palate.

Even with a full mouth, his spellcasting for the next scene change boasted the correct diction. A garden manor appeared on stage with stately trees and manicured flower beds. Some part of Zefta's facile mind registered the audience's expected reactions as the scene progressed. Everyone was having a good time.

———◆◆◆———

Well, not quite everyone. In the woods, not far from the village of Teasdale's Copse, a day's travel to the west, Darna shivered in the increasing cold and pulled her luxuriant stole tighter around her shoulders. Woven from the softest wool of the highland goats, brushed a thousand times by the old peasant women before being spun into fine thread, then dyed the deepest cobalt, it was highlighted by silver threads of silk, so that it looked as beautiful as it felt. It was an extravagance to be sure, even though her father owned the store selling the stole, as well as a variety of other wondrous dresses, robes, cloaks, hats, silks, yarns, and bolts of fine and exotic fabrics. After their "special" evening together, Darna wanted to look radiant for Gantry. Besides, Father could afford it.

Darna's brows knit together as she thought of her father and the mean things he often said to her as she slaved away at the ceaseless chores and tasks he gave her at home and at the store. Her friends knew that mentioning her father always ruined her mood. The only thing that would brighten it again was spending his money. That always cheered her up.

No spending spree was necessary to lighten this occasion, however, although fingering the richness of the stole probably helped a little. Tonight, everything bad in her life would disappear. Gantry would ask her to marry him. Her life with Gantry would be perfect.

However, the hour was late, and Gantry had not appeared.

She focused on not letting his lateness annoy her. Understandably he was nervous. Like her, he wanted the marriage proposal to be perfect. She determined not to spoil the perfection of his words of love with the slightest rebuke.

More time passed, and she began to pace. Her lips pursed together in a straight line with no hint of a smile. Her dress, her hair, her stole, all perfect for her loved one when the evening began, began to wilt. Her hair began to frazzle as the evening mist sprang up. The dimming light no longer caused the silver strands in her cobalt blue stole to sparkle fetchingly, and the growing chill caused her to clutch the stole even tighter about her . . . a chill that was not limited to the air.

She shivered. Her annoyance was interrupted with sudden fear. Had something happened to him? An accident, or was he attacked by bandits or a wild beast when on the afternoon hunt with the other rich scions of the town? It was well past the appointed time of their rendezvous. She decided to go back into the town and inquire.

As she approached the Juggling Bear Tavern, her fear turned to cold anger. Boisterous and bawdy singing was coming from the tavern. A chorus of young men singing of drinking and conquest. She could clearly hear Gantry's voice above the rest—the rich, baritone voice that had promised her happiness, security, and love, forever love. He was hoarsely singing a particularly off-color ditty about women and skirts and, well, things unsavory to her ears, though Gantry seemed to be lustily enjoying the song.

The scene which followed was a jumble of words, of anger, betrayal, and accusation, mixed with words of drink, dismissal, and arrogance. Darna could not remember it all precisely when it was over, but one thing was clear above all else. Gantry had used her, had conquered her, had boasted to his besotted friends about her, and had discarded her out of hand. He had never loved her.

Fornarius wasn't happy either. He paced with long, precise strides back and forth along the length of his shop in Wyldetree. His fiancé, Mirinda, sat meekly at his desk, watching him. She had been silent and he had been pacing since she had remarked that he needn't get so worked up about the details for their upcoming wedding. Now he made a precise, military-style turn, and his pent-up words rushed out as he whirled to face her.

"It is all well and good that you are content with a simple wedding, even an elopement, but you don't understand my position. Though but a merchant in some

people's eyes, I am also . . . a retired Solamnic Knight."
He looked at her with stern self-importance.

"Even Knights, active or retired, fall in love. Certainly, some of them elope just like anyone else." Miranda made her statement quietly, with a tone of puzzlement. She just didn't understand the import of his revelation.

"A true Knight could never do something as casual and frivolous as elope. Vows are very serious things— sacred things—to a Knight. Even a retired Knight."

Miranda did not know what to say.

His speech continued. "Something small and informal in terms of a ceremony would simply be out of character for one of my heritage. Order. Precision. Formality. Vows aren't made willy-nilly, like kender promises."

"I hadn't meant to upset you, dear Fornarius. The planning just seemed to make you tense. A wedding is a wonderful thing. It shouldn't cause unhappiness." She looked as if she might begin to cry.

Fornarius strode purposefully toward her and put the sheaf of parchment atop the desk in the bottom drawer. No sense risking the fine, cloth-fibered parchment getting wet spots on it from Miranda's over-emotional state.

"You confuse organization and attention to detail with unhappiness. I should involve myself in the planning. Obviously, the logistics of the situation have overwhelmed your delicate sensibilities. I will see to all the details."

Miranda stood to depart, moving toward the door. "I'm sorry if I've been selfish. Appearances, as you say, are important in business, and I know that you just want us to have a perfect wedding."

"Not only for business purposes, my dear, but for social standing. There is your family to consider as well."

"You are right, as always. I shall not trouble you further tonight. Now, I have surprise for you, if I may."

Fornarius sighed, the corners of his mustached mouth turning down into a frown.

Merinda hurried on. "I know you don't really like surprises. After all, you have a busy schedule, and surprises are disruptive of it, but I thought a scheduled surprise would be another thing altogether."

"A scheduled surprise?" answered Fornarius warily.

"Two weeks hence, a play, in Fillendale. A traveling troupe will be performing."

Fornarius relaxed visibly. "A play is quite acceptable. Support of the arts is, after all the cultured thing to do, the *Solamnic* thing to do." He pecked her on the cheek and sat down at his desk to continue his planning. He did not look up as she left the shop.

Darna's crying and depression lasted an entire fortnight before it began to wane. Her father ignored her troubles, just as he always ignored her feelings. Her mother clucked condescendingly about the passion of young love but did not really understand what had happened. Benoit, the apprentice in her father's shop, knew all the grisly details—he had heard her friend, Katrice, gossiping about Darna's betrayal and humiliation to a coterie of Darna's girlfriends as they shopped. He had probably stared like an obvious fool as he had eavesdropped, but the girls paid him no more mind than Darna's father did her.

Benoit spent the next several days trying to figure out how to avenge Darna's honor, but by the time he had composed a little speech in his head that would tell off that cad, Gantry, the sobs from upstairs had diminished.

Then one night, as he was closing up the shop, the wailing started again with renewed vigor. So distraught did Darna sound that Benoit ventured up the stairs to the private quarters above. Darna's father and mother were out or he would not have dared. Still, his heart pounded at each step toward his beloved's door.

Finally, he knocked.

"Go away!"

"I j-just wanted to make sure you were all right."

"No, I'm not all right. I'll never be all right again." The sobbing started again.

"Is there anything I can do or get or—"

Suddenly, the door flew open. Darna stood there quivering, defiant, and weak. Her silken robe was loosely tied and half-open over her night clothes. Her hair was disheveled and stringy, her eyes puffy and red from crying. She sniffled.

"Get Katrice. Something terrible has happened."

"Katrice has gone to Fillendale, like your parents did, to see a play. Some traveling band of players is putting on a comedy. I . . . I can be back with her in about four hours."

Darna looked as if the world were about to end.

"Two hours if I s-s-steal a h-horse."

The thought of poor, honest Benoit stealing a horse on her behalf broke Darna's despair. She laughed feebly. "No. No need for anyone to become a criminal on my behalf. My life is over. I just need a friend to talk to."

"I'm your friend, Darna. I always have been."

So Darna talked to Benoit about Gantry and his betrayal and her foolishness in believing his words of love. Even though Benoit already knew much of what she said, he listened and sympathized. Almost an hour had passed before she admitted what had rekindled her crying. She was pregnant. Her prospects of a respectable life with a nobleman were ruined. She could never face her parents, especially her father. He would be shamed. He would certainly take out his dishonor on her. She would be disowned or even beaten. What would she do? She began to cry softly again.

To his surprise, that is when Benoit proposed marriage in his own awkward, stumbling way. They could leave this very night. At first, she protested his motives, then the practicalities of it all. Finally, she sat quietly for several minutes, reflecting.

"Yes, I will run away with you."

A look of radiant joy flooded Benoit's face as she said these words. He began to get up to help her pack—his mind already rapidly forming decisions and plans about their elopement. Darna put a hand on his shoulder to stop him—his joy was not matched on her tearstained face. "I will run away with you, but I won't marry you. I don't love you. You're not the type of man I mean to marry."

Darna could see the disappointment crashing down upon his face. She misinterpreted it.

"That doesn't mean that I won't . . . that we can't . . . be together." She laughed softly to herself. "It's not like I'd be risking getting pregnant."

Benoit blushed crimson. "I would n-never take advantage . . . I mean, you're in a t-t-tight spot. . . ."

Darna misinterpreted his words again. "Of course, I mean, why would you want me."

"It's not that I don't want you," Benoit interrupted, "not that, at all." He hesitated, looking down at the floor. "I have hopes, not expectations. N-n-never do anything you d-don't want to do."

She nodded. "We'd best get packing. I don't know what we would do if Father came home."

The couple quickly determined to set off for Fillendale. Darna suggested that by joining the traveling band of players they could, perhaps, make their escape with new professions. Benoit, in turn, refused to let Darna "borrow" any of the shop's cash, as she frequently did when going shopping. Packing what the two of them could readily carry, they started down the road to Fillendale late enough that they would arrive well after the performance began but before the evening's entertainment ended. They hid in the woods a few times along the way when they heard people approaching. Darna thought it best if her father did not know exactly where she was or that she was pregnant.

"He can keep his honor if he doesn't know."

Benoit quickly agreed, knowing that Darna's father would be mad enough that his apprentice had absconded from his responsibilities. He would be forced to work double-shifts until a new employee could be found.

In Fillendale, Sebastius, the rotund yet robust leader of the Traveling Players of Gilean, clapped his hands and, with a hearty "Yowza," called for all of the players to put aside their after-performance chores and gather round for a moment. His puffy, malleable face beamed with pride and happiness. "Well done, my friends, well done, indeed. The audience loved you. They cried, they laughed, and most importantly, they threw money on the stage at the end."

"Huzzah!" cried Gilf, a bit player and stagehand, from the back of the circle. "We lesser lights like it especially when they throw money. No one buys us drinks at the inn afterward, like they do for the prima donnas."

Crawford, the leading actor for the night's performance, this time in the short comedy *The Trouble with*

Dwarves, turned sharply and gave Gilf a vicious stare. Gilf paled visibly under his stony gaze until Crawford winked and broke into a broad smile, laughing at the momentary fear he had inspired in the young man.

"It is called acting, young sir, acting. I drink . . . because I act."

Everyone laughed heartily, most of all Sebastius.

"You see," the master of the troupe bellowed, "laughter is infectious. The mood permeates to the soul. After an evening of fine comedy, well-performed, even Gilf and Crawford team up for sly guffaws!"

"With that . . . and the throwing of money. Let's not forget that. Perhaps we should continue to perform this play for a spell," volunteered Gilf meekly.

"I would not be doing my job," replied Sebastius, "as your humble—" several chuckles broke out—"leader if I were to allow your repertory to grow stale—" the chuckles subsided—"and excellence tends to suffer—" two sighs were joined by an audible groan—"when the same play is performed *twice* in a row."

"How about twice in one lifetime?" called out one of the old-timers, for it was true that Sebastius never let the players do the same performance twice. He was always fiddling with the scripts, rearranging the scenes, combining vignettes, adding new characters, and the like. The more recent additions to the troupe suspected that this was always true. The old-timers could vouch for it, although the old-timers were not necessarily very old. Everyone who joined the Traveling Players of Gilean was marked with a peculiar black tattoo, which protected them completely from aging and death. Should someone leave the players, however, the tattoo vanished of its own accord, and their aging began again.

"Nor would repeating a performance achieve what we need to accomplish as artists of the stage," finished Sebastius seriously.

The old-timers knew that the Players always performed for a dual purpose—entertainment for the audience, yes, but also a special goal that only Sebastius knew and somehow planned in order to teach a lesson to someone present.

Some whispered that Sebastius was a god, the brother of Astinus, who chronicled all of history and life in the Library of Palanthas. Knowing all history the instant it occured, Astinus was able to guide his brother to people in need. Sebastius was very secretive, however, and no one had the temerity to ask him about these matters.

"As you know, friends, we have a bit of travel before our next performance. Our run of comedies has been quite successful and should, I believe, be extended. I was thinking of the famous kender musical comedy *Who, Me?*

There were several groans. Kender were maddening enough, but the songs in the play were nonsensical, the blocking incomprehensibly complicated, and the props frighteningly numerous. "So Many Pockets, So Little Time," an unceasingly cheerful number actors could never seem to get out of their heads once it found its way there, called for forty-seven different props to be deposited in twenty-nine different pockets of eleven different players, so they could be pulled out, studied, traded, dropped, fondled, and re-deposited elsewhere as the verses progressed.

Almost immediately, someone started humming the blasted song, causing several of the others to promptly throw shoes at the perpetrator.

"Now," said Sebastius, "I have a few notes. Let me go through the assignments."

Zefta cringed, because he knew what was coming. With a complicated play like this, with a huge number of performers, and multiple speeches, jokes, and songs, Sebastius always approached organization in the same way.

"Aaron, I would like you to play Bottomsup Stumblebum, but in the first act, I think that you should revise the 'Shiny Marble' ditty to repeat the 'Cats-eye, All mine' chorus while you swing across the stage. Next, Badar . . ."

A number of the cast and crew scrambled to produce parchment, pens, and ink, in order to take copious notes of Sebastius' instructions. A middle-aged gnome named Patentworthy Pathwanderer began to set up his "spring-powered automatic transcribing enlarger and reducer with collapsible easel on hydraulic telescopic height adjusters" for the same purpose, to the experienced dismay of all about him. The most knowledgeable scrambled safely away before he began to wind the mechanism. Cathar Bellowstroke, the dwarf who acted as crew chief, rolled up a sleeve and produced an edged piece of graphite in order to make notes on his arm. "If I lose my cues," he once quipped, "I have more serious problems than whether the furniture is properly arranged for the next scene."

Zefta slumped down in a nearby corner, conjured up a swarm of gnats, and practiced zapping them out of existence with electrical charges fired from his fingertips.

"Gloria, the costumes will need more spangles for the dwarven mine number."

After scoring five simultaneous hits on the hapless gnats with his five fingertips, Zefta interrupted his casual violence to scrounge up a mirror to make his game more challenging. The left/right reversal threw him off for a bit, but soon the gnats' prospects were once again hopeless. He needed a bigger challenge. He began to work on figuring out how to make Cathar's beard, but not the rest of the old dwarf, invisible. He fussed with area effect calculations for almost three minutes before he realized, disgustedly, that all he really needed to do was formulate a variation of a *disguise* spell—hardly challenging at all. He then began to count the number of plays for which he had provided magical sets since his apprenticeship to Sebastius more than a century ago but gave it up as a lost cause. If it wasn't too many to count, it was certainly too many to care. He returned his focus to Sebastius, who still seemed genuinely enthusiastic whenever he doled out these endless assignments and downright garrulous whenever he stepped before an audience.

"Taewynd, you really do need to put on a few pounds for the kender seductress dance. Remember, even though you know that the kender are going to keep stealing your veils, you need to act surprised. Maybe slap a hand or two playfully or shake your finger. . . ."

Sebastius glanced over at Zefta, smiling indulgently, though their relationship was not always a happy one. Sebastius had, for instance, been quite displeased about the growling in the wardrobe cabinet during the performance of *Mistaken Identity* a few weeks back, suggesting that maybe the time had come for Zefta to move on. Zefta was convinced that he had said that only to make a point and could not possibly have meant it literally. Still, for all the grief he'd gotten, Zefta almost wished he had loosed a slavering monster on poor Crawford on stage—at least *that* would have been worth the stern looks and words of disapproval and criticism.

"Zefta. *Zefta!* Pay attention, man. As I mentioned earlier, we're dropping the 'kender roll' scene. The Kender

Anti-Defamation League got all over the playwright about that one. No use stirring up trouble or insulting the little fellows. Remember that night should begin to fall immediately after the 'Happy In Each Other's Pockets' song." Looking up from his notes, Sebastius nodded to himself, his double-chin wrinkling and unwrinkling with the motion. "Yep, that's it, I think."

"Sebastius," began Zefta, somewhat tentatively, "I was thinking that the meadow scene could use a bit more pizzazz. Maybe a group of woodland animals could come to drink at the brook and be enchanted by the song and gather round little Buttonbutton as she sings."

"Hmmm. I don't think so, Zefta. The 'Outstanding in My Field' number is the only real ballad in the whole show. It's a change of pace thing. You don't want to busy that up. It sets up the whole 'turkey liberation' sequence to look even more madcap than it is. No, let's just stick with your basic meadow. No animals."

"But, Sebastius, in a kender musical, by the gods, there is so much frenetic movement and chaos and chattering, that unless I do something spectular the audience will scarcely notice the scenery at all."

"Exactly as it should be—"

Sebastius' reply was cut off by an extremely well-dressed gentleman who had found his way backstage.

"You must be Sebastius," the gentleman observed, nodding his head perfunctorily in greeting. "I require a word with you about something of the utmost importance."

"Sir, if you will kindly wait a moment, Sebastius and I—"

"Now, now, Zefta. That's no way to treat a customer. Besides, we're through with our discussion, I think. Quite through. You would do well to focus on your assigned tasks should you wish to continue to perform them."

Zefta stood motionless, mouth agape, at the public nature of this assault upon his professionalism. Forgetting about the assembled players and the interrupting customer, he responded in heat.

"Who else would perform my tasks? You? You haven't conjured a set in decades, not that you could match my efforts even then!"

The troupe was shocked at Zefta's outburst. Most simply looked on, silent and appalled. The more superstitious began to fumble for talismans or charms to ward off the backlash that was sure to follow. Near the back of the crowd, Gilf started to make book on who would win the fight, immediately quoting ten to one odds in Sebastius's favor. "Always bet on the god. . . ." he muttered under his breath, as Maybar bet in favor of the fuming mage, Zefta.

"If *you* can learn, I'm sure that anyone can do the same."

"Not one of the players has shown any flair for set illusions," retorted the mage. "Skill like this takes time to develop."

"True enough," replied Sebastius with an uncharacteristic smirk, "even for immortals. So maybe it's a good idea to find an apprentice and begin training one immediately."

In the back of the crowd, Gilf pocketed his winnings.

With a dismissive wave in Zefta's direction, Sebastius walked the inquiring patron around the corner of the backdrop, toward the wings of the stage itself.

Instead of leaving in a huff as the rest of the troupe disassembled, Zefta stewed silently, waiting to continue his confrontation with Sebastius again when the stranger finished talking with their imperious, cheese-faced leader. He could hear their conversation from around the post.

"Now, sir, what can I do for you?"

"My name is Fornarius. I am to be married to my beloved Mirinda ten days hence in Wyldetree, the small town not far south of here along the main trade route. The Wyldetree Boy's Choir was scheduled to perform at the wedding, but, well, frankly, their rehearsal performance was not really acceptable. I think some of those boys have been in the choir for too many years. There was definitely some wavering, even some cracking, on the higher parts."

"Certainly that happens with all boys at an age, sir. We can each perform a certain role only for so long, eh?" responded Sebastius, appraising the appearance of Fornarius—the Solamnic style of dress, the unwieldy longsword that somewhat unbalanced the man's natural gait, the unfamiliar heraldry on the man's belt buckle, the unfashionably antique style of his haircut.

"I would know nothing of performing roles, sir. I am an honest merchant versed in theatre only through my extensive reading. It is the duty of a Knight to be well read. Even in retirement, I take my duties seriously."

"Ah, I thought I had noticed you in the audience tonight. Perhaps I was mistaken."

"My duty tonight was to accompany Mirinda to your performance. She found it quite amusing. When I mentioned that the boy's choir was simply unacceptable for our wedding, she . . . uh . . . suggested you be retained."

"And you concurred?"

"Well, of course, I did some checking at the end of the performance and was assured of your reputation, both as to reliability and consistency of quality. Most importantly, I was informed by one of your . . . performers . . . that your little band has an extensive repertoire."

"You would, of course, prefer a different comedy for your wedding, since some members of the wedding party were here tonight."

"No. I mean yes. I would prefer another *play*. Certainly not a comedy." Fornarius shuddered, as if something had left a bad taste in his mouth. "Nothing so frivolous as tonight's production, certainly nothing featuring dwarves lacking directional sense. This is a wedding, sir. The finest houses of Wyldetree will be in attendance, as well as fellow members of the Knights of Solamnia. All quality people, you understand."

"I see. No riffraff invited."

"You understand completely. Not all of Mirinda's family knows me well. I wish to make sure that the wedding and entertainment properly reflects that Mirinda has chosen wisely."

"We do have a fine instrumental group and some elf singers of considerable voice."

"Please, sir. Nothing so mundane. This is my wedding, and it must be a perfect reflection of me."

Sebastius racked his memory but could not think immediately of a play sufficiently pretentious, priggish, and pompous as to be a perfect reflection of the prospective client who stood before him. "I see," he temporized.

"Are you familiar with the play *The Oath and The Measure*? I have it in my library and could—"

"Zounds, my man! *The Oath and The Measure* must be three and a half hours long if it is a minute."

"Ah, then you do know it."

"The complete explanation of the code of the Old Knights of Solamnia, as told in excruciating detail through a series of simple vignettes exemplifying each of the virtues of Knighthood. The vignettes punctuate a recitation of the historical antecedents of the code."

"Yes, that is the very one," Fornarius said, nodding approvingly.

"The stilted style and meter is enough to sear it into every mind that has ever read it. I have never actually heard of it being performed, however."

"That is why it is perfect for the wedding. A unique experience that will demonstrate my literary breadth and expound my virtues in a structured and ordered way. Structure, order, and perfection are very important to the Knights of Solamnia . . . us Knights of Solamnia, you know. Most plays simply are too chaotic, too free-form, to be proper for such a formal situation as a Solamnic wedding, but this one . . . well, this one is unique."

"That it is, but three and a half hours is long for a wedding entertainment. What with the ceremony itself, the traditional recitation of the Vows of Binding, and the receiving line afterward . . . certainly I could trim down the slower, less central portions of the play."

"Please, sir! That would be like trimming ivy with a sword."

"At least let us have an intermission, an opportunity for a sip of wine and some cakes, perhaps. The audience, especially any children, may get restless."

"You miss the point, my dear Sebastius. The ordered tone and unusual length of the piece will be a testament to the fortitude and endurance so beloved by the Old Knights of Solamnia."

"It certainly will."

"Then it is decided?"

Sebastius cupped both his chins in his massive, callused left hand and rubbed his graying stubble thoughtfully. His thick eyebrows tilted toward his slightly red nose in a **V**, almost touching in the center. Long tufts shot up in the middle of each brow, giving him a slightly comical look, even at his most serious.

"There is, of course, the matter of the fee. Normally, we solicit donations from the crowd, but at a private affair such as this . . ."

Fornarius's posture straightened even more, if that were possible. His chin lowered slightly and his teeth clicked softly together as his mouth clenched in perturbation. His sword rattled slightly as it bumped into a support post.

"This is my wedding, sir. Everything must be as it should. Everything must be flawless in each and every particular." He waved his gloved hand in a dismissive flutter that was obviously well practiced from dealing with servants and menials of various sorts. He snorted, a bit less genteelly than he obviously intended, but recovered quickly. "Money is no object. Simply submit a statement at the performance once you have calculated your costs and margin."

"I shall simply average our take at our last ten performances. I would not wish you to feel that I would in any way take advantage of your . . . situation." Sebastius replied casually, fixing upon Fornarius's soft hand as it gripped the ornate hilt of his pristine sword. Fornarius reddened briefly, the flush beginning in the neck and suffusing upward across his thin, drawn face and almost to the top of his ears.

"I am an retired Knight and a merchant of considerable wealth and standing. My only *situation*, as you put it, is that I require . . . no, I *demand* that the play be performed completely and exactly as written. Nothing short of perfection will suffice for my guests, my wedding, my bride."

"As you wish, Fornarius." Sebastius bowed deeply, flourishing with his right hand outstretched. It was the type of grandiose bow he used after his introductory greetings on stage.

Zefta had not budged from his listening post as Sebastius and Fornarius had rounded the corner of the set to talk. Instead he had remained, eavesdroping. Even without approaching the wooden support of the set or leaning toward the conversation, he had, by remaining quiet and motionless, heard the entire conversation.

"You can quit holding your breath, Zefta," Sebastius rumbled from around the corner, "and come here. The merchant has left."

Zefta did his best to round the corner in a dignified fashion but was unconvincing. He was no actor.

"Gather the others, if you would, mage," said Sebastius with a sigh. "It seems we must do assignments all over again." With that, the leader of the Players ambled toward his wagon, his mind already occupied.

By the time Zefta, grumbling through the entire chore, had gathered up the rest of the players, Sebastius had returned from his wagon. He sat on a tall wooden stool on center stage, one black-booted leg on the floor of the stage, the other crooked with the heel of his boot hooked onto the lower rung of the stool. His rugged hands held a thick book, bound in maroon leather, with the seal of the Knights of Solamnia stamped in gold-leaf upon the spine. On the front, similar gold-leaf set out the title: *The Oath and the Measure: A Play Exemplifying the Virtues and Statutes of the Knights of Solamnia in Five Acts and Ten Vignettes by Sir Galvin Hunter Tardanius*. Neither Zefta, nor anyone else, seemed surprised that Sebastius should have such a tome at his ready disposal. He always seemed to have whatever script they required, though it was a minor mystery how he fit such a library, as well as his own not insubstantial girth, into his small private wagon.

By now, even the stragglers among the audience were long gone. Some of the actors and support personnel been been tracked down in the local saloons or wakened from slumber.

" 'Tis a long play," growled their leader, as he looked up from the maroon and gold tome. "I'm afraid that the scribes will be quite busy during the night copying your respective parts and cues. But it is also more *orderly* than our planned kender musical."

"So is a whirlwind in a china store!" a stagehand called out from the fringes.

"In any event," continued Sebastius after the laughter subsided, "I hope no one is disappointed in the change of plans." His bushy-browed eyes scanned the gathered throng to see if all were in attendance. "Very well, let us start. Aaron, you are to play the young Knight in the vignette on humility. It has come time in your progression to cast you against type."

The weary crowd chuckled. Sometimes the assignments were as entertaining to them as the plays were to the crowds that visited them.

Zefta, however, sighed. Once again, he had a long wait with little expectation.

"Certainly," Zefta complained, when his time finally came, "a squire's room must have some accoutrements besides a wooden pallet and a washbasin."

"I do not make these things up, Zefta. Fornarius is clearly familiar with the text and has demanded that the performance perfectly exemplify his Solamnic sensibilities. You know how fussy Solamnics can be." Sebastius looked at the sky apologetically and lowered his voice to a whisper. "No offense to any of our Solamnic friends, mind you, but 'tis an undeniable fact that a Knight of Solamnia is practically the antithesis of a kender, and in much more than just whether they can be trusted to watch your coin pouch. The Knights simply seem unable to abide chaos. The man . . . this Knight . . . wants his wedding to be a perfect reflection of himself, understand? A perfect reflection."

Zefta started to protest, but Sebastius cut him off. Zefta was annoyed, but this time he decided to count to ten before he said anything.

He lost his chance to say anything at all.

The discussion was interrupted by a pretty young girl and her awkward male companion.

"Excuse m-me, k-kind sir. The dwarf d-disassembling the benches s-said you were in charge here."

"I am Sebastius. Welcome to the Traveling Players of Gilean. The answer is, of course, yes."

The young man looked confused. "I-I haven't asked a question yet."

"Ah," said Sebastius, his countenance warming and softening, "but I am an actor." He leaped from the stool to bow and flourish as before. "Actors ply their craft by observation and simulation."

He stood, elbows out, his muscles taut, his hands on his wide hips, as he appraised the young man and the young woman clutching the fellow's hand a bit too tightly. She feigned confidence, but there was a wild look in her eyes, a deep-seated fear not of Sebastius or this place, but of something else.

"You seek refuge, no?"

The fellow swallowed hard and stepped forward to offer his hand to the large man. "My name is Benoit. This is my . . . p-partner . . . Darna. We seek . . . employment with your troupe."

"What is refuge but employment with a home on wheels which leaves your troubles behind? Pardon my bluntness, but you do not seem to have the confidence, the swagger, the unfettered egotism of actors. May I inquire as to your qualifications to join our band of merry adventurers and theatrical performers?" His face was stern, but his tone was light.

Now the young maiden stepped forward and spoke for the first time. "I know a lot about fabric and sewing and accessories."

Sebastius could tell from her attire that she spoke the truth, or at the least that she knew of such things from the wearing of fine garments. Although she wore traveling clothes, the fabric was a fine, sturdy brocade, lined with a dark and complementary satin. The ruffles at the sleeves of her white underblouse were bright. The stitching was intricate and densely tight. More importantly, her slender hands showed a classic sewing callus.

"Benoit is a very organized fellow and hard worker, also knowledgeable about fabrics and supplies and such."

"Oh, well then, we could always use an organized fellow and hard worker." Sebastius turned his gaze toward Zefta and let it linger a moment before turning back to the young man. "Our next play involves a large number of set changes—a *meticulous* person could be quite useful. There is even a small part or two—nothing much, two, three lines at the most—that is not yet filled."

Benoit winced slightly. "I-I-I'm n-not sure I'd m-make much of an actor," he stuttered. "M-my best skill is intricate handwork, for detail, in s-s-sewing."

"Intricate handwork *and* meticulous. So be it," declaimed Sebastius royally. "You may apprentice here with our mage, Zefta, to create the illusions necessary for our theatrical craft."

Zefta glowered hot coals at Sebastius but said nothing. Benoit, although taken aback by his assignment, determined to say no more lest he be given an even more daunting task to perform as a member of the company.

Their large leader turned next to the young woman. "As for Madame Darna, a costume mistress—" Darna reddened slightly at emphasis of the word mistress, but Sebastius noted the involuntary flush and took it in stride, hardly skipping a beat"—costume *matron* is sorely needed by the troupe. As you can see," the big man continued gesturing broadly at his own clothing, a sky-blue tunic over brown leggings with an improbably garish yellow-and-orange-patterned silk sash at the overextended midriff, "I have no sense of fashion myself. Or, at least," he continued, looking again meaningfully at the fuming Zefta, "my sense is not fashionable with some."

"Thank you," said the young couple in unintended unison, then looked about anxiously, knowing not what to do next.

"Zefta, here, will show you to an empty wagon, which you may use during your stay with us, and he can help you put away your things. He is quite an expert when it comes to wardrobe cabinets."

Zefta clenched his teeth together tightly.

Sebastius continued, "If you go by the fire, I am sure that there is some hot elderberry tea left still. There is no sense getting a chill in your condition . . ."

Darna's eyes darted wide open. Benoit face registered alarm a half-second later.

". . . as weary travelers who have obviously, from the brambles on your clothing, traveled far this evening on else aside the main roadways," continued the master thespian smoothly. "In the morning, Zefta can introduce you around and Benoit can start his apprenticeship."

Zefta bristled visibly at being dispatched on such trivial errands and turned an appraising eye on his new

DONALD J. BINGLE

apprentice and the fetching young maiden. "Intricate handwork . . ." he harumphed under his breath.

He bowed perfunctorily toward the couple, a sudden gleam in his eye. "This way, young ones. I exist only to make Sebastius's desires into reality." He stepped toward the fire, without even looking to see if they were following, muttering to himself, ". . . No matter how drab, unimaginative, and boring his desires may be."

Fornarius found Mirinda waiting patiently by the "mushroom fountain" in the town square. The water gurgled out from an irregular oval at the center of a wide, slightly convex, rough stone supported by a squat pillar. The cool, sparkling fluid cascaded unevenly down the circular edge to the pond. Mirinda sang softly to herself as she trailed a delicate finger in the clear water.

"My negotiations were a complete success. The Traveling Players of Gilean will perform their show immediately before the Vows of Binding." Fornarius beamed with pride, as if contracting the troupe was a master stroke of diplomatic subtlety or an honor-bound mission entrusted to a Knight's duty.

"I never doubted that you would be successful. You know I trust you in all things."

Fornarius reddened subtly at her last words. He gripped the hilt of his over-sized sword to fight back the blush. Mirinda did not notice, continuing gaily, "I still do not understand why the boys' choir suddenly displeased you. They perform often at weddings, even outside of the Wyldetree itself."

"My very point, my love. I attended their last rehearsal and can assure you that though pleasing, they are quite unremarkable, even mundane. Certainly not the unique and unparalleled performance that should accompany the vows of the perfect couple at the perfect Solamnic wedding ceremony."

"You strive so valiantly, darling Fornarius," whispered Mirinda, as she lightly stroked his cheek with her hand, her fingers still cool from the water of the fountain. "You must have made an excellent Knight. You need not try so hard on my account. I am quite content with the wedding because I will wed you. All else is simply brown sugar on the porridge."

Being compared to porridge caused Fornarius's brow to furrow momentarily.

"Ah, but your approval I already have," he said graciously. "I do not believe your aunts and uncles, even your grandmama, feel that you are making a good match."

"Fortunately for us both, you are not wedding my grandmama, so her opinion is not really so important. Still, I am sure that she will be pleased and impressed with a light comedy instead of the more ordinary choir performance."

"But it is even better yet, my dear. I have convinced the troupe to perform *The Oath and the Measure,* the play I told you about last fall. To my knowledge, it has never been performed in its entirety anywhere. It is quite the milestone."

"A premiere! How exciting! But I recall, you said that play was quite lengthy."

"True, but to learn the lessons of each of the virtues held true by the Knights of Solamnia is no small task. No facet is hidden, and all is revealed."

It sounded more like schooling than a celebration, the way he spoke of it, but Mirinda smiled and took Fornarius's arm, hugging it to her as they turned to begin their late walk to the stable where their carriage and fine horses waited to return them home to Wyldetree.

"I'm sure everything will be just as you want it, dear, absolutely perfect."

Over the next ten days, many preparations were made.

Benoit fashioned fake armor and weapons from wood and fabric and painted background colors onto a phalanx of prop shields before they were turned over to more delicate and trained artists to fashion heraldry upon them: roses, dragons, kingfishers, stars, and the like. He also spent an inordinate amount of time practicing, for indeed he was assigned a small part in the play. It was just a few lines, late in the first act in a vignette about the virtue of honesty, then again at the close of the play. Though his character did not even have a name (he was denoted as "Second Guardsman" in the pages that had been handed to him by the weary and ink-stained scribes), he fretted about his responsibility.

"We have retrieved the scroll, sir," Benoit practiced, as he picked up another shield for painting, holding forth the paintbrush stiffly, as if it were the scrollcase that he was supposed to proffer to Crawford, who would be playing Sir Derrick.

He was sure the intonation was wrong, and he was afraid he might stutter before the crowd. Worse yet, he feared he would trip and fling himself upon the much more experienced actor. Somehow on stage, in front of all those people, the thought of actually walking and talking at the same time seemed like an insurmountable challenge.

"We have retrieved the scroll, sir," he tried again.

PERFECT

After three shields and more than two dozen incantations of the same line, Benoit turned his rehearsal to his second line. This one really terrified him. It was not that it was lengthy or a tongue-twister or required him to cry real tears, or any of those things that true actors could do on a bet. It was just that it was the very last line of the play. It would make the last impression upon the audience.

"And so, all being in order, was measured well and proper." For such a simple line, it somehow seemed very crucial. It was the universal message meant to be conveyed by the entire performance, he was sure. It was, however, hard to tell for certain, as he had only been given his own scenes for studying. He didn't really know what the whole play was all about. The weary scribes had been much, much too busy to produce extra copies of the whole thing. Apparently, the whole text was massive. Sebastius had insisted that each and every line copied by the scribes be proofed and verified to make sure that there was not a single mistake. Something about meter, or cadence, or rhyme, or reasons beyond the ken of a simple clothier's apprentice—even one who was now also an apprentice mage.

Benoit had other worries, for on top of his prop-construction duties and his lines, Zefta had, indeed, taken him as an apprentice illusionist. Sebastius was right that magic required an organized mind and excellent manual dexterity, but a capable apprentice needed something more—a willing teacher and a strong desire to learn magic. Thus, the training was made more difficult than it otherwise might have been, as Benoit had no real desire to become a mage, and Zefta was providing the training only reluctantly, on Sebastius's order. Accordingly, long hours would go by without a mention of illusions or spellcraft when suddenly Zefta would bark instructions and recite arcane formulae and lists of ingredients at the overwhelmed shopkeeper. Whether these bursts of activity were a method of instruction or merely the reaction to prodding by Sebastius was not clear to poor, bewildered Benoit. He tried to do his best whenever something was demanded of him.

"Why is it that some spells require physical components, while others just require hand-motions and verbalization?" queried Benoit after one frustrating session.

"Listen, young Benoit," replied the exasperated mage, "I'm sure I could tell you something about optimizing the sub-harmonics of the magical fields, as it relates to the probability function in inverse relationship to the field of magic invoked, but I can't imagine how that would help the situation. Once you have mastered at least some minor bit of magic—a *sneeze* cantrip, faerie lights, something, anything—perhaps I will be more of a mind to discuss the theoretical underpinnings of things mystical."

"I-I'm just trying to d-do my job."

Zefta sighed heavily. "And I mine." He smiled and put his arm around the young man. "I tell you what. For now, you just take everything I tell you as true—even if you don't understand it. In turn I promise that I will tell Sebastius that you are a fine pupil and a good fellow."

So between tense but intermittent sessions of instructions, the two men became friends, or at least friendly.

It was in such a context that Benoit expressed to Zefta his fears that he or someone else would make a major mistake in a play of such complexity. The mage reassured him.

"Things go wrong all the time. You just make something up to cover the mistake and go on. It's called 'extemporaneous ad libbing.'

"Oh, oh I could never do that," said young Benoit, his eyes wide open in terror at the very thought of having to think as well as walk and talk at the same time.

"Well, you can't just have the whole performance come to a crashing halt," scolded Zefta.

"I'm sure Crawford or one of the other more experienced actors would step in and make sure that wouldn't happen."

Zefta's right eyebrow arched and his upper lip twitched twice. "Ye gads, man. Do you wish to curse us all?"

"No. I wouldn't ever . . . I mean . . . I m-meant no offense . . . I . . . er . . . w-whatever do you mean?"

Zefta thought a moment before speaking.

"Actors and theatre people of all types are great respecters of luck and fortune, to the extent of extensive superstition and charms and all."

"But that's just stuff and nonsense . . . isn't it?" blurted out the sensible shopkeeper.

Zefta gave him a look of alarm. "Don't say that." He quickly mumbled a few magical phrases that were meaningless to Benoit and sprinkled a bit of shiny dust over the two of them. "There. I think we'll be all right."

Zefta lowered his voice to a whisper, though Benoit could not imagine who might be listening. "Luck is as real as magic and much more powerful. This troupe has been around. The players know a thing or two, and they respect luck and curses."

Benoit pursed his lips, frowning skeptically.

"Why do you think they never wish one another luck? 'Twould be misfortune and folly of the worst sort. No, the one who messes up, that's the one who has to fix it. If you bollix your line, you're the one who has to make it right or you curse yourself and the rest of us too."

A distraught and terrified expression appeared on young Benoit's face. Zefta's hands moved subtly but intricately, hidden in the folds of his robe. A sudden noise behind the nearest wagon arose, and Zefta used the excuse to get up and leave, smiling wryly. Benoit sat alone for a few moments—one more pressure set upon him in his new life—then went back to rehearsing his lines from the play. He was so worried about it all that he broke out in a rash.

————◆◆◆————

Fornarius spent the several days before the wedding in a rush of concentrated high energy. The impending groom was an unrelenting taskmaster, completely distrustful of anyone else's judgment or competence, unable to delegate even the most minute details. After the set-up crew hired from Fillendale had spent almost two hours arranging rows of chairs, Fornarius showed up to check on things and immediately flew into an apoplectic rage.

"Did it not occur to your simpleminded brain that there is a play to be performed at this wedding and that there will be a significant contingent of Knights of Solamnia in attendance?" he railed at the foreman. "The chairs, man, the chairs. Do those seem appropriate to you for Knights?"

The foreman looked about anxiously for some clue as to the problem. He was totally bewildered by Fornarius's question. All of the Knights he had ever seen used chairs, normal chairs, just like these. Was there something special about Solamnic wedding ceremonies? If so, he had never heard of it. He stammered a few times and fell silent. He had no idea what to say.

"The spacing, man. Look at the spacing. It is hardly adequate."

The foreman focused on the center aisle. It looked perfectly adequate to him. Both Fornarius and Mirinda were slender. It was not like two giants or trolls were getting hitched (not that he would rent chairs to barbaric monsters such as those).

Fornarius followed the foreman's gaze, snorting with disgust. "Not there, you imbecile! The spacing between chairs. It's . . . it's . . . designed for *non-combatants*. Not only do warriors and Knights tend to be above-average in height and build—" Fornarius reflexively straightened his posture as he spoke—"but they generally wear armor and carry a sword or other battle accoutrements, even on ceremonial occasions."

The foreman understood the words (except, possibly, for "accoutrement," which he guessed to be a fancy kind of sword), and his mind was beginning to work itself around to what they meant, but Fornarius had no patience for the stout laborer's pedestrian cognitive ability.

"Accordingly, the chairs must be farther apart, to allow for extra room at the side, for a Knight's sword to dangle without becoming entangled in the rungs of the neighboring chair."

The foreman nodded; that certainly made sense.

"The rows need to be farther apart to provide a more oblique angle for each guest to be able to see the performance on stage without his or her line of sight being occluded by the guest sitting immediately in front of him."

The foreman's shoulders slumped in minor despair. He had no idea what "occluded" meant. Truth be told, it was not a precisely correct use of the term, but, of course, he did not know that. His head stopped nodding in agreement and, instead, cocked to one side in a kind of puzzlement often seen in young children when their parents are talking about things beyond their ken.

Fornarius threw up his hands in despair and pique. "They won't be able to see, because the head of the person in front of them will be so close it will block their view."

A wave of understanding crashed upon the beach of the foreman's brain. "Oh, yeah, sure. I get it," he said truthfully as the client prattled on about blockage and sightlines.

The same type of scene repeated itself with the flower arranger, the caterer, the musicians, the trellis-builder, the ushers, even the priest. Most had worked weddings before and had some experience with the type of hyperactive tension that sometimes accompanied such events. They dealt with the problems, rearranging this or that to satisfy the customer, and went on about their business, weary from the encounters but not unduly aggravated by them. Fornarius, on the other hand, grew more keyed up with each incident, his phobic attention to detail becoming more and more compulsive.

Eventually, Mirinda arrived, her mood the silver lining to her groom's dark and stormy cloud. She gushed about how beautiful and wonderful everything looked. She thanked and complimented the workers and artists with praise so effusive yet innocent that it could be nothing but heartfelt. To everyone's joy, she ended her visit by persuading the overwrought Fornarius to leave with her and get some rest before their perfect day on the morrow.

———◆◆◆———

The day of the wedding came, the day all had worked so hard to make perfect for Fornarius and Mirinda.

The day itself cooperated fully. It was bright and sunny but not overly hot or humid. White, puffy clouds lazed overhead, breaking the glare of the sun as they moved on the slight, refreshing breeze. A pleasant day filled with promise.

The Traveling Players of Gilean breakfasted before the dawn so they could move from Fillendale to Wyldetree at first light. They had packed the night before, the stage components numbered and stacked for rapid deployment. Everything was organized and ready. They arrived at the wedding site without difficulty, and after unloading the necessary supplies and components in their proper places they moved the wagons out of sight so as to not disturb the beauty or serenity of the wedding tableau. The workmen (everyone but those with the largest parts to perform) quickly and efficiently set up the main stage, with blocking marks intact as well as the two lower, semicircular sub-stages, which projected to the very edge of the audience's chairs from the front corners of the main stage. These would be used for some of the minor vignettes.

Darna had been hard-pressed to make the necessary costumes perfect. She had sewed until her fingers were practically numb. She also endured the dubious joys of morning sickness, confirming her pregnancy, but that was good, from Benoit's point of view. It distracted her from second-guessing her difficult decision to leave with him or worrying about whether her father was on their trail.

Darna was working harder than she had ever worked for her father, and she was kept busy with the arrangement of the costumes and final touches of color and detail. Not only that, but Zefta had dropped in that morning to tell her that the openings on the pockets on the guardmen's costumes were too large for proper Solamnic style, so she had spent the bumpy ride to Wyldetree sewing them partially closed. Sebastius, it seemed, was both generous and demanding.

Benoit spent the entire trip fidgeting, beads of sweat gathering at his forehead as he repeated his lines endlessly.

"I swear you are more tense this morning than the night we fled Teasdale's Copse," Darna observed between tight stiches. " 'Tis only a play."

"You don't understand."

She halted her sewing momentarily. "You're not casting any beginner's spells during the performance, are you? Even Zefta wouldn't demand so much so quickly, would he?"

"No, no. I'm not really even a beginner yet."

"Then there's nothing to worry about."

"There is. I could still ruin everything."

"Ruin everything?" queried Darna, her tone sliding down the scale from skepticism towards sarcasm.

"Yes, don't you see? We could get kicked out of the troupe. Why, I almost wished someone luck this morning! That would never do!"

Before Darna could question him about that odd comment, however, the wagons arrived at Fillendale, and Benoit rushed off to perform his crew duties. His hands were shaking as he arranged the props for the performance. Zefta noticed Benoit trembling and came over to him.

"My dear boy, the morning air seems to have chilled you. Take this." The mage produced a dark flask from his deep pockets.

Benoit eyed the flask warily. "What is it? A p-potion of warmth? I'm not really c-cold. . . ."

"No, no, no," replied the mage, his voice dropping conspiratorially. "Just a mild ale to take the edge off the breeze and calm your nerves. Drink it all at once. It has a bit of a bite."

Benoit did as he was told, downing the flask. His throat burned with fire. He coughed once but immediately felt a rush of warmth and confidence.

He looked about at the fancy preparations being made for the wedding ceremony and accompanying feast: the food, the music, the guests, the doves and flowers that would make a girl's wedding dreams come true. He rememembered Darna, back before she paid him any mind, talking to Katrice and her other girlfriends about wedding day hopes and plans.

"Poor Darna," he muttered to himself. "Stuck with me."

"What's that you say?" inquired a relaxed, even jovial Zefta as he dropped the empty flask back into his robe pocket.

"Oh, nothing."

"Well, then, I leave you to your performance. You do, of course, have your steel."

Benoit patted his wooden prop sword, dangling from his belt. "I am fully costumed, Zefta, I assure you."

Zefta was right. The ale had warmed and relaxed him—his words flowed so fluently they almost seemed to run together.

Zefta looked at Benoit in a combination of astonishment and horror.

"No, no, dear boy. Your steel." He held up a steel coin. "Every participant in a play in which a Knight of Solamnia appears must carry a steel for luck, or disaster will befall us all." He pressed the coin into the pocket of Benoit's costume. "Keep it near at all times," the mage cautioned seriously. "I pray no one else has forgotten!"

Before Benoit could ask more about this strange new superstition, Zefta rushed off to others of the troupe, occasionally pressing a steel into their hands as he went. Most of the actors happily acceded to the mage's request, tucking the coin into a vest pocket, a pouch, or a shoe and matter-of-factly going about their business.

Finally, it was almost time to begin. Sebastius walked about checking costumes, arranging props, and counting actors. Finally, he came to Zefta's customary post. The mage had his feet up and out of boredom had conjured a swarm of butterflies to dance about his toes.

"It would be best if you were to make some effort at concentrating on your duties," warned the troupe's leader.

"My dear Sebastius, I would never do anything but that. I have taken an apprentice as you asked. Despite my prodigious talents, I sit here before the performance practicing my bits so as to make them as perfect as possible."

"I recall no butterflies in this play." Sebastius's face darkened. His right foot began to tap involuntarily as he awaited what would no doubt be an impertinent answer.

" 'Tis a long play, Sebastius, and I merely thought that the soliloquy by Sir Guye is, well, a bit pedantic and that maybe having some butterflies chasing each other about in the clearing would provide some needed distraction."

Sebastius's eyes flashed. He took a deep breath.

"Zefta, we have been through this before. You are not here to grandstand. Just because you have developed more extensive talents does not mean that the nature of the services the troupe requires has changed."

"Certainly you must admit that this play, in particular, warrants some livening up," retorted the mage.

"Butterflies are hardly in keeping with the somber nature of the soliloquy. One must be true to the heart of the play, Zefta, just as one must be true to their own heart."

Zefta unconsciously fingered his tattoo. "Then the pennants, perhaps. The background pennants could be in more lively colors, and as the sun sets and brightens them a breeze could pick up from the east and cause them to flutter so the insignia can been seen."

"Good gracious, man, to make out the insignia the pennants have to stand stiffly in the breeze, not flutter about. You can't have a full-force gale on stage as the man is trying to explain the virtues of truth!"

"Not a gale, just a bit more color and an eastern breeze . . ."

Sebastius sighed heavily. How many times had he had this same discussion?

"Very well, but, mind you, just a breeze . . ."

Neither man had seen Fornarius approach as they conversed. The last they had seen of the groom, he had been berating the jeweler for not polishing the rings properly. Now it was to be their turn.

"I thought I made my instructions about the play quite plain. I understood, Sebastius, that yours was a troupe of professionals who could be depended upon to perform any play in the manner in which it was intended."

"Fornarius, dear sir, no need to be troubling yourself about these minor details. Please, take your seat for the performance. We were just discussing the background of the truth vignette—"

"Mocking it, you mean. Is this the approach you are taking to all of the virtues expressed in the play?"

Zefta had never seen Sebastius put so on the defensive. He stifled a chuckle.

"Mocking? How does a breeze mock anything?"

" 'Tis a vignette on truth by a Knight of rank in the Whitestone Glade on the Island of Sancrist."

Both Zefta and Sebastius stared at Fornarius, uncomprehending. Their benefactor continued, "You are mocking it with colorful pennants and eastern breezes."

"Mocking?" repeated Sebastius.

"Everyone knows that the local dyes on Sancrist are dark, not bright. Worse yet, the breeze on Sancrist comes from the west. It is a prevailing *western* breeze. It is the *truth* on Sancrist, and you mock the truth by making it otherwise."

Despite their differences, Sebastius and Zefta found themselves unified in their desire to appease Fornarius. Sebastius recovered his composure.

"Your mastery of the detail of this complex play is amazing, Fornarius. You are most assuredly right in both substance and manner. Fret no more. The play will be *exactly* as it should be, in each and every detail."

Fornarius's eyes darted to Zefta, daring the mage to disagree. Zefta looked at the ground, merely nodding in agreement.

Fornarius turned and walked away, vendors and contractors ducking for cover as he approached.

"Come, Zefta. The troupe is gathered. It is time to start."

The two men quickly made their way to the gathering point backstage, a hubbub of talk and preparation.

Sebastius's booming voice cut through the backstage chatter, interrupting all of the conversations. "As you know, people," he lectured, "this play, *The Oath and the Measure*, has never in the history of the entire world been performed in its entirety."

He paused for dramatic effect, which was somewhat lessened by Gilf's muttered observation that he thought it was Sebastius's brother who was the history buff.

"Our benefactor, Fornarius, is to wed the lovely Mirinda in a formal Solamnic ceremony close upon the heels of our somewhat extended performing time. Our performance shall reflect directly upon Fornarius's knightly heritage and Solamnic sensibilities. Every action, every detail must complement the wedding ceremony."

Everyone in the troupe nodded curtly and dispersed to take their places for the performance. Sebastius made his way to the stage.

"Ladies and lords, Knights of Solamnia, friends, family, and countrymen of the betrothed, harken to me, your loyal servant, Sebastius. This day's performance is a world premiere of a classic of literary verse and virtuous verisimilitude, *The Oath and the Measure*. While told in the context of a squire's quest to learn the duties and qualities of a Knight of Solamnia, the lessons of truth, honor, justice, courage, chivalry, reflection, sacrifice, and endurance will be imparted to all of you, most especially endurance, though I know from the character of our benefactor, Fornarius, and the legends of Solamnic lore, that you are all well acquainted with honor, truth, and virtue."

Fornarius sat ramrod straight in his chair in the first row of the audience, slightly uneasy. Perhaps it was simply nervous jitters over his imminent nuptials or perhaps Sebastius's emphasis on the word "endurance," or even that he looked straight at Fornarius when he said the word "truth." There would be serious consequences later if this rotund, glib fellow did not deliver the show promised for his fete, but it was out of his hands now. He was relying on others. And he hated that.

Crawford and Benoit stood backstage as Sebastius made his grand introduction. Benoit was sweating profusely, though the day was not hot.

"Don't worry, son. It is a small part."

"N-nothing to fear. I have my steel," responded Benoit.

"Your what?"

"My lucky steel. Don't you have one? Zefta was handing them out."

Crawford shook his head, a perplexed look upon his face. Zefta was generally not among the superstitious segment of the Players. His nose picked up the unmistakable order of dwarven spirits on the young man's breath.

It was too late—the play was upon them. Crawford assumed character and walked onto the stage.

Benoit swallowed hard and really began to sweat.

———◆◆◆———

Unlike Benoit, Fornarius calmed as the play began. Everything was precisely as it should be. The actors delivered their long, metered, and complex lines of dialogue, verse, and instruction flawlessly and with proper solemnity and moral timbre. The crests, heraldry, and costumes appeared rich and authentic to his eye. The stage, a wooden set of alarming simplicity and few embellishments, somehow subtly became the castle keep of the Knights, then the squire's room above the stables, then the king's throne room, then the forests of Sancrist, all with a fullness that was simultaneously breathtaking and entrancing.

For the better part of the first act, all was well from Fornarius's perspective. No coughing, no shifting about in seats, no movement from the audience disturbed the perfection of the performance. In fact, the audience made no sound at all, not a laugh or a sigh or an exclamation of admiration.

To Fornarius, this was as it should be.

To the players, it was frightening. They were used to playing to a receptive audience, to obtaining a reaction of some kind as they performed, to teasing emotions from an audience, supplying encores, and getting ovations.

This audience sat unmoving and silent. It could have been that the quality of the performance was simply such as to strike them mute. Certainly that was the case with Fornarius, who sat rapt, savoring every tedious recitation and overextended lecture. But the play, so long and belabored, so preachy and lecturing in tone, so plotless in exposition, and so structured, orderly, measured, and metered in its words, had bored the audience.

Not simply bored, no, exquisitely and profoundly bored, most especially the assembled Knights of Solamnia, who had endured sufficient lecturing on the virtues during their training to last them an entire lifetime and more.

In a commercial performance, there no doubt would have been attrition, patrons giving up and quietly moving to the exits—first from the back and aisle seats so as to not disturb those who really viewed this primer on virtue as great theatre—but eventually from all quarters as early departures emboldened others. Here, given the fact that the wedding vows and celebration were due to follow, the audience simply sat silent. Trapped.

To their credit, none of audience slept, which would have deeply insulted the performers, who were doing an excellent job of performing the play exactly as written. Instead, they sat with erect posture and folded hands, eyes forward, seeing everything but registering no reaction.

They say that true warriors have a talent for this motionless watching. It certainly is a skill much useful in times of war. A spy or border patrol can wait motionless for hours, ready to swoop down from nothingness in times of turmoil and battle. Honor guards at tombs are similarly trained to remain motionless and silent in their vigil over the honored dead.

Most Solamnic Knights learn the skill of patience and watching in their daily civic virtues class. Although not all in the audience were Knights, their stillness was as infectious as laughter is at a party. The quiet was, as the Knights themselves were known to be, ordered, unhurried, and unsullied by imperfection. A perfect stillness it was but as frightening to the actors as catcalls and boos. It was unnatural.

When his first cue came, Benoit marched stiffly to his spot, eyes forward as befitted a guard, ready to perform his part in the vignette on honesty. Mostly, the job of the Second Guardsman was to stand to the right of the First Guardsman while Crawford, playing Sir Derrick, berated and lectured a servant boy who had been caught stealing magical potions and scrolls. Finally, Benoit heard his speaking cue.

"And what evidence proclaims the guilt of this petty thief?"

Benoit stepped forward stiffly, thrust his hand into his suddenly too small pocket and pulled out the prop scroll as quickly as the tiny pocket allowed.

"We have retrieved the scroll, sir," Benoit boomed out in a stiff monotone. As he spoke he saw a glint shimmering in the air about chest-high several feet before him.

When he pulled out the scroll from the tight pocket, the "lucky steel" Zefta had given him had apparently been carried with it and was flung unfettered into the air. It hung for a moment, spinning at the apogee of its arc before continuing its brisk flight onto the sturdy wooden floor, bouncing noisily away.

"Keep it near you," the horrified Benoit heard Zefta say in his mind as the coin bounded across the stage.

Instinctively, Benoit dove for the offending steel, flinging himself at it with an alacrity and abandon that was totally unexpected to everyone in the audience and on stage—including himself. Sliding across the stage as the coin continued to bounce and skitter downstage and to the right, the adroit Second Guardsman snatched the steel out of the air just past the forward edge of the stage itself, inches from the startled, wide eyes of Fornarius, who was reeling in apoplexy from the sudden disintegration of the perfect performance.

Picking himself up as Fornarius sputtered in shock at both the unscripted action and the clear smell of spirits on the actor, Benoit drew himself back into the formal pose of the Second Guardsman, wavered slightly, marched crookedly back to his place and thrust the coin toward Crawford's unbelieving eyes. Then, fulfilling his duty as an actor to cover his own error, Benoit ad libbed with enthusiastic sincerity, ". . .and a steel!"

The audience, roused now completely from its uncomprehending artistic stupor, howled in laughter, Fornarius excepted.

Crawford swiftly took the coin from Benoit and, to the audience's delight, fingered it across his knuckles before returning it to the Second Guardsman and beginning the next soliloquy, which he now felt the liberty of shortening considerably.

Freed from the constraints of perfection, the players began to play to the audience and feed off its laughter and approval.

Zefta smiled to himself as he watched this unfold. He could no longer be singled out. Everyone was making slight and appreciated alterations to the script. A few murmured magical phrases later and things really began to change—an extra dash of color here, a few extra butterflies there, a breeze strong enough to tousle the hair of Crawford as he launched into yet another modified, yet still pedantic soliloquy.

Zefta lit up with excitement and glee as he concentrated harder on his work. For the first time, he, or at least his magic, could be the star of a performance. He would save this stupefyingly tedious and now imperfect show with a set of tricks so dazzling and imaginative that it—and he—would be the topic of conversation for weeks. All the years, the decades, the centuries of arduous training and practice and repetition of magic, had prepared him for this moment. He now had more confidence and capability than he had ever dreamed possible when first he had joined the players to become a stage mage. Now his illusions were so powerful that they could entrance a vast audience and transport them to places they had never been, to fantasies they would otherwise never hope to imagine. And tonight! Tonight the worlds he created would be beautiful, colorful, fantastic.

"An apprentice," he cackled between fevered magical incantations. "See if an *apprentice* will ever give you effects like these!"

Eyes in the audience focused and chins tilted up as the audience's attention to the play increased. As the colors on stage brightened, so did Zefta's mood and his zest for embellishment. In a matter of minutes, he had clearly gone too far, farther than he had ever really intended, and much beyond his proper role. The vividness of the sets went past reality or even wildest fantasy. The sets overshadowed the actors and became the key element of the performance.

Pennants blew gaily, fluttering noisily in the breeze.

Butterflies, ladybugs, and dragonflies swarmed and wheeled above brightly blossomed wildflowers.

Forest creatures gamboled underfoot, while slick and shiny trout leaped from burbling, white-watered brooks.

Castle fortifications sported reliefs and gargoyles amidst the crenellations.

Room furnishings became busier and ornate.

Zefta's embellishments challenged the actors. The carefully designed blocking of their movements was disrupted by velvet ottomans and flowering bushes; their concentration was broken by the unexpected sights and sounds that they shared with the audience.

To their credit, they adapted—or did their best. Indeed, Zefta's continued magical improvisations spurred the performers on to their own fancies of creativity. The measured meter of the script gave way to animated dialogue, the blocking became more flamboyant, fluid, and unstructured, and the performers began to ad lib with apocalyptic abandon.

Every so often a performer managed to work his own "lucky steel" into the business of the play. One flipped a steel coin absentmindedly while he discussed beauty and truth. Another bit his coin exaggeratedly to test its genuineness when receiving payment for a tankard of ale. Several placed coins on the eyes of their fallen comrades at the denouement of the battle scene. One actor even used his to level an unsteady table, by tucking it under the short table leg in the relatively somber trial scene.

The audience was delighted by it all. They leaned forward in their seats so as not to miss a moment of the action, trying to anticipate the next spectacular setting as well as the next way a steel would be worked into the action, laughing heartily and clapping often. The actors began to enter the stage from the audience, rather than from the wings, engaging non-performers in conversation and revelry along the way. In the dining etiquette vignette on the left sub-stage, one of the actors nudged an audience member and asked him to kindly pass the salt, then tipped him a steel for his "excellent service."

Eventually, the laughter and gaiety infected even Fornarius. The tension of the past few weeks of preparations fell away as, despite himself, he hugged his side with laughter.

By the time Benoit strode forth upon the stage a second time at the close of the play, happiness and contentment reigned both on-stage and off. Rather than mumbling his line in a monotone upstage, the youth marched energetically downstage, thrust out his chest and declaimed: "And so, all being in order, was measured well and proper." Bringing forth his coin, he added with a broad, drink-induced wink at the crowd, "For honor is real, which is tested with steel." With a curt nod, he tossed the coin to Fornarius in the front row. Stiffly, the groom stood, holding it up for all to see.

The audience roared its approval, cheering and applauding wildly for the players. The standing ovation lasted for more than three minutes, with some standing on their widely spaced chairs.

Fornarius, himself, was conflicted. The comedy and gaiety of the play had penetrated his brusque and formal exterior and enlivened his soul, but it had also shone a bright lantern on the secrets of his past.

"The only steel I wield," he whispered amidst the tumultuous ovation, "is coinage."

The wedding went forward in the boisterous spirit of the last acts of the play. Miranda, radiant and gay, was invigorated even more than usual by the energetic levity of the players' performance and delighted by the tentative smile on Fornarius's usually stern face.

Fornarius pulled his bride aside before the Vows of Binding could begin, a flutter of panic showing on his usually controlled countenance. Miranda shushed him with an embrace.

"Love is always honorable," she whispered. "Nothing else matters."

Holding hands, the couple ran up to the cleric for the formal words of binding, all of which went unnoticed amidst the smiles and looks of love between the two betrothed. When, in his excitement and the wonder of the moment, Fornarius confused the rings—he was supposed to hand Mirinda's to the cleric for blessing—no one noticed, except for the cleric, who grinned and switched the rings back as all eyes were closed in meditation.

When the cleric announced the wedding couple joined, Fornarius grabbed the lithe Mirinda and swept her back into an arching kiss, passionate and honest and not at all ordered or measured or proper. And, being a fine and observant actor, Crawford took his cue and mimicked Fornarius's flamboyant embrace backstage, sweeping Gilf back for a kiss that would have been the stuff of girlish dreams, had Gilf been a girl and not sputtering in apoplexy at his treatment by the elder actor.

Applause, more thunderous even than that which ended the performance, erupted from friends, family, Knights, and colleagues, as well as the onlooking players of the troupe. As the orchestra struck up an energetic and sprightly tune, Fornarius and Mirinda took their first steps together as husband and wife, stepping lightly toward the food and wine of the post-ceremony festivities of their perfect wedding. As they did, the guests spontaneously reached into to their pockets, purses, and pouches . . .

. . . and showered their path with steels.

<hr>

Zefta left the players as the festivities rollicked from afternoon toward evening, his black tattoo fading from his arm forever as the light faded on the wedding day feast. He knew now that his reasons for joining the troupe had long ago been satisfied. It was time to show his magic and his imagination to the world, to live the life he had always sought but had been afraid to embrace.

He reached into the air, plucked a steel coin from nothingness, flipped it merrily, and relaxing his concentration, let it fade back to nothingness.

Fornarius broke away from the dancing for a few moments to find Sebastius cozying up to yet another fine ale, as the twilight dwindled behind the forested hillside overlooking the wedding celebration. Opening his pouch, he deposited a generous payment on the bench next to the relaxing fat man, without waiting for an invoice. Fornarius smiled and nodded to Sebastius in salutation.

"An unusual performance."

"I should not be taking any payment, sir, especially not such an ample one. You sought perfection, and my band of players failed to deliver it to you."

"Sometimes," mused Fornarius, as he gazed contentedly toward the revelry of the feast, "perfection is not about order and structure, or even truth. It is about recognizing and enjoying all that you have."

" 'Tis also the case," agreed the large man, "that the central theme of a wedding is not perfection. It is joy."

Fornarius smiled tentatively in agreement.

"Yet your joy seems tempered," observed Sebastius.

Fornarius opened his mouth to speak then closed it again.

"Even the best actors can become stale in their roles. How long have you played at being a retired Knight?"

Fornarius flushed deep red. His eyes widened then darted about, finally settling upon the ground.

"I did not mean to deceive Mirinda. It began years ago, when I first arrived at Wyldetree. Villagers can be finicky, even suspicious, about doing serious business with outsiders, but everyone knows you can trust a Knight of Solamnia to deal honestly—even a retired one. It was good for business."

"Ah, yes. Money does fuel the arts."

"Besides," continued Fornarius in a plaintive rush of words to justify his behavior, "I adore all things Solamnic. I am sure I could have become a Knight if I tried."

Sebastius sat quietly, catching the glimmer of the evening's first stars.

"Still, I must find a way to tell Mirinda."

"Pah," snorted Sebastius. "The audience always knows more than you suppose. You have a new role and a new outlook. Perform those well, and happiness will be with you."

As Fornarius turned back to rejoin the dancing, muffled laughter drifted toward the pair from the wagon newly occupied by Darna and Benoit, along with the jingle of a steel coin falling to the floor of the wagon.

Inside the wagon, Benoit looked in startlement at the steel coin that had fallen from his costume pocket.

"But how . . .?"

A Matter
of Honor

Richard A. Knaak

In and near the town of Brumen,
located on a peninsula in the northwest part of Ansalon

Thirteen years after the War of the Lance

Have at you, monster!"

As the armored figure charged him, Golar did his best
to make the man look like a competent swordsman, in
spite of his out of control swings. With his great war
axe, the ruddy brown minotaur could have easily cloven
the man in two, but Golar deliberately counterattacked
high over the head of the smaller human.

"This ends here and now," Heston snarled, overdoing
his show of anger. "No more will you threaten this land!"

"And will you be the one to stop me?" Golar rumbled.

"I will be . . . with the aid of the Sword of Hope!"

The two battled back and forth across the wooden platform. A cheer went up as Heston lunged and nearly ran
the shaggy minotaur through. The crowds always cheered
when they thought Golar was about to be vanquished.

Golar was playing the evil Pretor, a dishonorable pirate captain who preyed on the peaceful villagers of the southern reaches of the continent of Ansalon. The Traveling Players of Gilean were performing in a small town on the northwestern peninsula that had likely never before played host to any member of the minotaur race, and certainly knew nothing about their great history and culture. The citizens of this small town knew only one minotaur—the villain presently on stage.

Golar liked to think that it was his great acting ability that made the audience despise his character, although some humans feared his kind on general principle. When townsfolk noticed him in the troupe, they tended to edge away or reach for their weapons, but once they saw him act on stage, they treated him with respect, even, occasionally, with friendliness. Because of this, Golar pictured himself as an ambassador of sorts for his kind.

Heston stumbled, nearly running the minotaur through again, this time by sheer accident. Knowing that they were well in advance of the climactic death scene, Golar nimbly stepped aside to avoid the blade, turning toward the audience as he did.

Standing far beyond the crowd, clad in a voluminous travel cloak that disguised the wearer's identity, appeared the same watcher from the last two places the troupe had stopped. Golar knew then that he had finally been tracked down.

A gasp from the crowd, combined with a strong pressure to his abdomen, surprised the massive warrior. The minotaur looked down and saw his foe's sword tip, piercing his torso . . . and immediately he slumped to his knees. The great war axe fell by his side.

"You are undone!" Heston shouted. "Undone, Pretor!"

Golar put his hand over the spot where the blade had penetrated. He wove back and forth slightly, trying to recall his next line. Glancing out beyond the crowd, the minotaur noticed that the cloaked figure had suddenly vanished.

"You've slain me," he finally managed to rumble to Heston. "I scarce believe it. This is the end of me. . . . "

Golar fell over, sprawling across the stage.

He paid scant attention to Heston's grand speech, the epilogue of the play. Golar's mind was fixed only on the cloaked figure he had seen three times now— the one following him.

A booted foot prodded the prone minotaur. "Play's over, Golar," Heston whispered. "Time for the bows."

Grunting, the minotaur rose. Alongside Heston and the other members of the troupe, he took his bows, receiving a fair amount of applause from the beings who had just cheered his demise. Humans were a curious sort, but here in their midst Golar could at least pretend to be something he was not. Among his own people . . .

The head of the troupe came out to take his bow. Jovial Sebastius marched out in his finest robe, arms outstretched as if he sought to embrace everyone present. He made a point of congratulating Heston and Golar, then hugged a few of the others. After that, Sebastius stepped up to the edge of the stage.

"Thank you, my friends, for your deep appreciation of our little show! We will be here for one more night, this time with a tale of love and comedy! I hope you'll join us again! Thank you for coming!"

As the crowd dispersed, many talking excitedly about the various highlights of the play, Sebastius turned to his actors and, in a lower tone of voice, murmured rather absently, "Hopefully we'll all remember our lines tomorrow, eh, Golar?"

The minotaur did not reply immediately. He was thinking about what the rotund Sebastius had just announced. The Traveling Players of Gilean would be here for yet another night. That meant another chance for Golar to be confronted by the hooded figure.

"Golar? Are you listening to me?"

"I'm sorry, Sebastius. . . . I'll remember my lines next time, I promise."

The balding man's brow furrowed for a moment, then Sebastius shrugged.

"Well, as you're not actually in the next play, it probably doesn't matter." He turned to one of the other actors, seemingly dismissing the minotaur from his presence. "Twayne! I want to speak to you about certain rewrites I've done for your part! A new refinement of your role, if I do say so."

As the troupe's master hurried away, the minotaur inspected his abdomen where Heston had accidentally wounded him. No blood flowed; no mark existed. He had known that it would be so.

"I'm sorry about that," Heston said, joining Golar as the latter left the stage. "I'll be more careful next time."

"Doesn't matter, though, does it? Not like it did me any harm."

The younger human smiled grimly. With his jet-black hair and well-groomed mustache, Heston looked like the sort of hero he often played on stage. Unfortunately, in real life he had been anything but a hero, having spent many years as a lowly steward in a great man's house—until he had fallen in love with his master's beautiful daughter and left her with child. Fearing what her father would do to him when he discovered the responsible party, Heston had run away . . . and found a new home in the troupe shortly after. Now, three years later, he still felt guilty about everything—especially leaving his beloved to face her disgrace, alone.

Once Golar would have found his story revolting, but over the twelve years he had spent with the players, he had learned much about human frailties. He had learned much about his own.

"This town is supposed to have a good tavern," Heston commented, cheerfully changing to one of his favorite subjects. "Judging by the applause you drew, the patrons would probably buy even you a round or two. What do you say to that, Golar?"

The two often searched out the local taverns and inns, sampling the brews. They never imbibed too much. One thing Sebastius did not condone was an actor who could not recall his lines because he had been too deep in his cups the night before. While the master never explicitly said such activity would spell ouster from the troupe, the threat was implied, and Golar, who found life as an actor most fulfilling, usually watched his drink.

His thoughts turned again to the mysterious watcher. If the figure was watching him, then perhaps he should avoid the taverns.

"I'll stay by the wagons tonight, Heston. You go on."

"Not much sense on going if you're not coming with," Heston muttered in genuine disappointment.

While Heston's good looks always attracted the women in taverns, Golar knew that his companion's heart would always belong to the disgraced lady he left behind. Heston did not even look at another woman, even though some of his prettiest fellow players, playing those parts, dropped hints his way, through the years.

With a disgusted snort that he hoped was convincing, the minotaur turned away. "Don't depend on me for your merriment, human! I'm not leaving the encampment tonight and that's that!"

He marched off to his own wagon, without even glancing over his shoulder at the human. Golar did not care if Heston thought him angry or arrogant, as long as he did not realize the truth.

For the first time in years, the minotaur was afraid.

<hr>

I am afraid, the hooded watcher thought as he skirted the people and the wagons. *I should not be, but I am! It makes no sense!*

Night had come and with it more ease of movement. Some of the townsfolk noticed his presence, but perhaps assumed he was part of the troupe. Karas did not care what the humans of this town thought of him, so long as they did not interfere. He had a mission to fulfill, a mission on which he had spent several long years of his life—since first he had reached adulthood.

Karas pulled back the hood of his cloak, revealing the horned head and bovine snout of a minotaur warrior. In the dark, his tawny fur gave him a pale, ghostly look—very unlike the one he sought.

"It had to be Golar," Karas muttered to himself. "It had to be!" Yet, the Golar he had been searching for should have been older by now, graying, even stooped. The minotaur on stage had seemed in the prime of life, though, only a few years older than Karas himself . . . but how could that be if it was Golar?

There remained only one method of verification. Karas had to get close enough to see his face, to identify him for certain. From a distance, it had been impossible to tell whether or not the actor carried the birthmark of Golar. Up close, Karas would be able to see . . . then he could deal with the situation as warranted.

From within his cloak the young fighter drew a long sword and fingered it warily, reassuringly. While many minotaurs preferred to wield a war axe, Karas had found this blade to be good company and manageable in a sudden fight. Thirteen years might have passed since the War of the Lance, but the other races still recalled that most minotaurs had served as soldiers of the Dark Queen and Emperor Ariakas. Never mind that the minotaurs had been slaves and puppets; to many, Karas's people were as guilty as the Dragon Highlords.

Precious minutes passed, and still the one he suspected to be Golar did not leave the safety of the encampment. Karas grew impatient but couldn't just charge in and confront the whole troupe. Even if Karas fought well, the struggle would alert the humans of the town—who, undoubtedly grateful for the entertainment they had just enjoyed, would come to the aid of the actors. The young warrior did not fear the whole town, but if he was captured or slain, he would be unable to send word to the clan that he had succeeded—that the stain had been lifted at last.

More time passed, and still his quarry did not appear. Karas silently cursed. Virtually every other player had left the camp. Even the mustachioed human that Golar had been speaking with earlier had gone out. Yet, where was the minotaur actor?

That settled one issue. Karas had been seen. Despite his precautions, despite having stepped out of hiding only briefly, to scrutinize the face of the minotaur on stage, Karas had evidently been spotted by Golar. No other explanation sufficed.

That made his task trickier now. With his adversary on the alert, Karas might have to wait weeks, months, before he managed to find him alone and confront him. Oh, to be so close . . .

"I've waited this long, though," Karas quietly rumbled, chiding himself for losing heart. "And the clan's waited even longer! We'll see justice done! If you are Golar, you'll yet pay, so I've sworn on my very life! By Sargas, Lord of Vengeance, honor will be restored, even if it means my own sacrifice!"

Only the low moan of the wind responded to his murmured words. Calming himself, the tawny minotaur settled back down to wait. Sword in hand, he watched the camp, and waited.

He wondered how even Golar had sunk so low as to become an actor.

"No, no!" Sebastius pointed low to the ground. "The ballroom curtains must reach all the way down! All the way!"

As Golar struggled with the ragged sheets, part of the minimal set for the evening's play, he wished for the hundredth time that the master of the troupe would invest in proper equipment. The sheets were supposed to represent the golden, silky curtains of a royal house; a rickety wood frame formed the walls from which they hung. Surely Sebastius could have done better, and yet, come tonight, the minotaur knew, the crowd would see an elegant palace, for the elaborate ballroom scene. What amazed Golar more was that he himself would experience its splendor. A magic surrounded the Traveling Players of Gilean, one that not only turned rags into silk, but actors into heroes. . . .

Heroes . . . ?

"Golar? Can you help me with this scenery?" one of the female troupe members asked sweetly. "I can't reach high enough."

"Coming, Dardella." The minotaur helped the young, raven-tressed woman trying to tie faded ribbons on some tree branches. Dardella was lithe and lovely and never seemed to mind his own fearsome appearance. The troupe treated all races the same. The play was the thing, after all, and everything else unimportant.

With no part in the coming production, the minotaur spent much of his day working hard to help the others prepare for it. Besides helping with the background scenery, he made certain that the stage itself was strong enough to withstand the big wedding scene near the end of the play. Sebastius did not always use stages—or much scenery—but recently he had grown fond of high platforms, so that even those standing in the back of large audiences could see the actors clearly. Unfortunately, these high platforms often creaked when someone as heavy as Golar walked upon them. With more than a dozen actors in the wedding scene, the minotaur had to make certain the posts and supports were firm.

He sat with Heston during the afternoon meal. The young, mustachioed human had been chosen by Sebastius to play the lead, a man who, after a long journey and several trials, comes back to marry the woman of his dreams, despite the ill will of her rich father. Although Heston swore that he had never told Sebastius about his shameful past, he couldn't help but find his role uncomfortably close to his own life story. He had a case of the nerves.

"I don't know if I can do this, Golar. Each time I read the lines, I think of you know who. I've spent these past few years trying to decide whether or not I should return and face her and her family, but—have you ever known what was the right thing to do, yet still feared to do it?"

"Do you fear that her father will kill you—or have you arrested?"

Heston considered this question. "Actually . . . these days I think I fear more her opinion of me and what I failed to do . . . "

Golar grunted, and went back to his meal. He would never entirely understand the behavior and thinking of humans.

The play went on, as planned.

Sebastius promised the audience a wonderful treat—a promise he rarely failed to deliver. Despite his earlier misgivings, Heston threw himself into his role, so much so that Golar actually found himself in complete sympathy with the character. The ballroom set, of course, overwhelmed the onlookers; it looked every bit as majestic as the play demanded. No one saw rags and ribbons; a domicile of kings lay before the enchanted spectators.

As the wedding scene neared, the minotaur thought to peer out at the audience from behind the wagons. This night he had seen no sign of the immense, hooded figure. Had he been wrong to worry? Had the stranger some other business; or perhaps he was simply a traveling pilgrim, whose route had taken him along the same road as the troupe for a time. That seemed likely, on such a peaceful night.

By the climax of the play, in which Heston convinced the heroine's father to accept both him and the marriage, Golar had once again become caught up. He wondered if it might be possible to convince Sebastius to rewrite the play a bit, so that Golar might have a small scene in it, the next time. The master rewrote all the time; surely he could make a place for the minotaur. . . .

The play was over. The audience clapped and clapped. The players took bow after deserved bow. Tonight had been Heston's finest performance yet.

The human actor evidently thought the same, for he came over to the massive minotaur a few minutes after the last ovation, flush with pride. "Did you see me out there, Golar? I don't know when I've felt this confident! Did you see my performance?"

"I did. You performed exceptionally well, human."

Heston's eyes grew brighter. "You know what? I fell so deep into the role, I imagined facing up to old Draclyn himself, telling him that his daughter and I were meant to be together forever—no matter what he might do to me! I imagined her in the audience, Golar, listening to me! Imagined her watching and smiling, all forgiveness and love as she drank in the words I meant for her long ago!" He sobered slightly. "But, of course, that's silly, isn't it? I just wanted to believe that . . . "

"You were good just the same—" the minotaur began.

"Listen, Golar!!" Heston fairly shouted. He waved the previous matter away. "Tonight I definitely need a good drink . . . or two . . . and I need a drinking partner! Please come!"

His first inclination was to say no, but Golar hadn't seen any mysterious watcher tonight, and he relaxed his guard. If there was one thing Golar—any minotaur— enjoyed, it was drinking a few . . . after a hard day, and all that needless worrying.

"All right, human," he rumbled good-humoredly. "We'll go. I could use some distraction myself." The minotaur paused, a notion occurring to him. "But first, I need to take care of something in my wagon. Wait here. It'll only take a moment. . . . "

———◆———

Karas saw his opportunity. He needed a moment, a single moment, in order to achieve the completion of his oath-sworn quest. If the other minotaur would just step into the open, away from the wagons and his companion, then Karas could act.

How many warriors had failed to find Golar over the years? How many had never returned home, loath to let their kin know that they had not lived up to their blood oaths? Like those who came before him, Karas had to return with proof of Golar's death or . . .

He touched the hilt of the dagger at his waist. Karas would not return to the clan empty-handed. He would be shamed, like the others.

Today he had avoided showing himself at the play in the hopes that his quarry would relax and dare to move about beyond the wagons. Then darkness had nearly fallen, and still there was no sign of the one he pursued. He had nearly decided to abandon his watch for the night, when suddenly the human actor stepped into sight. The player looked impatient to be somewhere, but clearly awaited someone else. The young warrior's hopes rose a little.

And a few minutes later, when an unmistakable figure joined the man, Karas's heart beat faster, and his hand immediately drifted toward the hilt of his sword. Golar at last!

The two players clearly were heading into town to find a place to drink. Karas considered rushing to block their path, but then other members of the troupe appeared. Cursing silently, the hunter pulled behind a tree and watched as the actors talked amongst themselves.

Their conversation seemed to go on for an eternity, but at last the pair separated from the rest and journeyed on. By then Karas had decided to follow them silently, at a distance. Too many folk were still wandering around. Better to hold off any confrontation until later, after the activity had died down. In a town this small, they couldn't go far. After so long a pursuit, Karas could wait a couple more hours, knowing that this evening he would rectify a dishonor to his clan more than a decade old.

"Enjoy your merriment this evening, Golar," the minotaur warrior murmured. "for tonight this matter of honor between you and the rest of the clan will finally be settled."

———◆◆◆———

"I'd just like it settled, once and for all," Heston muttered. "If I knew that she never wants to look at me again, if I knew that she hated my guts, I could live with that . . . I guess. It's wondering about her that does me in. You know what I mean, Golar?"

The shaggy minotaur poured some more ale for his companion, hoping to drown his incessant sorrows, but to no avail. The human had been going on and on about his lost love. He scarcely noticed that the minotaur had tuned out his guilt-ridden talk. Golar was busy emptying mug after mug of his own, drinking more than Heston, thinking how the taste paled compared to he had been used to back home. How he missed the taste of Mithian Blood Ale, especially . . .

Although the minotaur's presence had cowed him, the innkeeper steeled himself to approach the pair and say, "Forgive me, players! After the performances you two put on—and very good ones, I might add—I hate to sound anxious, but it is late—"

"And you must return to your dear wife!" Heston burst out resentfully. He shook his head in overdone regret. "Well, my friend," he said, turning to Golar, "surely we cannot keep this poor soul from his happiness, even if we know not how to find ours."

"Suppose not," Golar grunted. He downed the last of his drink then dropped the mug on the table with a loud bang.

"Gods, Golar! You'll be owing this kind man a new table if you do that again! Hurry up and pay him now, and let's go back! Sebastius is probably waiting to chew us out!"

"It's all right! It's all right!" the anxious owner returned. "Please, consider that last round on me! May you have a pleasant journey tomorrow!"

The players would be heading toward the large town of Brumen to the southeast. A journey of some three days. Sebastius hoped to spend nearly a week in the area. The minotaur looked forward to the move; bigger towns meant bigger crowds and better roles.

Despite the innkeeper's offer, Golar tossed the necessary coins on the table. He accepted charity from no one. With Heston leading the way, the minotaur departed into the night.

"Aaah, another fruitless evening, eh, my friend?" his human companion asked, as they walked along the darkened street.

"How many drinks do you think we had, Heston?"

"Apparently not enough. I still feel as sober as a rock. And you?"

"No better. I think they water the ale here—"

The sound of running feet suddenly pushed away all thought of drink from the minotaur's mind. He reached for his axe, then recalled with a grimace that he had left his weapon back in the wagon. Golar went for his dagger instead, but Heston placed his own hand on the minotaur's, restraining his fellow player.

"Easy! It's only a boy! Looks like he wants to tell us something."

Sure enough, a young human, perhaps twelve summers at most, ran toward them, oil lantern in one hand and folded scrap of parchment in the other. Pausing just before the pair, he took a minute to catch his breath, then, with a nervous glance at Golar, faced the mustachioed man. "Be you the one they call Heston?"

"That's me, my lad! The self-same Heston, worthy of the stage! You're up a little late! What can I do for you?"

"Was told to give you this." The boy handed him the parchment, which had been tied up with a string.

"What is it?"

"Dunno, sir. Just been told to bring it to you. You're supposed to know what to do after you read it."

"Aaah, a mystery!" Heston untied the string. Unfolding the parchment, he held the message up to the lantern. Golar peered in mild curiosity, but could not make out the words. It hardly mattered, anyway. Most likely one of the good ladies of the town had taken a fancy to the dashing hero of the play and now sought a rendezvous. It had happened before, many, many times.

An abrupt change came over his companion. Heston's expression grew slack. He stared at the messenger as if the boy had just turned into Takhisis. Golar reached for the note, but Heston shook his head and stuffed the parchment into a pouch.

"This is for me alone, friend." Heston eyed the boy. "How long ago did you receive this?"

"Only a few minutes, sir."

The man nodded. "Take me there!"

"Aye, sir!"

The minotaur put a heavy hand on his companion's shoulder. "Where? What goes on, Heston? Do you need my aid?"

Again the mustachioed player shook his head. "No, no, my friend, this is something I must deal with on my own. Can you make it back to the wagons?"

Golar snorted. "I can hold my drink, human!"

"Then I'll bid you farewell now! I really must be going!" He turned to the youth. "Lead on, boy!"

The minotaur watched as Heston followed the young messenger into the darkness. He considered shadowing his friend, but then decided that, surely, Heston faced little threat in this peaceful town. Yes, likely a maiden had watched the stage hero in action and had swooned. It would not have been the first time.

Golar started back to the wagons. He looked forward to sleep after so many mugs of ale. Besides, with the wagons on the move tomorrow, he would need all the strength he could recover—

Suddenly he became aware of a furtive movement near the building to his right. As he reached for his dagger, a cloaked shape detached itself from the darkness there. At first the minotaur wondered if some messenger of the dead had come for him, but then, even in the dim light of the single moon shining tonight, Golar could make out the protruding shape of a sword sheath, the clink of metal against metal, the markings of a warrior.

"Golaritimoni de-Barash . . . " a voice from within the cloak uttered. "Golar the God-marked . . . "

Despite the urge to turn and run, Golar stood his ground. He had been so preoccupied all day, he had forgotten all about the watcher. For so many years he had half-expected this moment, but today he had deluded himself into thinking the watcher had been a figment of his mind, and he had forgotten to be alert.

"My name's not Golar," he returned, desperately trying to stave off recognition. "I'm Broka of clan Teseri."

An accusing hand—a minotaur hand—thrust forward from the confines of the robe. "No! You are Golar! I know this even though you look too young! You are Golar the God-marked!"

"God-marked?" Golar snorted. "The only deity who's marked me is the one of drunkenness, young warrior!"

"On the left of your muzzle! The crescent-moon birth mark that—" The shadowy hunter paused as Golar turned to show him that side—and the lack of any birthmark whatsoever.

"You've got the wrong one, hunter. I'm just a wanderer. I've not seen or heard of this Golar the Pockmarked, in this area!"

"I was so sure!" The newcomer stepped closer, removing his hood.

Golar had to bite back his shock. He knew that face, or rather, he knew a very similar face. Even in the darkness, he could recognize the features of his cousin, Juris. Juris would be older and grayer now . . . but Juris had also bore a healthy legion of children, most of whom resembled him more than his mate.

"No birthmark . . . " the cloaked minotaur warrior muttered, half to himself. He peered closely at Golar's muzzle. "No, none at all . . . " He reached up as if to touch where the birthmark should be.

Golar flinched. The reaching fingers threatened to

undo his trick. The minotaur had used the artful tricks of the stage to cover up the tell-tale crescent. It had always been conspicuous, a black slice down the side of his muzzle. People used to say that such a mark predicted greatness and leadership. Instead, it had portended dishonor—the ultimate crime among minotaurs.

Golar tried to push the hand back, but it was too late. The other warrior had noticed his reaction and rubbed the spot.

"Actor's paint and false hair!" the minotaur warrior rumbled angrily. "You hide the truth under a disguise! You are Golar!"

The cloaked minotaur leapt back and drew his sword. Golar tried to step past him, but the warrior blocked his way.

"Move, young one! I've no quarrel with you!"

"I've one with you, Golar! I am Karas of clan Barash, your own clan, and I come to right the wrong you've done to all of us!"

"I don't know what you mean!"

"The shame of more than a decade!" Karas snarled. "A dishonor haunting us since the last days of the war, Golar! Surely your memory hasn't failed!"

Golar tried one last bluff. "The war? That would mean at least twelve to thirteen years ago! Look at me, Karas of clan Barash! I'm scarcely older than you! I can't have seen much action in the war! I wouldn't have even been quite an adult then!"

Karas faltered, if only for a moment. "More of your stage tricks, then! You might look young, but you talk old and that mark shows who you really are! Besides, the more we speak with one another, the more I recall you myself . . . for we met more than once when I was a child!"

He spoke the truth there. Golar recalled having met this young minotaur warrior, Karas, when visiting with

Juris's family. The sixth of his cousin's children and the fourth-born of the males. A bright, eager child whom Golar himself had predicted would some day make a brilliant and dedicated commander.

"You're still mistaken," Golar insisted, but he knew that Karas had convinced himself, and so he was finally trapped.

"I know you, cousin! Now face up to the shame and dishonor you've brought upon our kin! Face justice, coward!"

"Justice?" rumbled the older minotaur, no longer able to hold back the words he had wanted to say in his defense for so very long. "I see no justice, just a child doing the will of a bunch of stiffbacks!"

"And I don't see a warrior—but a spineless coward who fled from his comrades in battle, leaving them to their deaths!"

Golar forced himself to stay calm. He could feel his rage rising. If he did not keep himself under control, they would come to blows there and then . . . precisely what the younger minotaur wanted.

"I don't hear any denial, cousin!" Karas edged closer. "Were you or were you not part of the legion at Crosspoint? Wasn't your unit supposed to hold back the Ergothians at all cost, borrow time for the Dragon Highlord to move his cavalry into the fray?"

In his mind, Golar again saw the two massive forces converging on one another—the shiny armor of the Ergothians sweeping against the darker colors of Takhisis's warlords. Golar's legion had been sent to a volatile region of the front, a place where the battle would surely be the worst, the bloodiest.

The Dragon Highlord had preached the necessity of giving no ground. He said each warrior had the blessing of the Dark Queen. This last had not impressed the minotaurs much; they were soldiers, whose loyalty had been bought with blood. They served and served well, but the cause had never been their own . . .

"You were not there," Golar hissed to Karas. "You were not there!"

The other minotaur stood snout-to-snout with him. "Are you saying that you did not abandon your comrades at the height of battle, fleeing before the eyes of many?"

Golar's heart beat madly. The remembered cries of war rang through his mind. He saw the charging warhorses of the Ergothians, recalled the great lances skewering warriors right and left, pictured the armored figure atop one animal hurtling down upon him, swinging a sharp and gleaming blade.

"Let me pass!" he suddenly snarled.

"No! You'll stand and fight! You must! If you refuse to defend your honor here, then come back with me and meet a proper death in the arena! Erase the shame you've brought upon our clan!"

Karas reached for Golar, but the older minotaur reacted quickly, seizing his attacker by the wrist and twisting him around. Golar smashed his heavy fist into the warrior's jaw.

Karas's sword dropped. He teetered. Golar struck him again, driving his fist into the stomach. As his adversary doubled in pain, the minotaur unleashed a final blow to the back of his head.

Karas sprawled on the street, unconscious.

Golar eyed his fallen foe. Quickly deciding, he took Karas's sword and replaced it in the sheath. Then, with surprising gentleness he lifted the minotaur warrior over his shoulder. Golar surveyed the area, then hurried off with his heavy burden.

He found a safe place in the woods south of town. No one would find Karas here. Golar considered tying him up, but he felt certain that the warrior would stay unconscious until the troupe was gone. Then perhaps the young fool would rethink his quest.

His task completed, Golar hurried away from the scene and hurried back to the wagons of the theatre troupe. The darkened wagons were a welcome sight. For a long time they had been his home. Golar quietly wended his way to the wagon where he slept.

"A late night, my friend?"

Sebastius, a lantern in one hand, suddenly materialized to block his path, his posture and manner far too innocent.

"No later than some," Golar tersely replied. "Have you seen Heston, by the way?"

"As you and he departed together, I assume that you would know better than I do, where he might be now."

"He went ahead of me. He had another engagement."

"Well, so long as it doesn't affect his performance tomorrow," shrugged the rotund master of the troupe. "I'm sure he'll turn up soon enough—or not, as the case may be. In the meantime, let us talk about you. You look as if you've had an interesting evening."

"What do you mean by that?"

Sebastius looked startled by his suddenly vehement tone. "I am merely concerned about your well-being, Golar. That is all."

The massive minotaur turned away, reminding himself to be careful with the master. Who knows what he might accidentally blurt out? "Nothing happened tonight. Everything's fine . . . just fine."

"Well, make certain that you get enough sleep," the troupe master called after him. "Weariness affects your stage skills." As the minotaur disappeared, the master muttered under his breath, "So does surliness."

Golar's only reply was a deep grunt. For one of the few times in over a decade, he wasn't thinking about his responsibility to the group. Instead, the memories of a day in the distant past swept across his mind like a relentlessly advancing army.

The minotaurs had fought with resolve that day. Their foes died in droves but there seemed an eternal number of them. Archers far out of their range rained death upon the beastmen. Golar saw friend after friend of his perish by arrow, lance, or sword. He had fought in many battles but with each passing second, his own death seemed to be inevitable—and for what would he be dying? Defending something that had not been worth defending in the first place, for a Dragon Highlord who had already fled the battlefield? There was no honor in the battle. Better that he should flee and live to fight another day . . . those were the strange, dishonorable thoughts running through his head.

So Golar had backed away from the crumbling line, knowing that he could never rally his comrades to retreat. He had backed away, at first pretending the need to bind a wound, but then the minotaur had turned around . . . and ran, and kept running.

He didn't stop until he had encountered the Traveling Players of Gilean. At first he had joined the troupe in order to hide among them, but then Golar had come to appreciate and enjoy his new way of life. In fact, he had grown proud of being an actor. He felt as though he was an ambassador for his misunderstood people. Disgraced by their part in the War of the Lance, the minotaurs were more than ever shunned. Golar no longer thought of what he had done with any shame; he had rebuilt his life, and was helping in a small way to rebuild the world.

Of course, the old traditions died hard, and few mino-taurs would see things his way . . . as Karas's appearance had reminded him.

"He won't return," the ruddy brown minotaur mut-tered to himself, rubbing his upper left arm. "He wouldn't dare!" Golar continued to absently rub the spot as he neared his wagon. There on his arm was where Sebastius had etched the mark of the troupe—a black lotus tattoo. All the players wore the symbol, even the master himself. The Traveling Players of Gilean was the minotaur's true clan now, and he bore its emblem with pride, however odd that would have seemed to one of his own race.

Climbing up into the wagon, Golar threw himself onto his bed and immediately fell asleep. However, he did not sleep his normally peaceful slumber. Instead he dreamed variations of the old dreams he had first suffered after he deserted his comrades. He saw his friends dying over and over in his dreams, but each now wore the accusing face of Karas. Golar struggled to wake himself, but the dreams gripped him. The bloody scenes repeated again and again, seemingly all night long.

A hard banging against his door jarred the minotaur from his troubled sleep. At first he thought that it was Karas coming for his retribution, but the muffled voice outside the door was familiar.

Lighting a lamp, he swung open the door to find Heston standing in the dark, a drawn look on his face.

"What sort of madness are you about, human? If—"

"I'm leaving!" the mustachioed player gasped. "I'm leaving, Golar!"

"You're not making any sense!" the half-asleep mino-taur rumbled. "In the middle of the night? Where do you think you're going! Sebastius won't like being awakened by your foolishness!"

Heston rolled up the sleeve of his left arm, the turned so that the other could see the bareness of his limb. "He already knows."

Holding the lamp close, Golar snorted in astonishment.

Heston's black lotus tattoo had disappeared.

Only those who left The Traveling Players of Gilean lost their telltale mark. And not many chose to depart. In a dozen years, Golar had only witnessed it two, maybe three times.

"I've just come from him, Golar! I told him everything, told him that I needed to leave. He knew it was time, he said, and shook my hand. Then when I looked, the tattoo was gone!"

"Why're you leaving, though?" Heston's imminent departure stunned Golar more than he dared admit. For many months Heston had passed for the nearest thing to his comrade . . . his friend.

"Because of her . . . " The man glanced over his shoulder. Looking past his companion, Golar made out the vague shape of a rider atop one of a waiting pair of horses. A woman with long hair . . . and a squirming form half-wrapped in her travel cloak.

"She was in the audience, just like I imagined she would be one day," Heston went on. "She came to look for me, to show me the . . . my girl." His head slumped. "I'm not worthy of her, Golar, but she insists on having me back. She has searched and found me. She even gave her father an ultimatum—and now we will return to face him."

The minotaur snorted softly. He could not blame the human for wanting to set things right. Heston had talked about it so often, during all the time they spent together.

"You'd best get going, then. From what you've told me, you've got quite a journey ahead of you."

"But I wanted to say goodbye to you." The former actor extended a hand. "And wish you the best in everything."

As Heston shook his hand, Golar realized that all this time, as he had listened to the human's repeated tale of woe, he had never trusted Heston with the truth about his own background

"Travel well, Heston. Live well."

The mustachioed human smiled briefly, then hurried off toward his beloved. Golar watched the shadowy figures turn their horses, then with a last wave from Heston, the family rode off.

Golar closed the door and returned to his bed. He sincerely wished his friend all the luck in the world. Unlike the minotaur, Heston had never truly been happy with the troupe. Oh, he had enjoyed himself, to be sure, but remorselessly the past had tugged at him. That wasn't at all the case with Golar, who felt absolutely at home in the Traveling Players . . . and would never leave the troupe, even under threat of an oathbound young warrior.

Karas would have preferred to return home, but sadly that option was not available to him. As the young warrior rubbed his chin and struggled to his feet, he knew that he had no choice but to continue his oathbound pursuit of the coward, Golar.

Trust someone like Golar to resort to tricks in defending himself. Karas hadn't expected the older minotaur to strike him when he wasn't prepared. Karas had offered him ritual combat, and instead the cowardly minotaur had knocked him senseless and fled.

RÍCHARD A. KПΔΔK

Stumbling through the woods, Karas located his horse, still tethered to a tree. Despite the added delay, the hunter took time to take care of his mount, then, getting his bearings, he rode off.

Karas soon found clear evidence of the wagons' route. Fresh wheel ruts led toward a large town called Brumen. The minotaur warrior considered his next move. Golar would surely stay within the safe confines of the wagon train until the troupe reached Brumen.

He would have to surprise him in Brumen, somehow. Karas would not let the minotaur actor fool him again. This time, one way or another, he would force Golar to redeem his honor.

Did Golar not realize the extent to which his family and kin had been affected by his heinous act? When word had spread of Golar's retreat in the midst of battle, the coward's own brother, Markyn, had defended him, at first, challenging those who would slur the reputation of the soldier missing in action. During the third such challenge, Markyn had been slain—and then someone reported having seen the telltale mark on a minotaur far from home.

Because of the shame Golar brought down upon them, the clan Barash had spiraled downward. Who could trust the honor of a clan willing to hide such a lie, while the unrepentant coward still lived? Markyn had perished, believing that his brother's body still lay on the battlefield somewhere, but the telltale mark couldn't be denied, and now all knew the dishonor of Golar.

Other clans broke contact with the clan. The emperor himself turned away the elders when they sought intervention.

And so, in desperation, the patriarch had sent out the hunters, each sworn by their lives to come back with

Golar. The patriarch chose first and foremost from those who had known the coward personally, the better to identify him should he don some disguise. Karas had been among the first, and the patriarch placed hope on him, for Karas had known Golar when he was young and was therefore all the more determined to avenge the clan. That was a long time ago. Until he had accidentally crossed paths with the players and noticed the minotaur actor in their midst, Karas had begun to wonder if his quest would ever end.

Late at night Karas finally caught sight of the wagons, set in a circle. Karas heard music and laughter from the actors inside the circle. It angered him that Golar could be enjoying his life so much, and he nearly charged down into the camp there and then. Only the futility of such an act held him back. He would fail his quest if the players fought back and killed him. Karas could afford to wait. He knew now that time was on his side.

For three days and nights, the tawny warrior shadowed the Traveling Players of Gilean. By the second night, Karas not only resented Golar, but also regretted that he himself could not join the troupe for what seemed their perpetual merriment. Since his departure from Mithas, Karas had spent little time with others. He had forsaken a life for himself. He knew he could have no future, no pleasure, until he had been released from his blood oath. But the members of the troupe seemed carefree ...

On the fourth day, the troupe finally reached Brumen. Situated on a trade route, Brumen constantly welcomed travelers. Minotaurs, however, were still rare in the region, and so Karas skirted the population, seeking a vantage point from which he could keep an

eye on the troupe while preventing others from notic-
ing him. Karas had seen Golar once or twice during the
journey, and knew that he had not fled. Karas could
still bide his time. The coward Golar seemed quite satisfied to spend the rest of his existence in the dubious
company of the players.

Karas developed a plan—a very clever plan, if he
dared say so, which would use the actors themselves to
achieve his goal.

The players would not perform on the first day. They
needed time to prepare the show and to spread the news
of their arrival. By tonight there would be handbills
nailed on walls and posts everywhere.

Which fit into Karas's plan.

He waited until the dead of night to enter Brumen.
Anyone who saw him would surely guess that a minotaur hid beneath the bulky cloak, but Karas would simply
tell them that he was the one of the troupe, and hurry
on. He almost chuckled to think they would confuse
him for Golar. Most humans couldn't tell the difference
between one minotaur and the next.

The wind had a wet chill, and Karas wrapped the
cloak tightly around him as he walked the darkened
streets. In the distance he could hear activity from
one section of Brumen, and he turned away from that
area. He had no intention of mingling with crowds.
What he needed he would readily find anywhere in
town. He already had that much faith in the players—
and their master.

Sure enough, he saw a piece of paper fluttering from
a hitching post. In the dim light he had to squint to read:

The Traveling Players of Gilean present . . .

He tore the handbill from the post and stuffed it into
a pouch. A sound made him turn, but it proved only to

be a dog, which took one look at the cowled minotaur and promptly darted away.

Karas snorted, then hurried back out of town to where his mount waited for him. He had what he had come for. He rode back up to a clearing in the wooded hills that he had chosen for his camp. There, warmed by a small campfire, Karas pulled out the crumpled handbill and perused the full text.

The master of the troupe, Sebastius, seemed to claim credit for doing nearly everything in the coming play. Karas counted his name at least half a dozen times. Unfortunately, the one name that he sought, Golar's, did not appear anywhere. He puzzled over that.

He did not recognize the title of the play. Some king's name, he supposed. But he noticed some important words below the title, describing it as "an adventure in an exotic land of monsters, treasure, and love!!!"

An adventure. With monsters.

Surely that would include minotaurs.

Everything was just as Karas had hoped. This time he would force Golar's hand and make the coward face him. This time, the matter would be settled.

———◆———

Golar had not noticed any sign of his pursuer since arriving in Brumen and, as the day passed, he turned his thoughts completely to the coming production. He went about his work with great enthusiasm, and looked forward to the night's show. It was one of Sebastius's more lurid, flamboyant pieces, which audiences enjoyed almost as much as the actors.

With Heston gone, the role of hero had been inherited by a half-elf named Twayne. Golar knew the half-elf fairly well. Twayne always treated him courteously, and certainly he was an able actor, but the minotaur found himself missing his friend Heston.

Golar threw himself into the day's combat practice, fighting with such abandon that Twayne could barely defend himself. At one point, his war axe broke the sword in two and nearly cleaved the half-elf as well.

"According to the play," grumbled Twayne, tossing aside his broken blade. "I am supposed to win this battle, you know."

"Sorry, Twayne."

"I know that you are used to performing these sequences differently with Heston, but as he has seen fit to leave us, it would be best if you accustom yourself to my style."

Golar readied his axe again. "Don't worry. I will adjust, half-elf. Find yourself another sword and let us begin again."

Twayne did so, and the two went at it again. This time the minotaur focused his moves and corrected himself for his new opponent's methods. The pair worked on the choreography of their big fight scene throughout much of the day. By late afternoon, they had the scene down to perfection, with one or two fresh ideas they intended to throw in, if Sebastius approved.

"We are moving together like dancers now!" Twayne gasped. "I think, though, that we both need a rest. At least I certainly do."

Golar felt exhausted, too. In truth, he had thoroughly enjoyed the mock combat. The rehearsal had stirred his old feelings of battle lust. He retired to his wagon, but, inside, suddenly felt so claustrophobic that he nearly tore down the door in his haste to go back outside. He gripped his ax tightly, as though looking around to see if anyone wanted more practice.

"Are you all right, my friend?"

As ever, Sebastius had popped up when he was least expected. The minotaur looked from down his superior height at the figure of the master, almost laughable compared to his own massive bulk.

"You've got a show to do, Sebastius. Better be about it."

The heavyset human seemed unperturbed by his deliberately aloof attitude. "And you are an important part of that play, friend Golar, which makes my question worthwhile, don't you think?"

"I'll remember my lines, follow all my footwork, and in the end die a proper death, don't you worry! I won't let you down."

"I should hope not! There will be a good crowd tonight. A receptive crowd, you understand. They too must not be let down."

Golar nodded. Tonight, this play would touch someone in the crowd. The plays always did. Not necessarily in a predictable manner, but the Traveling Players of Gilean always left their mark.

The old feelings of battle lust had faded. Golar drew a heavy breath. "I'll be at my best tonight, Sebastius, I promise."

The master of the troupe smiled. "That's all I ask, my friend!" He gingerly pushed aside the head of the minotaur's war axe, which dangled just a few inches from his protuberant girth. "Now, come, put that dangerous weapon away and let us go over your lines one more time! A little effort, and I think that tonight we might see your finest performance yet, Golar! What do you say?"

Such unusual praise from Sebastius lightened the minotaur's mood. Hefting the ax over his shoulder, he cheerfully nodded. "I'll try my best, Sebastius! I won't let down the troupe!"

All memory of his fiery past vanished. The other players depended on him. Sebastius was counting on him. Golar would not let the troupe down. Tonight, he would indeed give his utmost. Maybe tonight, he thought, I'll give a perfect performance.

———◆———

Karas's plan had to be perfect.

Only minutes remained before the curtain opened to begin Act One. Karas had his mount tethered a short distance away. From here he could see backstage and the actors' wagons.

It amazed him that his cowardly cousin had not abandoned the players and fled. True, the troupe afforded Golar some protection, but there must be some other reason why he clung to them.

A human from the town suddenly came up a path behind him, whistling softly. Karas silently cursed. He started to pull his hood forward over his horns, but the local had already spotted him.

To Karas's relief, the man hesitated only a moment before nodding to the minotaur. "Getting some air before your show?"

The man must think he was one of the troupe. "Yes. It's been a long journey."

"Didn't know there were two of you. Uh, minotaurs, I mean. "

"We're cousins." That was the truth, so why not?

"Well, I'm Tomas, chief watchman of this town. We don't get too many of your kind around here. Good thing you two came in with the show, or there might've been a little too much curiosity on the part of some of our boys, if you know what I mean." He winked good-naturedly.

After the minotaur nodded, Tomas added, "Nothing personal, believe me. I say, live and let live, eh?"

Considering his mission, Karas could hardly agree, but again he nodded assent. He only half-paid attention to the human's prattling. Still, Tomas presented both a potential problem and added boost to his plan. "It looks to be quite a crowd tonight."

"We don't get much in the way of such entertainment up here."

"Will there be guards posted just in case something should happen?"

Tomas shrugged. "Don't expect much to happen, but I'll probably have a couple of men standing 'round just in case."

Karas leaned forward and in his friendliest tones whispered, "Then maybe I should let you in on one of the surprises of the play, one I don't want your men to misinterpret when it occurs."

"Oh?" The town watchman's eyes widened. "A surprise for the audience?"

The minotaur nodded. "Yes."

———————◆◆◆———————

Quite a crowd had gathered. From behind the scenery, Golar surveyed both the throng and the streets beyond, but to his relief saw no sign of Karas. That settled it for him. His young cousin had come to his senses and given up. By now, the other minotaur must be well on his way back to the islands of their people.

Sebastius abruptly materialized among the players, clapping his hands high in the air. "Places, everyone! Places! The show is about to begin!"

Twayne, clad in a simple cloak and carrying a sturdy

but rusting sword, stepped up beside the minotaur. It still amazed Golar that the moment the half-elf presented himself to the audience, he would transform, in their eyes, into the dashing, well-clad hero of the piece. His cloak would look as though it were spun with gold, and his common sword would gleam as if freshly cast. Twayne himself would change and grow in stature.

"A good crowd out there."

Golar grunted. "Yes."

"Were you expecting someone? I've never known you to watch the audience so intently."

The minotaur did not glance at the half-elf. "The music's about to begin. You should take your place."

The other player frowned, but evidently did not take any offense at the minotaur's tone. As Twayne left him, Golar peered once more into the audience. Still no sign of the watcher. So much for the brief unease he had felt. Karas was gone. Golar could concentrate on the play—and only the play. The minotaur silently ran over his lines, savoring them. Yes, he was fortunate to have found a new life. He truly belonged among this troupe. . . .

The opening notes of the music were sounded, and the first actors took their places before the assembled townsfolk. A simple fake door became the entrance to a vast castle. A few scraggly shrubs were transformed into an impenetrable forest. Twayne's cloth cloak and the old breastplate he had donned just before stepping out onto stage made him now appear a glittering prince.

Golar watched, almost as fascinated as the crowd, though it was old hat to him. Perhaps because of his relief at Karas's disappearance, he fell deeper into the play than ever before. He experienced the love and betrayal in the first act then suffered alongside the hero as the epic journey began in the second. As his own part did not begin until the middle of the third act, the minotaur inasmuch as joined the audience and drank in everything.

For the first time, he paid attention to the lead character's struggle to discern the true meaning of honor. Golar could not recall that theme ever playing quite as significant a role in the telling of this tale, but tonight it seemed at the very forefront. Twayne's character even made a desperate decision that in some ways echoed Golar's path in life. In a scene that paralleled the ignominious incident that was the secret of the minotaur's past, the half-elf abandoned his comrades in the midst of battle. But tonight, the play clearly demonstrated that his comrades would have died regardless of whether Twayne had stayed behind; the similarity to his own story was so close, that the minotaur was astonished. He leaned forward, eyes never leaving the play, wondering how the character would resolve his inner torment —

"Golar! Prepare yourself!"

The minotaur started at Sebastius's voice. He looked out on stage and realized that, yes, his entrance was due at any moment.

Gripping his axe, he took his place and waited for Twayne to speak the necessary cue.

"—and but a few hours to safety!" the half-elf called out heartily. "If nothing more bars our path, we are to freedom!"

Brandishing the axe, Golar burst from the wings, confronting Twayne's character and roaring, "Halt! You are in the domain of Raxas the Terrible! None may enter but those who wish to die at my hand!"

Twayne raised his sword. "Nay, beast! If anyone perishes this day, it will be you!"

"Aye!" shouted a voice beyond the audience. "So it shall!"

To Golar's horror, a familiar cloaked figure burst from one side of the audience. The newcomer charged the stage, waving a long sword. The nearby town guards did nothing to stop him and, in fact, seemed to be watching the newcomer with undisguised relish.

As he leaped onto the stage, Karas pushed the startled half-elf away, sending Twayne sprawling into the meager scenery. The old sword went flying from the hero's grip. The rest of the players backed up uncertainly. Was Sebastius improvising again? But the troupe's leader seemed to have vanished from the area.

"What do you think you're doing?" Golar muttered low, so the crowd would not hear.

"Forcing you to do what should have come naturally, cousin! Forcing you to do battle for the sake of your honor!"

"Not my honor! More the clan's pride! I've done nothing I regret! I would've died for no good reason at all!"

Karas thrust, trying to force the other minotaur into fighting him. "By keeping yourself alive you have besmirched the clan! You have your chance now, Golar! Redeem yourself!"

"By slaying you, or letting you slay me? What point does that serve, you young fool?" Golar blocked another thrust by his young cousin. He heard the crowd cheer. They thought this was part of the play. "Well, Karas? Am I supposed to return to Mithas and tell the clan that your death has restored my honor?"

The younger minotaur tore away the hood of his cloak, the better to see his dodging opponent. Karas gritted his teeth. "No, you've got it right. It would be better if you came back with me to face the arena—but if you refuse, then perish now by my hand."

"A fate no better than awaiting certain death on a lost battlefield. The Highlord left us to die for a worthless cause!"

Golar swung the axe wide, trying to keep Karas at bay. Even as he traded words with Karas and dodged blows, he desperately sought some way to escape the logical outcome of this combat.

The crowd continued to cheer as the two minotaurs shifted for advantage. Golar's ax gave him a better reach, but Karas had fierce determination on his side. He sought to slay his opponent, whereas Golar simply hoped to stave off his young foe.

Karas had clearly trained long and hard, for his sword darted in again and again, flicking in surprising directions at the last moment. Golar managed to deflect him, but Karas gave no quarter.

Twayne suddenly appeared, his sword recovered. The half-elf was alone among the other actors in seeing Karas as a real threat not under Sebastius's control. He made his way toward the minotaur warrior, who had not noticed him. He raised his sword.

"No! Get back, Twayne!" shouted Golar.

Karas immediately saw the threat and stepped back to face both adversaries. He sneered. "You possess such little honor that you must call upon this half-breed for help? I grew up thinking you were a fine warrior, cousin, and I hoped that some of that still remained, but you're a disgraceful villain!"

"We can charge him together, from both sides," Twayne coldly said.

"My sword is more than a match for both of you, half-breed!"

The half-elf, waving his sword, glared at the minotaur intruder. "Say the word, Golar."

"No!" The minotaur actor stepped between Karas and Twayne. He suddenly understood, with a clarity that had eluded him until now, what he must do. "Leave this to the two of us! No one else must get involved!"

Karas eyed Golar. "So! You have a crumb of decency left!"

"This is a minotaur matter, Karas! If there must be a fight, let it be between the two of us. No others should suffer!"

"Of course. That is how it should be."

Twayne, looking puzzled, edged away. As he did, suddenly the minotaur warrior thrust close, nearly catching Golar in the chest. The older minotaur stumbled, then slashed wildly at his enemy. Karas retreated deftly, then lunged at Golar's left arm.

The blade came within inches, but Golar's axe came up to block with Karas's sword. For a brief moment, the two warriors were locked, each trying to force down the other's weapon. Finally Golar twisted around, freeing himself and his axe.

In doing so, however, he left an opening. Karas moved fast, driving his blade toward the minotaur actor's stomach.

Golar let out a harsh cry. The axe slipped from his grip as he lurched away from his foe. He stumbled to one knee then fell.

He heard Sebastius's voice rise above all the other commotion—shouts and scuffling and scattered applause.

"So ends our experimental play!" boomed the master of the troupe. "Thank you one and all! I hope you enjoyed it! Tomorrow, we will repeat the show, albeit without deviating from the traditional script! Everyone here is welcome to witness the next performance free of charge!"

"Get away from me!" Karas snapped from somewhere

above Golar. "I need to see if he still lives! He deserves a quick death, at least, for finally owning up to his shame!"

Twayne's voice sounded loud and clear. "Of course he is dead! No one could have survived such a blow!"

"But wait, there's no blood on my sword!"

"Are you so young and untried that you have never pulled your blade free of a foe, minotaur? In my seventy years and more, I have done so several times! That is surely what happened."

"Yes, but his wound! I need to see—"

"You have taken his life, and now you demand to rummage his corpse! Are all your race so bestial and uncaring?"

A gentle hand touched his shoulder. With his eyes closed, Golar could not at first tell who had bent down beside him, but then he heard Dardella whisper, "Lie still and hold your breath as much as possible! Sebastius is trying to settle the matter."

He made no motion, no sound. So, the master and the players were trying to aid him in his improvised subterfuge. Golar felt some gratitude, yet at the same time, his conscience haunted him, for the falseness and evasion went against the grain of his race.

It had come to him in a flash of inspiration. Karas needed to see him dead. Only then would the young warrior be satisfied that his quest was completed. Therefore, why not let him strike a killing blow? Golar hoped that his death would be enough, that Karas would not demand his corpse as proof for the clan patriarch.

"Easy, my young friend!" Sebastius said in a conspiratorial tone, bravely interposing his body between Karas and the fallen form of Goldar. "Let us finish this unfortunate tableau in the seclusion of the wagon train! We have no good reason to let the fair people of Brumen think this other than a part of the script!"

Karas snorted. "All right, human! Just so long as I have evidence . . . "

"Oh, you will have evidence, I believe! Twayne! Would you be so kind as to gather a few of the other strong fellows and bear our dear departed fellow off the stage?"

"Where shall we put him, Master Sebastius?"

"Mmmm . . . his own wagon for now. He will not be going far in his state, will he?" After a pause, Sebastius continued, "Now then, my brave warrior, come with me for a moment."

Golar remained as still as possible. He felt ashamed, however. Did a minotaur lie down and let others save his hide?

But he did this for young Karas too, Golar reminded himself. He was saving himself, but he was also saving the young minotaur.

Rough hands grabbed his legs and shoulders. It took four of the players to lift him up and their heavy breathing proved the effort.

"To his wagon . . ." Twayne grunted. They carried Golar's swaying body out of sight of the townsfolk and away from Karas. Sebastius had a grip on Karas's arm, pretending to comfort him.

A short time later, he found himself inside his wagon. All left, save Twayne, who shut the door.

"He is still out there," the half-elf muttered tensely. "Sebastius is trying to convince him that he does not need your body to prove that you are dead, but the fool seems insistent."

"Give him my war axe," said Golar, nodding at Twayne with gratitude as he stood and brushed himself off.

"Your beloved axe?" Even the half-elf knew how minotaurs valued their weapons as virtual extensions of their bodies. Willingly giving up his axe was akin to Golar surrendering a limb.

"Do it. Make the suggestion as though you just thought of it. It's the only way he might leave without me."

Twayne nodded. "As you wish."

It was not what he wished; it was what might work. As the half-elf departed, Golar gritted his teeth at the thought.

Surrendering his treasured axe . . .

One deception after another. Truly now, he had shed the last vestige of any claim to being an honorable warrior. Truly now, all that remained for him was his life in the troupe.

All that remained . . .

There remained only a few loose ends, but it seemed that this corpulent human intended to make Karas work as hard to finish the matter as he had worked to track down his quarry in the first place. Did the man understand nothing about the minotaur race? Karas could not simply return home empty-handed and claim he had slain Golar. The patriarch would require proof to present to the emperor. Clan Barash could not reclaim its former glory without proof—and the emperor's blessing. There would always be suspicion otherwise.

"I tell you for the last time, fat one! I lay claim to my cousin's body! Let me bring it back to Mithas, and once his death is verified, he'll receive full burial honors as befits the warrior he once was . . ." At least, Karas hoped that would be the case. Since slaying Golar, he had felt more and more uncertain, although for what reason he could not say. Golar had given his clan no choice. By finally accepting his fate, the older minotaur had salvaged his honor. Surely the elders would recognize that and grant his spirit a proper farewell.

Surely they would.

"But you must understand, my young friend," the one called Sebastius insisted again. "That Golar was one of us! He has been a player for over a decade! We watch over our own. Think how long a journey you will have back to the minotaur isles! Forgive me for being blunt, but how will you preserve his remains?"

Karas had not considered that. In his mind, everything had seemed simple. Yet, the human had a good point. When he had started on his quest, Karas had never imagined ending up in this distant land, with a body to bear all the way home.

"I'll try to find a mage, someone who can cast some sort of spell . . . "

"That could take a long time in and of itself, my dedicated young warrior friend. Longer even than the trip home!"

Too true, but what other choice did Karas have?

"I heard what you just said," interrupted the half-elf who had tried to confront Karas on stage, as he hurried around a wagon. "And if I may make a suggestion, Master Sebastius?"

"Why should I trust your suggestion?" the minotaur pressed, torn and exasperated. "What is your suggestion?"

"Take his axe."

Karas blinked. "His axe?"

"It is the one that he has carried since warrior days. His mark, his clan symbols, are all etched into it. You can see it for yourself. Whatever you may have thought of him, Golar would not have willingly parted with his weapon, if he was still alive."

Sebastius eagerly took up the suggestion. "Yes, for

when all is said and done, my young friend, a minotaur
is still a minotaur!"

The tawny warrior considered this interesting idea.
If it was the same axe that he recalled, it had a family
history. Originally it had been passed on to Golar by his
father, a champion in the arena.

"You may have something, half-breed . . . but I would
prefer to take his horns as well. Those would survive
the journey."

The rotund human shuddered. "Is that your idea of
what is honorable, now that in death poor Golar has
redeemed himself?"

In truth, Karas wasn't sure. He felt guilty enough
about taking the axe, which, by rights, should be passed
down to Golar's eldest son—or buried with him. These
were peculiar circumstances, and he didn't need to offend
the troupe. Surely if he brought the champion's axe back
to Mithas, that would prove Golar's death and Karas could
leave his cousin's horns. No minotaur should go through
the afterlife without them.

"Bring me the war axe, half-breed. If it is the one I
remember, it should serve my purpose."

The half-elf scowled at being called a half-breed, but
nodded and left. A few moments later, he returned with
the axe. The unusual heft of the weapon clearly put a
strain on the lithe creature.

Karas inspected the axe from head to handle. The axe
had been well used and not just by Golar's father. Golar
himself must have killed many with it. The young warrior could sense the history in the weapon. He would
not have minded wielding it himself.

On the shaft he found the marks designating the
war axe as originally belonging to Timon, Golar's
father. The symbols for Clan Barash had been etched

into the opposite side. Karas needed no further proof. This was a great weapon that no minotaur, however cowardly, would abandon without fighting to the death.

"This will do," he rumbled.

Sebastius clapped him on the back, an audacious thing to do. The minotaur had to admire his nerve. "Then it is all settled, my young friend! You must be anxious to be on your way now—"

"I can't leave until after the burial. I owe my cousin that much."

"You have a long journey ahead. If you are as eager to return home as you seem to me to be, surely you should get going! I am, of course, versed in the rituals of minotaur funerals! You may trust in me to give Golar the proper honorable farewell."

Karas indeed was eager to move on. Golar had been family, and slaying him made him feel strangely queasy. His father, Juris, had been a close cousin with Golar— almost a brother. Karas could still recall the look of regret that had passed over his father's face when he pledged his life to tracking him down.

He hefted Golar's axe over one shoulder. "You may be right, human. There is a time to tarry, and a time to go. Very well, as long as you promise me that he'll be buried properly, I'll leave him in your hands. The axe is all I need, and I have far to travel."

"A wise choice." Sebastius led him away from the wagons. "I believe your mount is this direction?"

The troupe master accompanied him all the way to the edge of town and even beyond, but curiously, Karas did not mind his presence any more. Indeed, he felt almost calmed by the human's presence. By the time they reached his mount, Karas was feeling oddly at peace with what had happened—and his decision to go.

"I thank you for your consideration, human," he rumbled awkwardly to the stout, robed figure as he mounted. Karas glanced down at Sebastius. "It had to be done," he muttered. "For the good of the clan."

This time Sebastius said nothing. The tawny minotaur urged his horse forward, trying to think about the journey ahead and not at all about the dead body he left behind him. He should have felt proud, vindicated, but instead all Karas felt was confusion.

Confusion . . . and regret.

Golar sat in the darkness, waiting for someone to come tell him that the crisis had passed. Sebastius finally did, knocking politely on the door, then peering in without waiting for Golar to answer. "He is gone, my friend. You can come out of hiding."

The minotaur player bristled at the last remark, even though Sebastius clearly did not mean to insult him. Several of the other players stood nearby, including Twayne and Dardella.

"Well!" Sebastius exclaimed, with a clap of his meaty hands. "Quite a day we have had for ourselves! I trust that tomorrow we will return to a more normal routine? Twayne! You should help with striking the set! Dardella! Would you see to organizing the back-stage for tomorrow's show? I will join you shortly . . . " He looked at the others staring at Golar. "And the rest of you all have duties and responsibilities, I should think."

After the others had dispersed, Golar asked him, "How did you convince him, Sebastius? Did he seem satisfied?"

"He appeared so."

"Did he—did he say anything?"

"I gather he showed some remorse."

Golar winced. He couldn't forget he had tricked his young cousin into believing that his clan's honor had been upheld.

"It's better this way," the minotaur muttered, more to himself than to Sebastius. "He'll go home happy and be hailed a hero, while no one else'll waste their lives searching for me."

"As you say."

Golar sighed. "Sebastius, I need to talk to you about something. I—"

The snort of a horse made him whirl. Golar gaped as a rider suddenly entered the encampment . . . a minotaur rider who stared back with even worse shock evident on his tawny features.

"By Sargas's axe! *Golar*?"

Karas sat atop his tall mount, his expression shifting rapidly from one of astonishment to betrayal and disgust.

"Bah, more actor's tricks, cousin? I must be a world-class fool. I thought the covering of your birthmark was spineless enough, but this charade truly proves how dishonorable you are!"

"Karas—what are you doing back here?"

The warrior dismounted, Golar's axe gripped tight in one hand. As he walked toward the minotaur actor, his other hand slipped to touch the hilt of his sword.

"I came—dear cousin—because I thought it over and decided I should attend your funeral! After your *brave* death, I thought it the least I could do for the friendship once held between you and my father! Now I see that he and even I sorely misjudged your worthiness."

"You don't understand—"

"I understand all I ever need to understand about

you, Golar." Karas threw the axe down at Golar's feet then drew the sword. "Now pick up your weapon! I don't know how you managed that trick before, but this time I'll make certain that either you come back with me to face your clan, to face your disgrace, or we end it here and now, and I witness your death . . . in truth, this time!"

"I'll not fight you."

Karas grew incensed. "Must I force you? You will fight me one way or another! Pick it up, I say!"

He jabbed at Golar with such sudden speed that the older minotaur could not dodge him. Maybe Karas intended only to prick Golar's skin, but the sword point dug deep. Golar gasped and pulled away as best he could.

The younger warrior stared.

No cut, no trace of blood, marked where he had struck Golar.

"That's not possible!" barked Karas. "There must be a wound!" He raised his sword up and studied the tip. "No blood!" His gaze returned to his cousin. "Not even the smallest scar."

Several figures came rushing up from the wagons, among them Dardella and the half-elf. Twayne carried a sword of his own.

"Back again? Should we take care of him, Golar?"

"Please, please!" Sebastius, who had said nothing up till now, interjected. "There will be no unnecessary violence here, Twayne!"

Karas ignored them, his gaze fixed on Golar. "What sort of sorcery is this, cousin? Do you not bleed like any mortal?"

The minotaur actor clenched his fists. Despite every effort, he had failed to elude Karas. All that remained now was to tell him the awful truth. "You can't harm me,

Karas, much less slay me." He tapped the black lotus tattoo near his shoulder. "You see this mark? Those who bear this, those who are members of the Traveling Players of Gilean, can neither be injured nor killed, cousin. So long as we remain a part of this group, we're immune from all forms of death, including aging. It's part of the pact we make in order to devote ourselves to becoming players."

"Madness! More trickery! More guile! It can't be!"

Golar turned to Twayne, holding out his hand. The half-elf knew exactly what he wanted him to do, for Twayne immediately turned over his sword.

"Let me show you, Karas."

Turning the point of the blade toward himself, Golar did the unthinkable. With one thrust, the minotaur actor impaled himself on the sword.

Karas gasped then stared as Golar slowly pulled the sharp blade out of his stomach. It had been lodged in there, several inches deep, but still no blood flowed, and as the minotaur pulled the last of the steel free, the wound slowly sealed itself.

"For others in the troupe, it may work differently, cousin, but this is how it works for me. So you cannot slay me, Karas. I hoped you wouldn't find out the truth, but you had to come back."

The younger minotaur looked so shocked at this news that Golar felt pity.

"You tried your best. No one could have done better. When you leaped up on the stage, you truly caught me by surprise. Under other circumstances, I likely would've been trapped there and then."

The other minotaur stared down at his useless weapon. "I can't harm you."

"No."

"What if I forced you to come back to Mithas with me?"

"I'd surely escape at some point. I've no interest in going back, Karas, not that I could make you understand. Not only do I consider what I did on that day to have been necessary, but since becoming part of the troupe I've grown to feel that I am doing something even more necessary now—giving something positive to the world, not tearing it asunder for yet another baseless cause."

Golar half-expected his cousin to rage and rant at him. Instead, though, a clearly crestfallen Karas sheathed his sword, then stared at the minotaur he had sought for so long. His voice was very calm, almost flat.

"You've defeated me. I've failed my blood oath. Trust you, cousin, to find your way out somehow."

"Karas, I—"

Karas shrugged. "I'll bother you no further. I see how you picture the matter. But I know what must be done. The clan will have to find another way to regain its honor. I can do no more for them here. . . . I can do no more, even for myself."

With that, he picked up the axe and started back to his horse. Once mounted, though, Karas glanced over his shoulder. With what Golar realized was a trembling hand, the young warrior held up the great war axe.

"I've changed my mind about some things. I'll not be needing this." Karas tossed the weapon toward Golar.

As the heavy axe struck the earth, a chill sensation passed through Golar. He bent to retrieve his beloved axe, intending to say a few last placating words to the tawny minotaur warrior.

Karas didn't wait, however. As his cousin bent to pick up his axe, the minotaur warrior steered his horse toward the forest then urged the animal on. By the time

Golar had straightened, Karas was a tiny figure among the distant trees.

"Well, that's the end of that," Dardella remarked. Beside her, Twayne nodded.

"What do you think?" Sebastius asked Golar.

The minotaur did not answer at first, staring from his axe to the woods. "No," Golar finally answered. "It's not the end, not yet." He eyed the troupe master. "Sebastius, I must go after him."

"Why, Golar?" Dardella asked, surprised.

Twayne added his concerned voice. "All is well now, minotaur. You are still with us and your young pursuer has given up the hunt. By tomorrow, he will be well on his way home!"

Sebastius said nothing.

Golar hefted the axe, feeling its solid weight and knowing it would serve him well for what he planned. "No . . . no, he isn't going home."

———◆———

He could not go home. He could not go home and face his family, the patriarch and the clan elders. He had failed, failed miserably. Despite his blood oath, Karas had failed his quest.

His blood oath. Others had sworn blood oaths. He wondered if any of them had come across Golar, in the past. If so, had they, too, been unable to return home, knowing that their failure would add to the shame of the already-battered clan? If such was the case, then they had no doubt chosen the only route remaining to them, the one route left open, Karas realized, to him.

The minotaur reined his mount to a halt. Karas peered around, deciding this place was as good as any.

He was already some distance from Brumen. Likely they would not find his body until long after the wolves or scavengers had had their way with it.

Karas dismounted, trying to come to grips with what he had to do. That the wolves might ravage his corpse did not bother him so much, he reflected. After all, the woods were a natural place to die, and a place that was fitting for a warrior.

He chose a small clearing. Ironic that it should come to this, and that it was Karas, not Golar, the dishonorable one, who must die. The thought made him bristle, but he could do nothing about it. Golar had placed himself forever beyond the reach of his people, beyond, apparently, the reach of his own conscience. He cared not what he had left behind for others to endure.

"I will not be like him," Karas muttered. "I will do the honorable thing."

Unbuckling his sword sheath, the tawny warrior reverently laid the blade on the ground before him. As an afterthought, Karas returned to his mount, removing both saddle and bridle from the animal. He did not bother to tether the creature, knowing that the trained steed would remain nearby for the time being. Eventually the horse would wander off, hopefully to live out the rest of its life in freedom and peace. Certainly the animal had been loyal to him, and deserved a proper future.

Karas knelt before his sheath. However, instead of drawing the sword, he pulled his dagger free from his belt. The minotaur stared at the small, sturdy blade, focusing on the clan symbol just above its hilt.

There were several methods by which the ritual could be performed, but the dagger seemed quickest. Karas could have impaled himself on his sword, but after watching Golar perform the deed without any repercussions, the young warrior just could not bring himself to go through the same motions. Besides, the dagger had always seemed to him more personal.

More precise.

Still kneeling, Karas begin whispering. He called to his ancestors, listing those most accomplished first. He asked each to help guide his hand, so that his pain did not linger. The tawny minotaur then asked the same favor of the gods most prominent among his people—Sargas the Avenger and Kiri-Jolith the Just. Although the two gods were often rivals, Karas knew that first and foremost they cared for their chosen children. If they deemed him worthy, they would join in aiding him.

He touched the tip of his dagger onto the sword sheath, asking that the greater weapon add strength to the lesser. In truth, before this moment, Karas had been like many young warriors, paying little attention to the formal rituals, save when required to memorize them for the instructors. He had always dreamed he would die in glorious battle, not in this way.

At last, he began the final litany. Karas raised the blade high, then murmured, "Ancestors, Sargas and Kiri-Jolith, Barash, for whom my clan is honored to be called, guide this weapon to its mark! Let the shame and dishonor that flows within me for failing my blood oath spill free with my life's fluids, never to taint kin and clan! Let my failure to accomplish my task be erased by my sacrifice now! I, Karisijurisi de-Barash, ask this of you now—as I give to you my unworthy life!"

With both hands, he thrust the dagger toward his heart . . .

And paused with the blade but a fraction of an inch from his chest, unable to push it any nearer.

Karas's hands shook. He gritted his teeth and tried to finish the job, but a sudden yearning for life kept him from accomplishing any more than barely piercing his tough hide. Tears slid down his face as he struggled against himself, but still the minotaur could not do what must be done.

Karas dropped the knife. Propping himself up with both hands, he gulped for breath as, through blurry eyes, he stared at the blade. He had sworn an oath on his life! On his very honor! He had failed miserably in his quest; for what remained of the honor of Barash, Karas had to slay himself now!

Seizing the dagger, he tried to shove it in between his ribs—but again couldn't finish the gesture. A trickle of blood mocked the seriousness of his effort. Karas swore under his breath, feeling in his heart that he shamed his kin as terribly as Golar.

"Barash, guide me!" the frantic warrior cried to the heavens. And *still* he could not do it.

"The concept seems so simple, so right," a voice from behind him said, tinged with sarcasm. "The execution of the ritual, though, is another thing entirely, isn't it?"

Dropping the dagger in surprise, Karas turned to face Golar. The older minotaur eyed him grimly. In his hands he carried the massive war axe, the edges of its sharp double-blades gleaming.

"I knew you'd try this," Golar added. "When you left the ax behind, I knew with certainty that you'd try this, and so I followed."

"Did you come here to try to stop me, then?" Karas asked, studying the other. Golar did not look like a rescuer. The minotaur actor had a decidedly murderous gleam in his eyes.

"Stop you?" Golar swung the axe around wickedly, close to Karas. "I came to make certain that you'd succeed, cousin."

"You want me dead?"

Golar's expression grew emotionless, and when his words spilled out they seemed devoid of all inflection. "If you were dead, no one would know I was still alive, would they? No one would come searching for me any more, would they?"

Karas's weapon was out of reach. He tried to think. Nothing could truly harm the other minotaur, but maybe he could fend him off long enough to leap onto his mount, which still stood nearby.

"So, by slaying me you believe you can safely go back to the sanctuary of the acting troupe, Golar? Is that it, cousin?"

The darker minotaur stepped toward him, eyes never seeming to blink. "What do you think, Karas?"

Karas's left foot brushed the dagger he had dropped earlier. Karas tried to guess how long it would take to scoop up the weapon. It was a long shot, for Golar's war axe gave the minotaur player a longer reach.

Golar swung again, this time coming even closer. Golar wielded his massive weapon with the ease of years of practice.

Karas could not match those years. He had been a fool to ever think that he could. In truth, Karas had expected to find a sniveling coward, someone who had let his skills rust over the past decade. Golar had clearly kept in shape.

"You don't want your secret known?"

Gola's voice tightened. "Enough questions, young cousin."

The tawny warrior had only but to reach to grab the dagger. "This hardly seems a fair combat."

A shrug. "You may get lucky."

With that, Golar again brought the axe into play. The blade would have severed Karas's head at the neck, but the older warrior misjudged the distance by a few precious inches.

Karas, however, had already leaped aside. He seized the dagger. A paltry weapon against the axe, the desperate warrior did the only thing he could think of doing— he threw it.

The dagger *sank* into Golar's chest.

The older minotaur grunted in pain, dropping his axe. He fell to his knees, then slipped backward to the ground.

Karas froze, certain this had to be some trick. Golar had made himself invulnerable. He could not have been wounded.

Golar did not rise. A groan escape his mouth, though, one that clearly spoke of pain and approaching death.

At last recovering his senses, the younger warrior hurried over to his dishonored cousin, kneeling beside the minotaur player. Golar lived yet, but judging by the blood and the fact that only the hilt protruded from his chest, he had little time.

"W-well struck . . . cousin."

"Golar! What madness is this?"

The stricken minotaur spat blood. "No madness . . . no madness . . ." He indicated his shoulder. "Look . . . no lotus . . ."

Karas glanced and saw that the black lotus tattoo had somehow completely vanished. "I don't understand! What does this mean?"

"C-couldn't let—couldn't let you kill y-yourself . . ." Golar coughed. "Hoped you'd go home, but when . . . you

left the axe . . . I knew you intended to follow the ritual
. . . you would have d-died . . . for the sake . . . the sake
of the clan's honor . . ."

"Your secret would have been safe! You goaded me
into striking you! You knew that you weren't protected
any longer!"

"My f-finest performance . . . " A brief glow returned
to Golar's eyes. "Better this . . . than the Circus . . . all
the faces. I wanted to die as a warrior . . ." The minotaur coughed again, this time violently. "Karas . . . what
I did in the war . . . in the war . . . I still don't regret!
My death wouldn't have b-brought life to any of my
. . . my comrades . . . but in your case . . . your death
. . . that would have weighed more heavily on my soul
than I could . . . could bear! Your death . . . I would've
blamed myself forever . . ."

He started to choke. Karas held him up. He forgot
all about his clan. He only knew that a warrior and a
kinsman lay dying.

"N-now you can t-tell the others . . . the clan . . . the
. . . the stain is lifted from Barash! Th-thirteen years . . ."
Golar choked. "Thirteen years, and they finally have
their damned honor back . . ." His eyes suddenly swam
with fear. "Finally . . . they . . . can rest."

The minotaur's gaze froze, and his body grew limp.

"Golar!"

Karas knelt there for a long time. Finally the minotaur warrior shifted position, and lifted the body up.
He looked around, saw Golar's steed waiting. After a
moment's thought, Karas brought his cousin's body over
to the animal, then draped him across the saddle. He then
led the horse back to his own mount.

Karas had retrieved his weapons and saddled his steed
when he finally realized that someone else was there.

Reacting with alarm, he whirled to face his new foe, sword already out.

"You need fear no violence from me," Sebastius said quietly.

"Have you and the others come to avenge him?"

"Avenge Golar? He would never have wanted that, my young friend. It was his decision to leave the players, and his decision to revoke the safety that being one of us offered him. No, I merely came to honor his choice and see how you fare."

Karas sheathed his sword. "What do you mean by that?"

"You look troubled. Is not the honor of the clan restored? Are you not satisfied with the outcome? Are you not pleased?"

At first, Karas did not answer. Purposely turning his back on the rotund figure, he mounted his horse. However, even then he felt the gaze of Sebastius on him, so much so, that the minotaur could not bring himself to simply ride off without some reply.

Taking the reins of both horses in his hand, Karas finally looked back to meet Sebastius's eyes. "No, human, I'm not satisfied. I take little pleasure in fulfilling my oath, in lifting the stain from the clan of Barash. When I started out on this quest, it seemed simple. A matter of honor, that was all. I never considered the choices Golar had to make . . . nor the ones I'd be forced to make myself." He snorted. "I failed my own blood oath. I failed to take my life. How can I fault Golar for doing the same, especially after his final sacrifice for my sake?" He shook his head. "I understand him far better now, Master Sebastius, and know that I'll not forget him or this day . . . *ever*."

With that, he turned away from Sebastius and urged

his mount slowly ahead, steering the animal toward the direction of distant Mithas. Golar's horse followed obediently behind.

"Wait!" called Sebastius. "You plan to take his body back after all?"

"I must," Karas answered, reining the animals momentarily. "For him. He deserves to go home . . . even if I must ride day and night to see that his body makes it back in one piece. The clan will—they must—hear his story and honor him as one of their own."

"I wish you well," came the troupe master's quiet voice. "And a safe journey."

Sebastius said no more, and the minotaur did not look back.

Rewrites

Aron Eisenberg
and Jean Rabe

Farmlands south of Estwilde
Present day

The red-bearded dwarf stood on his tip-toes, sweaty feet jammed uncomfortably into hard leather boots, stomach pressed against the craggy trunk of a thick oak. He stretched a hand over his head, laying a curling playbill to the bark. With his other hand he tugged a nail from his pouch, held it to the top of the playbill and pushed it in. Then he reached for the gold-tipped warhammer on his belt. One good whack and the nail went in all the way.

The dwarf stepped back and looked up.

The playbill read:

Knights of Passion
A play in two acts

There were plenty of other words. In fact, the dwarf was certain the troupe had never before posted so verbose a notice about an upcoming production. All the letters were neatly and fancifully printed, looking like insect soldiers marching in precise formation across the sheet.

> *People of the Provinces: You are cordially invited*
> *to the premier of an original play presented*
> *by the Troupe of Gilean.*
> *'Knights of Passion' is an updated rendering*
> *of the classic 'Laurinda and Jewyel',*
> *the tragic story of a Qualinesti in love with a Silvanesti.*
> *To reflect these troubled times, the play has*
> *been deftly reinterpreted with a Dark Knight*
> *in love with a Solamnic Knight.*
> *Since our drama is in the process of being fine-tuned,*
> *we will happily accept your compliments and criticism.*
> *The curtain rises at sunset on the fifth day of Dry Heat*
> *in the meadow near Forthan's Creek.*

> ***Knights of Passion***
> *Written by Thronden Blackmoor*
> *Directed by Sebastius*
> *Dark Knight Commander—Aleena Lee'Ander*
> *Solamnic Knight—Thronden Blackmoor*
> *Solamnic Squire—Edger Bower*
> *Dark Knight Lieutenant—Catal Rorig*
> *Goblin Emissary—Heart*

The cast listing continued.

The dwarf's name wasn't listed, not even in the finest print, as he had a relatively minor part this go-round. Because of this minor part, the dwarf had been told he wasn't needed at rehearsal this morning. That meant he had plenty of time to decorate the countryside with these effusive posters.

The dwarf snorted and looked to the south, spying a massive shaggybark tree about a half-mile away. He started in that direction, reaching over his shoulder and into his backpack for another playbill.

"Wha . . ."

The wind caught the poster just as he pulled it out, taking it high over his waggling fingers. Like a big ungainly butterfly, it fluttered to the east. The dwarf watched it disappear with a sigh.

"One fewer to hang," he said. "Maybe I ought to toss all of 'em into the wind." He gave a chuckle. "After all, it's not a particularly good play. Not a single funny bit in it."

———◆———

The wind played havoc with the Solamnic Knight's scarlet cape, whipping the hem around his ankles and threatening to trip him as he strode across the field. The wind blew dust into his eyes and tangled his long brown hair, blew hotly against his face and added to his agitation. He was soaked beneath his gleaming silver plate mail, rivulets of sweat running down his legs and into his boots, his feet sliding back and forth with each step, promising blisters by evening. He clenched his gloved hands tight around a stack of pages he carried, and rehearsed his lines as he strode:

"I cannot continue like this, for I believe in protecting the weak, rallying the strong. . . ."

"And defending the righteous," said another voice.

Thronden turned around.

A young man dressed in loose fitting garments approached. "I love that line, Thronden. Good line. I just wanted to tell you."

293

"Please refer to me as Sir Giles Bronzewood. It helps me get into character."

"Of course, Thrond . . . Sir Giles. The stage is almost finished. Your presence is requested."

Thronden nodded.

"Thron . . . Sir Giles . . . why the armor? Dress rehearsal isn't for another two days."

"To truly get into the character of a Solamnic Knight, you should *become* a Solamnic Knight, act like one at every opportunity. Wear your armor, endure the heat. *Feel* the heat. Feel the weight of the plate and learn how to move in it. Feel everything as though you were a knight. In fact. . ."

His attention abruptly shifted as the wind carried a hint of jasmine his way.

Thronden saw her coming. She was wearing the glossy black armor of a Dark Knight, fog-gray cloak swirling like a cloud around her polished black boots. The wind was combing her long auburn hair and bringing to him the heady scent of her perfume.

"Aleena," Thronden softly announced.

Her face was both angular and smooth, her pale complexion flawless. Her eyes were closed, and the lids, the color of pink rose petals, were edged in impossibly long lashes. Her chin was tilted up, the heat of the sunshine making her skin glisten like a wet pearl. Though she was still nearly two dozen yards away Thronden could make out every striking detail.

She was the most breathtakingly beautiful woman he'd ever known. She was lanky without being too thin, tall but not overly so—the Dark Knight plate armor could not hide all her exquisite curves. Thronden suspected that elvish or faerie blood ran faintly somewhere in her family tree, as her features were so delicate and perfect and her grace was . . . beyond human. Suddenly she opened her eyes wide—ginger brown eyes like a doe—and took in the set. Then she turned and saw Thronden.

"Aleena," Thronden said with a hush. A pause, and then louder so she could hear: "Aleena."

She walked toward him. Floated, Thronden thought. Walking was too simple a word for how she moved. The wind was escorting her, not daring to blow the curls into those sweet doe eyes.

"Sir Giles, are those more corrections?" she asked, drawing close. She pointed a slender finger at the stack of papers in Thronden's hands. Her voice was feminine and delightfully musical. She was standing so close to him.

"I'm glad you're wearing armor today, Sir Bronzewood," she continued. "I didn't want to be the only one strutting around in this stuff. It's uncomfortable, but I thought it would help me get into the part. I have to learn how to move in this Dark Knight outfit." She gently drummed her fingers against the breastplate. "The gods know how real Knights can wear this much metal every day. So heavy and . . ." She paused, letting out a breath. "To think they fight battles in this uniform, all the time! Amazing. I hope the audience will appreciate that we're using authentic armor for this play."

Aleena pointed to the pages that an open-mouthed Thronden was holding.

For the briefest of moments he stared into her eyes. In that instant, he felt like he was drowning, and so he swiftly raised his gaze and focused on a curl that hung artfully down the center of her forehead. He had lost the one love of his life before joining the players—indeed it was that loss which drove him to the troupe—and he had vowed never to become smitten again. He took a step back. The wind rustled the edges of the pages, and the sound of hammers against wood drifted across the meadow toward them. Thronden awkwardly passed Aleena the top several sheets. He watched as she read the first few lines.

"Thank you, Sir Bronzewood," she said. "Why, I think this will be much better!"

She floated away toward the creek and the stage that was taking shape, fog-gray cloak swirling around her polished boots, the scent of jasmine trailing her.

Thronden followed at a distance, angling his course so he could talk to Jalas. The elf, assistant director of this production, scowled when he spotted the rewrites in Thronden's hands.

Jalas met him halfway to the stage. His long hair was tied back tightly, giving him an uncharacteristically dour countenance. "Does Sebastius know you've rewritten scenes again? Sebastius is the director. He should decide if you can still rewrite."

"I haven't really *rewritten* anything. Not completely anyway. I've just made a few corrections here and there, fine-tuned it," Thronden returned. He handed the stack to a passing Solamnic Knight actor and told him to hand them out. "Jalas, the changes this time aren't all that much. In fact . . . .no!" Thronden's face grew pale as the wind gusted fresh, liberating dozens of sheets. "No! No! No!"

He stared hopelessly as the actor in Solamnic garb tried to grab the sheets, borne aloft by the breeze. Thronden watched for a few minutes, as the actor plucked a few pages from the ground and snatched at others in the air.

"When you've retrieved them all," Thronden shouted, "put them back in order." He released a deep sigh and struck out toward the stage. "And be fast about it," he muttered half to himself. "Rehearsal will be starting in a few minutes." He spotted Sebastius by the stage.

Initially Thronden thought Sebastius was supervising the stage crew, but soon he realized the big man was watching the creek that flowed behind the stage. The wind sent ripples across the surface, appearing to hurry the water along its course. Sebastius cocked his head then looked over his shoulder, hearing Thronden clank toward him.

"Places!" Sebastius called.

Enough of the stage was finished so the actors could rehearse their movements, and the workers backed away, brushing the dirt from their clothes and wiping the sweat from their faces. Thronden envied those who hurried to the creek to wade and refresh themselves.

"Places!" Sebastius repeated. His voice cut across the expansive meadow and over the scattered noise and conversations. Everyone quickly quieted, and four men in summer tunics moved onto the bare wooden stage. They arranged themselves shoulder-to-shoulder and stood at attention.

"We'll take it from the very beginning of Act One," Sebastius announced. "We have the Dark Knight sentries looking out across their encampment. We have the music rising."

"About the armor . . ." Jalas approached Thronden. The elf talked so softly Thronden had to concentrate to hear him over Sebastius and the four Dark Knights on stage. "As the assistant director, it is my duty to warn you . . . that, well, with all this armor which'll be clanking . . ."

"Armor clanks," Thronden said dryly.

"Well, we should change that. I've talked to one of the sorcerers and she thinks perhaps she can cast a—"

"I want the audience to hear the armor. It's part of the atmosphere."

Jalas tugged on his lower lip. "I concede you have a point—"

The sounds of wood splintering cut off the rest of the elf's words. One of the Dark Knights on stage had put his foot through a half-finished floor and was suddenly stuck up to his hips in broken boards. "My leg!" he shouted. "I think I've broken my leg!"

The world was filled with commotion then, as actors and stagehands alike set off to pull out the wounded actor.

"The wood's bowing in another spot!" shouted the ogre in charge of construction. "We are going to need some time to fix it." Those working on the sets hurried to patch the stage.

With a frown, Sebastius watched as a thickset half-elf ordered the injured Dark Knight carried away from the stage. The half-elf knelt by the moaning actor's side and tugged up his shredded pantleg.

"Should've been wearing your armor," the half-elf scolded. "The plate would've likely protected you."

"If all of us had been in armor the whole stage would've collapsed," the actor sharply returned. He rested back on his elbows and watched as a warm orange glow magically appeared above him and settled over his broken leg. Whatever force kept the actors in the troupe from aging also kept them in reliably good health.

"You'll be good as new soon," the half-elf said. "Ready for this afternoon's rehearsal."

"Bring some more planks!" Thronden shouted. The set crew was hard at work reinforcing the stage. "We'll need to make this much sturdier. And we'll need to replace this whole section."

"The stage has never collapsed before," someone said.

"Should have waited until everything was completely finished before rehearsing on the stage," someone else grumbled. "Should've—"

"Places!" Sebastius barked. "Instead we'll practice in front of the stage."

"I'll stand in for the injured Dark Knight," Jalas volunteered.

"Places!" Sebastius called again. "We'll take it from the top of Act One. Music!"

A gnome scurried forward, humming, waving his arms to guide invisible musicians. His gyrations made him look like a plump bird trying hopelessly to take flight.

"The music swells and . . ."

The gnome stopped humming, and the four Dark Knights stepped up. Jalas stood at one end.

Behind Thronden the actress playing the Dark Knight Lieutenant, Aleena's second-in-command, was pacing. Her stage name was Catal Rorig, and she was quietly practicing her lines.

"You can't be serious, Commander," Catal said, "agreeing to meet with a Solamnic Knight. Alone." She paced faster, and Thronden could hear her steps as he watched the rehearsal. She began to rhythmically thwack her rolled-up script against the palm of her hand. The ground was damp from recent rains, and Thronden was certain she was wearing a muddy path.

"It is a waste of time, this meeting you've planned," the actress recited.

Thronden gritted his teeth. Catal had just botched the line. It wasn't the line, actually, Thronden knew she had all the words down correctly. It was her inflection.

"But if you go ahead with it, this absurd meeting, watch his eyes," Catal continued. "They'll tell you if he's lying."

Catal thumped the script so hard this time Thronden imagined her hand stung. He glanced over his shoulder and saw the actress stuff the script into her pocket and massage her palm.

Catal caught Thronden staring at her.

"It's not bad, Thronden, this play you've written," she said brightly, touching the rolled-up script in her pocket.

He raised an eyebrow.

"In fact, it's surprisingly good for a first effort."

Thronden was about to thank her, but she kept babbling.

"Still . . . I don't think you've given me enough lines. I think I should have a lot more to say, being a lieutenant and all. Lieutenants are important, and would talk more about all manner of things. I should have more time on the stage, too. Much more. I think a lieutenant—"

A great flapping sound stopped her, and snared everyone's attention. The wind had caught one of the curtains that was stretched out on the grass and was tugging it toward the creek. The people working on the sets instantly abandoned their projects and dashed after it, whooping for those wading in the creek to help.

Thronden watched the curtain whipping toward the creek, its velvety sheen shimmering in the sun. An ogre, the one supervising the set construction, was the first to make a grab for it. He set his feet and with his great strength kept the huge swath of fabric from reaching the water, which could have ruined the material. It flapped loudly, looking like a huge kite straining to take flight.

"Got it!" he hollered proudly, just as the gnome stopped humming on Sebastius's cue. "I got it!" A dozen other hands joined his, and together they pulled the curtain back a safe distance and anchored it with a few rocks. Then they returned to their hammers and paintbrushes.

"To a man!" cried one of the Dark Knight actors in front of the stage, continuing the rehearsal. "To a man we will contest our hated Solamnic enemy!"

"To a man," Jalas echoed.

"Victory will be ours!" said the third.

"And may songs, great glorious songs, be sung of us," Jalas said, reading from the script. "May . . . May . . ."

Sebastius looked to the elf. "What's wrong?"

Jalas looked up from the page. "Sebastius, Thronden . . . I don't think a Dark Knight would say a line like this—'may songs, great glorious songs, be sung of us.' It's . . ."

Thronden's attention was divided, to say the least. "At least it's not my line," Catal murmured from behind him. Out of one eye he watched the curtain struggle to rise with the breeze.

"That's enough!" Sebastius bellowed. "Jalas, you will please speak what is written. Follow the script. Now . . . let's take it back to the very beginning."

"The beginning, again?" This came from the gnome. He started his spirited humming again, waving his arms.

Sebastius cued the music to swell, then to stop, motioning for the Dark Knights to begin once more.

"Jalas is right," Thronden interrupted too stridently, judging by the sharp look from Sebastius. "Hmmm. Perhaps 'may we hear glorious songs of our exploits on every man's lips.' "

"On every man's lips?"

Thronden turned. The actress playing the Dark Knight Lieutenant was still lurking near him. Catal was thumping her rolled-up script against her hand again. "Man's lips. What about women's lips?"

He made a face, and noticed that the other actors were also shaking their heads.

She persisted. "And speaking of lips, don't forget that my lips ought to be uttering more lines."

"I want to speak to you about my part, too, Thronden." The speaker was a pint-sized goblin. He brushed by the Dark Knight Lieutenant, rapping his tiny red fist against Thronden's plate mail. "I'm the goblin emissary, right? Well, my grandfather was an emissary to Takhisis, and I heard stories about his exploits in Neraka. Based on what I know of my grandfather, I figure an emissary ought to be loquacious and eloquent. The very word emissary implies that, right?"

Thronden stared at the goblin, trying to strike a patient pose while shutting out the continued muttering of Catal—trying to mull the right wording for the 'glorious songs' lines, all the while worrying if Sebastius really liked his play.

"Right?" the goblin asked louder.

Thronden smiled indulgently at the small creature. The goblin, Heart—as he was fondly called by the members of the troupe—was dressed in his costume, a shabby tunic over which he wore a breastplate cobbled out of bits of leather and chainmail. He held a spear in his hand, waving it at Thronden.

"I like all the other parts, Thronden. Good job for your first effort. Excellent effort, in fact. But my characterization seems all wrong. For an emissary."

"Sir Giles Bronzewood," Thronden told the goblin. "When I'm in costume, I'm . . ."

"Thronden. Bronzewood. Whatever, whoever," Heart continued. "My dialogue's wrong. Listen to this." The little creature dropped his spear and pulled a script from beneath his breastplate. "Me help you, Dark Knight. Me help you good. You pay me good." The goblin's features drew forward until they looked painfully offended.

"Pardon me if I say you don't know goblins, Sir Giles. Goblins don't talk like this. At least the goblins in my clan certainly didn't. And a goblin emissary certainly wouldn't. I should be saying something more like . . . 'Dark Knight Commander, it is time for our agreed upon exchange. My valuable information for your valuable coins.' What do think? You may want to add these changes." Heart grinned wide.

Thronden frowned. "I have already tinkered with your part, Heart. It's in the corrected pages." Thronden pointed to the actor in Solamnic costume who was slowly making his way across the meadow, shuffling and ordering the pages as he went.

"Good!" Heart said a little too loudly. "That's good, Thronden! Good! Good!"

Sebastius spun away from the actors rehearsing and in two steps was at Thronden's shoulder, looming over him. Sebastius was a large man, very tall and rotund, with big hands and a round, doughy face that looked a bit like the moon when it was full.

"Will you please be quiet? I can't hear the actors for your arguing. And what's this about corrections?"

"Yes, they're coming," he said, pointing. Thronden's knuckles were white and the frustration was thick in his voice.

"Why didn't you tell me? We shouldn't be rehearsing at all, until the actors have the latest version."

"Mostly it's the later scenes," Thronden apologized. "I was hurrying over to tell you, but . . . by the gods!"

He was looking beyond Sebastius now, past the Dark Knight actors rehearsing to the stage, where the ogre and half a dozen humans were setting up the first backdrop. The panel was large and nearly in place, appearing impressive with all its color and considerable detail. It was obvious hours and hours of work had gone into it. They were trying to force it, to hold it steady against the wind, trying too hard. The ogre's fist went through the canvas, in a spot near the center. That would have been easy to fix, had not one of the other workers stumbled and fallen through the canvas. The split panel teetered then toppled back off the stage with a crash.

Glaring at the ogre, Sebastius walked back to stand squarely in front of the Dark Knight actors. "Okay, let's try it again," he said irritatedly. "Pick up the pace this time.".

"I hope the corrections add a little humor," someone said.

"It's a drama," Thronden said absently. "There's nothing funny about it."

"Dramas can have some funny bits. This play needs some funny bits."

Sebastius again cued the gnome, who started humming again, softly, increasing the tune's tempo as Jalas read from the script.

"Our enemies marshal in a field filled with flowers. The white petals will soon turn red with Solamnic blood." Jalas looked up, seeing Thronden approach Sebastius.

The gnome hummed louder.

"Sebastius?" Thronden said hesitantly, drawing his shoulders back. "Sebastius, I've been giving it some thought, and I don't think the Dark Knights should enter from that side of the stage. That's east as the audience is facing, and according to allusions in the script the camp is actually in the west."

Sebastius turned slightly and looked down, eye to eye with Thronden. It was a stare that could wither most people. Only inches separated them.

"So," Thronden continued bravely, "I think we should have all the Dark Knights enter from the opposite side of the stage. It would be more fitting."

"Anything else?" The words had an edge to them.

"The script corrections for Act One are here." Thronden said. "Maybe we should pass out the corrections and start over one more time, as there are a few small changes . . ."

"And enter from the west."

"Yes, the Dark Knights." Thronden said.

Faintly, came the sound of canvas ripping as another panel of the set fell down.

"Do you disagree with the way I'm directing your play?"

"No."

Sebastius tilted his head.

"Aye. All right. I'm disagreeing with you. A little."

"A little? You disagree a little," Sebastius said ominously. The director's cheeks were reddening, and Thronden realized it was not from the sun.

"Aye. Just a little. Mainly it's about some of the blocking and interpretation." Thronden paused and decided to be forthright—as a Solamnic Knight would be. "All right. I guess I disagree with you more than a little. There are a few spots where I think there should be more music. And then there's—"

"An emissary should sound dignified," Heart came up to interject, squeezing himself between Thronden and Sebastius.

Another piece of canvas ripped.

The scattered conversaions of the actors grew in volume, as they discussed the play and its latest rewrite.

"Then you direct it," Sebastius told Thronden.

The conversations stopped.

The hammers quit pounding.

Someone sat on a flapping piece of curtain to keep it quiet.

Heart squeezed himself back out and looked up at Sebastius in astonishment.

"Me direct it?" Heart spit out.

Sebastius ignored the goblin. "You obviously think you can do a better job, Thronden. Well, direct it yourself, then."

There was a gasp from somewhere amid the assembled actors.

"I said, you direct 'Knights of Passion.' It is *your* play, after all."

Thronden paled. "But Sebastius . . ."

The big man turned and walked to the east, toward a copse of trees where the actors' tents and wagons were largely hidden from view. "You direct it," he repeated over his shoulder.

Whispers started, soft at first and then growing until they sounded like a swarming, buzzing insect chorus.

"That's never happened before, Sebastius walking off like that," Catal hissed.

"Ever," muttered Heart.

"I've been with Sebastius two hundred years and I've never seen him do that."

"Never ever."

"Hey, Thronden!" a craggy voice shot over the buzzing. "Thronden! I'm back! I hung up all your playbills!" The dwarf tromped toward the actors and the stage, stroking his bushy beard. He put on a puzzled look when he noticed no one was breathing, much less rehearsing. "What's going on? Why ain't you all going through your lines? Where's Sebastius?"

Thronden stood dumbstruck.

"Okay, so we've got the new pages. Now what, *Sir Giles Bronzewood*?" This came from one of the actors playing a Solamnic Knight. He fluttered the fresh script pages.

Thronden swallowed hard and looked around. The stagehands were waiting for him. The goblin Heart was jumping up and down, rejoicing in his new lines. Catal was still thumping her script, dissatisfied. All the other actors looked at him. Jalas was heading in his direction.

"Maybe I will direct it," Thronden said after a moment's panic. His voice was unusually soft. "Maybe." He gathered his copy of the script, registering with frustration streaks of grass stains, folded corners, a few dirt smudges. He stared at the pages in his hands for a full minute and listened as the buzz of conversations grew louder still. "Everyone can spend the rest of the day looking over the changes in the scenes. We'll start to rehearse again in the morning."

Jalas stared at him as Thronden brushed by, colliding with the dwarf. Once again the script flew from his fingers. He swiftly grabbed it up from the ground, and kept moving.

"I posted all your playbills Thronden," the dwarf grumbled as he untangled himself from Thronden. Then he added, "Well, all but one of them."

———◆◆◆———

An oil lamp burned low inside the large tent. Its flickers chased ghost-shadows across the canvas and the weathered features of the old man who paced behind a desk. The medals on his cloak collar and the etchings on his breastplate marked him as a Dark Knight Commander. The insistent chirping of crickets, irritating in its monotony, could be heard outside, while in the distance, a great owl hooted. Other sounds intruded too, someone walking in long, measured steps just outside the tent, the soft crackle of a nearby fire, a muted conversation about hobgoblin weapons—this latter proving mildly interesting to the commander. He listened to it as he moved effortlessly despite his obvious years. He'd kept himself lean and fit and brutally active.

"Sir?" It was the tent's other occupant, an adjutant, a sturdy woman also garbed in the night-black armor of the Dark Knights. She'd been quietly watching him for several minutes.

The pacing stopped. The commander seemed to study his chair a moment before sitting in it. He leaned forward, fingers stiff against the wood, heavily lined face set in a grim expression eerily highlighted by the oil lamp.

"This thing you've chosen to interrupt me with had better be important," he said.

The adjutant stood at attention on the other side of the desk and respectfully lowered her eyes. "I found this, Commander, blowing across the field. At first I paid it no heed and intended to toss it aside. But I chanced to read it. And I thought you might care to know about it, sir." She laid a piece of grass-stained parchment on the commander's desk.

"A scrap of paper." The air whistled through his clenched teeth. He stared at the adjutant.

"I considered it important, sir."

A shake of his head, and he turned his gaze to the parchment. "People of the Provinces," the commander read. His voice was thin, an old man's voice, but each word was crisply enunciated. "You are cordially invited to the premier of an original play presented by the Traveling Players of Gilean." He looked up. "A play. You thought I might care to see a posting about a play? I haven't time for such frivolities. We've a battle with hobgoblins to plan."

The adjutant nodded and gestured at the playbill, urging the commander to keep reading.

"*Knights of Passion* is an updated rendering of the classic *Laurinda and Jewyel,* the tragic story of a Qualinesti in love with a Silvanesti. To reflect these troubled times, the play has been deftly reinterpreted with a Dark Knight in love with . . . bah, utter foolishness!" The commander slammed a fist down on the parchment, the force of his blow rattling the oil lamp.

"I didn't like the idea of it either," the adjutant said. "A Dark Knight could never love a Solamnic Knight. I think it is a fatuous, impossible notion for a play."

"You were right to bring it to my attention." The commander eased all the way back into his chair and read the poster again. "Hmmm. I am seventy-five years old. Did you know that?"

The adjutant nodded, then added. "Yes, sir. You are the senior commander in the Provinces, the most decorated survivor of the Chaos War and . . ."

". . . and in my day, I have heard of such things," he said, cutting her off. He rose from the desk and walked to the open tent flap, staring out into the field. "I've heard of Knights of different orders falling in love. Or foolishly thinking what they felt was love. All the battles and fragility of life playing havoc with their senses and sending them into each other's arms." He returned to the desk. "But it doesn't happen nowadays, thank the Dark Queen. We've become more disciplined through the decades." Softer, "We've no time for love anymore."

He dropped a finger to the desktop and traced a whorl in the pitted wood. He allowed his thoughts to wander for a moment. "We cannot allow the notion of a Dark Knight in love with a Solamnic to be promoted to the masses," he said finally. "We would be remiss to ignore this."

The adjutant shifted her weight back and forth between her feet. "I agree, sir. It just wouldn't happen, a Dark Knight in love with a Solamnic."

"And therefore this performance—*Knights of Passion*—is dangerous heresy. And it will not be allowed to happen."

"Yes, sir. It would be a very dangerous precedent. One does not physically embrace the enemy. Not even in play-acting. It would be bad for our image and the morale of our troops."

The commander crumpled the poster and threw it in a corner of his tent. He steepled his fingers under his chin. "Some say I am too old to be out here on active duty," he said, the words soft and no longer crisp, and strangely, as though not meant for the adjutant. "They say I've spent too many years in the field. Should've retired years ago." He paused. "But without this noble work, what would I do?"

"Sir?"

"There are important causes and people to concern me. The hobgoblins to fight." He closed his eyes. "Actors pose no real threat to our Order. Yet . . ."

"Sir?"

After several moments of silence, he returned his attention to the adjutant. "This notice you've discovered says that this acting troupe will . . . 'happily accept your compliments and criticism.' "

"Yes, sir."

"Well, they will happily or otherwise accept our dictum. Forthan's Creek is not terribly far from here. Leave at first light. Visit this Sebastius . . . the so-called director of this travesty . . . and warn him not to put on his play—here in the Provinces or elsewhere. It would be unhealthy for his troupe. The curtain must forever be closed on *Knights of Passion.* "

The commander rose and walked around his desk, brushed by the adjutant, and slipped outside the tent. Row upon row of tents and wagons stretched out before him under the stars. At the edge of his vision he saw sentries patrolling. The commander's force was considerable. Beyond the camp were bands of gray and black, the mountains in the distance. A faint light on the horizon indicated a small town they'd stopped in recently for supplies.

The day's heat had abated somewhat, but it was still warm so the Dark Knight campfires were kept small. Orange glows dotted the night, the fires looking, the commander mused, like giant fireflies come to ground. The slight breeze brought to him the scent of wild pig and vegetables that were roasting. The quiet snap of flames from the closest fires mingled with the sounds of the crickets and the hushed conversations of his men.

"Will you be joining the men for dinner, sir?" the adjutant, coming up behind him, asked.

The Dark Knight Commander shook his head. "No, I've lost my appetite," he said, "and I've changed my mind."

"About the play, sir?" The adjutant seemed disappointed.

"Yes. You'll not leave first thing in the morning to deal with this Sebastius fellow and his audacious actors. You will leave now."

Thronden took off his cloak and tugged at the fastenings of his breastplate, and laid the pieces carefully on his cot. The tunic beneath was thoroughly soaked with sweat.

"Sweating like a dozen pigs," he said. "Perhaps I should visit the creek." Or perhaps not, he instantly decided. There would be actors and stagehands there, and all of them would have questions for him.

He plucked at the wet fabric with his fingers and tugged the tunic off. Thronden was a muscular man, though he usually concealed that fact in voluminous shirts. His face was strong, and his nose straight—"strikingly handsome," he'd heard others call him. Unlike many in the troupe, though, he put no effort into his appearance—except when he was on stage. In fact, when he wasn't on stage he went out of his way to look plain and to avoid drawing attention to himself. He found a dry shirt and put it on.

Thronden had a large tent, having inherited it from a minotaur who left the troupe suddenly several years ago. It was sparsely furnished with only a cot, a small desk piled with papers, and a clothes chest that doubled as a chair. It didn't have a mirror, like nearly all the other tents and wagons. Thronden didn't need one—he knew well enough what he looked like. And it lacked any personal decorations or touches hinting at his life before he became a Player of Gilean. The tent was as austere and enigmatic as the man. Now he paced from one end of the tent to the other, flattening the grass into a path, his leg plates clanking with each step.

"I only wanted it to be perfect," he said to himself. "I didn't mean to anger Sebastius. I just wanted my first play to be memorable. The gods know I've been involved with the theater long enough that I should get it right."

He'd been a member of the Players of Gilean for nearly fifty years. It seemed a good stretch of time, though there were actors here who'd been with Sebastius for centuries. Sebastius had told him, one evening in Palanthas, that he should try his hand at writing a play. "You're one of the finest actors I've had the pleasure to direct," Sebastius had said. "No role is too much of a challenge. But can you write a play? I think that would challenge you—to go beyond acting."

Go beyond? Thronden enjoyed acting, as it allowed him to assume other lives for a time. All the parts he played were more interesting than his real life, he thought. More often than not his stage characters triumphed over great odds and won true love in the end. He rarely had a small part and often served as the leading man. He could pass for a man in his early-twenties to mid-forties depending on the make-up. And with his rugged good looks, he could also play a convincingly roguish type or scoundrel. On rare occasions, he played the villain.

But he'd never before played a Solamnic Knight who was completely noble and heroic, selfless and flawless and virtuous. So when Sebastius encouraged him to write a play, he wrote himself into the heroid lead, giving himself the part he'd always dreamed of. In real life he had shirked responsibility, and was more of a follower. This play made him a leader of men

In his youth he had briefly considered joining the Solamnic Order, sincerely wanting to do something to better the world. But he ended up admiring their deeds from afar, as he traveled Krynn and tried to find a place for himself. The only real place for him seemed the players.

It was nearly a half century ago to this day that he discovered his home amid the actors and musicians who figured in Sebastius' traveling troupe. He had written this play to fulfill his thwarted ambitions of becoming a knight—but also to create an imagined romance between himself and Aleena. Beautiful Aleena. Romancing her on stage sent his senses reeling. He would never allow himself to pursue her in real life. There would be no more failed romances.

"Ah, my Lady Dark Knight," Thronden said, reciting a line from the play. "Your beauty makes the stars envious."

Thronden had not admitted to a single soul in the troupe that he once loved someone as beautiful as Aleena. That was nearly fifty years ago, and he was certain she was dead now.

"I lose myself in your eyes, Lady Dark Knight," he continued to rehearse. "I lose my soul and my honor."

They were good lines, he thought, and it was a promising play. But it looked like Sebastius—for whatever reason—had given up on it. Maybe Sebastius didn't like the play and therefore didn't want to direct it. He frowned. Could he really direct this play himself?

"No," he told himself. "I am not capable of directing." Being in a play and writing a play were enough. Well, more than enough.

"Aleena," he said in a hush. What was she thinking about all of this? About his arguing with Sebastius and causing the director to storm off? About his constant fine-tuning? He'd put so much work into the play, all of himself into it. Every last detail. He wanted it to be perfect. He constantly thought of ways to improve it. He couldn't just abandon it now, could he?

"Can I direct this?"

"Certainly not as well as Sebastius could." That was Jalas, standing just inside the tent flap.

"I didn't hear you come in," Thronden said with mild surprise.

The elf shrugged. "Can't imagine you'd hear much of anything with all that clanking from your leg plates."

"How could Sebastius do this to me? How could he abandon my play? Do this to everyone? In my decades, I've never seen him quit a production before."

"Ever," the elf agreed. "And I've been with him centuries. He's never quit. You must have really gotten under his collar. All your changes and suggestions and second-guessing. One giant irritating burr, I'd say you were."

Thronden ignored Jalas. "How could Sebastius do this to me? To all of us? To my play? How could he?"

Jalas watched Thronden for several long minutes before he spoke again. "They're all in their tents and wagons, memorizing the new lines."

Thronden leaned over the desk and looked at the stacked pages on it. They were blank, but they were something to look at other than Jalas's penetrating stare.

"They'll be expecting you to guide them confidently, tomorrow morning."

Thronden stiffened. "Sebastius shouldn't have quit."

The elf stepped closer. "I'm your assistant director now. What do you want me to do?"

"Maybe you should direct it instead of me."

"It's your play."

"My play?" Thronden exploded. "Is it? I think Sebastius has made a mess of the staging so far. He cast Catal in a role that Marlenna could have played ten times better. The actors don't yet have the feel of Knights. And there are still some scenes that need to be revised!"

"What time in the morning, Thronden?"

Thronden stared into the eyes of his friend, then looked away. "Leave me, Jalas. I need to be alone." Thronden looked up to see the tent flap fluttering in the wind.

Thronden absently shuffled the pages of the script, lost in thought. He could go to Sebastius and apologize. That would be the very best thing to do, and perhaps what Sebastius wanted. But that plan settled coldly in Thronden's stomach. Why should he apologize for wanting his play to be perfect?

Thronden could go ahead and try directing. But he'd never been truly in charge of something. He'd never been a leader.

Or he could retire from the players, which was at the forefront of his mind right now. Pack up his meager belongings, or just leave them here for the next member of the troupe. Maybe Sebastius wanted him to do just that. Maybe Sebastius wanted him to strike out across the Provinces and find something else to occupy his time. That would be the easy way out—leaving.

"The ending . . ." Thronden said to himself. "I still need a good ending."

A soft orange glow spilled out the tavern's windows, the light coming from merrily burning lanterns on the walls and tables. Conversations spilled with it, most centered on the same topic: the upcoming play.

"My wife hasn't been quiet since she saw the notice," the barkeep told a customer. "She's been going through her clothes, deciding what to wear. I've never seen her so excited in many years."

The customer took a pull on his mug of ale. "I'm not sure what all the fuss is about. I've never seen a play before. And I've lived round here my whole life."

"You've never seen one because there aren't any out here usually," the barkeep chuckled. "They're in the cities, places where there are theaters. Palanthas, New Ports, places where there are lots of people."

The customer shrugged. "I figure I'll go give it a watch anyway. Then at least I can say I saw one."

The barkeep had a wistful look in his eyes. "I saw a play a long time ago. I wasn't much more than a boy. I was visiting my uncle in the north, and there was a troupe of actors. They put on a great show about pirates and sorcerers. I went away wanting to be a pirate. I still remember it."

Across the room a young human woman stared into the eyes of her elf companion. He held her hands.

"I saw a production of *Laurinda and Jewyel* a long time ago," the elf said. "It was a sad tale, but superbly acted. To think they've rewritten the story, and that they're performing it here, out in the middle of nowhere, is amazing. I'm tempted to see it again."

"It is wonderfully exciting, isn't it?" the young woman said. "I can't wait to see it. It's all everyone's talking about. We must go very early so we can sit up close."

"Very, very early," the elf said, "as I suspect everyone has the same notion. If the play starts at sunset, we should be there shortly after dawn to get a place in the front row."

Across from the tavern were three small wood and brick homes. Families sat around the tables in each.

"I read *Laurinda and Jewyel* in school, as I recall," one mother said. "I was a child, and it was part of my studies. I read it three times."

"I recollect reading it, too," the father said.

"But that was back before the present war," their young son observed.

"When they had a school here," the mother said. "So many schools closed during the war. So sad."

"I don't think I would have liked school, anyway," the son said good-naturedly. "But I think I would have liked to read *Laurinda and Jewyel*. Can we go to the meadow tomorrow and watch them rehearse?"

The mother beamed. "That would be nice."

Next door:

"I don't think I can stand to wait for the curtain to raise. There's never been anything so thrilling happening here. A play, imagine that! Actors and a stage, out here! I just can't believe it. Too good to be true!"

And the next:

"No more watching the cookfire burning for entertainment, Artor. It's gonna be like the big city in a few days. The big, big city!"

"Wonder if the actors are any good?"

"Does it matter, Artor? It's a play. A romance! It will be marvelous fun!"

"I thought that the notice called it a tragedy."

"Does it matter? It's a play. We are sure to have a marvelous time."

———◆———

"The most changes are in Act Two," Thronden announced the next morning. "Let's start the rehearsal there."

An ensemble of flutes, strings, and small horns started playing in front of the repaired stage. The gnome conducted them, as Thronden, dressed in his full Solamnic plate mail, cued the actors to make their entrance.

Aleena came on first, her black plate mail shining in the early-morning sun. Her hair was pulled up and away from her face, intending to give her a severe, military look, but nothing could make that beautiful face severe, Thronden thought.

Jalas was at his side. "You're putting too much effort into directing Aleena," he whispered. "It's the others you really need to worry about. She has her lines down fine."

Thronden made a noncommittal "mmming" sound.

"Speaking of worries," the elf continued. "What about the fourth scene in Act Two? Is it done now, or are you still revising?"

"Mmmm."

"And the ending?"

"One more rewrite . . ." Thronden cued the music to diminish. Then the gnome gestured to a horn player. A lone, low note cut above the rest of the instruments.

A drum banged softly, and two Dark Knights came on stage and stood on each side of Aleena, a few feet behind her. The goblin Heart scampered on, looking over his shoulder as though he might be followed.

Thronden nodded at the two dozen villagers who were gathered to watch the rehearsal with rapt attention. "Won't they tell everyone we don't have an ending yet?" he told Jalas.

"The play opens in four days," the elf said. "Will it have an ending by then?"

"It will have an ending," Thronden said a trifle too loud.

"You can't rewrite forever, my friend."

Thronden paused. "My friend." He liked the sound of that. "I want it to be perfect, Jalas."

"Nothing is perfect," the elf answered, as he walked away. "Nothing is ever, ever perfect."

Except, perhaps, Aleena, Thronden thought.

"Commander!" One of the Dark Knights on stage shouted.

Aleena nodded to the small audience.

"Commander!" the other Dark Knight announced. "Comes hither your spy. If he brings news, he shall live."

"No spy am I," Heart said, as he strode to the front of the stage. His back was straight as a plank.

Thronden shook his head. "Your posture," he hissed. "Walk like a typical goblin!"

"I'm walking like an emissary," Heart shot back.

Thronden's glower forced the goblin into a less rigid pose. Heart thrust his head forward and bent his neck, an uncomfortable posture to be certain, but it met with Thronden's approval.

"No spy am I, Dark Knights," Heart repeated. "I am an emissary from the great goblin kingdom."

Aleena slowly turned to face the creature, her fog-gray cloak billowing behind her. Two flutes started then, their notes haunting and dissonant. "And does the emissary from the great goblin kingdom have news for me?"

Heart extended his lower jaw so that his teeth poked above his top lip. He worked up some saliva and let a thick ropy strand fall to the stage.

"Good, good," Thronden whispered.

"News," Heart hissed. "Yes, I have news."

"Then it is time to make an exchange," Aleena said.

"Yes, yes," Heart said. He wrung his hands together and smiled maliciously. "My valuable information for your valuable coins."

A horn joined the flutes, and the drum beat softly. Thronden watched as the four actors on stage continued to recite their lines. Only once did a Dark Knight stumble and have to refer to the script in his pocket. Thronden was just about to start the scene over again, when he was interrupted by the dwarf, thumping on his leg plates.

"I've been watching all this," the dwarf began, "sitting back there with the . . . uh, audience."

"And . . ."

"And I think it needs a little humor. A funny bit or two. You didn't pull a single chuckle out of Act One."

"This is a drama," Thronden said. "I don't want the audience to giggle."

The dwarf poked out his bottom lip. "Needs a little humor, Thronden."

"Not even a smile," Thronden returned. "This is a serious business."

The dwarf nodded. "I'll say it's serious all right." He pointed a stubby finger to the east.

A Dark Knight, a real one from the look of the shield strapped to her back and the sword hanging from her side, approached, leading an impressive black war-horse. She stopped to talk to the ogre stage manager, who waved his arm toward the copse of trees, where Sebastius's wagon was parked.

"Damn serious." The dwarf waddled back to the audience and settled himself between a pair of off-duty tavern wenches.

Thronden watched apprehensively as the Dark Knight led her horse to Sebastius's wagon. "Start from scene five, Act Two," he called to Jalas. "And tell Heart he is doing a terrific job. The saliva is perfect."

Then he hurried across the meadow to Sebastius's wagon, the strains of the flutes and strings following him. Sebastius's wagon was the largest and most ornate of those in the troupe. The Knight's horse was tied to a nearby tree. Thronden momentarily stared at the muscular and expertly groomed animal before climbing the three steps to Sebastius's door. He hesitated only a moment before entering unbidden, clanking with each step.

It was remarkably cool inside, and full of shadows. Diffused light filtered in through gauzy curtains that were pulled closed across a window above a table. Nearby stretched a bed piled high with pillows. Sebastius was propped up amidst them, with a silk coverlet pulled up to his waist. He had a book in his lap, though how he could read it in the dim light was questionable. Sitting beside him was a flagon of wine.

The big man gripped the flagon, looked idly at Thronden, then at the Dark Knight standing next to the bed. He uncorked it, took a deep pull and settled back deeper into the pillows.

"Didn't you hear me?" the Dark Knight asked Sebastius. She had a rich, silvery voice that Thronden thought would do well on stage.

Sebastius's lips turned slightly downward as he rolled his eyes. "There's nothing wrong with my hearing. Is there something wrong with your manners?"

The Dark Knight bristled.

"Doesn't anyone knock?" Sebastius persisted, switching his attention to Thronden now.

Thronden barely managed to swallow the apology that was rising to his lips.

The Dark Knight turned to regard the actor in Solamnic plate and bristled even more visibly. She cast the Solamnic an icy look then turned her attention to Sebastius again.

"Master Sebastius," The Dark Knight pointedly shifted her posture, showing only her back to Thronden. She looked down at the imposing man in the bed. "I am First Adjutant to Commander Karel of Neraka. He bids me bring you this message: You will ring down the curtains on *Knights of Passion.* You will burn all the scripts, and you will never consider putting on such a play ever again." She clicked her heels together to punctuate the order.

Sebastius yawned and placed the back of his hand against his forehead. "I've got a terrible fever," he said. "Can't you let a sick man rest?" He took another draw from the flagon. "Because I'm under the weather, I'm not really involved with this play. I'm no longer the director. Indeed, I've nothing to do with this particular production."

The Dark Knight inhaled sharply.

Sebastius yawned wider. "So it's not my decision whether the 'curtain closes' on the play." Suddenly his words were terse. "I've no say in the matter. That's up to the director."

"And that would be . . . ?" The Dark Knight pressed.

Sebastius gestured with the flagon. "Thronden Blackmoor, over there. He's also the author and leading man. The whole of it is his show. *Knights of Passion,* written by Thronden Blackmoor, starring Thronden Blackmoor, directed by Thronden Blackmoor." Yawn.

Thronden fought the blush rising to his cheeks. Hearing his name over and over made him feel foolish, or arrogant. Was he indeed arrogant? he wondered.

The Dark Knight spun about. "Director Blackmoor. I am adjutant to Commander Karel of Neraka. He bids me bring you this message: You will close down your production of *Knights of Passion.* You will burn all the scripts, and you will never, ever consider putting on such a play again. It is an insult to our Knighthood. A complete affront to our Order. To go against Commander Karel's instructions could result in your arrest, imprisonment, or death."

Thronden looked for help from Sebastius. The big man had put his knees up and was balancing the book against his thighs. He was paying neither visitor much attention.

"Commander Karel insists I get your word on the matter," the adjutant continued.

Surprisingly, Thronden felt more angry than afraid. "And if I don't give you my word?"

The Dark Knight's eyes glimmered menacingly. "As I said, there will be repercussions. Your welfare—and that of your actors—will hang in the balance. You cannot put on this play. We will not allow it."

"From my understanding, it's not even finished yet," Sebastius muttered, sarcastically.

Thronden stole a look at Sebastius, who pointedly ignored him. Then he turned to meet the defiant gaze of the Dark Knight. Thronden stared at her for more than a few moments. He felt a sudden swell of pride within himself, and in that instant he found a courage he didn't know he possessed.

"Adjutant, *Knights of Passion* will open to the people of the Provinces in five days. The play will go on, despite your threats." He pivoted, clicked his heels, and stepped to the door. Almost as an afterthought, he glanced over his shoulder, and added: "If you're marshaled in the Provinces you're welcome to attend. There's no charge for this performance."

———◆◆◆———

It was a surprisingly large turnout. The actors were amazed at the number of farmers, goatherds, and merchants who made their home in this area and who turned out for the production. Practically all the seats were filled by late afternoon, and Jalas, the ogre, and a handful of others were busy setting up more chairs for the people who were still streaming toward the stage. Some of the locals were in awe of the ogre, and he was quick to demonstrate his strength, picking up a trio of giggling children and gently depositing them in chairs. It was as large of a crowd as they could expect in most any city. And everyone seemed excited.

Sebastius would have been happy with the crowd, but he refused to leave his wagon. Thronden couldn't figure out why. No one in the troupe was ever sick—it just wasn't possible.

Jalas told Thronden he'd checked on Sebastius a short while ago, and that the big man was still in bed, reading and drinking wine, and occasionally peering out the window at the growing audience. Sebastius claimed he was still under the weather and would, therefore, and most regrettably, miss the premiere of *Knights of Passion.*

To keep his mind occupied, Thronden focused his attention on preparations for the show. The stage was finally finished, made of carefully constructed wooden sections, now reinforced, that came together and apart easily. Torchlights—and a few well-placed magical globes—illuminated the sets. Thronden's script called for the interior scenery to be simple, while the outdoor backdrops were quite intricate and enhanced with illusions. Perhaps, despite his instructions, the sets were too elaborate. He worried that they would overshadow the themes of the play.

The music started, the flutes trilling low and the drum beating steady. The murmurs from the audience all but disappeared, and the curtains drew back. The four Dark Knights stepped to the fore and began Act One.

Thronden retreated to the back of the stage and began his customary nervous pacing. Jalas joined him before the tall Dark Knight's soliloquy ended.

"You shouldn't be so nervous, my friend," the elf said. "They're just farmers and herders. I suspect most of them have never seen a play. And so if your play stinks, they might not even realize it."

"Even farmers and herders have opinions, Jalas. Every opinion counts."

"But who are they going to tell? Word of it won't travel anywhere. Isn't that why we came out here for the premiere? You can still rewrite it, if necessary, before we hit the cities."

"I . . ."

"I know, you want it to be perfect." Jalas sighed. "You kept making changes right up until this very afternoon. It is as perfect as can be."

"What about the ending? I just finished it this morning. I hope Aleena had time to memorize everything."

The elf cocked his head as the music picked up tempo. "That's your cue, Sir Giles Bronzewood. You're on."

Thronden made his way up the steps behind the curtains. He took a deep breath and stepped out onto the stage. The Dark Knights hung to the west side of the stage, in the shadow of the curtains, just visible to the audience.

Suddenly the wood floor of the stage seemed to melt away, becoming a grassy plain, the curtain transforming into a ridge of distant mountains. The painted backdrop became even more picturesque. The lights on the stage dimmed to simulate dawn. There were gasps of amazement in the audience, the youngest asking their parents how it had been done, the elders shushing them and saying it was all magic. A painted piece of wood made to look like a young red maple was pushed onto the stage; the fabrication somehow looked as though a real tree had taken root.

"Here I am in Hinterlund," Thronden announced in a strong stage whisper that carried well. "I, Sir Giles Bronzewood of Edgerton, find myself in Hinterlund once again." Thronden looked resplendent in his Solamnic armor, cape fluttering gently around his ankles. His hair was long and straight and shiny, falling to his shoulders. "My love is here in Hinterlund," he said loudly. "My love and my doom spun into one."

He walked across the stage, and the backdrop changed

slightly as he went, hinting that he was traveling a good distance.

"Windswept Hinterlund," Sir Giles Bronzewood stated now, his sonorous voice easily reaching to the very last row. Behind him, the four Dark Knights closed. Within moments the music became fast and furious, and three of the Dark Knights were circling and jabbing with their swords, the fourth remaining outside and looking for an opening, darting forward but unable to land a blow. Sir Bronzewood crouched, just as a sword pierced the air, and he slashed out, cutting the straps that held one of the Knight's leg plates. A second slash and a line of blood grew visible across the Dark Knight's thigh. The Dark Knight dropped to his knees, and Sir Bronzewood effortlessly leapt over him to gain some breathing room.

"I slay my love's enemies," he cried. "Love curses me!"

The crowd was gasping, shouting for Sir Bronzewood to look behind him, cursing the Dark Knights, screaming questions:

"Is that real blood?" a little blonde-haired girl gasped to her mommy.

"Is that actor truly hurt?" a man asked his bewildered wife.

"I-I don't know. I . . ."

"Get them, Giles! Get the Dark Knights!"

Sir Bronzewood wheeled, slashing at the Dark Knight who was still on his knees. The man pitched forward and lay still. The remaining three circled him again. This time Sir Bronzewood feinted to his left, spinning right a second later, barreling into one of the Dark Knights and pushing him off the stage and nearly into the laps of the folks in the front row. In that same instant, another Dark Knight stabbed forward. He

would have wounded the Solamnic, had Sir Giles not
been quick. Instead, his blade sunk mistakenly into the
chest of his fellow Dark Knight. The Dark Knight had
killed one of his own!

"It is only you and I now," Thronden told the remaining Dark Knight.

"I cannot fail my commander!" the Dark Knight cursed.

"I love your commander," Thronden said. "With
every breath, I love her."

"Your Solamnic blood will . . ." Suddenly the Dark
Knight actor dropped his sword.

Thronden started, whispering that the Dark Knight
wasn't supposed to surrender, he was supposed to die
valiantly now. Before Thronden could figure out what
was going on and improvise his next move, he heard the
audience utter a collective gasp.

"My Solamnic heart . . ." Thronden began, trying to
keep up the momentum. He was staring into the crowd,
noting the fear etched on many faces.

"It's Dark Knights!" a large man in the middle of the
throng shouted. "Real ones!"

"Real Dark Knights!" a shrill voice echoed. "They're
not part of the play! There are too many of them!"

Nearly half the audience ran then, tripping over chairs
and each other. Those who weren't calling for family
members and friends were shrieking in utter disbelief
and terror. Some fell to their knees, trembling. A few
passed out in fright. Many of the remaining audience, all
of them sitting as though nailed to their seats, were quivering and turning paler by the second.

Thronden looked past the last row. There, gathering
at the top of the hill—night-dark armor and night-dark
horses making them ominous—was a veritable Dark
Knight army.

"They're going to kill us, Thronden!" It was Heart, and he was running up the center aisle, narrowly avoiding being trampled by the fleeing patrons. He barely managed to claw his way up onto the stage. "Thronden, the Knights were serious when they said this play should fold. They're here now and they're going to fold it for us!"

All the actors knew about the adjutant's appearance in Sebastius's wagon, and about the threats. Thronden had mentioned it to Jalas, and the elf had spread the news.

Backstage, Jalas looked out, at the top of the hill. He sucked in a breath. He couldn't tell how many Dark Knights were up there, but he knew they seriously outnumbered the actors and what was left of the audience. White flowers shown faintly in the dim light. "Our enemies marshal in a field filled with flowers," he said, reciting one of the Dark Knight actor's parts. "The white petals will soon turn red with Solamnic blood." Jalas's fingers trembled.

On stage, the "slain" Dark Knight actors got up and crawled through the slit in the back of the stage. Behind the backdrop, Thronden heard the worried voices of the actors, many of them piteously calling for Sebastius. He faintly heard the voices of the real Dark Knights approaching, the nickering of all the war-horses, and the angry and frightened words of the remaining patrons.

"C'mon, Selas," someone in the audience yelled. "We've got to run. Dark Knights! There must be a hundred of 'em."

"I'm not leaving, Emil. If them Dark Knights're gonna kill us, they'll kill us whether we run or stay put. So I ain't runnin'."

"Nobody should be running," Thronden said, at first to himself, and then louder. "Nobody should run! Don't run!" He bellowed. "Don't be afraid! The play will continue regardless!"

"Are you crazy?" This came from Heart, who was clinging to Thronden's leg. "The Dark Knights are going to close the curtain on all of us!" The goblin's tiny knees knocked together, and he waved toward the back of the audience. "Lots of Dark Knights, Thronden, and they have lots of weapons."

Thronden squinted to make out the details. The Knights were dismounting and pulling lances and pikes from their saddles. In military precision they began marching down the center aisle.

"They're not going to shut us down," Thronden said determinedly. "The play will—must—continue."

Heart shook his head in disbelief.

"Places, everyone," Thronden called. "The play is still going on. We will take it from . . ."

The rest of his words were drowned out by the clanking of the Dark Knights' armor. He realized there must be well more than a hundred soldiers. It truly was a small army. Half of those approaching had swords drawn. They wore glossy black armor, all with shadow-gray cloaks that swirled round their heels. At the lead was a most impressive elderly Knight, with an elaborate braid on his shoulders and etched scrollwork on his breastplate. Directly behind him came the Knight he'd seen yesterday in Sebastius's wagon, the female adjutant. So the old man in the fancy armor must be the Commander. Were they indeed here to lay waste to the stage? Were they here to make an example of him for defying their order to shut down the production?

The Dark Knight Commander raised his arm, and the men following him surprisingly broke away and began to claim the seats left empty by the deserting villagers. More of the villagers left as the Dark Knights moved among them. Thronden guessed there were six or seven dozen Knights settling in. The rest remained back by the horses, standing alertly.

"I'm not leaving, Emil!" one of the patrons announced loudly. "Dark Knights aren't keeping me from seeing how this play ends."

"W-we're not going anywhere, either," a heavy-set man in the second row worriedly said for all to hear. "W-we're here to see a play." There was nervous clapping of encouragement around him. "Can't outrun Knights with horses, anyway," he added.

On the stage, the goblin Heart rapped his fist on Thronden's leg plate. "The townies are rallying," he said, "but the actors backstage are talking about bolting."

"We can't let the Dark Knights shut us down, Heart."

"Shut us down? It's only me and you on this stage, Thronden. I think they have already shut us down."

Thronden reluctantly drew his gaze from the Knights and looked at Heart.

"No actors, no show," the goblin summed things up.

"One minute, ladies and gentlemen," Thronden announced. "One minute, and our production will continue." He hurried out the slit at the back of the scenery, Heart on his heels.

The troupe was clustered together, most of them trembling. Aleena was in the middle. She was standing on something.

"You've performed before ogres and hill giants," she was saying. "Before armies that stopped fighting only long enough to watch a play. You've performed in front of Dark Knights before."

"Though not ones who don't want the play to be performed," Catal cut in. "Not ones who've threatened our lives."

"Not without Sebastius," someone else volunteered.

"We risk too much," Catal added.

"It would be easy to pack up and move on," the dwarf suggested. "It would be the safe thing to do."

Thronden glared at the dwarf.

"But we've never quit," the dwarf continued. "No one's run us out of any town. Ever."

"And no Dark Knight army is going to run us out of this meadow," Jalas said. The elf joined Aleena on her makeshift platform. "Thronden's put a lot of effort into 'Knights of Passion.' We've put a lot of effort into memorizing all the script changes. We're not going to let our friend Thronden down."

"So we're not going to run," Aleena said. "We're going to put this play on for Thronden, for ourselves, and for that audience out there. We'll put on a show that these Dark Knights won't soon forget. A show for the few farmers who are staying, who have more courage than some of us." She looked to Thronden. "Director . . . Sir Giles Bronzewood . . . where do you want us to pick up the performance?"

Thronden swallowed hard. He was speechless at their grit and loyalty, and he fought to keep from shedding an appreciative tear. "Why don't we start again from the beginning of Act One?" he said. He instantly began dispensing directions and advice, bolstering the courage of the troupe. Leading them.

⬦

The Dark Knight Commander had found a prime spot in the very first row, near the center of the stage. The adjutant sat immediately to his left, occasionally looking over her shoulder as if taking stock of the shifting audience. The commander was reading seemingly intently from the program, while the handful of villagers nearest him continued to shiver timidly.

On stage the actors were doing their best to master their fears and refuse to wither under the Dark Knights' glares. Still, Heart kept dropping his spear, and Catal, the Dark Knight Lieutenant, tripped and stumbled against a backdrop. They juggled and dropped props, which soon prompted laughter from the commander and his adjutant. Titters ran through the rest of the audience, too.

"It's not supposed to be a comedy," Thronden fumed backstage.

"Oh, it's turning out to be funny all right," Jalas said with a sad smile. "Darkly funny."

"A real black comedy," the dwarf mused.

From his wagon, Sebastius watched out the window.

Thronden eased around to the side of the stage, where he could get a good close look at the commander and his adjutant. They were huddled in discussion between scenes, but when the actors quieted before the next scene, and the music died down, he could overhear them.

"This play is too long," the commander observed.

The adjutant nodded.

"Though I do enjoy watching the Dark Knight Commander. She is beautiful." He paused. "And, though this play seems long, it has its captivating moments. I want to see how it turns out."

"Then we'll close the curtain on the play forever?" the adjutant asked hopefully. "Slay the playwright, and take the actors prisoner for good measure?"

The commander drew a gloved finger to his lips and nodded toward the stage.

Act Two was just beginning.

"Commander!" One of the Dark Knights on stage shouted.

Aleena stood at the edge of the stage, poised as though she might take flight. She wore little make-up, only paint on her lips and a little color on her cheeks. And she looked singularly beautiful. The armor couldn't hide her beauty. If anything, it accented the softness of her face. Doe eyes looked over the audience.

In return, all eyes were on her. Thronden knew everyone in the crowd found her as captivating as he did—as the Dark Knight Commander did. Perhaps he should pursue her off-stage, was his fleeting thought. Then he instantly abandoned the notion. He'd lost his true love once, and he wouldn't allow himself another foolhardy chance.

Thronden noted that her lips didn't tremble. She was not only beautiful, but brave.

"Commander!" the other Dark Knight actor announced, as his fingers fumbled and he dropped his sword. The actor bent to pick it up, but only lost his grip again. He gave up and let the weapon lay on the stage, nearly tripping over it as he moved to deliver his next line. "Comes hither your spy. If he news brings . . . he news brings . . . he shall live."

The audience chortled at the botched line.

"No I spy am I," Heart said, glancing nervously at the Dark Knights in the audience, as he walked to the front of the stage. His back was straight and his head was held high, but his knees knocked together audibly. "I spy no spy," he said. Heart closed his eyes, trying to remember the words. "No spy am I sky. No. No. No."

More laughter from the audience.

"No spy am I," he repeated, grinning widely when he got it right.

Thronden felt a tug on his cloak. "The audience is warming up to your play," the dwarf said. "I told you it needed some comedy. Even a drama should have a few funny bits. Maybe you ought to get another army of Dark Knights to show up at the next performance. Make it all part of the act."

Thronden shot him a withering look.

On stage, Heart aimed his head forward and bent his neck, making him look more like a demented creature. "I am a seminary," he said, his eyes darting around the audience.

The commander laughed and slapped his leg.

"No spy am I, Dark Knights," Heart said more firmly, struggling to recapture his focus. "I am a seminary . . . I mean, I am an emissary from the great koblin gingdom."

Amidst the chuckles, Aleena slowly turned to face the goblin, her fog-gray cloak billowing behind her. Two flutes started then, their notes haunting and dissonant. "And does the emissary from the great goblin kingdom have news for me?" she asked authoritatively.

Heart extended his jaw so his bottom teeth poked above his upper lip. He worked up some saliva and let a strand fall to the stage.

"News. Yes, I have news," he hissed.

"Then it is time to make an exchange," Aleena said.

"Yes, yes," Heart said. He wrung his hands together. "I make a motion that . . . I make a motion that." He looked exasperatedly at the audience, then raised his voice. "A motion, a motion . . ."

"A motion?" the Dark Knight Commander boomed. "I'd say you're making a commotion!"

More laughter.

Heart stomped his foot and listened. Jalas was backstage feeding him his next lines. "Yes, yes, it is time to make an exchange. My valuable information for your valuable coins."

Thronden put his head in his hands.

"Are you going to do some funny bits, too, Thronden?" the dwarf asked him. "When you go back on stage, soon?"

"This is a drama," Thronden said between clenched teeth.

Jalas whispered more lines to Heart.

The play continued.

"Too long," the Dark Knight Commander said, after the scene finished.

"Shall we end it now, mercifully?" the adjutant asked. She drummed her fingers against the pommel of her sword.

The commander shook his head and leaned forward, intently. "Not yet. It is dreary long, but I confess I find it rather intriguing." It was stirring an old memory.

Aleena was back on stage, this time dressed in a flowing black robe, cut low to show her stately neck and a heart-shaped pendant that dangled there. "We can't see each other, my love. Ever again," she said.

Thronden moved into full view of the audience. He, too, had abandoned his armor and was dressed in a fine tunic and leggings. But his Solamnic cloak remained.

"I must see you," he said. "You know I love you deeply." The words were simple, but they brought sighs from the women in the audience. "I love you more than life." An elderly lady near the Dark Knight Commander brought a handkerchief to her eyes. "I love you," Thronden repeated. "Beyond our station and our causes, beyond all of Krynn I love you. Beyond my honor, and beyond my oath."

They stepped into each other's arms.

"Love doesn't care about war," Thronden continued.

There wasn't a sound from the audience now. All eyes were on the couple.

"Love doesn't care about honor. Love has no enemies. Love rises above battlefields. It reduces the noblest Knight to a trembling child." Thronden dropped to one knee. "It turns the weakest man into an undefeatable giant. It has no prejudice. It doesn't care whether you are a Dark Knight or a Solamnic Knight."

"But love cares," Aleena said.

"Love cares," Thronden echoed.

A lone tear slid down Aleena's cheek. It glistened like a string of miniature diamonds in the starlight.

"Love is all that matters," Thronden said.

Aleena leaned forward and kissed his forehead. "And were there enough love in this world, there would be no wars," she said. "There would be no Dark Knights and no Solamnic Knights. There would be meadows, and not battlefields. Love is all that *should* matter."

Then she turned away from Thronden and pulled a knife from her robes, its silver blade sparkling with a faint glow. She held it to her breast. "Love is all that should matter," she repeated. "Love transcends wars and causes." She pressed the tip to her throat.

Someone in the audience gasped.

The Dark Knight Commander leaned forward, fingers laced under his chin. The old memory continued to dance. He raptly watched Thronden, peering into the actor's eyes.

For a moment Thronden caught the Dark Knight Commander's stare, then turned his attention back to Aleena. The Dark Knight Commander sat back and watched.

"You are wrong, my beloved Solamnic," Aleena continued her lines. "You are wrong, though I wish it were otherwise. Love is *not* stronger than war. And love does *not* transcend honor and our Orders." She whirled and with a move that shocked every single patron, she plunged the knife into Thronden's chest. He crumpled on the stage.

ARON EISENBERG AND JEAN RABE

"And it does *not* transcend duty."

She let out a sob then knelt on the floor and cradled him, her shoulders shaking as the last of his life spilled out. She tugged the blade free, held it to the sky. "But love endures! May love remember us."

The knife flashed as she plunged it into her own heart.

The stage went dark, and a single flute played a sad melody.

"May love remember us," came a whisper from the empty stage.

The audience was quiet for a moment, then sobs burst from all parts of the crowd.

The Dark Knight Commander was silent, staring into the darkness of the stage as if he was frozen. Near him, the adjutant brushed away a tear and began to clap.

It was several minutes more before the actors filed out onto the stage. Aleena and Thronden came on last and bowed deeply. The commander nodded to his men then, giving them permission. The applause swelled, and after another moment, the commander joined in the clapping.

<hr>

Backstage, Thronden wiped at his make-up. Sebastius was finally up and about, standing several yards away, keeping his distance and talking with Jalas. Thronden strained to hear some praise from the mouth of Sebastius, but couldn't hear what they were talking about.

However, something close to praise came from the Dark Knight Commander, who made his way backstage after the show. He paused to idly inspect a table filled with make-up jars and hairpieces, prodding them with his gloved fingers.

"Quite an interesting production," the Commander muttered, looking at a small pot filled with glitter.

He didn't meet Thronden's gaze, in fact pointedly ignored him. Next he turned over a mirror then held a comb up to the light of a lantern. It was as if he were looking for clues to a crime.

"Who is the director of this troupe?" the commander asked after he'd finally lost interest in the paints and dyes.

Sebastius hesitated then stepped forward. "Of the troupe," he said, "though not of this play."

"Interesting production," the commander repeated. "Rather long, though, and too deliberate in parts. Very accurate in terms of the costumes and especially regarding the Knightly protocol, but it could use some more intentional comedy."

"Told you," the dwarf whispered to Thronden.

"I found, as far as love stories go, that it was a bit improbable. A Dark Knight in love with a Solamnic Knight? Improbable indeed!" He paused and theatrically swept his cloak behind him. "I will admit it had an appropriate ending."

"A tragic ending," Thronden ventured.

The Dark Knight Commander turned to acknowledge him, stepping away from Sebastius and closing on Thronden. He dropped his voice to a near-indiscernible whisper. "I, too, loved a woman once," he said. They locked eyes, but the commander said nothing else.

The next moment, the Dark Knight Commander was gone. They saw him making his way back up the center aisle, his men falling in behind him. Within minutes the soldiers had mounted their horses and were thundering away.

Sebastius returned to his wagon and gazed out his window as normal activity resumed. He watched one man move through the company. The crew and actors cast Thronden respectful glances as he threaded his way toward his tent.

Sebastius watched as the actors began to chatter quietly amongst themselves—about the Dark Knights and the stalwart farmers who held their ground, about their parts and their lines, and what needed to be improved before the next presentation of Thronden's play.

Jalas entered Thronden's tent.

"What, this time?" Thronden asked wearily. He was rubbing at the last of his make-up.

"It was a good play," Jalas said, "and it had a fine director." The elf said nothing else. He turned and left, making sure the tent flap closed behind him.

"Improbable?" Thronden allowed himself a faint smile as he tugged off his tunic. "An improbable love story?"

A strange, almost wistful expression played across his face as he sat at the desk and put a quill to a fresh sheet of parchment. "Yes, improbable, and far too serious. I rather liked the comedy, inadvertent though it might have been. I think the dwarf is right. It could use a few more funny bits. Heart has a real knack for comedy. I will have to remember that as I rewrite."

Thronden's quill began to move across the page.

The War of Souls ends now.

**The *New York Times* best-seller from
DRAGONLANCE® world co-creators**

Margaret Weis & Tracy Hickman

available for the first time in paperback!

The stirring conclusion to the epic trilogy

DRAGONS OF A VANISHED MOON
The War of Souls, Volume III

A small band of heroes, led by an incorrigible kender, prepares to battle
an army of the dead led by a seemingly invincible female warrior. A dragon
overlord provides a glimmer of hope to those who fight the darkness, but
true victory—or utter defeat—lies in the secret of time's riddles.

March 2003

The Minotaur Wars

From *New York Times* best-selling author Richard A. Knaak comes a powerful new chapter in the DRAGONLANCE® saga.

The continent of Ansalon, reeling from the destruction of the War of Souls, slowly crawls from beneath the rubble to rebuild – but the fires of war, once stirred, are difficult to quench. Another war comes to Ansalon, one that will change the balance of power throughout Krynn.

NIGHT OF BLOOD
Volume I

Change comes violently to the land of the minotaurs. Usurpers overthrow the emperor, murder all rivals, and dishonor minotaur tradition. The new emperor's wife presides over a cult of the dead, while the new government makes a secret pact with a deadly enemy. But betrayal is never easy, and rebellion lurks in the shadows.

The Minotaur Wars begin June 2003.

The original Chronicles

From *New York Times* best-selling authors Margaret Weis & Tracy Hickman

These classics of modern fantasy literature – the three titles that
started it all – are available for the very first time in individual
hardcover volumes. All three titles feature stunning cover art
from award-winning artist Matt Stawicki.

DRAGONS OF AUTUMN TWILIGHT
Volume I
Friends meet amid a growing shadow of fear and rumors of war.
Out of their story, an epic saga is born.

January 2003

DRAGONS OF WINTER NIGHT
Volume II
Dragons return to Krynn as the Queen of Darkness launches her assault.
Against her stands a small band of heroes bearing a new weapon:
the DRAGONLANCE.

July 2003

DRAGONS OF SPRING DAWNING
Volume III
As the War of the Lance reaches its height, old friends clash amid
gallantry and betrayal. Yet their greatest battles lie within each of them.

November 2003

Before the War of the Lance, there were other adventures.

Check out these new editions of the popular Preludes series!

DARKNESS & LIGHT
Sturm Brightblade and Kitiara are on their way to Solamnia
when they run into a band of gnomes in jeopardy.

February 2003

KENDERMORE
Tasslehoff Burrfoot is arrested for violating the kender laws of
prearranged marriage – but his bride pulls a disappearing act of her own.

April 2003

BROTHERS MAJERE
Desperate for money, Raistlin and Caramon Majere agree to take
on a job in the backwater village of Mereklar, but they soon discover
they may be in over their heads.

June 2003

RIVERWIND THE PLAINSMAN
A barbarian princess and her beloved walked into the Inn of the
Last Home, and thus began the DRAGONLANCE® Saga.
This is the adventure that led to that fateful moment.

October 2003

FLINT THE KING
Flint Fireforge's comfortable life turns to chaos
when he travels to his ancestral home.

November 2003

TANIS: THE SHADOW YEARS
When an old dwarf offers Tanis Halfelven the chance to find his father,
he embarks on an adventure that will change him forever.

December 2003